"DO YOU

A VAMI

When she nodded, ~~~~~~~~~~~~~~~~~~~~~~~~~~w her into his arms. "If you change your mind, if what I am gets to be too much for you to handle, just tell me. I can't promise I'll never hurt you and it scares the hell out of me."

"We'll just have to learn to trust each other."

"Yeah. I'll see you tomorrow night."

Sheree frowned. "I saw your mother during the day. How is that possible?"

"She's Mara, Queen of the Vampires," he said, starting down the steps. "Most of the rules don't apply to her."

"Hey! Aren't you going to kiss me good night?"

She was wrapped in his arms before she had time to blink. His mouth covered hers in a searing kiss that burned every thought from her mind and left her weak and wanting more.

"Tomorrow night," he said, and it sounded like both threat and promise.

Other titles available by Amanda Ashley

A WHISPER OF ETERNITY

AFTER SUNDOWN

DEAD PERFECT

DEAD SEXY

DESIRE AFTER DARK

NIGHT'S KISS

NIGHT'S MASTER

NIGHT'S PLEASURE

NIGHT'S TOUCH

NIGHT'S MISTRESS

IMMORTAL SINS

EVERLASTING KISS

EVERLASTING DESIRE

BOUND BY NIGHT

BOUND BY BLOOD

HIS DARK EMBRACE

DESIRE THE NIGHT

BENEATH A MIDNIGHT MOON

AS TWILIGHT FALLS

Published by Kensington Publishing Corporation

Night's Promise

AMANDA ASHLEY

ZEBRA BOOKS
KENSINGTON PUBLISHING CORP.
http://www.kensingtonbooks.com

ZEBRA BOOKS are published by

Kensington Publishing Corp.
119 West 40th Street
New York, NY 10018

All Kensington titles, imprints, and distributed lines are available at special quantity discounts for bulk purchases for sales promotion, premiums, fund-raising, educational, or institutional use.

Special book excerpts or customized printings can also be created to fit specific needs. For details, write or phone the office of the Kensington Special Sales Manager: Attn.: Special Sales Department. Kensington Publishing Corp., 119 West 40th Street, New York, NY 10018. Phone: 1-800-221-2647.

Zebra and the Z logo Reg. U.S. Pat. & TM Off.

First Mass-Market Paperback Printing: February 2014
ISBN-13: 978-1-4201-3043-0
ISBN-10: 1-4201-3043-9

First Electronic Edition: February 2014
eISBN-13: 978-1-4201-3044-7
eISBN-10: 1-4201-3044-7

10 9 8 7 6 5 4 3 2 1

Printed in the United States of America

To Shirley Brashear
My sister from another mother

Chapter One

Derek Blackwood had grown up knowing he was a vampire. And not just any old vampire. His mother, Mara, was a legend among their kind, the only vampire who had ever regained mortality, and then given it up. He had never known his father. Kyle Bowden had died shortly after Derek's birth. Logan Blackwood, his mother's second husband, was the only father Derek had ever known.

Seeking a few minutes of solitude, Derek went out on the balcony of his mother's home in the Hollywood Hills. Taking a deep breath, he gazed out over the moon-shadowed valley below. He enjoyed being alone from time to time. Enjoyed the peace and quiet, something that was sorely lacking just now.

Derek glanced over his shoulder. His relatives were gathered inside, here to help his parents celebrate their twenty-fifth anniversary. He grinned faintly. He had a family like no other. Of course, they weren't kin in the usual sense of the word. Roshan and his witch-wife, Brenna, slow danced cheek to cheek in the middle of the kitchen. Their adopted daughter, Cara, sat in the living room, chatting with her husband, Vince, who had been turned by Mara. Cara and Vince's twin sons, Rafe and Rane, were watching a baseball game in the den, while the twins' wives, Kathy and Savannah, sat in the kitchen with his mother. Vampires all, born or made.

Watching them, hearing their easy laughter filled him with an aching loneliness, made him wonder, not for the first time, if he would ever find a woman to share his life.

Suddenly restless, he headed for the garage. Sliding behind the wheel of his brand-new convertible, he backed out of the driveway and headed for his favorite hangout.

Driving down the twisting narrow road to the highway, he contemplated his past. Although he had known early on that he was a vampire, he was still coming to terms with who and what he was. As a child, he had been like any other kid, able to run and play outdoors, eat mortal food. Unlike other children, he never got sick; when he was injured, he healed immediately. His only restriction was that he needed to wear sunglasses during the day.

When he reached puberty, his life changed drastically. One day he was a relatively normal teenager; the next he was overpowered by a desperate need for blood. A need that could not be ignored, or satisfied by anything else. He discovered the sun was no longer his friend, though he could endure it for short periods of time if necessary. He could drink anything he pleased, but solid food made him violently ill.

Turning onto the freeway, he put the pedal to the metal.

The night was growing short and he was thirsty.

Chapter Two

Sheree Westerbrooke stood in the front of the full-length mirror in her bedroom, admiring her new Goth look. It had taken her days to find just the "right" ensemble, but it had been worth it. If one wanted to fit in, one had to look the part. After all, she couldn't just waltz into a vampire club looking like a tourist. She needed fake fangs, some black Goth-style clothing, shoes, and jewelry. She had debated dying her shoulder-length dark blond hair black, but decided to buy a long black wig instead. Her own mother wouldn't recognize her. Neither would her best friend, Shirley, she thought with a grin. Perhaps she'd send her a photo.

Sheree smiled at her reflection, pleased. She had always loved vampires—the ugly ones with pointy ears and hairy hands, like Nosferatu; the suave, handsome ones, like George Hamilton, Gerard Butler, and Frank Langella; the comic ones who spoke with funny accents, like Leslie Nielsen; the scary ones, like Gary Oldham and Christopher Lee. She loved them in comic books and movies, in novels and fantasy magazines.

She had vampire posters on her walls, a collection of

vampire figurines, a Lady Dracula costume she wore on Halloween. She had seen every movie and play about the undead she could find, read every book of fiction and non-fiction about them in the local library. She had even tried her hand at writing vampire poetry, which, you should pardon the pun, sucked.

It didn't matter that Sheree's parents and friends told her there was no such thing. They insisted that vampires by any other name—Nosferatu, undead, Dracula, vampyr, blood-sucking creatures of the night, whatever—simply didn't exist except in low-budget horror movies and gothic novels.

But Sheree refused to accept that. People had believed in vampires for thousands of years. Since the beginning of recorded history, every culture and civilization had its own vampire legend. Surely, if vampires were only a myth, any interest in them would have faded away long ago.

Ergo, vampires must exist. There were vampire chat rooms online, vampire nightclubs and hangouts. Out of all those hundreds and thousands of people who were pretending to be vampires, there had to be at least one who was the real deal.

And Sheree was determined to find him—or her—no matter where he or she was hiding.

Being rich, single, and bored, Sheree had decided to visit every vampire hangout between California and New York until she found what she was looking for. Hence, her new look.

Taking a deep breath, Sheree picked up the new Ferragamo black leather bag that held her make-up, cell phone, wallet, and a sharp wooden stake.

She plucked a small bottle of holy water from her dresser, then dropped it into her bag. "Don't leave home without it," she said with a grin. A last quick glance in the mirror and she hurried out the door.

Drac's Dive, located in Hollywood, California, was Sheree's first stop. She paused inside the entrance, letting her eyes adjust to the dim lighting. At first, it looked like the place was empty, but, gradually, she realized it looked that way because the walls were painted black and everyone in the place—waitresses, bartenders, the band and patrons—was attired in black clothing.

The air reeked of alcohol, perspiration, and incense.

As soon as she took a seat at the bar, three men approached her, all wanting to "get to know her better." The first was tall and thin, with greasy blond hair, close-set brown eyes, and a long, thin nose. The second was short, with brown hair, blue eyes, and regular features. The third had short black hair and dark brown eyes. And fangs that were obviously fake when he smiled at her.

She declined each invitation. After thirty minutes and several more questionable offers, which she also refused, she left the club. So, she hadn't found a real vampire at Drac's Dive, but there were other clubs out there that catered to the Goth crowd. And what better place for a vampire to hang out than in the midst of a bunch of undead wannabes?

After pulling a slip of paper from her pocket, she perused the list of names she had found on the Internet: Blood and Wine; The Black Rose; Nosferatu's Den; Demon's Delight.

A check of the addresses showed Nosferatu's Den was only two blocks away. Maybe she would have better luck there.

* * *

Derek sat at the bar, his gaze moving over the crowd, considering and rejecting one patron after another. Many were familiar to him. He had dined on a few. It never failed to amuse him the lengths humans would go to make themselves look like vampires, though he had rarely known a real vampire with skin as pale, or lips as red, as those of the wannabe bloodsuckers in attendance. The men were all dressed like Bela Lugosi: black suits; crisp white shirts; long black capes, some lined in red, some in white. A few even mimicked Lugosi's accent. The women also wore black—mostly long flowing gowns with plunging necklines that displayed their cleavage, real or enhanced.

He had never understood the human fascination with vampires. His kind were, for the most part, merciless hunters of mankind. Some, like the members of his family, resisted the urge to kill their prey. Knowing how tempting it was to drain mortals dry, to drink their blood, their warmth, and their memories, he admired his family's determination to take only enough to survive.

He was thinking of changing his hunting ground to Hollywood Boulevard when a bewitching scent tickled his nostrils, drawing his gaze toward the entrance and the slender woman who stood framed in the doorway. Like the others, she wore black, from her hooded cloak to her high-heeled boots. When she lowered her hood, he saw her hair was also black. Dyed, he thought, or perhaps a wig. Her eyes were a deep golden brown beneath thick lashes.

His gaze followed her progress into the club. He noted that she had attracted the attention of several other men, as well.

She sat at the other end of the bar, the slit in her skirt parting to reveal a slender calf clad in black silk.

In spite of the music and the low rumble of conversation,

he heard her order a Bloody Mary, which she sipped slowly as she glanced at the club's occupants. Was she looking for someone in particular, he wondered. Or just looking?

During the next half hour, he watched her reject the advances of one man after another, finally agreeing to dance with a tall, dark-skinned man with an Italian accent.

Derek stared at them through narrowed eyes as they swayed to the music. Seeing her in the arms of another man aroused an unexpected stab of jealousy. It was a new emotion for him and he examined it closely, wondering what had provoked it. He didn't even know the woman.

Almost before he realized what he was doing, he crossed the floor to cut in on the woman and her partner.

Sheree offered a tentative smile to the man who took her partner's place on the dance floor, felt a jolt, like an electric shock, sizzle through her as he gathered her into his arms.

Startled, she looked into his eyes—deep gray eyes that seemed to pierce her very soul.

"Good evening, lovely lady," he murmured. "I hope you don't mind my cutting in."

"Uh . . . no. I guess not."

He smiled, revealing even, white teeth. "Have you a name?"

"Of course," she replied tartly. "Everyone has a name."

"Care to share yours with me?"

She stared at him, unable to shake the feeling that it would be dangerous to tell this stranger who she was.

He lifted one brow, his expression amused. "It's just a name."

"Names have power."

"Only if you're a witch." He cocked his head to the side. "*Are* you a witch?"

"Perhaps."

"I think not." His gaze moved over her from head to heel. "A dark angel, perhaps."

Sheree smiled in spite of herself. "No, but you're getting warmer."

"Ah. A vampire?"

She batted her eyelashes at him. "Why, however did you guess?"

He laughed softly. "Just a hunch, darlin'. Let me see your fangs."

"I'm sorry, but I left them home tonight. Can I see yours?"

"Maybe later. Can I buy you a drink?"

Sheree intended to say no but found herself accepting instead. She wasn't sure if it was because he was without doubt the sexiest man she had ever seen, or if it was his smile, or if it was the way her heart had skipped a beat when he called her darlin'. She grinned inwardly, thinking *all of the above*.

When the music ended, Derek led her to a table, excused himself to get their drinks. She had asked for a Bloody Mary and he decided to make it two, though his drink of choice was something warmer. And redder.

She was swaying to the music, her eyes closed, when he returned.

For a moment, he found himself staring at her. What was it about this woman, he wondered, that enchanted him so? She was pretty. She smelled good. She had a winning smile and she laughed easily. But it was more than that. What more, he had no idea.

"Here you go," he said, placing her drink on the table.

She opened her eyes and smiled as he sat across from her.

"A toast?" he suggested, lifting his glass.

"All right." She lifted hers as well. "What shall we drink to?"

"New beginnings?"

"New beginnings," she repeated, and touched her glass to his.

Her scent tantalized him, as did the steady beat of her heart, the sight of the pulse throbbing in the hollow of her slender throat. He clenched his hands when his fangs brushed his tongue. Damn. He needed to get away from her, needed to feed now, before he did something reckless.

"Will you be here tomorrow night?" he asked, his voice tight.

"Are you leaving?"

He forced a note of humor into his voice. "It's feeding time."

"Oh, of course," she replied, playing along.

"Tomorrow night." He had intended to return to his own home in Sacramento sometime tomorrow, but that could wait a few days. Pushing away from the table, he brushed his knuckles across her cheek. "Ten o'clock."

Before she could answer, he was moving toward the exit.

Sheree stared after him, then shook her head. She was either drunk or seeing things, but she could have sworn she'd seen a faint red glow in his eyes.

Chapter Three

Mara sat on the sofa in front of the fireplace, reminiscing about the past. She told herself she wasn't waiting up for Derek. He was a grown man. He no longer needed her to look out for him, nor would he appreciate it. But she waited anyway.

It was an hour before dawn when he entered the house. He scowled when he saw her.

"Dammit," he hissed. "I'm a big boy now. I don't need my mother waiting up for me."

Mara lifted her head, nostrils flaring, but said nothing.

"I didn't kill anyone."

She smiled faintly. "All things considered, I could hardly condemn you if you did." How could she? She had killed more than her share of mortals in the long centuries of her existence.

Derek dropped into his favorite chair and stretched his legs out in front of him.

"You smell of perfume and alcohol," she remarked.

"I met a woman. I didn't feed on her."

"But you wanted to."

He didn't deny it. "Do you mind if I stay here for another few days?"

"Of course not. The others are all going home tomorrow night."

There had been a time when the DeLongpres and the Cordovas had maintained homes in Oregon, but they had all moved shortly after Derek's birth. Now, they lived in California, though not all in the same town. Derek made his home in Sacramento. Roshan, Brenna, Vince and Cara had homes in San Jose. Rane and Savannah owned a ranch-style house located on several acres near Auburn, while Rafe and Kathy lived in Red Bluff. Mara owned a home in Northern California, but this house in the Hollywood Hills was her favorite.

"Where's Logan?" Derek asked.

"He went out for a run."

Derek nodded. Long ago, Logan had been known as Hektor. Mara had turned him over nine hundred years ago. Derek knew of no other vampires who had lived as long, or possessed such strength and power. His own preternatural abilities were almost as strong, bequeathed to him through his mother's ancient blood.

Like his stepfather and his mother, Derek could run for miles, faster than the human eye could follow, and never get tired. He would never be sick, never age beyond what he was now. Not a bad life, if you didn't mind existing on a warm liquid diet. Not that he didn't enjoy hunting as much as the next vampire, but he remembered all too clearly the taste of mortal food: hamburgers and French fries, chicken and mashed potatoes smothered in gravy, beans and rice, apple pie. Sometimes he thought he would willingly trade fifty years of his existence for a steak, thick and rare.

"Tell me about the girl," Mara said.

"She's young, pretty." He grinned wryly. "She likes vampires."

"How nice for you."

"Yeah." Blowing out a sigh, he gained his feet, then kissed her on the cheek. "I'm going to bed."

Mara watched him climb the stairs to the second floor. He remained a miracle in her eyes, the child she never should have had. She had never wanted a baby, never intended to keep him. She had never had any experience with children, no idea how to care for one. Yes, she had been certain giving the baby away was the right thing to do.

Until she had held him in her arms. One look at her newborn son and she had known why women throughout the ages were willing to endure the pains of childbirth. One look and her heart had swelled with a rush of love unlike anything she had ever known or imagined. One touch, and she had known why mothers fought like grizzly bears to protect their young, why they were willing to live and die for their children. Why she couldn't give him away.

She had watched him grow, marveling at each new accomplishment: his first tooth, his first step, his first word. His first day of school.

His first taste of blood.

Mara remembered it well. She had received a phone call from his kindergarten teacher. A little girl had fallen on the playground and cut her arm. The teacher had found Derek comforting the girl, and licking the blood from the wound.

Later, at home, Mara had taken him aside and explained that he must never do that again, that mortals would not understand. He had looked up at her through dark gray eyes—eyes wise beyond their years—and nodded that he understood. For a short time before he reached puberty, he had developed a sudden craving for raw hamburger, or for steaks so rare Logan had opined there was little point in cooking them at all.

She had taken Derek hunting the first time, and wondered, as she watched him stalk his prey, if, indeed, it was his first time. There had been no hesitation when he summoned his prey, no sense of uncertainty as he bent the young woman over his arm and buried his fangs in her throat.

He would have taken it all had she not stopped him. Even now, Mara could clearly recall the way he had glared at her, lips drawn back, fangs dripping blood, eyes blazing red with anger as he surrendered his prey.

Unchecked, untutored, he would have been a savage predator.

She had seen no sign of that brutality in the years since then, but deep in her heart, she feared the danger still existed.

Chapter Four

Sheree rolled onto her side and stared out the bedroom window, her thoughts immediately turning to the man she had met last night. She had never known a man who intrigued her as he did, nor one as breathtakingly handsome, or as blatantly sexy.

Almost, he looked too good to be real, as if some benevolent genie had read her mind and conjured a man who was everything she had ever dreamed of. Long dark hair: check. Dusky skin: check. Dark gray eyes: check. Tall and broad shouldered: check. Long muscular arms: check.

She loved the way he looked, with his high cheekbones and eyes that were slightly slanted, the way he moved, as if his feet hardly touched the floor, the way he held her when they danced, the way he looked at her, as if she was the most beguiling woman he had ever met.

Slipping out of bed, she stretched her arms over her head, wishing it was nine at night and she was about to get ready to meet her mysterious stranger instead of nine in the morning on her way to the dentist.

* * *

Sheree had arrived at Nosferatu's Den at nine-thirty that night. She had waited as long as she could, but there was just no way to ignore her eagerness to see him again. She had thought the day would never end. It wouldn't have been so bad if she'd been able to go to work. At least that would have been a distraction. But she'd been laid off weeks ago. She could have gone job hunting, but none of the ads in the paper appealed to her, and she wasn't qualified for the ones that did.

Donning a pair of shorts and an old T-shirt, she had plunged into her usual weekend chores: dusting, vacuuming, changing the sheets on the bed. She cleaned the bathroom, did two loads of laundry, and was done by noon. A quick lunch, and the day stretched endlessly before her.

With hours to kill, she had gone shopping for something new to wear that night. Wanting to stand out from the crowd at the Den, she had bought a long silver sheath with a slit up the side her mother would have found scandalous, new underwear—just in case—and a pair of heels.

Back at home, she had showered, shaved her legs, washed her hair, and been ready to go by eight-thirty.

And now it was a quarter after ten, the club was crowded, and he still wasn't there. Maybe he wasn't coming. She had just decided to go home when something drew her gaze to the entrance. And he was there, striding toward her, oozing testosterone. He wore black slacks and a black silk shirt, open at the throat.

Warmth spread through her as she watched him draw closer. And then he was close enough to touch, his smile caressing her as he took her hands in his.

"Sorry I'm late."

She shrugged. He was there now; that was all that mattered.

"You look very pretty this evening, shining like the sun at midnight."

Cheeks flushing, she murmured, "Thank you."

"Not playing the vampire tonight?" he mused, gesturing at her gown.

"No. Disappointed?"

"Not at all. There are enough fake fangs and black wigs in this place already." He lifted a lock of her golden hair and let it slip through his fingers. "Don't you know you're prettier as God made you?"

He guided her to a booth in the back, slid in beside her, his thigh brushing hers, sending little frissons of anticipation rocketing through her. "So, will you tell me your name tonight?"

"If you tell me yours."

"Derek."

"Sheree."

"A lovely name for a lovely lady. So, what are you in the mood for?"

You. She bit back the word, the heat in her cheeks growing warmer as her gaze met his. She breathed a sigh of relief that she hadn't spoken out loud, that he couldn't read her mind.

He lifted one brow, a mysterious glint in his eye. "Can't decide?"

"I don't know. I always order a Bloody Mary but I think I'd like to try something different tonight."

"How about a Vampire's Kiss?"

She stared at him. "A what?"

"A Vampire's Kiss. It's a French martini."

"I don't believe you."

"It's good."

She eyed him skeptically. "What's in it?"

"Finlandia Vodka, Korbel Champagne, Chambord, and a bit of sugar tinted red for the rim of the glass."

"What's Chambord?"

"It's a black raspberry liqueur. It gives the drink its dark color. For a more realistic look, some bartenders drizzle red syrup or grenadine on the inside edge of the glass so it looks like blood dripping."

"Have you had it before?"

He nodded. "It's an elegant drink. Really quite good. Are you game?"

She hesitated. Something in the way he said "game" conjured a quick mental image of a fawn being brought down by a hungry lion.

"Sheree?"

She realized the waitress had arrived and was waiting for their order. "I think I'll just have a glass of chardonnay."

Derek smiled at the waitress. "Make it two." He leaned back, his arm resting on the top edge of the booth. "Not feeling daring tonight, after all?"

She laughed, suddenly self-conscious without knowing why. "I don't think I want to drink anything that looks like blood."

"Ah."

Disliking the silence that fell between them, she said, "What do you do for a living?"

"I play the stock market from time to time."

"Seriously?"

He nodded.

"Seems like a risky way to make a living. Especially these days."

He shrugged. "I do all right. And I can afford to lose."

"Oh?"

Leaning forward, he whispered, "My parents are very rich."

Lowering her voice, she murmured, "So are mine."

He wasn't surprised. Everything about her screamed

money, from her shoes to her handbag. "You don't work, then?"

"I used to. I was laid off three weeks ago. You don't know anyone who wants to hire someone with absolutely no skills, do you?"

"Why do you need a job?"

"A girl has to do something with her time. The only thing is, I'm not really qualified for anything."

"No?"

She shook her head. "I majored in folklore in college. Not exactly in demand these days."

"I guess not. You should have been taking classes in aerospace engineering and computer programming."

"Tell me about it."

Derek smiled at the waitress when she delivered their order.

Sheree noticed the tip he left was more than the cost of their drinks. A good sign, she thought. She had dated a lot of guys who claimed to be wealthy, but expected her to pay for dinner.

Sheree took the glass he offered her. "Last night we drank to new beginnings," she said. "What shall we drink to tonight?"

His gaze moved over her, blatantly bold. "Getting to know each other better?"

Everything female within her responded to the heated look in his eyes, the sexual intimacy implied in his suggestion.

With a nod, she lifted her glass, felt his gaze linger on her throat as she swallowed.

Derek glanced at the dance floor. Several couples were locked in each other's arms, rocking back and forth in time to a low, sensual beat.

He jerked his chin at the dancers, then held out his hand. "Shall we?"

Her hand was small and warm in his as he led her onto the floor and drew her into his arms. Wonderful pastime, dancing, he thought. The perfect excuse to hold her close, feel the welcome heat of her body against his. Being this close to him made her nervous. He knew it by the sudden uptick in the beat of her heart.

"So, I gather you're really into the whole vampire scene," he remarked after a moment.

"They fascinate me. Of course, rationally I know they don't exist, but . . ." She shook her head. "I can't help believing they do."

"And what do you think they'd be like, if they were real?"

"I'm not sure." It was hard to focus when he was so close, when his breath was warm against her cheek. He held her lightly, yet she was aware of a barely leashed power lurking just beneath the surface. "What do you think?"

"I suppose it would depend on the vampire."

"Oh? In what way?"

He drew her closer, inhaling the fragrance of her hair and skin, the faint coppery scent of the warm red tide that flowed silently through her veins. "I imagine vampires are like people in most ways. Some good, some bad. Some brave, some not. Some happy with their nocturnal lifestyle, some wishing for relief."

"Hmm. I never thought of that."

His knuckles stroked the side of her neck. "You've obviously never considered the danger, either."

She shivered at his touch. "What do you mean?"

"Vampires are born predators."

"Even the good ones?"

"Even the good ones."

"But you don't believe they really exist, do you?"

He was about to say he knew they did when a familiar scent wafted through the air. Looking toward the entrance, he swore under his breath, then led Sheree back to their table.

"Is something wrong?" Sheree asked, sliding into the booth.

"Oh, yeah," Derek said, still standing. "My sister is here." The lie rolled easily off his lips. After all, he couldn't very well introduce Mara as his mother, not when she looked younger than he did.

Sheree glanced past Derek to see a slender woman gliding toward them. "She's lovely," Sheree murmured, although lovely didn't really do the young woman justice. Her skin was smooth and clear, her figure slim and perfect. Hair as black as ebony fell down to her hips.

The woman smiled as she approached. "Derek, how nice to see you."

"Sister, dear." He didn't ask what she was doing there, but the question was implied in the tone of his voice.

"You must be Sheree. I'm Mara."

"I'm pleased to meet you. Won't you join us?"

"No, thank you." Mara laughed softly. "I just stopped by for a drink."

"Do you come here often?" Sheree asked.

"Now and then, when I'm thirsty. I don't want to intrude on your evening, but it was lovely meeting you, Sheree."

Rising on her tiptoes, Mara kissed Derek on the cheek, then melted into the crowd.

"You two seem very close," Sheree remarked. "I always wanted a sister, or an older brother."

"Yeah, me, too." Derek slid into the booth, his gaze following his mother's progress toward the bar. What the hell was she doing here? As if he didn't know. "Do you want another drink?"

"I don't think so." Sheree frowned. "Mara. That name sounds familiar somehow."

"Does it?"

She leaned forward, one elbow propped on the table, her chin resting on her hand. "I overheard a couple of men mention it one night. But they were talking about vampires, so I'm sure it was another Mara."

"Of course. What were they saying about her?"

"Something about her being the oldest, most powerful vampire in existence." Sitting back, she made a dismissive gesture with her hand. "They claimed she knew Cleopatra."

It was nearing one A.M. when Derek walked Sheree to her car. After kissing her good night, he returned to the Den and ordered a real vampire martini: a glass of red wine laced with blood. Sipping it slowly, he thought about what she had said. People—other vampires? hunters?—were talking about Mara. He had to wonder who they were and what, exactly, they had been saying. His mother had kept a pretty low profile for the past twenty-six years. Few outside their family knew she had somehow evolved from vampire to human, a mystery no one could explain, or that she had willingly given up her humanity because of him.

At Mara's urging, his stepfather had bestowed the Dark Gift upon her. Her preternatural powers had returned stronger than ever, perhaps because Blackwood's blood was Mara's blood. She had always been a force to be reckoned with, but never more so than now. If those talking about her were humans hoping to do her harm, they were in for a hell of a surprise, one that was likely to be their last.

Like the rest of his family, Derek was in awe of his mother. Although she looked younger than he did, she had been born in Egypt in the time of the pharaohs.

His mother. She was the most beautiful woman he had ever seen, her eyes a deep emerald green, her hair thick and long and as black as night. Not only was she the most beautiful, but she was the most powerful creature in existence. He had grown up on stories of her life—how she had been raised as a slave in the house of Chuma, one of Pharaoh's trusted advisers, and how, just a month shy of her fifteenth birthday, her master had given her to Shakir, a wealthy ally, as a gift. There had been no male slaves in Shakir's household, no eunuchs. Mara had skimmed over the years she'd spent in Shakir's palace, but it had been easy for Derek to imagine what she had suffered there. She had run away so many times that her master had finally locked her in a cell, releasing her only when he desired her to warm his bed.

Had it not been for Dendar, the vampire who had come to her in the dark of night, Mara likely would have perished in that foul prison. Dendar had turned her and deserted her, leaving Mara to discover for herself what she had become and how to survive. Fueled by rage infused with preternatural power, she had avenged herself on the men who had used and abused her, and then destroyed the vampire who had made her.

She had confessed once that she regretted killing her sire. *Had I known how wonderful it is to be a vampire,* she had said with a sigh, *I might have kissed him instead.* Knowing his mother would blow off his concern, Derek made a quick call to Logan, advising his stepfather that Sheree had overheard some men talking about Mara.

He might be worrying for nothing, Derek mused when he ended the call, but why take chances?

Chapter Five

Sheree drove home slowly, her thoughts on Derek. And his sister, who was as beautiful as her brother was handsome.

While getting ready for bed, Sheree tried to remember exactly what the men she had heard talking about Mara had said. Of course, it couldn't be the same Mara, just an odd coincidence.

She tried to imagine what it would be like to have lived since the time of Cleopatra, to have watched the world change so drastically. Every new invention must seem like a miracle to someone born back then.

How did you adjust to such radical changes in your life? But then, modern man had to adjust to changes, too. Horses replaced by cars, candles replaced by gas lights and then electricity. Paperback books going the way of the dinosaur. Landlines being swallowed up by cell phones that grew increasingly more powerful and did practically everything but the laundry. Not that people did much laundry these days, what with disposable clothing and material that shed dirt the way ducks shed water.

She grinned, thinking about the new iPad Z12, and cars that talked to you and were capable of driving themselves if you didn't want to be bothered holding the wheel, or if you wanted to take a nap during a long journey.

After brushing her teeth, Sheree slipped under the covers and closed her eyes, all thoughts of vampires and technology fading away as Derek's image rose in her mind and followed her to sleep. . . .

And he was there, so real she knew she couldn't be dreaming. He whispered her name as he drew her into his arms, his hands sliding up and down her back, his palms skimming the sides of her breasts, his mouth covering hers in a kiss that sent a shaft of heat straight to her core. His tongue tangled with hers in a provocative duel that had her clinging to him as the only solid thing in a world rapidly spinning out of control.

Sheree closed her eyes, gasping with pleasure as he kissed his way to her throat, his tongue like lightning as he laved the tender place beneath her ear. In a distant part of her mind, she realized he was biting her, but it felt so good, she didn't care. Pleasure spiraled deep within her, spinning outward to every fiber of her being, more sensual and satisfying than anything she had ever imagined.

She smiled when he kissed her good night. At his word, she sank into oblivion.

Sheree was sweet, Derek thought as he drove home from her house. Far sweeter than anyone he had ever known. Or tasted. Slipping inside her mind had been all too easy.

He smiled with the memory, thinking just one taste would never be enough, although he would have to wait a day or two before drinking from her again.

Taking from her too often would leave her weak, listless.

Taking too much could leave her dead.

He had been tempted to seduce her while she was in thrall, but while it might have been physically satisfying, he preferred his partners to be awake and willing.

Pulling into the driveway of his mother's house, he noted that the lights were on. No doubt she was waiting up for him again. Derek slammed the door as he got out of the car. Dammit, he was twenty-five years old and a vampire. What was she worried about?

As expected, Mara was waiting for him in the living room, a vision in a long white velvet robe, her hair like a black nimbus around her shoulders. His vampire senses told him the rest of the family had gone.

She lifted her head when he entered the room, her nostrils flaring, a knowing look in the depths of her deep green eyes.

Derek dropped onto the sofa across from her, folded his arms across his chest, stretched his legs out in front of him. And waited.

"How was your evening?" she asked.

Derek clenched his hands in an effort to hold on to his temper. "I've told you before. I don't need a keeper."

She dismissed his objections with an airy wave of her hand. "I'm your mother. It's my job to worry."

"What, exactly, are you worrying about?"

"I still have enemies. Not all of them are dead, you know. None of them would hesitate to avenge themselves on me by destroying you."

He nodded, wondering if two of those enemies had been in the Den tonight, talking about her. "I'm a big boy. I think I can take care of myself."

"Perhaps." She rose in a smooth, sinuous motion. "But you can't blame me for worrying. After all, you are my only son." She dropped a kiss on the top of his head. "And I'm not likely to have another. Good night."

He watched her walk toward the stairs; then, with a wry smile, he muttered, "I love you, too."

He grinned when she waved a hand to let him know she'd heard the words he spoke all too seldom. She might be proud, vain, sometimes annoying, often demanding, but there was no denying that he loved her more than words could say.

Which made him more determined than ever to find out who was looking for her. And why.

Knowing Logan was waiting for her, Mara put a little extra swing in her stride when she entered the bedroom, smiled smugly when her husband whistled under his breath. Although she had known him for centuries, her lust for him, her need for him, had never waned. Even when she'd told herself she didn't love him, didn't need him or any other man, it had been a lie.

"Did you find out anything?" Throwing back the covers, he patted the space beside him, his eyes hot as she slipped out of her robe, revealing a diaphanous black gown that was little more than a whisper of silk.

"No." She slid into bed beside him, her body pressing against his.

"You met the girl?"

"Yes. She doesn't know anything. She's just a foolish little vampire groupie."

Logan laughed softly. "I guess she hit the mother lode."

Mara tossed her head. "I don't want to talk about her or hunters, or wannabe vampires."

"No?" Wrapping her in his arms, he nuzzled her breasts. "What do you want to talk about?"

"Nothing." She traced the width of his shoulders, raked her fingers down his chest. He was a magnificent creature, with the physique of a Greek god and honest, deep-set brown eyes. She had turned him on a whim. Another man might have hated her for it, but not Logan. He had never bewailed the loss of his humanity. To the contrary, he had readily accepted his new way of life, and her, without reproach. She had always admired him for that.

"Derek thinks you're in danger."

Eyes flashing, Mara pushed him back on the bed and straddled his hips. "I said I don't want to talk."

Throwing his arms out to the side in a gesture of feigned surrender, he grinned at her. "I'm all yours, woman. Have your wicked way with me."

Mara leaned forward, her hair falling around the two of them like a black velvet curtain. "That is exactly what I had in mind."

Chapter Six

Pearl Jackson leaned back in her chair and swirled the wine in her glass. "I'm bored."

"You're always bored," Edna replied, refilling her own glass.

"Well, can you blame me? It's been years since we had any fun." Pearl sipped her wine. "Do you ever wonder what happened to Mara's baby? He'd be a grown man now. Do you think he turned into a vampire?"

Edna shrugged. "I don't know. What difference does it make?"

"None, I guess. But aren't you the least bit curious to know if he survived?"

Edna stared at her friend. "What made you think of him after all this time?"

"I don't know, dear. I was just sitting here reminiscing about the past, thinking about how drastically our lives have changed."

Edna snorted. "Changed? That's putting it mildly, don't you think? If it hadn't been for Rafe turning us, we'd both be long dead by now."

"True." Pearl sighed. "I'd be a hundred and six and you'd be . . ."

"Never mind! Age is a number, and mine is unlisted."

Pearl shook her head. "You always were secretive about your age. I never understood why. It's nothing to be ashamed of."

"Maybe not, but saying it out loud . . ." Edna shook her head. "It just sounds so old. If I don't say it, then I can pretend I'm still young."

"Well, then, I guess it's a good thing you can't see your face in a mirror!"

Edna glared at her, then burst out laughing.

After a moment, Pearl laughed, too. She and Edna Mae Turner had shared a room in the maternity ward in a Texas hospital decades ago. They had hit it off instantly and had been the best of friends, both as mortals and vampires, ever since.

"So," Edna said, wiping the tears from her eyes. "What do you want to do?"

"Let's go find Mara's son."

"Are you out of your hundred-and-six-year-old mind? If Mara finds out we're looking for him, you'll never see a hundred and seven!"

"Oh, pshaw. I'm sure she's over it by now, dear."

"We helped Dr. Ramsden kidnap her son," Edna said dryly. "Mothers don't get over things like that."

"Aren't you the least bit curious to see if the boy went fanged or furry?"

Edna frowned, then exclaimed, "Oh! His father's latent werewolf gene!"

"Exactly. Derek carries it, too."

"I wonder if he shifts during the full moon?" Edna wondered aloud.

"Even if he does, I shouldn't think it would be a big deal. I mean, vampires can already shape-shift," Pearl said, and then frowned. "Vamp or wolf, how will we ever find him?

We don't know where he lives. Or if he's even in the country. It would be like looking for a needle in a haystack. Damn, it was such a good idea, too!"

"I know how to find him," Edna said, warming to the idea.

"You do?"

"I drank from him, don't you remember?"

"That was years ago, dear, when he was a baby." Pearl shifted in her chair, then crossed her ankles. "Why, he must be twenty-five or twenty-six by now. Do you think the bond is still effective?"

"Why wouldn't it be?"

"Well, you've never used it. I don't know how long such a bond lasts when it's just one-sided. I know it's different if there's a blood exchange."

"It could be a moot point," Edna mused. "For all we know, the boy could be dead."

Pearl shook her head. "Always looking at the negative."

"I'm just being practical," Edna retorted. "Do you think Mara knows about the werewolf gene?"

"I doubt it, unless the boy's shifted." Pearl slapped her hand on her knee. "Come on, it will be an adventure. I'm tired of sitting around doing nothing. Even if we never find him, at least it'll give us something to do. A purpose! A quest! Are you with me?"

"Of course I am," Edna retorted with a smug smile. "You won't find him without me." She paused a moment before saying, "We never did avenge Travis's death."

Pearl nodded. Lou McDonald had destroyed Travis years ago. Pearl had fully intended to avenge her grandson's death, but, what with one thing or another, it had never happened. But it wasn't too late, she thought, grinning. Thanks to Rafe Cordova, if there was one thing she had plenty of, it was time.

Chapter Seven

As was her wont, Sheree slept late. On waking, she spent half an hour meditating, took a quick shower, and then went downstairs for breakfast.

She had often thought of hiring a housekeeper, or maybe a chef. Or maybe both. But cooking and cleaning the house gave her something to do, and though her mother would never understand, Sheree found a certain satisfaction in knowing how to cook and keep house. Of course, once she got married, she would never have to lift a hand again, especially if she married a man of her mother's choosing.

Sheree pushed a stray lock of hair behind her ear as she waited for her toast to pop up. She kept hoping her mother would stop her eternal matchmaking. In a letter received only a few days ago, her mother had touted her two latest choices: Ralph Upton, only son of a prominent surgeon and a successful lawyer who was on the fast track to becoming a millionaire in his own right, and Neil Somerset of the New York Somersets, who had recently invented a new and improved weapons system that was going to make his company richer than it was already.

She shuddered. All the money in the world wouldn't get her into bed with Neil, or Ralph, either.

After buttering her toast, Sheree poured herself a glass of orange juice and sat at the table. She had met Ralph Upton at a benefit last year. Nothing her mother said would persuade her to consider him for a husband. As for Neil Somerset, he was a playboy, just like his father.

In the living room, Sheree practiced her tai chi, her thoughts wandering to Derek. How did he spend his days? Was he thinking of her? Would he be at the club tonight? He hadn't said anything about meeting again.

Nevertheless, later that day she haunted the shops on Rodeo Drive looking for just the right outfit. She found it at her third stop: a pair of slinky red leather pants; a low-cut, see-through white sweater paired with a white tank top; and a pair of red, high-heeled sandals. She nodded as she looked at herself in the mirror. If this didn't make Derek sit up and take notice, nothing would.

Sheree glanced at the club's entrance, then at her watch. It was after eleven. Time to call it a night. She felt suddenly foolish for sitting there waiting for Derek. Surely, if he had any interest in seeing her again, he would have been there by now. There was no denying she had been attracted to him. Had she read more into their meeting than was there?

Just as she was about to leave two elderly women entered the club, a sort of female Mutt and Jeff, Sheree thought, grinning. One was tall with white hair, the other shorter with bright red hair. She had never seen two people who looked more out of place. They both wore long black skirts and brightly colored blouses. They had to be in their seventies, Sheree mused. What on earth were they doing in a place like this? Arm in arm, they circled the edge of the dance floor until they found an empty table.

Slipping off the bar stool, Sheree settled her handbag over her shoulder, then headed for the door.

And bumped into the very man she had been waiting for all night. "Derek!"

"You're not leaving, are you?" he asked.

Pride and hurt feelings urged her to say yes and sweep past him. But there was nothing waiting for her at home. And she was all dressed up. . . .

"Sheree?" He flashed her a megawatt smile. "I know we didn't say anything about meeting tonight, but I was hoping you'd be here."

"I guess I have time for one drink," she said, and hoped she didn't sound too eager.

"Great." Taking her by the hand, he led her to a small table and held her chair. Whistling softly, he sat across from her. "You look terrific."

"Thank you."

"Is that a new outfit?"

"This old thing? Heavens no, I've had it for hours." Her shopping spree had cost her over eight hundred dollars, but when he smiled at her again, she considered it money well spent.

"Sit tight," he said. "I'll be right back."

Sheree smiled as she watched him thread his way through the crowd toward the bar. She couldn't help noticing that several other women were also tracking him, including the two elderly women, who had their heads together. She would have given up her new Jimmy Choo's to know what they were saying.

Derek returned a short time later with their drinks.

"Thank you." Feeling as though she was being watched, Sheree glanced at the two old women again. They weren't looking at her, but at Derek, an expression that looked almost like avarice in their eyes. "Do you know those two women?" she asked. "The ones in the brightly colored shirts?"

"No," he said. "Should I?" But even as he spoke the words, he had the strangest feeling that he should know the red-haired one.

"They've been staring at you ever since you came in." Not that she could blame them. He was gorgeous.

Derek shrugged, his eyes narrowing as he realized the two women were vampires. "What do you say we blow this place and go for a drive?"

"I don't know. Where do you want to go?"

"Just someplace where I can be alone with you."

Warning bells went off in the back of her mind. She hardly knew him, had no way of knowing if anything he had told her was true. He could be just another fortune-hunter. Heaven knew she had met more than her share.

"Too soon to trust me?" he asked.

"Maybe a little. I mean, I don't even know your last name."

Nodding, he pulled his wallet out of his back pocket and flipped it open to display his driver's license.

"Derek Blackwood," she said, reading the details out loud. "Sex: male. Hair: black. Eyes: gray. Height: six feet two. Weight: one hundred eighty. Date of birth: October twenty-fifth," she noted with a grin. "Almost a Halloween baby. It says here you live in Sacramento. What are you doing in L.A.?"

"Visiting my parents. They celebrated their twenty-fifth anniversary a few days ago. So, what about that drive?"

Sheree opened her mouth, fully intending to refuse. Only the words that came out were, "Yes, I'd love it."

His car was parked at the curb—a sleek white sports car

with black racing stripes and black leather seats. Unless he had borrowed the car, he really was rich. A top-of-the-line convertible like this one didn't come cheap.

He held the door for her, slid behind the wheel, and punched the ignition. She wasn't surprised that he preferred to drive instead of programming the destination autodrive. She didn't know him well, but she had already determined that he liked to be in control.

It was a beautiful night. The sky was clear, dotted with millions of twinkling stars, glowing satellites, and a full moon.

Derek drove the way he did everything: masterfully. It was a trait she found attractive. "Where are we going?"

He shrugged. "No place in particular. It's nice to breathe some air that's just air."

"True." Nosferatu's Den was a high-class nightclub, but the combined scents of perspiration, liquor, and perfume were occasionally overpowering.

A short time later, he pulled onto the freeway, headed toward Angelus Crest Highway. Sheree had been there before, during the day. It was a lovely ride, with a spectacular view. The air was filled with the fragrant scent of pines and earth. Some people claimed ghosts roamed the hills.

They climbed steadily upward for a while, and then Derek pulled into one of the turnouts along the side of the road. After shutting off the engine, he got out, opened her door, and offered his hand.

"I've never been up here at night," Sheree remarked. "The view is breathtaking."

"Yes," Derek said, gazing into her eyes. "Breathtaking."

She flushed at his compliment. "You like the night, don't you?"

"What do you mean?"

"I'm not sure. It suits you somehow."

A wry grin tugged at the corners of his mouth. She had no idea, he thought. "What about you? Are you a night person?"

Not until I met you. Aloud, she said, "I'm more of a morning person. Sunrises and early morning walks. Dew on the grass. The sense of newness that comes with each day."

"I guess opposites do attract."

"So they say." Silence settled between them. Sheree looked out over the valley. "It's a long way down. I remember reading about some man who accidentally drove over the edge and fell five hundred feet."

"Don't worry," Derek said, slipping his arm around her waist. "I won't let you fall."

The trouble was, she was falling already. Falling for a man she scarcely knew, but desperately wanted to know better.

His arm tightened around her waist, drawing her closer to his side. When she looked up at him, he lowered his head and claimed her lips with his in a searing kiss that made her toes curl with pleasure. He had kissed her before, but never like this. Surely no one had ever been kissed like this.

His tongue skated across her lower lip and hers darted out to meet it, eager to taste him.

Murmuring her name, he drew her into his arms, holding her body flush against his. They had danced together but he had never held her so tightly.

When he drew back, she released a deep, shuddering breath. "Wow."

He smiled down at her, his dark eyes glittering in the moonlight. "Wow, indeed," he agreed, and kissed her again.

He was breathing heavily when he released her. Taking a step back, he turned away from her, his hands tightly clenched at his sides. Her nearness aroused his hunger, tempting him almost beyond bearing. His whole being ached with need, urging him to take what he wanted. She was close. Too close. The steady beat of her heart, the scent of her blood, her desire. It was almost overpowering.

"Derek? Is something wrong?"

"No," he said, his voice oddly thick. "I just need a moment."

She stared at his back. Even in the darkness, she could see the tension in his shoulders. She reached out to him, then withdrew her hand. "Is there anything I can do?"

"No." He took several deep breaths before he turned to face her. "Sorry."

Confused, she murmured, "It's okay." Was he apologizing for kissing her?

"We should head back," he said. "It's late."

Nodding, she got into the car as he held the door for her. What the hell had just happened? What was he sorry about? Had she said something wrong, done something that offended him? She replayed everything that had happened in her mind, but could find no reason for his odd behavior. She knew he was attracted to her, knew he'd been just as turned on by that kiss as she had.

He said little on the ride back to the Den. Lost in thought, she hardly noticed.

When they returned to the club, it was closed. Sheree glanced at her watch. How had they gotten down the hill so fast?

Derek handed her out of the car, walked her to her own, and kissed her lightly. "Good night, Sheree. Sweet dreams."

"You, too." Sliding behind the wheel, she started the car, then pulled out of the parking lot. A glance in the rearview mirror showed Derek standing on the sidewalk, hands shoved into his pockets, as he watched her drive away. "Weird," she muttered as she turned the corner toward home. "The whole evening was just plain weird."

* * *

Derek watched Sheree's car until it was out of sight. What must she think of him, kissing her like there was no tomorrow one minute and then taking her home with no explanation? But he couldn't very well explain that the scent of her blood had been driving him crazy, or that it had taken all his willpower to keep from sinking his fangs into her throat.

Well, it was over and done, he thought, as he strolled down the street to a dive that was open for another half hour. Plenty of time to find what he was looking for.

He paused inside the doorway. The crowd was thin, with only a dozen men and women. Several couples were wrapped in each other's arms on the dance floor. The music was slow and heavy, darkly sensual.

Derek made his way toward the bar, aware that the three women seated there watched his every move. One was on the verge of passing out. One looked way too young to be in the place. But the third . . . she was older, not pretty, but striking. And bold. She met his gaze without blinking.

Intrigued, Derek made his way toward her. "Do we know each other?"

She laughed, a deep, throaty laugh. "Surely you can come up with a more original line."

"I could, but I don't have time. The club's about to close."

"Maybe you could think of a better one while you drive me home," she suggested.

"Fine by me," he said. Anything to get her outside.

Smiling, she unfolded from her chair in a sinuous movement that caused the slit in her skirt to part, revealing a glimpse of her leg from ankle to thigh.

"Shall we?" he asked.

"We shall." She took hold of his arm and they left the club. "Where's your car?" she asked in a sultry purr.

"Right here." He turned his back toward her to open the door, heard the soft swish of a wooden stake slicing through the air.

He cursed himself for being careless as he darted to the side, hissed as the stake pierced his flesh, mere inches from his heart. Spinning around, he drove his fist into the woman's jaw.

She dropped like a stone.

The faint snick of a gun warned him the woman hadn't been alone. Moving faster than the eye could follow, Derek whirled around, jerked the gun from the man's hand, and tossed the weapon aside. A quick twist broke the hunter's neck.

Grimacing with pain, Derek jerked the stake from his back, then tossed it into the storm drain. Breathing hard, he glanced up and down the street. There was no one in sight.

Never one to let a meal go to waste, he buried his fangs in the man's neck. Most vampires shrank from drinking from the dead. But he wasn't most vampires. The woman's blood, sweeter than the man's, served as dessert.

The scent of fresh blood drew Mara downstairs. She found Derek in the kitchen, rummaging in one of the drawers. "What's going on?"

"Nothing," he said brusquely. "Go back to bed."

"Nothing? You're bleeding." She ran her hand over his bare back. "Someone stabbed you. Who?"

"I don't know. Some woman I picked up in a bar."

Mara pulled a dish towel from one of the drawers. "Not that little blonde I saw you with!"

"No. A stranger. We left the club together. When I turned my back on her, she stabbed me. There was a man with her."

"Hunters." Mara wet the towel in the sink, and wiped the

blood dripping steadily from the ragged hole in her son's back. The wound should have healed by now, she thought, frowning. "Does it still hurt?"

"What do you think?"

"I think a part of the stake is still lodged inside."

"Well, don't just stand there. Get it the hell out."

Reaching into the cupboard over the sink, Mara withdrew a large brown wooden box. Inside, among other odds and ends, was a stainless steel probe. "Hold still."

Derek hissed, then swore as she began to explore the wound. "Geez, woman, what are you doing in there? Digging for gold?"

"Hold still! I've almost got it."

Moments later, she tossed a long wooden sliver into the sink, along with the probe. Wetting the towel again, she washed the blood from his back. And smiled. The wound was already healing, the deep gash knitting together seamlessly, leaving no scar behind.

"About the hunters," she said, wiping her hands. "I trust you cleaned up the mess."

Derek nodded. He had taken the man's ID and left his body in an alley. The police would assume he'd been the victim of a robbery, or a drug deal gone bad. After dumping the body, he had wiped his memory from the woman's mind and left her in her car, lucky to still be alive.

"I don't like this," Mara said, tossing the bloody towel into the sink on top of his ruined shirt. "I haven't heard of any hunters in the area. Did you get their names?"

"The woman's driver's license identified her as Julia LaHood, thirty-six, with an address in Porterville. The man, Selkirk, was in his forties. Home town in Washington."

"LaHood." Mara hissed out a breath. "From Porterville."

"You know her?"

"No, but I killed a hunter named LaHood about thirty years ago. She could be his daughter." Leaning against the counter, Mara crossed her arms. Her family had left Porterville twenty-five years ago. She might have thought it was coincidence that LaHood came from that part of the country, except she had never believed in coincidence.

"I know what you're thinking," Derek said. "Forget it. There's no way anyone could find you after all this time. We've all been careful."

"There's always a way," Mara retorted. "I haven't lived this long by making assumptions."

The barb stung, but he couldn't argue with her. He had been damn lucky tonight. If his reflexes had been a shade slower, it might have been his body lying in an alley.

"You're forgetting one thing," he said. "They weren't after you. They were after me."

And with that parting shot, he went upstairs to bed.

Mara glanced at the arched doorway that led into the kitchen. "You can come in now."

With a wry grin, Logan sauntered into the room. "I didn't want to interrupt."

Mara smiled, thinking how lucky she was to have him in her life. He'd had doubts about being a father, but she had no complaints. He had been firm with Derek, stern when necessary, but he had never interfered between mother and son.

"You heard what happened?" she asked.

Nodding, he gathered her into his arms. Being a vampire, it was hard not to eavesdrop.

"Why would hunters be looking for any of us after all this time? We've kept a low profile since before Derek was born. Our old enemies are no longer a threat. We haven't made any new ones." She looked up at him, thinking, as always, that he was the most devastatingly handsome man she had ever known. And she had known many. "Have you nothing to say?"

He shrugged. "Unlike you, I don't see conspiracies around every corner. Derek was at a vampire club. What better place to look for a vampire? Like you said, we've kept a low profile. Hell, I doubt if anyone who would care even knows that Derek exists. I think it was just bad luck that a hunter found him."

"But you have to admit, destroying my son would be the perfect way for someone to avenge themselves on me."

"You think the LaHood woman intended to kill Derek to avenge her father's death?"

"It's possible."

"Anything is possible," he murmured. "A meteor could wipe out life as we know it. A tsunami could sweep us all out to sea." He lifted a lock of her hair and let it sift through his fingers. "Or I could take you to bed and make love to you until sunrise."

"I'll take door number three," she said, leaning into him.

Logan swung her into his arms, then carried her swiftly up the stairs to their bedroom. He was undressing her when she grabbed his hands, her brow furrowed.

"All of our old enemies aren't dead," she said, a hint of red glowing in her eyes.

Logan frowned, and then nodded. "You're thinking about those two old ladies, aren't you? The ones who were with Ramsden."

"Edna and Pearl," Mara said, her voice edged with malice. "I should have killed those troublesome creatures years ago."

Chapter Eight

"I told you I could find him," Edna said, her voice ringing with triumph.

"I know, dear. I never doubted you for a minute." Pearl kicked off her shoes, then sat back in her chair and picked up the glass of wine on the table beside her. It was a lovely room, done in shades of green and gold. "Who do you think that girl was?"

"I have no idea. His next meal, perhaps?" Edna sank into the other chair. "He certainly turned into a handsome specimen, didn't he? So tall and dark. Makes me wish I'd been turned at thirty."

Pearl rolled her eyes. "You always were boy crazy."

"You don't think he's attractive?"

"That's beside the point, dear."

"We should have said hello."

Pearl stared at her friend. "Have you lost your mind? What would you have said? 'Hi, Derek, you probably don't remember me, but I helped kidnap you when you were a baby'?"

"Don't be absurd!"

With a huff of annoyance, Pearl said, "Now that we've seen him, I think we should leave town."

"Leave? Why?"

"Because he's not here alone, you twit. Mara is here."

"Mara?" Edna glanced around the hotel room, as if she expected to find the ancient vampire standing behind her. "Are you sure?"

"I caught her scent inside the club. Didn't you?"

"I wasn't paying attention to anything but Derek."

"Boy crazy, like I said," Pearl remarked with a sigh. "Could you tell if the werewolf gene has kicked in?"

Edna shook her head, her brow furrowed. "No. We need to stay until the full moon."

"I don't think that's a good idea."

"How else are we going to find out if he's both vampire and werewolf?"

"What possible difference can it make?" Pearl asked irritably.

"None, perhaps, but wouldn't you like to know if he can reproduce? What if it was the werewolf gene that allowed Bowden to impregnate Mara? Derek carries Mara's blood and the werewolf gene. . . . We could be looking at the beginning of a whole new race of vampires!"

Pearl stared at her friend, her mind racing with possibilities, but, in the end, her fear of Mara made her shake her head. "True, dear, but, like I said, what difference does it make?"

Deflated, Edna sat back, hands folded in her lap. "What are we going to do if we go back home? You were the one who wanted to put some excitement in our lives, remember?"

"Well, I don't know about you, but the idea of meeting Mara face-to-face is more excitement than I had in mind. We not only kidnapped her son, for goodness' sake, we fed on her child's father. Everyone knows she's never been very big on forgiveness, or are you forgetting what she did to Dr. Ramsden?"

Edna chewed on her thumbnail. Word of the doctor's

death had spread quickly through the vampire community. It had carried Mara's warning loud and clear: mess with my family and you mess with me. "Perhaps you're right."

"Of course I am."

Edna tapped her fingers on the arm of her chair, then sprang to her feet. "We'll just have to stay out of Mara's way," she exclaimed.

Pearl shook her head. "And if we can't?"

"Now who's being negative?" Edna chided. "We can avoid her until the full moon," she said, patting Pearl's shoulder. "And then we'll go home."

Chapter Nine

Louise McDonald sat at her desk, idly thumbing through an old scrapbook. She found it hard to believe she had been in the vampire-hunting business for over thirty-five years. She had made a lot of kills in her long career. In all that time, she'd only let one get away. Mara. The so-called Queen of the Vampires.

Grunting softly, Lou sat back and propped her feet on the edge of her battered desk. Even though it had happened twenty-five years ago, she still recalled her meeting with Kyle Bowden, the foolish mortal who had fallen in love with Mara. Bowden was the only person she had ever met who hired her not to kill a vampire, but to locate one.

She had charged him extra for that. Good thing, too, she thought with a wry grin, since he'd still owed her money when he'd gotten himself killed.

She would have given a month's pay to know the full story behind that odd relationship, and twice that to know what had happened to Mara, and whether her baby had been a boy or a girl, human or vamp or both. The kid would be grown now.

Lou glanced around her office. Tomorrow was supposed to be her last day. She was fifty-four. Time to retire. Vampire hunting was a young man's game, or woman's, as the case may be. But thinking of Mara gave her pause. Taking out the Queen of the Vampires would be a hell of a last coup. Something future hunters would talk about long after Lou was gone.

She reached for her phone, then punched in her sister's number. Cindy answered on the second ring.

"Hey, Lou, what's up?"

"Have you ever wondered what happened to Mara and her brat?"

Cindy snorted. "Where would you even start to look after all this time?"

Lou pulled the morning paper from the pile on her desk. She subscribed to most of the big-city papers. It had long been predicted that newspapers would disappear, and they had, for a few years, but had recently made a comeback. "Three hunters have been killed in the last few days, one of them here, in California. You remember Julia LaHood? She's mentioned in one of the L.A. papers."

"LaHood? Wasn't her old man a hunter a while back?"

"Yeah. I heard Mara got him, although there was never any real proof. What if Julia got wind of Mara's whereabouts and decided to avenge her father?"

"That's a big stretch after all this time." Cindy paused. "You're not thinking of going after Mara, are you?"

"One last hunt," Lou said. "For the biggest game of all."

Chapter Ten

Sheree sat at the breakfast table, the morning paper spread before her as she sipped a cup of English tea. Having little interest in the latest Hollywood scandal or the president's upcoming vacation, she skimmed the headlines until the word *vampire* caught her eye.

Leaning forward, she quickly read the article under the headline VAMPIRE IN THE CITY? According to the article, the body of forty-year-old Ira Selkirk of Granite Falls, Washington, had been found in the alley behind Chin Lee's China Palace, the victim of an apparent robbery. A broken neck was listed as the cause of Mr. Selkirk's death. According to the coroner's report, the man had also lost a pint or two of blood, though there were no injuries to the body other than the one that had killed him. His companion, Julia LaHood, who reported Mr. Selkirk missing and identified the body, said she had last seen Mr. Selkirk at Nosferatu's Den the night before. She had no memory of leaving the club with Mr. Selkirk, and no information regarding his death.

Stunned, Sheree sat back. Drained of blood? Last seen at Nosferatu's Den. She and Derek had been at the Den last night. Had there been a vampire there, too? Stars above, she and Derek could have been the vampire's victims. It was a sobering thought.

Lifting a shaky hand to the side of her neck, she remembered Derek asking if she had considered the danger in looking for a vampire, his warning that creatures of the night were born predators.

If the article in the newspaper was to be believed, he'd been right. The thought troubled her. Blinded by her determination to prove vampires existed, she had blithely ignored the danger. A very real danger.

Suddenly, finding a member of the undead community didn't seem like such a bright idea.

Maybe it was time to stop looking for creatures of the night and turn her attention to something a little less life threatening, like walking barefoot on hot coals or jumping out of airplanes without a parachute.

Sipping her tea, she wondered if Derek had seen the morning paper.

With an irritated sigh, Mara tossed the newspaper on the floor.

"Bad news?" Logan asked, peering up at her through narrowed eyes.

"Some stupid editor splashed the word *vampire* in the headlines."

Logan uttered something unintelligible from under the sheets.

"Derek should have dumped the body where it wouldn't have been found."

"Yeah, and maybe he would have bled out while he was at it."

Mara glared at her husband even though he couldn't see it. The man could be infuriating. But, what was even worse, he was right. Vampires healed almost instantly from most wounds, but there were exceptions. Injuries caused by silver or by wooden stakes dipped in holy water tended to be more painful and last longer. Of course, she was immune to such things, but her son wasn't, though he would be when he was older.

Taking a deep breath, she slid under the covers and curled up against Logan's side. She ran her hands over his back and shoulders. His skin was cool and smooth. She knew every inch of it as well as she knew her own. He was the most incredible lover she'd ever had. She draped one arm over his waist, her fingers running back and forth over his belly, grinned when he sucked in a ragged breath. "You don't really want to go to sleep, do you?"

"It's why I'm in bed."

She ran her tongue along his spine. "There are other things to do in bed."

In a move that would have been a blur to anyone but Mara, he rolled over, ripped the nightgown from her body, and tucked her beneath him. "Is this what you had in mind, woman?"

She grinned up at him, then batted her eyelashes. "Why, you sweet ol' thing," she purred in her best southern drawl, "however did you guess?"

Derek woke with the setting of the sun. Kicking off the sheet, he sat up, listening to the sounds of the house. There was no one home.

After rising, he showered and dressed, then went downstairs.

The newspaper was waiting for him on the coffee table in the living room, folded in half so that the first thing he saw was the story about Selkirk's death. "Subtle, Ma," he muttered.

He read the story, then tossed the paper aside. He should have dumped the body where it wouldn't have been found. It was one of the first things his mother had taught him, but hell, he'd been bleeding like a stuck pig.

He'd been smart enough not to drain the man dry, had sealed the wounds in his neck so there'd be no trace, and figured that was good enough.

Apparently not. Damn reporter!

He'd have to worry about it later. Right now, he needed to feed.

Leaving the house, he paused beside his car and glanced skyward. Two things hit him at the same time: the moon was going to be full tonight, and he had a sudden craving for a thick steak, rare.

Damn. He was a teenager the last time he'd hungered for a steak. It had worried the hell out of his mother, but the cravings had stopped after his first hunt.

He slid behind the wheel, then headed for a popular steak house on Hollywood Boulevard.

The waitress looked a little perplexed when he told her he wanted a thick slice of prime rib, red in the middle, and nothing else.

"No salad? Potato? Rice?"

"Just the steak."

"And to drink?"

"Just the steak," he growled.

After the waitress left to turn in his order, Derek sat back in his chair, aware of the covert stares of some of the other diners. When he stared back, they quickly looked away.

When the waitress returned with his order, Derek had second thoughts. He hadn't eaten solid food in more than ten years. The steak was thick, swimming in red juice. Hoping he could keep it down, he cut a small piece, took a bite, and chewed it carefully, ready to bolt from the restaurant if it threatened to come back up.

It didn't.

He ate the whole thing, savoring every bite, and wondered what was happening to him.

After paying the check, he strolled down Hollywood Boulevard, hands shoved in his pockets. Hollywood was an interesting place, filled with an assortment of interesting people.

A myriad of sounds and sights and smells pressed in on him from every direction. It had taken some getting used to, at first, the constant overload of noise. In time, he had learned to shut most of it out. But the scent of blood was always there—warm, tantalizing, almost irresistible.

And with it, the urge to hunt, to feed, to kill.

His mother had taught him early on that he didn't have to take a life. He'd asked her once how many she'd taken.

"It doesn't matter what I've done," she said. "I did what I had to do at the time. What matters now is what you do. What kind of man you want to be."

The thing was, he wasn't a man in the usual sense of the word. Never had been. Never would be.

"Hey, good lookin', are you lookin' for me?"

He paused at the sound of a woman's voice. Turning, he saw her standing under the awning of a hotel. It was hard to tell how old she was under the layers of paint, but he guessed she wasn't more than twenty, if that. She had a mass of curly brown hair. Her clothes proclaimed her for what she was—a hooker.

"I can show you a good time," she offered.

"I'll bet you can."

Smiling, she moved out from under the awning and linked

her arm to his. "My room's just down around the corner, honey."

He let her lead him down the street until he drew her into a parking lot.

She balked when she realized where he was taking her. "No way!"

"What's the matter? Change your mind?"

"Yes. Let me go!"

"Not just yet." Keeping a firm hold on her arm, he led her into the shadows.

"What are you going to do to me?" She whipped her head back and forth, hoping to find someone to help her, but the parking lot was empty.

"Relax. This won't hurt a bit."

She looked up at him through brown eyes wide with fear. "Please let me go. I have a little boy. He needs me."

"Yeah? Then why aren't you home with him?"

"I've got to earn a living!" She was trembling now.

When they reached the back of the parking lot, Derek folded her in his arms, felt his eyes go red as the hunger rose within him, the brush of his fangs against his tongue.

"No." She stared at him. "No, please!"

Holding her immobile, he lowered his head to her neck, his fangs pricking her skin. Her blood was clean, though heavily flavored with tobacco and alcohol.

He had intended to drain her dry, but guilt rose up within him when his mind brushed hers. She really did have a son, a four-year-old named Danny. Her mother looked after the boy while Star worked the streets.

Lifting his head, he ran his tongue over the tiny wounds in her neck, then wiped the memory of his bite from her mind.

She blinked up at him, her eyes unfocused.

"How much do you charge for your time?" he asked.

"What?"

"What do you charge?"

"Forty credits for an hour. A hundred for the night."

"What's your name? I'll see that you get it."

"St . . . Star Anderson."

"Look at me." Capturing her gaze with his, he said, "You're going to go home now. You won't remember any of this. Tomorrow, you'll go look for a new job, one that lets you be home nights."

"Yes." She nodded, her expression blank. "Tomorrow."

He walked her to his car, then drove her home, noting the address as he walked her to her door. He released her from his spell when she stepped inside.

Bemused by his unexpected benevolence, Derek slid behind the wheel, only to sit there, staring into the distance.

And then he drove to Sheree's house.

Chapter Eleven

Pearl and Edna stepped out of the restaurant's shadow. "That proves it!" Edna exclaimed, nodding.

"He ate a steak, dear," Pearl said, strolling down the sidewalk. "That doesn't prove anything."

"Do I need to draw you a diagram? Vampires don't eat, not anything! Ever! Don't you see? The only explanation is the werewolf gene."

"Or maybe it's just that he's half human, and the human part is kicking in. Did you ever think of that?"

"No." Edna shook her head. "No, I don't believe that."

"Well, the moon is full and he didn't shift, so let's go home."

"Not yet."

"Why not? Why are you so obsessed with his becoming a werewolf? It's not like he'd be the first vampire/werewolf in all of recorded history. Remember Susie McGee?"

"Of course." Edna tapped her forefinger against her lower lip. "I wonder what ever happened to her?"

"She was both."

"But not at the same time," Edna said smugly. "She was a werewolf who was turned into a vampire. Derek could be both at the same time. It's . . . it's unprecedented!"

"So, what? You want to see him get furry, is that it?"

"Exactly." Edna smiled. "We need to buy a camera!"

"And what if he rips our throats out while we're watching?"

"Oh, stop being so dramatic. That isn't going to happen, and you know it. I just have to know if he'll go back to being a vampire once he turns into a werewolf. . . ."

"Assuming he becomes a werewolf," Pearl interjected dryly. "The change might be permanent, like it was with Susie."

"Well, that's probably more likely," Edna admitted. "But, whatever happens, I want to be there to see it."

They were in a residential area now. Pearl stopped to peek into the window of a large house. Inside, a young man and woman were sitting side by side on a long white sofa. A large calico cat lay curled up next to the woman, purring softly.

"What are you looking at?" Edna asked, coming to stand beside her friend.

"Nothing, dear," she said, a wistful note in her voice.

Edna tilted her head to the side. "They look cozy, don't they?"

Pearl nodded. "Do you ever miss being married?"

"Sometimes late at night, I wish I had a man to hold me," she said, sighing. "It's been so long, I've almost forgotten what it was like being held, being loved."

"They're in love," Pearl remarked. "You can tell by the way they look at each other."

"Yes." Edna sighed again. "Have you ever thought that we might be able to . . . Never mind."

"Edna Mae Turner! Are you thinking what I think you're thinking? At our age?"

"I might look old," Edna said with a shrug, "but I don't feel old anymore. I feel younger, better, than I did at twenty."

Pearl clucked softly as she started walking again. She had to agree with her friend. She felt terrific. In all her years as a vampire, she had never met one who had been turned in their seventies. Most vampires tended to be turned in their youth and, naturally, turned others of a comparable age. After all, no one wanted to look eternally old no matter how good they might feel once the deed was done.

"We look awfully good for our ages," Edna opined. "Some nice mortal, elderly men might find us attractive."

Pearl stopped again, her gaze moving over Edna's face. They had been turned over a quarter of a century ago. She had been with her friend every day since then, but had never really looked at her until now. Edna looked her age, and yet, in some remarkable fashion, the lines in her face were hardly noticeable. There was a radiance to her skin that belied her years. Her hair was thicker than it had been before she was turned, her brown eyes sparkled with vitality. "You know, dear, you're really quite lovely."

"Am I?"

"Yes."

Edna regarded her friend for several minutes. "You know, so are you," she said, smiling. "You look your age, and yet you don't. Why, I bet we could find a couple of good-looking men in their fifties to keep us company."

"Do you really think so, dear?"

"Why not?" Linking her arm with Pearl's, Edna continued down the street. "There are lots of good-looking men in Hollywood. No reason why we can't get ourselves some fancy new clothes and look for some nice gentlemen friends while we wait for the next full moon, is there?"

Chapter Twelve

Curled up on the sofa, Sheree wiped the tears from her eyes. Sad movies always made her cry. Of course, most people didn't think it was sad when Dracula was destroyed, but she couldn't help feeling sorry for the monster.

Who was she kidding? She wasn't feeling sorry for the vampire. She was feeling sorry for herself. She had finally found a man she wanted and she'd lost him before she had him.

She felt like a fool, crying her eyes out over a man she hardly knew. Maybe she should just go home, visit her parents, and give Ralph and Neil a second look. So, they weren't tall, dark, handsome, and mysterious. They were settled. Her parents approved of them. Both men came from the same background as she did. She knew what to expect with them—boredom, she thought, sniffling. No matter how she tried to convince herself to give Neil and Ralph a chance, she just couldn't do it. She wanted an alpha male, like Derek, not some wimp in a white button-down shirt and tie.

Earlier, she had considered going to the club to see if he was there, but her pride held her back. She wasn't going to chase him, though she couldn't help wondering what had happened between them the other night. One minute they'd been kissing like a couple of horny teenagers and the next he was driving her back to her car.

Sighing, she turned off the movie, switched off the lights, and went up to bed.

As he had once before, Derek sat in his car outside Sheree's house. It was a nice place, two stories high, made of red brick with white trim and a bright yellow front door. A white picket fence surrounded the tidy front yard; colorful flowerpots filled with cacti sat on a ledge in front of the windows.

He stared up at her bedroom window. He didn't have to see her to know that she'd been crying, that she was in bed, asleep. That she was dreaming of him, a strange dream, the jumbled images switching quickly from one scene to another. But, through it all, a tall, dark-haired man shrouded in a long black cape whose face sometimes resembled his own, and at other times that of actors who had portrayed Dracula, played a major part.

He found that disturbing on several levels. Was it merely her reaction to the Den? To the article in the morning paper? Or had she somehow sensed that he was not the man he pretended to be?

Gradually, the images slowed, became less chaotic, until it was just the two of them, alone on a dark moor, making love beneath a midnight moon.

Gathering his self-control, he jammed the car in gear and stomped on the gas, quickly putting some miles between them before he did the unthinkable, like materializing in her bedroom and making her dreams come true.

At home, he slammed into the house, his nerves on edge, his urge for Sheree riding him hard. Rationally, he knew he was in no condition to be with her. He paced for an hour, then slouched into a chair. Staring into the fireplace, he took slow, deep breaths in an effort to rein in his lust.

He was still seething inwardly when his mother and Logan appeared.

"You're home early." Logan removed his jacket and tossed it over the back of the sofa. Moving to a side table, he poured himself a glass of wine.

Derek grunted his reply.

Mara tossed her wrap on top of her husband's jacket. Lifting her head, she took a deep breath. And frowned. She glanced at Logan, who nodded, indicating he smelled it, too.

Derek shifted in his seat, his gaze still on the fireplace, his hands clenching and unclenching.

Tension sizzled in the air.

Glancing from mother to son, Logan drained his glass. "I'm going up to bed."

"I'll be up soon," Mara said.

Nodding, Logan left the room.

Mara regarded her son for several moments before asking, "What's worrying you?"

"Nothing."

"Don't lie to me," she said sharply.

Derek scowled at her. One of the first things she had taught him was how to block others from reading his thoughts. It was a talent he rarely used at home, but he was grateful for it tonight.

He should have known it wouldn't save him.

"You've eaten mortal food," she said thoughtfully. "I can smell it on you."

He didn't deny it.

"And the moon is full." She sat on the arm of his chair. "Are you craving raw meat again?"

"I don't want to talk about it."

"I can make you tell me, you know."

It wasn't a threat. Simply a statement of fact.

He blew out a breath, then nodded. "I don't know what's happening to me."

"It's happened before."

"I know, but I wasn't fully a vampire then. Why now? I shouldn't be craving food." He snorted. "Maybe I'm reverting."

"I don't think so."

"Then what's causing it?"

"I wish I knew." She placed her hand on his shoulder. "I'm sure it's nothing to worry about."

"I hope you're right." He didn't want to be mortal, yet even as the thought crossed his mind, he wondered if that was true. If he was mortal, the biggest obstacle to being with Sheree would be gone.

"Is there anything I can do?"

"Yeah. Stop treating me like I'm your little boy."

Bending down, she kissed the top of his head. "Sorry, love, but you'll always be my little boy."

With a shake of his head, Derek set her on her feet, then stood. "I'm going to bed."

Mara stared after him, more worried than she had let on. It wasn't normal for vampires to crave mortal food. She had dismissed it as some sort of hormone thing when he was a teenager, some crazy aberration because he was half human. But she couldn't ignore it now.

Troubled, she followed him up the stairs.

Logan was waiting for her in their room. After closing

the door, he took her in his arms. "What do you think's wrong with him?"

"I wish I knew!"

"Could he be reverting?"

Shrugging, she laid her cheek against his chest. "If anything happens to him . . ." She let out a long, shuddering sigh. She loved Derek more than her own life. The thought of him in pain, the thought of losing him . . . Tears stung her eyes. She had killed the man who'd kidnapped her son when he was a baby, killed Thomas Ramsden without a qualm, as she would kill anyone who hurt what was hers. But this . . . there was no one to fight.

Lifting her head, she sniffed away her tears, then shook her head. "I don't believe he's reverting. Except for me, I know of no other vampire who has ever reverted." She shook her head again. "He wasn't made a vampire. He was born a vampire." She grinned ruefully. "It's in his blood. He can't change what he was born to be."

"Then what is it?"

"His father was mortal. Maybe as Derek grows older, he'll be able to consume mortal food." She lifted her chin. "I'm not going to worry about it until I know there's a problem. What are you grinning at?"

"Nothing."

"You don't believe me?"

"I know you, darlin'. You're gonna worry over this like a dog with a bone until you figure it out."

"Maybe you don't know me as well as you think you do!"

"Darlin'," he said, wrapping her in his arms, "I know you better than you know yourself."

Closing her eyes, Mara surrendered to his kiss. Though she would never admit it out loud, Logan was right. In all her long existence, no man had understood her, or loved her, as he did.

She sighed when he lifted her in his arms and carried her to bed.

"I know just the thing to take your mind off your worries," he said, a wicked glint in his eyes.

"Yes." She grinned when he stretched out beside her. "And a wonderful thing it is."

Chapter Thirteen

Derek rose with the setting of the sun. Still troubled by his need for more than blood and not wanting to talk to his mother about it, or see the worry in her eyes, he dissolved into mist and materialized outside, in his car.

Once he was out of the hills, he hit the freeway. Putting everything out of his mind, he stomped on the gas and lost himself in the thrill of barreling down the road at 140 miles an hour. Not surprisingly, he soon had a cop on his tail.

Slowing, he pulled off the road, put the car in park, and waited.

"I guess you know why I pulled you over," the cop said.

Derek nodded. "I've got a pretty good idea."

The cop flipped open his ticket book. "You're under arrest. I'll need to see your license and proof of insurance."

Looking up, Derek trapped the officer's gaze with his own. "You don't want to arrest me, officer, or give me a ticket. A warning will do."

"A warning, yes, of course."

"Thank you, officer."

Looking slightly confused, the cop closed his ticket book and returned to his car.

Derek tapped his fingers on the steering wheel as he

watched the patrol car pull into traffic. He would have been happy to give the guy his driver's license, only the one he carried was fake. He didn't have insurance, or a birth certificate, either. As far as humanity was concerned, Derek Blackwood didn't exist. Usually, he didn't give it a thought, but sometimes, like tonight, it made him feel like the invisible man. It was a lonely feeling.

Swearing a pithy oath, he put the car in gear and drove back toward Hollywood.

Without conscious thought, he found himself in front of Nosferatu's Den.

Sheree sat at the end of the bar, listening to the music and wondering what insanity had brought her back here. Only three nights ago, she had decided it wasn't safe to frequent Goth clubs like this one. She had phoned her mother to let her know that she planned to come home, and would probably be there in a week or two. At least at home, she would never be bored. Life with her parents was like living on a merry-go-round. If they weren't on the golf course or playing tennis at the club, they were out on the boat, or dedicating a new wing at a hospital, or holding a charity auction to raise money for one cause or another. There were always parties to host and plays to attend, gallery openings, nights at the opera. Life was often hectic, but never dull.

She had left home because she wanted something different, wanted to spread her wings and try living on her own. Her parents had frowned on her decision, but it wasn't up to them. She had her own money, thanks to a healthy inheritance from her great-grandfather.

Living by herself had been satisfying, in its own way, but also extremely lonely. She didn't know anyone in California, didn't have the skills to get a good job. And looking for a vampire hadn't been as exciting as she had hoped, until she'd met Derek.

Damn. She had sworn she would not think of that man again.

"Can I get you a refill, miss?"

"What? Oh, no. Wait. I'd like a Vampire's Kiss." One last drink, and then she was going home to pack. It seemed fitting somehow that it would be the drink Derek had recommended.

The bartender grinned at her. "Coming right up."

The bartender had just served her drink when two men approached her. Both were built like linebackers, tall and broad shouldered. One had a long scar on his left cheek. They both wore long black coats.

Sheree felt a shiver of apprehension when the scar-faced man sat on the vacant bar stool beside her. He had blond hair, worn long, and eyes that were an odd color, not yellow, not brown, but something in between. The second man stood behind her.

"Could we talk to you for a moment?" Scarface asked.

Sheree shook her head. "Sorry, I was just leaving."

"This won't take long."

"Sorry." She stood, but the second man blocked her retreat. "What do you want?" She told herself there was nothing to be afraid of. She was in a room filled with people; the bartender was only a few feet away.

"We'd just like to ask you a couple of questions."

"What kind of questions?"

"You were in here earlier in the week."

"Yes."

"We're trying to get in touch with the man you were with. He's a friend of ours. We were hoping you could tell us where he lives."

"I thought you were friends?"

Scarface smiled. There was no warmth in it. "He moved recently and we lost touch."

"I'm sorry, I can't help you. I just met . . ." She paused at the eager look in the man's eyes when she started to say Derek's name. "I just met him."

Scarface looked at his companion, then shook his head.

Sheree glanced around. If she yelled for help, would anyone come to her aid?

"All right, let's go at this from another angle," Scarface said. "What do you know about him?"

Sheree shook her head. "Nothing. I told you, we just met."

"Did he do anything that seemed unusual?"

"Unusual? In what way? We had a few drinks, we danced. That was all."

Scarface looked at his companion again. "We're wasting our time here. She doesn't know anything." He nodded at Sheree. "Sorry to have bothered you."

Sheree watched the two men as they made their way to a table in the back corner, where they sat with their heads together.

She grabbed her handbag and practically ran toward the door. When a hand closed around her arm, she let out a startled cry.

"Let's go." Scarface pushed her out the door. "Where are you parked?"

"D-down there. The-the blue one."

Fear choked her as the second man wrenched her purse out of her hands and unlocked the doors.

"Keep your mouth shut if you know what's good for you," Scarface warned, crowding her up against the side of her car.

"Please, let me go!" Sheree implored. "I don't know anything!"

Scarface opened the rear door and pushed her inside.

With a cry, Sheree lashed out at him, raking her nails across his cheek, kicking out at him as hard as she could.

But Scarface was bigger, stronger.

He hit her once and she fell back on the seat, certain her life was over.

Derek had been sitting in his car across from the Den, debating whether he should go inside or head back home, when he saw Sheree exit the club, a man on either side of her. Her face was pale, her eyes wide and filled with fear. Her heart was pounding so loudly he was sure he would have heard it even without his preternatural senses.

The men had turned left, herding Sheree toward her car, which was parked at the end of the block.

Derek muttered, "What the hell?" when the scar-faced man started to shove her into the backseat, grinned when she fought back, even though it was a losing fight.

When the scarred man struck her, Derek went into action. Faster than the eye could follow, he raced down the street, grabbed the man by the hair, and slammed his forehead against the car. The man dropped like a stone.

The second man whirled around, his hand reaching inside his coat.

With a low growl, Derek broke both of the man's arms and shoved him out of the way. Whimpering, the guy fell to the pavement, all the fight gone out of him.

"Sheree?" Derek touched her shoulder lightly. "Sheree, are you all right?"

She stared up at him, her mouth agape.

"Come on." Taking her by the hand, Derek settled her into the passenger seat. "We need to get out of here."

She didn't argue.

He picked up her fallen handbag, dropped it in her lap, then fastened her seat belt.

Moments later, he pulled away from the curb.

"Who were those men?" Sheree asked, unable to keep the quiver out of her voice.

"Beats the hell out of me."

"They said they knew you."

Derek shook his head. "I never saw either one of them before." He slid a glance in her direction. Her pulse was still a little rapid, but the color had returned to her cheeks. "Did they say why they were looking for me?"

"No." She glanced out the window. "Where are you taking me?"

"To your place."

"What about your car?"

"I'll pick it up later."

"I could have driven myself home."

"It's okay. I don't mind."

She turned her head away from him, her hands clasped in her lap, obviously nervous in his presence. He supposed he couldn't blame her. He'd seen her a few times and then left her with no explanation, but hell, what was he supposed to say? *I'd love to pursue a relationship with you and get to know you better, but I'm a vampire and you're prey and I really don't see this ending well for you.* Yeah, right.

"How've you been, Sheree?"

"Fine. I'm going back home to my family."

"Because of what happened tonight?" The thought of her leaving filled him with a sudden sense of loss.

"No. Because . . . just because it's time."

His hand tightened on the steering wheel. "Where's home?"

"Philadelphia."

Pulling into her driveway, he put the car in park, then cut the engine.

"Thank you for driving me home," Sheree said.

Before she could open the door, his hand closed over her arm. "Don't go."

"It's late. I'm tired."

"I mean, don't go home. Stay here." The words *with me* hung unspoken in the air.

Sheree took a deep breath, then turned to face him, her gaze probing his. "Why?"

Releasing her, Derek raked a hand through his hair. "I know I behaved badly. Treated you badly. I'm sorry. There are things you don't know about me, things I can't tell you. . . ."

"Like why those men were looking for you?"

"Yeah, like that."

"Were those men cops? Are you in trouble with the law?"

"No." He shook his head. "Nothing like that. It's just that my life is . . . complicated."

Her eyes widened. "You're not married, are you?"

"No, not even close."

Sheree turned her head away again, hiding her expression from him.

Derek drummed his fingers on the steering wheel. Only minutes before he had convinced himself there was no future for the two of them. If he was smart, he would listen to his own good advice and let her go before she got hurt. He had no doubt those two men were hunters. They hadn't asked for him by name, so they didn't know who he was—just that he was a vampire. It was a unique talent some hunters possessed, being able to ferret out members of the undead community.

Still not looking at him, she said, "Good night, Derek."

"Dammit!" Grabbing her by the arm, he forced her to look at him.

And then he kissed her.

And she forgot all about going back to Philadelphia.

When Derek released her, Sheree blew out a deep breath. "So," she asked, "where do we go from here?"

"I don't know." He brushed a lock of hair behind her ear, then trailed his fingertips down her cheek. "All I know is that I need you, and I hope you'll stick around long enough to give us a chance to get to know each other better. It's up to you."

Her gaze searched his, but there was no hint of deception in his eyes, nothing but a look that bordered on fear. Puzzled, she wondered what he had to be afraid of.

"It's okay," Derek said, drawing back. "You're smart to keep your distance."

Taking his hand in hers, she murmured, "I'm not going anywhere. Walk me inside?"

Feeling reborn, Derek got out of the car, then opened Sheree's door. Slipping his arm around her waist, he walked her up the steps to the front porch.

"It's not as late as I thought," she said. "Would you like to come in for a while?"

He hesitated, wondering if it was safe. He'd not yet fed and her blood called to him ever so sweetly. His gaze moved over her. Slender shoulders, a tiny waist, softly rounded hips.

She glanced back at him, her hand on the latch. "Derek?"

"Maybe for a little while." He followed her inside, felt the power inherent in the threshold move through him like an electric shock. It was something he still hadn't gotten used to, that jolt of supernatural juice capable of keeping creatures like himself from entering mortal homes uninvited. Even Mara, with all her power, couldn't breach a threshold uninvited.

He stood inside the doorway, watching Sheree move around the room, turning on lights, straightening the news-papers and magazines scattered on the coffee table, folding the blanket lying on the chair.

She gestured at the sofa. "Please, sit down."

He sat at one end of the couch, his gaze sweeping the room. The furnishings were decidedly feminine, from the flowered sofa and matching chair to the frilly pink curtains at the window and the collection of dainty ballerina figurines on the mantel.

"Are you going to join me anytime soon?" he asked.

"Sorry." Biting down on her lower lip, she perched at the other end of the couch, her fingers toying with the hem of her jacket.

Derek smiled inwardly. Now that she had him here, she wasn't sure what to do with him.

"Would you like something to eat? Or drink?"

His gaze moved to the hollow in the base of her throat. He'd love something to drink, but he was pretty sure she wasn't offering what he needed. "No, thanks." He draped his arm along the back of the sofa. "Do you want me to go?"

"Go? No, of course not." Her brows drew together. "Why do you ask?"

"It's obvious that my being here is making you nervous."

She laughed self-consciously. "Why should I be nervous?"

"You tell me."

She chewed on a fingernail a moment, gathering her thoughts, wondering if she should put them into words or keep them bottled up. But holding back never solved anything. Best to get it out in the open now.

"It's this thing between us," she said in a rush. "It's so new and yet it's so intense. It's a little scary, and now you're telling me you've got secrets you can't share, and you say you'd like us to get to know each other better, and people are looking for you, and you don't know who or why, and . . ."

Derek pressed his fingertips to her lips. "Whoa, girl, I'm sorry I asked."

"I just think we need to be honest with each other or there's no point in going on."

Her words splashed over him like ice water. She was right: There was no point in their going on. "You're a wise woman," he said quietly. "I think maybe we'd better end this before you get hurt."

When she started to speak, he shook his head. "There are things about me that I can't tell you. That I'll never be able to tell you. Things that would make you hate me if you knew."

Leaning forward, he brushed a kiss across her cheek. "Good-bye, Sheree."

Before she could ask him not to go, he was out the door.

Outside, Derek took a deep breath. The scent of rain was in the air. Overhead, the wind chased the clouds across the darkening sky. A sharp crack of lightning released a whiff of ozone, followed by a distant echo of thunder.

He stood there for several minutes, staring at Sheree's house. A thought took him home.

For once, he was glad to find his mother and Logan in the living room when he arrived.

"We weren't waiting up for you," Mara said. "We just got home from a wrap party at Justin's."

Derek nodded. Justin Price was the grandson of Sterling

Gaylord Price. Sterling had been a famous Hollywood movie producer in his day. He'd also been a notorious lech, a trait apparently handed down to his grandson. Logan had backed Justin's latest project, a big-budget 4D remake of *The Ten Commandments*.

"This film's got Oscar written all over it," Logan said, glancing at the gold statue on the mantel. "I think Oscar is gonna have a little brother. But, enough about me. How was your evening?" he asked, then frowned. "There's blood on the sleeve of your jacket."

Derek glanced at the stain barely visible against the dark cloth. "Yeah. I got into a bit of a scuffle with a couple of hunters."

Mara's head snapped up. "Hunters? Where?"

"At the Den. Two of them." He held up a hand, staying his mother's next question. "They weren't looking for you or for me, by name. Apparently they saw me with Sheree a couple of nights ago and recognized I was a vampire. They got a little too physical trying to get my identity from Sheree and I put a stop to it."

"Did you kill them?" Mara asked.

"No." He'd wanted to, but not with Sheree there, watching his every move.

"Did you catch their names?" Logan asked.

Derek shook his head. "They were both built like Mack trucks. One had a long scar on his cheek. Sound like anyone you know?"

"The man with the scar," Mara said. "Was he blond, with funny-colored eyes?"

"Yeah. You know him?"

"His name is Aurland. Richard or Rudy, something like that. He's from North Carolina. I've never known him to come this far west. He usually pairs up with his brother-in-law, Silas Fortenberry. Another big guy, dark hair."

Derek nodded. "That's them."

"There haven't been any hunters in this area for fifteen, twenty years," Logan remarked.

Mara nodded. "So why now?"

It was a damn good question, Derek mused, but one for which he had no good answer.

"What are you going to do about the girl?" Mara asked. "Being seen with you could be dangerous for her."

"I know. It's over."

"You care for her?"

"Yeah. She . . ." He scrubbed his hands over his face. How could he explain how he felt when he was with Sheree? She soothed him in a way he didn't understand.

Logan stretched his legs out in front of him, his hands laced behind his head. "You know, she might still be in danger from those two thugs. Just because you beat them off once doesn't mean they won't come back."

Derek nodded. "Yeah, I thought about that."

"You should probably keep an eye on her."

"I thought about that, too. It's not a problem at night, but during the day . . ." He shrugged. "She'll be going home soon."

Rising, Mara stretched her arms over her head, then took her husband by the hand and pulled him to his feet.

"Don't worry, son. I'll keep an eye on the girl during the day," Mara said. "Good night."

Derek watched the two of them climb the stairs.

What had prompted his mother to volunteer to look after Sheree? It was another good question for which he had no answer.

Chapter Fourteen

Sheree slept late, her dreams filled with images of men chasing her, catching her, of a handsome knight in shining armor riding to her rescue, then leaving her behind. She shivered, remembering how terrified she had been when those two men had dragged her down the street. There was no telling what they would have done to her if Derek hadn't shown up when he had.

With an effort, she got out of bed, showered and dressed, and then decided to go out for an early lunch. She couldn't just stay home and worry about what might have happened, and she refused to sit around and mope over a man who didn't want her. She was probably better off without him. Yes, lunch and a movie and maybe a manicure. If that didn't cheer her up, nothing would.

Leaving the house an hour later, she drove to her favorite restaurant, where she ordered half a tuna salad sandwich, a cup of vegetable soup, and a glass of iced tea. Comfort food, she thought, that was what she needed. So she asked for a hot fudge sundae with double hot fudge and extra whipped cream for dessert.

She was leaving the restaurant when she saw Derek's sister walking toward her. The woman was even lovelier in the light of day. Sunlight glistened in the wealth of her ebony hair, her flawless skin seemed almost radiant, her green eyes were bright and clear.

"Sheree!" Mara said, smiling. "What a nice surprise."

"Hi. It's nice to see you again."

"Thank you." Mara glanced at the restaurant. "Are you going in for lunch?"

"No, I just ate. I'm on my way to a movie. It starts in a few minutes."

"I haven't been to the movies in ages. Would you mind if I join you?"

"Not at all," Sheree replied, pleased to have company. "I'd like that."

"Shall we walk?" Mara asked. "It's such a lovely day."

"Good idea," Sheree said, thinking it would give her a chance to walk off a few of those calories she'd just eaten.

"So, tell me about yourself," Mara said, falling into step beside her. "We didn't get to talk the other night."

"There's not much to tell. I came out here to spread my wings, I guess you could say, but it hasn't worked out. I'm going back home in a week or two."

"Oh? I thought you and Derek were . . . never mind, it's none of my business."

"Yes, Derek." Sheree bit down on her lower lip, wondering how much she should share with Mara, and how much, if anything, Derek had already told his sister. "It just didn't work out."

"That's too bad. He seemed very fond of you."

Sheree was searching for a reply when they reached the theater. Inside, she bought a small popcorn and a soft drink, then glanced at Mara, who stood beside her.

Mara shook her head. "Nothing for me."

There were only two other people in the auditorium, a teenage boy and girl sitting in the last row, their arms wrapped around each other. Sheree grinned, thinking they were probably cutting class so they could neck.

"If you need someone to talk to," Mara whispered, "I'd be happy to listen."

Sheree shook her head. "There's nothing to say." Sighing, she stared at the bag of popcorn in her hands. "I was hoping he was the one, you know? I've never felt this way about anyone before, but . . ." She twisted a lock of hair around her finger, then shrugged. "He said it would be best if we ended it."

"I see." Mara patted her arm. "Perhaps he's right."

Sheree stared at the screen, her eyes burning with unshed tears. "I miss him already."

Derek stood in the shadows, watching Sheree's house. Lights burned in the living room window, the curtains drawn against the night. But he didn't need to see her to know she was inside.

He shifted from one foot to the other. He was here to relieve his mother, who had spent the day keeping watch over Sheree. "How is she?"

Mara stood in the shadows behind him. "She told me she misses you."

Derek glanced over his shoulder. "It's only been one day."

"So, you don't miss her?"

"What are you now, my matchmaker?" he asked irritably.

"I just don't like to see you alone."

Derek turned to stare at Sheree's house again. He was twenty-five years old and he'd never had a steady girlfriend, never dated any woman more than once or twice. While other thirteen-year-olds were discovering and appreciating the differences between boys and girls, he'd been learning how to hunt, how to control the ever-present urge to kill his prey, how to hide what he was from humans, how to defend himself against hunters, how to protect himself if he was caught out in the sun's light. None of which had prepared him for what he felt for Sheree.

He knew it was possible for a vampire to find happiness with a human. His family was proof of that. Roshan and Brenna, Vince and Cara, Rafe and Kathy, Rane and Savannah—they'd all fallen in love and made it work. The only failed relationship was that of his father and his mother. Loving Mara had killed Kyle Bowden as surely as if she had personally taken his life.

"Derek?"

"What do you want from me?"

"I just want you to be happy."

"Happy, yeah. I'll work on that."

"I wish you would!" she retorted. "It breaks my heart to see you looking so miserable."

"Do you want me to leave?"

Sighing, she closed the distance between them and placed her hand on his shoulder. "Of course not. I love having you here. You must know that."

He grunted softly.

"Just think about what I said, that's all I'm asking, all right?"

"Yeah." Covering her hand with his, he gave it a squeeze.

"Good. I'll see you at home later."

A faint stirring in the air, and she was gone.

Derek stood there for several minutes, then dissolved into mist, crossed the street, and slipped under the crack in the front door.

Sheree glanced at the antique clock on the mantel, unable to believe it was barely nine. Would this day never end? She had considered going out, but she was somewhat unsettled after last night's incident. She didn't think she was in any danger from the two men who had accosted her, certainly not the one with the two broken arms. Still, going out alone didn't seem very wise, all things considered.

She had called her parents earlier in the evening to let them know she'd be coming home, probably next week. Her mother immediately suggested a welcome home party, as if Sheree had been gone years instead of only a few months.

Thinking about it now, she wondered if going back to Philadelphia was such a good idea. Did she really want to get caught up in all those social obligations again? On the other hand, there was no reason to stay here.

Blowing out a sigh, she closed her eyes. And frowned at the sudden feeling that she was no longer alone. Sitting up, she glanced around the room, certain someone was there.

Rising, she grabbed the fireplace poker and tiptoed through the house, turning on lights as she went, peeking behind doors, peering into closets.

There was no one there.

Convinced she was imagining things, and feeling more than a little foolish, she dropped the poker on the bed, then went into the bathroom and turned on the taps in the tub, thinking a nice hot bath might relax her. And if that didn't do it, perhaps a cup of warm milk or hot chocolate.

After adding some lilac-scented bubble bath to the water, she tied her hair up in a ponytail to keep it out of the way, then stepped into the tub and closed her eyes.

She was cracking up, she thought. First she was imagining an intruder in the house when there was no one there, now she was imagining the scent of Derek's cologne.

Derek lingered near the ceiling in Sheree's bedroom. Tempting as it was to slip into the bathroom and watch her bathe, he couldn't bring himself to do it. He wasn't a voyeur, after all.

Resuming his own form, he looked around her room, wondering if she had decorated it herself. The walls were papered in an old-fashioned blue and white stripe. Curtains the same shade of blue as the paper hung at the single window, the blue captured again in the quilt on the bed. The floor was hardwood, the furniture painted white. Several framed pictures—two landscapes, two seascapes—hung on the walls. A well-read copy of *Wuthering Heights* lay open on the nightstand.

He paused near the door. From the slow, steady beat of Sheree's heart, he knew she had fallen asleep in the tub. He swore softly. Was she covered in bubbles? Did he dare look? What if she woke up? How would he explain his presence in her house, in her bedroom, uninvited?

He swore again, all thoughts of being caught taking flight when he heard movement in the kitchen downstairs. What the hell?

Dissolving into mist, he drifted down the staircase. The front door was ajar. Two men holding pistols stood with their backs toward him. One of them had a fat white bandage wrapped around his forehead. Aurland, the scar-faced man from the Den. The other hunter was a stranger.

Aurland waved his gun toward the second floor. "She must be up there."

The second man had one hand on the banister when Derek heard Sheree's footsteps in the hallway upstairs.

"Get out of sight," Aurland hissed. "She's coming down."

Derek glanced at the landing, and sure enough, Sheree was on her way down the stairs, wrapped in a bathrobe, her slippers flip-flapping on the steps.

Shit! He couldn't materialize in front of her. Darting out the door, Derek resumed his own shape again, then stood just inside the threshold.

At the foot of the stairs, Sheree came to an abrupt halt when she saw him. "Oh, Derek, you startled me!"

"Sorry." He glanced around, nostrils flaring. Aurland was hiding behind the kitchen door. The other man was in the hall closet.

Stepping out onto the porch, Derek gestured for Sheree to follow him.

She frowned at him instead. "What are you doing here?"

"Come outside," he said softly.

"I'm not dressed."

"Dammit, woman . . ."

"Louis! Now!" Aurland shouted as he emerged from the kitchen. The second hunter sprang out of the closet, both firing when they saw Derek. The first bullet took him in the shoulder, the second burying itself in his right leg. The silver burned through skin and muscle like acid.

The sound of Sheree's high-pitched scream galvanized Derek into action. His fist a blur, he punched the hunter nearest him in the throat, killing him instantly.

Aurland fired a second time.

The force of the bullet slammed into Derek's chest, just missing his heart. Before the hunter could fire again, Derek grabbed the man's head between his hands and with a quick twist broke his neck and tossed the body aside.

A strangled sob reminded him he wasn't alone. He turned in time to see Sheree sink to her knees, her eyes wide as she stared at the fallen hunters.

When he took a step toward her, she thrust her hands out to ward him off. "What are you?"

Damn! Capturing her gaze with his, he said, "Sheree, look at me. A couple of men tried to break into your house while we were talking. I scared the intruders away. You didn't see anything unusual. There are no bodies in your house. But you didn't want to stay here alone, so I took you home with me. Do you understand?"

When she nodded, he reached into his pocket, pulled out his cell phone, and punched in his mother's number.

She answered on the first ring. "What's wrong?"

"I need you to come get me." Glancing at the blood leaking from his wounds, he added, "Hurry."

Wise woman that she was, his mother didn't waste time asking questions.

Three minutes later, Logan and Mara were standing on the front porch. Logan took a quick glance around and stated the obvious. "We've got to get those bodies out of here."

Mara nodded. Unfortunately, they couldn't go inside without an invitation from the owner, which meant, wounded or not, Derek would have to clean up the mess. "Derek, bring the bodies out here and then bring Sheree to me. I'll take her to our place. Meet us there when you can. Oh, you might want to find a nightgown and a change of clothes for her."

With a nod, Derek dragged the two men out onto the porch, then went back into the house for Sheree.

She stared at him blankly. "What are you doing?" she asked when he scooped her into his arms.

"Just relax," he said as he carried her outside and lowered her into his mother's waiting arms.

"Everything is just fine," Mara said, her voice low and soothing. "Close your eyes, Sheree. That's right. You're going to go to sleep for a while, and you won't wake up until I call you."

Derek waited until Logan and his mother were gone; then he closed the front door and began setting things to right. Grabbing a dish towel from the kitchen he started mopping up his blood, no easy task since it continued to drip onto the floor with every step he took. Muttering an oath, he grabbed two more towels. He stuffed one inside his shirt and wrapped the other around his leg.

When he finished cleaning up, he went upstairs to find a change of clothes for Sheree. Downstairs again, he took one last look around, tucked her handbag under his arm, turned off the lights, and locked the door.

Moments later, he materialized inside the house in the Hollywood Hills. His mother was waiting for him in the living room.

"Where's Sheree?" Derek dropped her purse on a small table.

"In one of the bedrooms upstairs. She's resting comfortably. Go in the kitchen and sit down. I'll be there in a minute."

Lacking the strength to argue, Derek did as he was told. He clenched his hands against pain that grew worse with every breath as he climbed onto a high stool. Tugging the bloody cloth from inside his shirt, he tossed it into the sink. The one around his leg quickly followed.

"Do you think it was a good idea bringing Sheree here?" he asked when his mother stepped into the kitchen.

"We'll worry about that later," she said, dropping a towel on his lap. "Right now, I need to get those bullets out of your stubborn hide before you bleed to death."

"Yeah." Taking shallow breaths, he watched her fill a large aluminum pan with warm water, then deposit rolls of gauze and tape on the table, along with a pair of scissors and a probe that looked all too familiar.

"This is getting to be a habit," Mara said, easing him out of his blood-soaked shirt.

"Yeah." He spoke through clenched teeth. "A bad one."

She tossed the bloody garment in the sink. "What happened this time?"

"Aurland and another hunter broke into Sheree's house while I was inside. They ambushed me."

"What? You couldn't take down two hunters before they shot you?"

"They're both dead, aren't they?"

"You're supposed to kill them *before* they shot you." Her eyes narrowed as she studied his wounds. "Hold still now."

He sucked in a breath as she probed the wound in his shoulder, let it out in a hiss when she withdrew a misshapen silver slug and tossed it into the sink. After cutting off a length of gauze, she folded it into a square, and taped it over the wound.

Mara looked up when Logan entered the room. "Is everything taken care of?"

"Not to worry, my sweet. They'll never be found." He jerked his head at Derek. "Stings like hell, doesn't it?"

"Yeah," he rasped, flinching.

"I said hold still," Mara admonished as she slid the probe into the ragged hole in her son's chest.

"This girl seems like a lot of trouble," Logan remarked.

"Tell me about it. Dammit, woman," Derek hissed, "be careful!"

"Got it!" She tossed the second slug into the sink, and after wiping the blood from Derek's chest, she wrapped several layers of gauze around his torso, then tied off the ends. "Two down, one to go," she said cheerfully. "Take off your pants."

Propping one shoulder against the doorjamb, Logan admired the sight of his wife lounging in a tub filled with frothy, scented bubbles. "So, what now?"

"You could wash my back." She lifted one slender leg and rested it on the edge of the tub. "Or massage my foot."

"That's not what I meant, and you know it."

"A massage still sounds like a good idea."

Logan pushed away from the door, then knelt beside the tub and began to rub her foot. She had pretty feet, small, well formed. But then, she was pretty all over, and no one knew it better than he did.

She closed her eyes, a sigh of pleasure escaping her lips.

His hand moved up her calf, his fingers gliding over her silky skin. "What are you going to do about the girl?"

"Wipe the incident from her mind and let her go."

"I'm not sure that's a good idea."

"What do you want to do? Make her disappear?"

"There's something going on." Logan's hand tightened on her thigh. "I don't like it that four hunters showed up here in the last week."

"So, what should we do? Run away and hide?"

He released his hold on her leg and stood up. "You know me better than that."

"What do you want, then?"

Heat flared in his eyes, the hunters forgotten as the scent of her desire reached him. "Don't you know?" he growled.

She smiled as he stripped off his shirt, stepped out of his trousers and briefs, and slipped into the tub behind her. She leaned back as his arms went around her waist, his big hands caressing her. Thoughts of hunters fled her mind when he rose in one fluid motion, water splashing over the edge of the tub as he carried her, soaking wet, into the bedroom.

Lowering her onto the mattress, he covered her body with his.

"I know," she said, her voice a low purr. "I've always known."

Derek's nostrils flared as the scent of musk filled the air. Sitting on the edge of the mattress in the bedroom down the hall from his mother's, he ran his knuckles lightly over Sheree's cheek, wondering if he would ever find the kind of love his parents shared. What would Sheree's reaction be if he told her the truth? What would his reaction be if she looked at him with revulsion? Was she strong enough, brave enough, to share her life with him? It was, he admitted, a moot point at the moment. He knew his mother intended to wipe the night's events from Sheree's mind, wondered if the smart thing would be to wipe his memory from her mind, as well.

And even as he considered it, he rejected the idea. He'd told Sheree the truth when he said he needed her. He didn't understand why he felt such a strong connection with her. Truth be told, he no longer cared. But one thing he knew for certain. He would never willingly let her go again.

She was dreaming, but her dreams were like none she'd ever had before. She heard voices—familiar voices—coming from far away. She was aware of fingers caressing her, of someone sitting beside her. She tried to wake up, wanted to wake up, and couldn't.

Filled with a sudden, inexplicable panic, she tried to scream, hoping the sound would wake her, but she couldn't speak, couldn't move. She was aware of sunlight falling across her face. Knew that it was day, knew, somehow, that she had been asleep for hours, and yet she still couldn't move. Her eyelids were heavy, so heavy.

The light faded, leaving her in darkness.

She would have wept, had she been able.

This was death, she thought, and surrendered to the darkness.

Chapter Fifteen

"All right," Mara said, glancing from Logan to Derek. "We need to get our story straight before we wake her up."

"I already told her some men broke into her house and I scared them away, and then I brought her here because she was afraid to stay home alone."

"Why didn't you just erase the whole thing from her mind?" Mara asked. "That would have been infinitely easier."

"I didn't want to leave her unprotected. Besides, I wasn't sure the suggestion I planted was strong enough."

"And how are you going to explain the day she lost?" Logan asked.

Mara shrugged. "I guess we'll just have to plant some memories. I'll tell her we all went to lunch at Spago and then we came back here and spent the day by the pool. When she wakes up, she'll ask to go home, and Derek can take her. Agreed?"

"Sounds all right to me," Derek said.

"Or you could just take her home and erase the last two days," Logan suggested.

"We could," Mara agreed. "But, like Derek, I'd like to keep an eye on her, just in case she remembers something she shouldn't."

Logan frowned at his wife. What wasn't she telling them?

"All right," Mara said. "I'm going to wake her up."

Feeling as though she had missed something, Sheree glanced around, momentarily confused by her surroundings. The room was large, with plush white carpeting and dark red velvet draperies. A pair of black sofas faced each other across a rosewood coffee table. In one corner, a round black table polished to a high shine sat between a pair of overstuffed red velvet chairs. Several expensive-looking paintings of landscapes decorated the walls. A sword in a silver sheath hung over the mantel.

She looked at Derek, sitting on the sofa beside her. Mara sat on the sofa across from them, holding hands with a handsome man. Was it her husband? Had they been introduced? If so, Sheree couldn't remember his name.

"Are you sure you have to leave?" Mara asked, leaning forward. "We've loved having you here."

"Thank you," Sheree said, rising, "but I think I should get home."

"I'll drive you," Derek said.

"I do hope you'll come visit us again," Mara said.

Sheree nodded.

"Are you ready?" Derek asked, taking her by the hand. "Your bag's in the car."

"My bag. Yes." She smiled faintly. "Thank you for having me."

Derek slid a glance at Sheree as he drove down the winding road that led to the freeway. Sheree stared out the window, her purse in her lap, a slight frown puckering her brow.

"Did you have a good time today?" he asked.

"What? Oh, yes. Your sister and her husband are very nice. I'm afraid I don't remember his name."

"Logan."

"Yes. Logan. They seem very happy together."

Derek nodded. He didn't know any mortal couples, but the couples in his family were all very much in love. Whether it was just another perk of being a vampire or the men all had a knack for picking the right women to spend their lives with, he couldn't say. "Are your parents happy?"

"Not like your sister and her husband seem to be. Oh, don't get me wrong. My folks don't fight or anything, but, well . . ." She lifted one shoulder and let it fall. "Maybe all couples get that way after they've been married a long time. I suppose eventually you run out of things to say to each other."

He shrugged. Mara and Logan had known each other for centuries, but they hadn't run out of conversation yet.

"Are you an only child?"

"Yeah." He pulled off the freeway, stopped at a red light. It would have been nice to have had a brother. He had always envied Rane and Rafe their closeness. "You?"

"Yes. My mother had several miscarriages before I came along. She didn't want to try again."

When they reached her house, Derek killed the engine, then draped his arm over the back of her seat. "Here we are."

"Thank you for bringing me home. I don't remember . . . did I thank you for scaring away the bad guys?"

"No thanks necessary." She didn't know it, he thought, stifling a grin, but the bad guy she needed to worry about was sitting across from her.

Sheree put her hand on the door, glanced at her house, and let her hand fall back into her lap. "Would you mind walking me in?"

"Of course not." As he got out of the car, he grabbed her

bag from the backseat, then opened her door and reached for her hand. It was trembling.

"I'm sorry," she said as they walked up the porch steps. "I thought I was braver than this."

"Hey, we're all afraid from time to time."

"Really?" She pulled her keys from her handbag and unlocked the door, then glanced over her shoulder, one brow arched. "What are you afraid of?"

Reaching around her, he pushed the door open and stepped across the threshold, tugging her inside behind him. "There's nobody here."

She turned on the lights in the living room. "How can you be so sure?"

"The house feels empty."

She wasn't a scaredy-cat, but there was something niggling at the back of her mind. Something besides the robbery that had happened last night, but she couldn't quite put her finger on what it was. It left her feeling unsettled. Why couldn't she remember?

"Sheree, are you all right?"

"Not really." She chewed on the inside of her cheek. "Would you . . . never mind."

"Do you want me to stay the night?" he asked quietly.

She stared up at him. Was she that transparent?

"I will if you want me to."

"I'm just being silly. I'm sure those robbers won't come back again, but . . ."

Derek dropped her bag on the floor, then closed the door. "I'll crash on the couch."

"Thank you."

"No problem."

Sheree glanced at her watch. It wasn't late but she was suddenly very tired. "I think I'll go up to bed."

Derek nodded. "Get some rest. Things will look better tomorrow."

Impulsively, she rose on her tiptoes and kissed his cheek. "Thank you for being so understanding."

He watched her pick up her bag and climb the stairs to her bedroom. She was going to remember, he mused. She was going to poke and prod the depths of her memory until she uncovered the truth of what had happened last night. And then all hell was going to break loose.

He chuckled softly as he heeled off his boots and stretched out on the sofa. He didn't know how she would react when she learned the truth, but it was sure to be a hell of a ride.

In her room, Sheree locked the door. She wanted to rest in a tub of warm bubbles, but she felt funny taking a bath with a man in the house. She took a quick shower instead, slipped into a pair of comfy sweats—no cute PJs tonight— and climbed into bed.

It was too early to go to sleep, so she picked up the book on the nightstand and began to read, but she couldn't concentrate on the story. What was she forgetting? And why couldn't she remember?

Setting the book aside, she thought about the events of the last few days. First, Derek had rescued her from the two men who had accosted her at the Den. Except in movies, she had never seen anyone move as fast as he had. He had claimed he didn't know who the men were, and she certainly had no idea.

Sheree had no recollection of what had happened at her house last night, except for what Derek had told her: two men had broken into her home and Derek had chased them away. She frowned. She didn't remember Derek coming to see her, didn't really remember anyone breaking in. Had it been such a traumatic event that she had blocked it out? It was possible, but . . . she frowned as the image of a dead man flashed before her eyes, and with it, the remembered scent of blood and death. But that was impossible. Wasn't it?

Feeling a headache coming on, she turned off the lamp, and scooted under the covers. The darkness closed in on her and it took all the courage she possessed to keep from reaching for the light. Lying there, she took slow, deep breaths. There was nothing to be afraid of. Regardless of what the newspaper said, there were no vampires. Everything that had happened in the last three days could be explained rationally . . . if only she could remember.

The bath was warm, soothing, carrying her away, until she heard a sound from downstairs. She got out of the tub, pulled on her robe, and tiptoed down the stairs. Derek was on the front porch, beckoning her. A man stepped out of the kitchen, another from the hall closet . . . shouts, shots, the sound of her own screams, the smell of gunpowder and blood. Derek's voice, low and soothing, his dark gaze capturing hers . . . telling her lies . . . the sound of a woman's voice, telling her to go to sleep . . .

Mara's voice.

Sheree bolted upright. Swinging her legs over the edge of the bed, she pulled on her robe and went downstairs, determined to learn the truth once and for all.

Derek shoved his hands into his pockets when the living room light switched on. Sheree stood in the doorway, her face pale, her arms folded across her chest.

"The truth," she said tremulously. "I want the truth."

"There are all kinds of truth," he replied easily. "What truth are you looking for?"

"I want to know why those men were looking for you at the Den. And who broke into my house. And how you happened to be there. And how I got to your sister's house, and . . ."

He held up a hand, staying her words. "I get the message. I don't know the men who were looking for me." That much was true. He hadn't known them, but he had known what they were. "I was here last night because I was worried about you. It was mere coincidence that I arrived shortly after the intruders did."

She nodded. "Two men broke into my house. You killed them. I remember there were gunshots and . . . and blood. Your blood." Her eyes grew wide. "You were shot!" Her gaze flew to his shoulder. "There. And . . . and there." She pointed at his chest.

"Do I look like I've been shot?"

"No." She frowned. If he had been shot in the chest, he would be in the hospital. At the least, there would be bandages.

Doubts assailed her. Had she dreamt the whole thing? "Yesterday, I was at your sister's house. Why are my memories so cloudy?"

He shrugged. "Probably caused by the stress of the last couple of days, I would think." Rising, he walked slowly toward her, half expecting her to back away. When she didn't, he drew her into his arms.

She stood there, stiff as a board for several moments, and then, gradually, she relaxed against him, her cheek resting on his chest. "I'm so confused. I think I must be losing my mind." She looked up at him, her expression one of bewilderment and fear. "Do you think I'm going crazy?"

Derek stroked her hair, afraid he was about to make the biggest mistake of his life. But he couldn't stand to see the panicky look in her eyes, hear the ill-disguised alarm in her voice.

"No, love," he murmured, hoping his mother would forgive him. "You're not going crazy. The truth is, you've found exactly what you were looking for."

Exactly what you were looking for. The softly spoken words sent a shiver down Sheree's spine. "What do you mean?"

Derek took a deep breath, well aware that he was breaking the code of his kind. "You wanted to find a vampire," he said quietly. "You found one."

She blinked at him. Was he kidding? He wasn't smiling or grinning. He looked dead serious. She felt all the blood drain from her face. The arms that had felt so strong and comforting only moments ago suddenly felt confining.

Sensing her distress, Derek let her go and took several steps backward.

And waited.

She shook her head. "If this is a joke, it's in very poor taste."

"It's no joke."

"You're a vampire?"

He nodded.

"Prove it." She regretted the words as soon as they left her lips. Did she really want to know the truth, especially when the best way for him to prove it was to do what vampires did best?

Derek smiled faintly. "I've already tasted you."

She lifted a shaking hand to her throat. "I don't believe you."

"It was just once, while you were sleeping."

"No." She shook her head. "It was only a dream!" But it had felt so real.

"Are you sure?"

Feeling suddenly chilled, she ran her hands up and down her arms. "Am I going to become a vampire?"

"So you believe me?"

"Yes. No. I don't know."

His gaze moved over her, a predatory gleam in his eye. "I can hear the beat of your heart, the sound of the blood flowing through your veins. I can sense your thoughts, taste the fear on your skin."

"That's impossible!"

She let out a shriek when, without warning, he dissolved into mist and surrounded her. Planting the words in her mind, he said, *Now do you believe me?*

A moment later, he resumed his own form, careful not to touch her.

"It's true." Face pale, body trembling, she stared at him as if she had never seen him before. And even as she acknowledged the truth, she told herself it couldn't be real. He couldn't be real. "Why are you telling me this now?"

"You need to know. We've been seen together. Any vampire who gets near you will know you've been with me. You asked me who those men at the Den were. They were hunters, and they were after me. I should have realized just being with you would put your life in danger. I'm sorry."

Feeling suddenly faint, Sheree sank onto the sofa, hands clasped in her lap, as she tried to absorb what he was telling her. She wanted to yell at him, to blame him for involving her in his life, but how could she?

He was right.

She had wanted to find a vampire. And she had found one.

Chapter Sixteen

"I seem to be asking this a lot lately," Sheree said, looking up at Derek, "but where do we go from here? What am I supposed to do now?" She was in over her head, she thought, treading in unfamiliar territory. Even though she had been certain vampires existed, she had never really expected to find one. Certainly not one she found as attractive and desirable as Derek. Just her luck, she mused glumly. She found a man who excited her and he wasn't even a man, at least not in the usual sense of the word. "Does your sister know? I mean, what you are?"

"Yeah. It's hard to keep a secret like that from your family."

"How long have you been a vampire?"

"Since I was thirteen."

"Thirteen! That must have been terrible. How did it happen?"

"I'll tell you about it sometime. Right now, there are a few things you need to know."

"Like what?"

"For starters, you can't tell anyone about me."

"Who would believe me?"

"It doesn't matter. For your sake and mine, this has to be our secret."

"All right. I promise. What else do I need to know?"

"Never invite a vampire into your house."

"A little late for that bit of advice, don't you think?" she muttered dryly.

"Invitations can be rescinded, so if you want me to leave, just say so and I'll be gone."

"Really? Just like that?"

"Just like that. Most popular vampire lore is true, which is why it's been around so long. I know you have a wooden stake in your possession. You need to keep it sharp and carry it with you whenever you leave the house. It's more effective if you dip it in holy water. Vampires are strong, but their flesh is easily penetrated with wooden stakes or silver-bladed knives. If you think your life is in danger, never hesitate to strike first."

He paced away from her to look out the front window, debating whether to tell her that his mother and Logan were also vampires, and that Mara was his mother, not his sister, then decided such information was on a need-to-know basis, and right now, she didn't need to know.

He turned to face her again. "Do you have any questions?"

She shook her head.

He didn't have to read her mind to know she was still reeling from what he'd told her. "I'd advise you not to go wandering around alone after dark. And to stay out of Goth clubs. Oh, one more thing. Vampires are pros when it comes to hypnotizing people, so if you meet someone you think might be a vampire, don't look into their eyes."

"Have you hypnotized me?"

"Not exactly, but I've erased things from your memory.

Things you remembered anyway. I guess I need more practice."

"The two men who broke into my house? You killed them, didn't you?"

"Yeah."

"Were they hunters, too?"

Derek nodded.

"It all sounds like something out of a horror movie. Vampires and vampire hunters. I . . . thank you for looking out for me."

"It's the least I can do, since I'm the one who put you in danger in the first place." He blew out a breath. "Like I said, I'm sorry I got you involved in this. Take care of yourself."

"You're leaving?" She should have been glad. He was a vampire, after all. But the thought of never seeing him again made her heart ache. It made no sense. She should be terrified of what he was, running for her life. But, strange as it seemed, she wasn't afraid of anything but losing him.

"It's for the best, don't you think?"

"But . . . who's going to protect me if you go?"

"You probably won't need protecting as long as I'm not around."

He was right, of course, but . . . Rising, she closed the distance between them. Resting her hands on his shoulders, she went up on her tiptoes and kissed him.

At first, he didn't kiss her back; then his arms went around her and he pulled her body against his, his mouth devouring hers in a kiss that burned away every thought, every need save the flame that smoldered between them, growing hotter and more intense as his tongue dueled with hers.

"Sheree . . ." Holding her away from him, he took a deep breath. "Damn, girl, what are you doing?"

"I don't want you to go. Please, Derek, I've never felt this way about anyone else. Maybe it won't last, maybe it isn't even real, but shouldn't we find out?"

"Oh, it's real enough, love. Don't ever doubt it."

"I hear a 'but' in there somewhere."

"I don't want to see you get hurt."

"I'm willing to take my chances." Moving closer, Sheree ran her hands over his chest. "Are you?"

She was old enough to know her own mind, he thought as he took her into his arms again, and there was no denying that he wanted her more than his next breath.

Muttering, "I just hope you don't regret it," he lowered his head and branded her lips with his. Right or wrong, he intended to stay with her as long as she would have him.

Mara glared at her son in disbelief. "Have you completely lost your mind? How could you do such a stupid thing?"

"She had a right to know," Derek said. "I put Sheree's life in danger and she needed to be aware of it. Don't worry, I didn't tell her about you or Logan."

Mara glanced at her husband, lounging on the sofa beside her, his long legs stretched out in front of him. "I don't believe this," she said. "Our people spent years and thousands of dollars obliterating every scrap of proof of our existence, so that, gradually, mortals went back to believing in the myth and not the reality." She turned her angry gaze on her son. "Now, we have hunters being killed and stories about it in the newspaper. And to top it off, you decided to tell Sheree. Sheree, who knows where we live!"

"He did the right thing," Logan said. "The girl needed to know."

"What?" Mara rounded on her husband, ready to do battle. "How can you say that?"

"Because it's the truth. What was Derek supposed to do? Just walk away and leave her in the dark?"

"If necessary," Mara retorted.

"He's crazy about her," Logan said, grinning at Derek. "That being the case, he had no choice but to tell her the truth."

Derek dropped into the chair across from the sofa. He had always admired Logan, and never more so than when he stood up to his wife. Mara might be the most powerful vampire in the world, but Logan wasn't the least bit afraid of her, even though she could easily destroy him.

"There's always a choice," Mara retorted, but there was no heat in her voice.

"You're worrying for nothing," Logan insisted. "She isn't likely to go around telling everyone she's dating a vampire. Who would believe her?"

"I hope you're right. At the moment, we have more pressing problems, like finding out if it's just coincidence that hunters are popping up all over the place, although you know I don't believe in coincidence, or if someone's hunting us specifically, and if so, who it is."

"Okay, wife, where do we start?"

"At the Den, of course. And then we need to find out if any of our old enemies are looking for us."

"The Den." Derek sat forward, his brow furrowed. "There were a couple of vampires there a few days ago. I had the feeling I knew one of them, although I couldn't place her."

Mara's eyes narrowed. "What did she look like?"

"She was old. . . ."

"Was she with another old lady?"

"Yeah, how did you know?"

Mara glanced at Logan. "Edna and Pearl."

"You know them?" Derek asked.

"Oh, yes, I know them." Mara's eyes glittered with menace.

"They kidnapped you when you were a baby. They were partly responsible for your father's death."

"How so?" It was a story she had never told him.

Mara looked at Logan, a question in her eyes.

"Maybe it's time he knows. Past time, if you ask me."

Mara's gaze grew distant. "I met Kyle Bowden at the foot of the Sphinx. He was a brilliant artist and I was captivated by him and in awe of his talent." She smiled at the memory. "He fell in love with me, and I suppose I loved him, too, in my way. We parted when he discovered I was a vampire. It was about that time I realized I was losing my powers. Not long after that, I ran into Logan," she said, squeezing his hand. "I hadn't seen him in centuries. I don't know what I would have done without him, especially after I discovered I was pregnant. He took care of me, found a vampire doctor to look after me. A few months later, Kyle hired a hunter to find me and your father and I were reunited."

She glanced at Derek. He was watching her intently, his fingers digging into the arm of the chair. She hesitated a moment before continuing, but there was no point in stopping now.

"Because I was human and pregnant with Kyle's child, I decided to marry him. I had lost all my powers by then and I was learning to be human again. Unknown to me, the doctor I had been seeing during my pregnancy had designs on you. With the help of Edna and Pearl, he kidnapped you and your father. Everyone in our family tried to find the two of you, but it was useless. Edna and Pearl had some sort of spray that completely masked their scent and yours, making it impossible to follow their trail.

"I knew there was only one way to find you, and that was to have Logan turn me again. I was certain the blood bond between us would lead me to you, and it did. I killed Ramsden when I found him. He had been doing some sort of experiments on your father's DNA, hoping to discover how Kyle had impregnated me while I was both vampire and human. Your father died in my arms."

"You could have saved him," Derek said, his voice filled with accusation. "Why didn't you bring him across?"

Mara stared into the distance, seeing it all again in her mind's eye—the cage where Ramsden had imprisoned Kyle, the love in Kyle's eyes when she cradled him in her arms, Kyle's voice as he declared he had always loved her, even when he hated her. She had carried the guilt of his death in her heart ever since.

"Why didn't you save him?" Derek's voice was sharp, filled with bitterness. "Why didn't you bring him across?"

"I asked him to let me, but he didn't want it." She shook her head. "I couldn't turn him against his will. He would have been miserable the rest of his life."

Derek sat there a moment, trying to process everything she'd told him, and then he left the room.

Mara stared after him. "Maybe I shouldn't have said anything."

Logan slipped his arm around her shoulders. "He needed to know."

"Did I make the right decision when I let Kyle die?"

"It was the right thing to do, darlin'. He never would have accepted what he'd become. I doubt if he would have endured it for more than a day or two before he would have taken his own life, or found someone to destroy him. He would have hated you for turning him against his will."

"You didn't."

He laughed softly. "There are very few men like me. And none who love you the way I do."

She nodded absently, thinking about the book she had written while she was pregnant with Derek. The story of her life, it contained everything she could remember from the time her mother had abandoned her. She had written of her years as a slave in Pharaoh's house, of the night Dendar had changed her and how she had found him and destroyed him for it. She wrote of the men she had known, the enemies she had made, her horror at reverting, her despair when she lost her powers, her mixed emotions when she learned she was pregnant, her joy in holding her son in her arms. It was a story filled with violence and war and bloodshed, of mistakes she had made, of lives she had ruined.

She had intended to give the book to Derek when he was old enough to appreciate it, but the timing had never seemed right. Now, she wondered if that time would ever come.

Chapter Seventeen

Derek stood on the balcony, his hands clenched over the wrought-iron railing. It was his fault his father was dead. If he had never been born, his father wouldn't have been kidnapped and subjected to Ramsden's vile experiments.

Derek slammed a fist against the side of the building. How was he supposed to live with that? And what about his mother? Had she been happy to be mortal again? Had he robbed her of the chance to live a normal human life?

Vaulting over the rail, Derek landed lightly on his feet. Filled with nervous energy, he began to run, darting around the trees in his path, vaulting over fallen logs. When he reached the bottom of the hill, he slowed his pace. It wouldn't do to be seen running faster than the traffic on the street.

But there was no outrunning the past.

He slowed when he realized he was approaching Sheree's house, and stopped when he reached her driveway. All the lights were out save the one in her bedroom. She was in bed. Asleep.

A thought took him to her side. "Sheree?"

She stirred, a faint smile curving her lips. "Am I dreaming again?"

He swallowed hard. "Only if that's what you want."

"I want you here," she murmured sleepily. "Beside me."

It was what he wanted, too. What he needed. Sitting on the edge of the mattress, he removed his shoes, socks, and shirt, then slid under the covers.

Sheree turned onto her side, her eyes widening in alarm at the realization that he was really there and not a figment of her imagination. "What's wrong? What are you doing here?"

"What makes you think there's anything wrong?"

She lifted one brow. "Why else would you be here at this time of the night?"

He longed to tell her what he had learned about his father's death, but there was no way to explain it without betraying the fact that his mother and Logan were also vampires, or that Mara was his mother. Stroking Sheree's hair, he whispered, "I just needed someone to hold me."

His words arrowed straight to her heart. "Well," she murmured, wrapping her arms around him, "you came to the right place."

"Okay if I stay for what's left of the night?"

Nodding, she snuggled against him, deeply touched that he had come to her when he was so obviously hurting. What did vampires worry about, she wondered. They were, in a manner of speaking, at the top of the food chain. Other than vampire hunters, they had nothing to fear. They didn't get sick. They didn't get old. Most of the troubles and ills of the mortal world had little effect on them. So, what was bothering him? Maybe, in time, he would trust her enough to confide in her.

Holding Sheree close, Derek listened to her thoughts. It surprised him that she had accepted the truth of what he was so easily. Perhaps it was because she had been convinced vampires existed. Whatever the reason, being with her was just what he needed.

He held her all through the night, content to be at her side while she slept, to stroke her hair and her skin, to breathe in her scent. For once, her nearness didn't spark his hunger. Instead, her presence soothed him.

He stayed until the first faint rays of the sun touched the sky.

Derek wasn't surprised to find his mother waiting for him when he got home. "This is getting to be a habit," he noted sourly. "Are you gonna tuck me in?"

"There's no reason for you to feel guilty about what happened to your father," she said. "None of it was your fault. You're not responsible for what I did, or for what others have done in the past. But if you need to blame someone, then blame me."

"I want to see his grave."

Mara stared at her son. She hadn't been surprised by much in her long life, but his request caught her completely off guard.

"Well?" he asked.

"I'll take you tomorrow night."

In the morning, Sheree wondered if she had dreamed the whole thing—Derek's unexpected revelation of the night before, sleeping in his arms.

Vampire.

Her hand flew to her neck. Had he bitten her again while she'd slept?

Jumping out of bed, she ran into the bathroom. Staring into the mirror, she turned her head back and forth, relieved when there were no telltale marks. But then, there hadn't been any marks the last time, either.

Gazing at her reflection, she wondered why his news

hadn't frightened her last night, because she was plenty frightened now. What to do? As if in answer to her question, she heard his voice in the back of her mind, warning her not to invite vampires into her house. Good advice, she thought dryly. Only it had come too late!

Slipping on her robe, she went downstairs, then paused at the bottom. What if he was still in the house? She wasn't ready to face him again, not until she'd had time to think, something she couldn't seem to do clearly when he was around. But there was no sign of him anywhere.

"The least he could have done was say good-bye," she muttered, even as she told herself she didn't care. Attractive or not, he was a vampire and that was the end of it. So why was she missing him?

Feeling foolish, she went to the front door and said firmly, "Derek Blackwood, you are no longer welcome in my home."

As soon as she spoke the words, she felt an odd tremor in the air around her and knew, in some ancient primal way, that it had worked.

Relieved, she went into the kitchen. She had just put the coffee on when the doorbell rang. She felt a rush of excitement, then chided herself for expecting to find Derek on her doorstep. Everyone knew vampires weren't out and about during the day.

Opening the door, she was surprised to find Mara standing on the porch. Clad in a bright red sweater and white jeans, with her black hair falling like a cloud of silk over her shoulder, Derek's sister was as beautiful as she remembered.

"I'm sorry to be here so early," Mara said. "But I had a fight with Logan and I didn't have anywhere else to go."

"No, it's fine. Please come in."

"Thank you." Mara felt a tremor as she crossed the threshold. Even after all these centuries, it still amazed her that something as mundane as a threshold had the power to repel her. Fortunately, humans couldn't feel it unless they were revoking an invitation.

"I was just about to make breakfast," Sheree said. "Can I fix you something?"

"No, thank you, I've eaten," Mara said, following her into the kitchen.

"Please, sit down," Sheree invited, gesturing at a chair. "Would you like a cup of coffee?"

"Not now, thanks."

With a nod, Sheree scrambled a couple of eggs and slid them onto a plate, then carried it and her coffee cup to the table and took the seat across from Mara's.

"I'm sorry you had a fight," she said. "I hope it was nothing serious."

"Not really." Mara hesitated a moment, then said, "You must have questions."

"Questions?" Sheree asked, frowning.

"About Derek. He told me he'd talked to you."

"Oh. Yes." So it hadn't been a dream.

"You're worried about the vampire thing."

Sheree nodded.

"How do you feel about him now?"

"I'm not sure. I'm a little bit . . ." She paused, then sighed. "I'm afraid of him. Not him, exactly, but what he is. I've seen how strong he is, and . . ." She lifted one shoulder and let it fall.

"You're wondering if it's dangerous to be with him? And you're worried about the blood thing, afraid he might bite you."

"He said he's already tasted me, but I'm afraid he might . . . you know. I mean, I don't want to be a vampire."

"I'm sure there's nothing to worry about," Mara said, covering Sheree's hand with her own. "Derek would never hurt you, or turn you against your will. What else did he tell you?"

"Oh, about hunters and how to protect myself and . . ." She shook her head. "I can't believe we're having this conversation. Anyone else would think I was crazy. Has he ever . . . ever . . ."

"Taken my blood? No."

"It must have been awful for him, being turned so young." She frowned. "If vampires can't go out during the day, what did he do about school?"

"We were home-schooled."

"Oh."

"I think you might be good for each other. He's such a sweet boy."

"A sweet boy?" Sheree shook her head. Sweet was hardly the word she would use to describe Derek. Handsome, yes. Sexy, yes. But sweet?

"I've always mothered him," Mara said. "You know, he's very fond of you."

"I like him, too, but . . . Last night, his being a vampire didn't bother me, but this morning . . ." She shook her head. "I just don't know."

"I understand. But enough about vampires," Mara said. "How would you like to go shopping with me? Whenever Logan and I have a fight, I always go buy something new." She laughed softly. "It's a good thing we don't fight very often. What do you say?"

"I'd love to," Sheree said. "Just let me go get dressed."

"You did what?" Derek stared at his mother, who was curled up on the sofa beside Logan.

"I spent the day with Sheree. We agreed to keep an eye on her, didn't we?"

"You were just supposed to keep an eye on her, not become her new best friend. What did you talk about?"

"You, mostly. She's a little . . . hmm, I guess you could say, conflicted at the moment."

Derek groaned. Just what he needed. His mother playing matchmaker.

"I'm sorry you're so upset, but I killed two birds with one stone, so to speak. I kept her safe, and I bought a new Donna Karan gown to wear to Justin's party tonight." Turning to Logan, she added, "Wait until you see it. It's black and slinky. You're gonna love it."

"You know I love you in anything. Or nothing," Logan said with a wicked grin. "So, what excuse did you give for being at her house so early?"

"I told her we had a fight."

Logan laughed softly, amused by her clever ruse. "Well, since we're fighting, I think we'd better go to bed and make up. How about it?"

"I'd love to," Mara said, caressing his cheek, "but it will have to wait. I promised to take Derek to see his father's grave. You don't mind, do you?"

"No." Rising, Logan headed for the door. "I'll just go grab a bite while you're gone."

Derek stared after his stepfather. "He's upset, isn't he?"

"No, but he was always jealous of Kyle."

"What was my father like?"

"He was a good man. Far too good for me."

"Am I like him?"

"No. You're more like me. Are you ready to go?"

"Yeah."

Rising, Mara linked her arm with his.

Moments later, they were standing in the small cemetery

located behind Mara's house in the mountains of Northern California.

It was an old cemetery, surrounded by a white wrought-iron fence with an arched gate. A wooden sign, carved with the words *Rest Ye in Peace*, hung from the top of the gate. A black marble headstone marked Kyle Bowden's final resting place. The words *Taken From Us Too Soon But Never Forgotten* were engraved beneath his name along with the dates of his birth and passing.

Derek stood beside his father's marker, his hands shoved into the pockets of his jeans. Overhead, wispy clouds covered the moon, while a lazy breeze whispered through the leaves of the trees. In the distance, a deer grazed on a patch of moon-silvered grass.

He glanced at his mother. Standing beside him, clad in a long white hooded cloak, she looked like a fallen angel. Dropping to one knee, she placed a dozen long-stemmed pink roses on the grave.

Not red, Derek noted bitterly. Everyone knew red roses meant love.

"Did you ever love him?" he asked.

"I thought I did, but the truth is, there was never anyone for me but Logan, only I was too stubborn to admit it. Your father would still be alive if I hadn't been such a fool. But I'll always love Kyle because he gave me you, someone who means more to me than anything else in this world."

"I wish I could have known him." How could he ever know who he truly was without knowing the man who had sired him? He had known early on that Logan wasn't his real father. As a child, it hadn't seemed important. Why was it bothering him so much now?

"When I was kidnapped, were you sorry you had to give up your humanity to find me?"

"No. I had always planned to ask Logan to turn me when you were grown."

"Why?"

"I was mortal only twenty years." She gazed into the distance, and he had the feeling she was looking into the past. "I was a vampire for centuries."

"So, you don't miss anything about being human?"

"Only the taste of chocolate."

Derek shook his head. What was it about women and chocolate?

"Anything else you'd like to know?" Mara asked.

"No. Let's go home."

Logan was waiting for them when they returned home. "Everything okay?" he asked, glancing from mother to son.

"Fine," Derek said. "I need to hunt. How about coming along?"

Logan looked at Mara. With a careless wave of her hand, she said, "Take your time. I'm going up to bed."

Grunting softly, Logan followed Derek outside. Not trusting his son to drive in his current state of mind, he said, "Let's take my car."

Moments later, they were headed down the hill. "Are we really going hunting?" Logan asked, "or is this just an excuse to get out of the house?"

"Both. Tell me about my mother."

"She's a remarkable woman."

"Tell me something I don't know."

"She's spoiled. Stubborn. Powerful. But you know all that, too. What's bothering you?"

Derek blew out a sigh that seemed to come from the very depths of his soul. "I'm feeling lost and I don't know why. Something's happening to me. . . ."

"You mean your craving for steak? Your mother told me."

"I know it worries her."

"Of course it does." Logan pulled onto a deserted side street and shut off the engine. "She loves you."

"Yeah. Why did she leave you all those years ago?"

"Because she loved me and it scared her. None of the men in her life ever treated her worth a damn. She didn't trust any of us." A muscle twitched in his jaw. "Not even me."

"That must have hurt."

"You have no idea. I've loved her my whole life. It wasn't easy letting her go, but I sure as hell wasn't going to beg her to stay."

Taking a deep breath, Derek asked the question that troubled him most. "Do you think I could be reverting?"

"No. I'll tell you what I told your mother. I think your human half is coming through. Who knows, you might be able to walk in the sun and eat human food one of these days. The best of both worlds, if you ask me."

"Would my mother have stayed human if it wasn't for me?"

"No. She talked about being turned when she was pregnant. The doctor told her that he didn't think it was possible and that trying to be turned a second time might kill her. Even if you'd never been in danger, sooner or later, she would have found someone to bring her over. If not me, then someone else. She was that determined."

"Was my father a good man?"

"I'd say so. I didn't know him very well, but he loved your mother. And you. So, what now?"

"You can go home," Derek said, opening the car door. "I need some time to think."

He stood on the curb, watching the lights of Logan's car fade into the distance. He had a great deal of respect for his stepfather. The man had always been there for him, always told him the truth, no matter how unpalatable it might have been. He was the only man Derek trusted.

Jogging down the sidewalk, he pondered what Mara and Logan had told him while he searched for prey. He fed quickly, then hurried to Sheree's house.

He stood in the shadows for several minutes, staring at the lights shining through the living room window. Her home looked warm and friendly, inviting. He had fed only a short time ago, but Sheree's scent stirred his hunger anew. He had tasted her once and had craved a second taste ever since. And knew even that wouldn't be enough.

He should leave now, before he did something stupid—something that, once done, could never be undone, like breaking down the door, sweeping Sheree into his arms, and making love to her until the sun chased the moon from the sky.

The thought of holding her, tasting her, making love to her drove all rational thought from his mind. After crossing the street, he waved his hand in front of the door. It opened at his command, but when he tried to enter, the threshold's power repelled him.

Frowning, he took a step back. What the hell had just happened, he wondered.

And then he knew. Sheree had taken his warning about inviting vampires into her house to heart and revoked his invitation.

Sheree frowned as a cool breeze wafted into the living room. How was that possible? All the doors and windows were closed. Weren't they? A sudden chill ran down her spine. Had someone broken into the house again?

Rising, she grabbed the fireplace poker, tiptoed toward the entry, and peered around the corner. "Derek!"

He arched one brow when he saw the poker in her hand. "A wooden stake works better," he said, a touch of bitterness in his voice.

"What? Oh." She lowered her makeshift weapon. "I thought someone was trying to break in."

"Someone was. Sorry I bothered you."

"Wait! Where are you going?"

"It's pretty obvious I'm not wanted here."

"Don't go."

"Just don't come in?"

Sheree blew out a sigh, her longing to see him, to touch him, warring with her innate fear of what he was. The word *vampire* whispered down the corridor of her mind, and with it the memory of what had happened outside the Den, and what had happened here, in her own home. "Can I ask you something?"

"Why not?"

"You won't get mad?"

"No."

"It's common knowledge that vampires need blood to live. . . ."

"Yeah?"

"Where do you get yours?" She lifted a hand to her neck, then jerked it away when she realized what she was doing.

He didn't miss the gesture, or the morbid curiosity in her eyes. "Just where you think I do."

"So, you kill people?"

"Only when they're trying to kill me." Hands clenched, he took a deep breath. "I knew coming here was a bad idea. I won't bother you again."

Sheree took a step forward when he started to turn away.

Everything that had passed between them—every word, every touch, every kiss—flashed before her eyes.

"Wait!" She ran toward the door, across the threshold, and down the porch steps. "Derek, wait!"

He stopped at the edge of the walkway but didn't turn around. "Let me go, Sheree. No good can come from this."

"I don't believe that." Coming up behind him, she placed her hand on his back, heard him suck in a breath at her touch. "We met for a reason, I'm sure of it. It's almost like I was drawn here, to this place. It can't be just coincidence that I was looking for a vampire and I found you."

"You're afraid of me. You can't build any kind of a relationship on fear."

"You're afraid, too."

He nodded. "I'm afraid I'll hurt you. Or worse."

"Can't we go inside and talk it over?"

Slowly, he turned to face her. He let his hunger rise up within him, felt the sharp tips of his fangs brush his tongue, knew his eyes had gone red with the need to feed.

"This is what I am," he said flatly. "Do you still want me to come in?"

Sheree stared at him for a moment. His countenance was frightening, there was no denying it. Had it been anyone but Derek, she would have run screaming into the house and slammed the door. But this was Derek, and even though she was still afraid of what he was, and even though she might be making the biggest mistake of her life, she simply couldn't let him go.

Folding her arms, she said, "Your sister thinks we'd be good for each other, and I . . . I think so, too."

"She's not my sister," Derek said. "She's my mother."

"Your mother!" Sheree stared at him. "Mara is your

mother? The same Mara those men in the Den were talking about? The Mara who knew Cleopatra? That Mara?"

Derek nodded. "The very same." With an effort, he forced his hunger into submission, felt his fangs retract, the red fade from his eyes.

"I don't believe it."

He shrugged. "Well, it's true just the same."

Sheree backed up and sat down, hard, on one of the porch steps, her mind reeling. Derek's mother had lived in the time of the pharaohs. She might look twenty but she was ancient. Sheree shook her head. She had invited the most dangerous vampire in the world into her house.

"You're not gonna faint on me, are you?" Derek asked. "You look a little pale."

Sheree looked up at him, surprised to find him so close. But then, vampires were supposed to be able to move faster than the human eye could follow. What other supernatural powers did he possess? Did he sleep in a coffin? Could he change into a bat? Did he cast a reflection in a mirror?

"I don't sleep in a coffin. I can't change into a bat. I don't cast a reflection in a mirror." He grinned faintly when she realized he was reading her mind. "You've seen me dissolve into mist. I can climb tall buildings in a single bound."

"Can all vampires read minds?"

"As far as I know. Are you all right with that?"

"I don't know. Do you read all my thoughts?"

"No. Just the good ones."

She glared at him, not certain if he was kidding or not.

Unable to resist the urge to touch her, Derek took a step forward. When she didn't recoil, he brushed his knuckles down her cheek. "There's no future for us," he said with regret, "no matter what the Queen of the Vampires thinks."

"I don't believe that."

"No? Why not?"

"Because I think I'm falling in love with you. And I think you care for me, whether you want to admit it or not."

Heaving a sigh, he sat on the step beside her. As always, her nearness soothed him. "Maybe you're right." Most of the men in his family had married mortal women. Rafe, Rane, Vince. Hell, Roshan had married a witch. They'd all had problems of one kind or another, sure, but they were all happy now. Maybe it was worth a try.

"You said you've been a vampire since you were thirteen," Sheree said, frowning. "I thought vampires didn't age."

"Normally they don't."

"And I thought they couldn't reproduce."

"They can't."

Head tilted, she stared up at him, waiting for an explanation.

"It's a long story."

"I'm not going anywhere."

"Do you really think we can make this work?"

"We won't know until we try. So, tell me how you became a vampire."

"Before she married Logan, Mara had an affair with a mortal. During that same time, for reasons no one knows, she started reverting to being human again. I was conceived somewhere along the way. My father died a short time later and Mara married Logan. For the first thirteen years of my life, I was like anybody else, and then, overnight, my vampire nature kicked in."

"I've never heard of anything like that."

"It's happened before. Vince—one of Mara's fledglings— was a new vampire when he fell in love with his wife, Cara. She got pregnant and had twins, Rane and Rafe. They grew up like everybody else until they reached puberty. They stopped aging when they turned twenty-five."

"Is that when you stopped?"

"Yeah."

"Did they marry and have children?"

"They're both married. Savannah was artificially insem- inated and she and Rane have a daughter. Rafe and Kathy are childless."

"Must be nice not getting older, but . . . what about their wives?"

"Savannah and Kathy are both vampires now."

"Oh?"

"It was their idea," Derek assured her. "No one forced them. Savannah waited until her daughter was grown."

Sheree contemplated that for a few moments. She couldn't imagine asking to be turned into a vampire, but if you wanted to spend the rest of your life with one, it was probably the only logical solution, unless you wanted to grow old while your husband stayed forever young.

"You still think we've got a chance?" He didn't have to read her mind to know what she was thinking.

"How old are you, really? I'm afraid to ask."

"Twenty-five."

"And you'll never look any older?"

"No."

"Does it hurt? Becoming a vampire?"

"I don't know. For me, it was a natural transition."

Sheree rubbed her hands up and down her arms as the night grew colder.

"You should go inside," Derek suggested, rising. "It's get- ting late."

"Will I see you again?"

"Do you still think dating a vampire's a good idea?"

When she nodded, he lifted her to her feet and drew her

into his arms. "If you change your mind, if what I am gets to be too much for you to handle, just tell me. I can't promise I'll never hurt you and it scares the hell out of me."

"We'll just have to learn to trust each other."

"Yeah. I'll see you tomorrow night."

Sheree frowned. "I saw your mother during the day. How is that possible?"

"She's Mara, Queen of the Vampires," he said, starting down the steps. "Most of the rules don't apply to her."

"Hey! Aren't you going to kiss me good night?"

She was wrapped in his arms before she had time to blink. His mouth covered hers in a searing kiss that burned every thought from her mind and left her weak and wanting more.

"Tomorrow night," he said, and it sounded like both threat and promise.

Chapter Eighteen

Pearl stared up at the house on the hill. "What are we doing here?" she whispered. "Have you lost your mind?"

"I just wanted to see where he lives," Edna whispered back, her voice edged with excitement.

"You idiot! Mara's in there."

"Mara!" Edna's eyes widened. "I was so busy following Derek, I didn't pay any attention."

"We need to get out of here, now!"

"Do you realize how many hunters would pay a fortune to know where she lives?" Edna asked.

"All the money in the world won't do you any good if you're dead, dear. And I mean really dead!"

"Just one more minute. I've been thinking. What if it wasn't Mara turning human that allowed her to get pregnant, but the werewolf gene itself?"

"If that's true, why didn't any of our experiments work?"

"Maybe artificial insemination won't work. Maybe the sperm loses potency when exposed to the air."

"Are you suggesting that Derek might be able to father a child?"

"It's a possibility."

"So is the danger of Mara finding us. Let's get out of

here! Oh, Lord," Pearl hissed. "It's too late." Heart in her throat, she glanced over her shoulder to find Mara standing behind her.

"Years too late," Mara said. "I should have destroyed you decades ago."

Pearl grabbed Edna's hand, intending to dissolve into mist and disappear, only to discover that she was powerless to do so.

"Any last words?" Mara asked, her gaze drilling into Pearl's.

"You can't kill us!" Edna exclaimed.

"Oh? And why is that?"

"Because we know something about Derek."

Interest flickered in Mara's eyes. "Go on."

Edna shook her head. "Not until you promise to let us leave here alive."

"No chance."

"He's been craving meat!" Edna said. "Don't you want to know why?"

Eyes narrowing, Mara glanced from one woman to the other. Dressed in black from head to foot, they looked like a pair of over-the-hill ninjas. "Does this have anything to do with Ramsden?"

Edna nodded vigorously.

"I'm listening."

"Your promise first," Edna said.

Mara cocked her head to the side. "I can make you tell me, just as I can make your death agonizingly long or blessedly short." Capturing Edna's gaze with her own, she willed her power into the other woman, planting thoughts of excruciating pain into Edna's mind until the woman screamed in agony. "I'm still listening."

Moaning, Edna dropped to the ground.

"Leave her alone!" Pearl shouted. "I'll tell you."

"I'm listening."

"Your son carries the werewolf gene."

Mara snorted. "You'll have to do better than that."

"It's true. Kyle Bowden was a werewolf, but the gene was latent in him. We think it's becoming active in Derek. It's why he's craving meat."

"That's ridiculous," Mara scoffed. "And even if it's true, wouldn't it have manifested itself long before now?"

"Obviously the vampire half has been suppressing his inner werewolf."

"So why is it emerging now?"

"Sometimes these things are sparked by internal changes."

Mara stared at Pearl, reluctant to believe her hypothesis, but what if it was true? The first time the craving had come upon Derek was at puberty. It had happened again just after he turned twenty-five, another significant milestone, in that he had stopped aging. "You think he's turning into a werewolf? Seriously?"

Pearl knelt beside Edna. "We won't know until the next full moon."

"Will the change be permanent?" Mara asked, thinking of Susie McGee.

Pearl shrugged. "Only time will tell."

"Yes," Mara mused. "Time."

Clutching Edna's hand, Pearl looked up at the ancient vampire. "I told you what you wanted to know," she said, hating the tremor in her voice. "If you're going to destroy us, make it quick."

Chapter Nineteen

"Where are the old ladies now?" Derek stretched his legs out in front of him, his chin resting on his folded hands.

Sitting beside him on the sofa, Mara smoothed a nonexistent wrinkle from her skirt. "I let them go."

Derek raised one brow, but said nothing.

"I know, I should have destroyed the two of them. They've had it coming for years."

"So why didn't you?"

Mara glanced at Logan. Reclining on the other couch, he gave a one-shoulder shrug in an "it's up to you" gesture.

Derek looked at his mother. "What's going on, Ma? What aren't you telling me?"

She bristled at his tone, but she could feel the tension building in him, so she let it slide. "They gave me some interesting news. After I heard it, I decided to let them live a little longer."

"Must have been some kick-ass news," Derek muttered. "You've said you wanted them dead more than once. So . . ." His gaze darted from Mara to Logan and back again. "What did they say?"

"It's their opinion that the reason I was able to get

pregnant had less to do with my reverting to humanity than with the fact that your father was a werewolf."

Derek sat forward, eyes narrowing. "What?"

"You heard me. I never knew it, and neither did he, but apparently Kyle carried a recessive werewolf gene, which means you also carry it. Only in your case, it seems to be dominant."

Rising, Derek paced the floor. If it was true, it explained a lot: his restlessness when the moon was full, his craving for raw meat. He paused in midstride. "Are you saying I'm going to turn into a werewolf?"

Mara glanced at Logan again before answering. "It's anybody's guess. Nothing quite like this has ever happened before."

Derek raked a hand through his hair. "What else?"

"There's no way of knowing if, once you turn into a werewolf, you'll remain a werewolf."

"So, I'll either be a werewolf, or a vampire, or both?"

Mara nodded.

"Well, it's a hell of a trifecta, isn't it?"

A thought took Derek to Sheree's house. Uncertain of his ability to keep either his hunger or his emotions under control, he stood in the shadows. What would she think if he shared what he had just learned? What could he say? *Hey, guess what? I might not be a vampire much longer.* Or, *Hey, did you hear the latest news? I might be a vampire* and *a werewolf.*

Yeah, just what she needed. Something else to worry about. That would go over really well.

He held his breath when he saw her looking out the window. His first instinct was to go to her. He fought it for a moment, telling himself it was too dangerous to be near

her in his current state of mind, but even as he told himself
to stay where he was, he was crossing the street, knocking
on the door.

She opened it with a smile. "Hi."

"Hi."

Taking him by the hand, she pulled him inside and closed
the door. "I thought you'd be here sooner. Your mother left
over half an hour ago."

"Is that right?" He still wasn't sure it had been a good
idea for Sheree to invite his mother inside; then again,
Sheree was probably safer with Mara than with him.

Still holding his hand, Sheree sat on the sofa, tugging him
down beside her. "What's wrong?"

"Nothing, why?"

"You wouldn't lie to me, would you?"

He shook his head. "I'll tell you some other time."

"More secrets?"

"Not exactly. I learned something new tonight and I'm
not ready to talk about it yet."

Worry furrowed her brow. "Is it something that affects us?"

"I'm afraid so."

"You're scaring me."

"I don't mean to. So, how did you spend your day?"

She pouted a moment because he wouldn't confide in her,
then blew it off. There was no point in being angry. He had
warned her there were things about himself he couldn't
share. "I didn't really do very much. I called my parents and
told them I wouldn't be coming home right away, after all.
My mother got a little upset with me. It seems as soon as I
told her I might be coming home, she went into party mode.
She seems to think I should be welcomed back as if I've
been away for years."

"She probably misses you."

"Maybe. And then I had a phone call from this guy she's

trying to set me up with. Neil Somerset." She shook her head. "I could tell my mother put him up to it. Neil and I have nothing to say to each other. It was very awkward."

A muscle twitched in Derek's jaw at the mention of another man, even one thousands of miles away.

"Your mother and I spent the rest of the day giving each other manicures," Sheree went on, "and watching old movies on TV. She's quite the movie buff."

"Yeah, well, she's probably seen them all."

"I can't imagine living as long as she has." Sheree looked at him, her expression thoughtful. "You could live that long, too, couldn't you?"

"Maybe."

"Can I get you a glass of wine?"

"No, thanks." He clenched his hands, fighting the urge to take her in his arms and drink from her.

She must have seen the hunger in his eyes, he thought, because she grew very still. In the sudden silence, the sharp intake of her breath was unusually loud. With his preternatural senses, he heard the sudden pounding of her heart, smelled the fear on her skin.

"I should go," he said, his voice thick.

"You need to feed, don't you?"

He didn't deny it.

"You can . . . I mean, if you need to . . . um . . ." She flipped her hair over her shoulder. "Just don't take too much."

He knew he should refuse, should get the hell out of there before it was too late. But the remembered taste of her, the sweetness of it, lingered in his mind.

He cursed under his breath as he took her in his arms.

"Will it hurt?"

"No, love." He claimed her lips with his in a long, slow kiss, held her until the tension went out of her and she was kissing him back, her fingers tunneling into his hair, her body yearning toward his. His hands moved over her, lightly, gently, learning every curve.

He kissed his way along the length of her neck until he found the soft vulnerable place just beneath her ear. His tongue laved the skin, and then, keeping a tight hold on his control, he bit her. She pressed herself closer as sensual warmth spread through her.

It took all of his self-control to hold back, to keep from savaging her throat and taking it all. But then a strange thing happened. One taste, two, and his hunger receded.

She moaned a soft protest when he lifted his head.

He gazed down at her, amazed that his voracious thirst had been satisfied with so little.

Sheree looked up at him, her gaze slightly unfocused. "Are you finished already?"

"Are you sorry?"

She nodded, a faint flush staining her cheeks. "It was—I don't know—amazing."

His life had been full of surprises, Derek thought, giving her a hug. But Sheree was the best one of all.

Chapter Twenty

Pearl filled two water glasses to the brim with red wine, handed one to Edna, then collapsed in a chair, heedless of the liquid that splashed into her lap. "I thought we were dead for sure!"

"Me, too!" Edna took a long swallow, then shook her head. "This isn't going to cut it. I need something warm to drink."

"In a minute, dear. Let me catch my breath." Pearl drained her glass, though it wasn't easy, her hands were shaking so. "Why didn't she kill us?"

"She must have decided we could be of use later. After all, no one knows more about werewolves than we do."

"That's true." Rising, Pearl refilled her glass. She and Edna had conducted numerous tests on the creatures in the past. "Who do you think the hunters in town are after? Mara? Or Derek?"

"I don't know. Two hunters have disappeared. One was reported dead. One seems to have lost her memory."

"If we're not careful, we could be next," Pearl said, resuming her seat.

"Funny, all those hunters showing up here at the same time."

"Almost as if someone's put out a hit," Pearl remarked, then frowned. "But that doesn't make sense, dear. Hunting vampires is what hunters do. It's in their blood."

"True," Edna said, "but maybe one of Mara's old enemies wants her dead and doesn't have the *cojones* to do the job himself."

"It's a possibility," Pearl agreed.

"If they're afraid to go after Mara, killing Derek would be the best revenge they could take. If anything happened to him, she would never get over it."

Pearl nodded, and then sighed. "Remember when we were hunters?"

"Yes, indeed," Edna said, grinning. "And we're still hunters."

"Yes, dear. Only the prey has changed."

Setting her glass on the table beside her chair, Edna stood. "Speaking of change, it's time to get out of these dreary outfits and into something a little more comfortable."

"Like a nice warm neck or two?" Pearl remarked.

"Girlfriend, you must be reading my mind."

Derek waited until Sheree was asleep before slipping outside to where Mara waited.

"What's up?" He glanced up and down the street, but all was quiet, the houses dark. A faint breeze carried the scent of skunk. Somewhere in the distance, a dog barked, a steady yapping that spoke of boredom.

"Would you believe me if I said I was just in the neighborhood?"

"Not likely."

"All right," she said with an airy wave of her hand. "I'm spying on you."

"Worried about me?"

"No, about Sheree, actually. I know the mood you were in earlier."

"And you thought I'd rip her throat out?" He laughed softly. "Why would you care?"

"I've grown rather fond of her these last few days."

"Yeah, me, too." Derek shoved his hands into the pockets of his jeans. "She let me drink from her tonight."

"You fed on her?" Mara exclaimed.

"No! No, it wasn't like that. She knew I needed to feed and she offered, but the thing is, after a swallow or two, the hunger left me. Nothing like that's ever happened before."

"Interesting, but not unheard of. So, you're going to stay with her?"

"For a while."

"Do you think that's wise?"

"Probably not, but . . . all I know is that I need her in ways I don't understand. It's like she's a missing part of me. I know, that sounds sappy as hell, but . . ."

"Believe it or not, I understand. It's how I feel about Logan. The hardest thing I ever did was admit that I needed him," she said, smiling. "Chauvinist that he is, he's never let me forget it, which would be unbearable, except that he needs me, too."

"Yeah."

Mara glanced at the house. "Are you thinking of spending the day here?"

"No. I'll be home before dawn."

"All right. I'll relieve you then."

"Thanks, Ma."

With a shake of her head, she vanished into the darkness.

* * *

Derek lingered in the shadows, enjoying the quiet of the night. Opening his vampire senses, he listened to the slow, steady beat of Sheree's heart, smiled when she sighed in her sleep. His mind brushed hers. She was dreaming of him.

Leaning against a tree, he felt himself relax—really relax—for the first time in months. And he owed it to Sheree. He had never expected her to accept what he was.

He lifted his head as a new scent was carried to him by the night wind.

Hunters! There was no mistaking that smell. Or the smell of vampires!

Dissolving into mist, he drifted down the street. Hovering in the air, he watched in amazement as the two old ladies he had seen in the Den fought a trio of well-armed hunters. The hunters, all big men in their prime, towered over the two vampires. Had life and death not hung in the balance, Derek might have found the battle highly amusing.

He had no intention of interfering until the fight turned against the vampires. Chiding himself for being a fool, he materialized behind the nearest hunter and choked him out.

The shortest of the hunters quickly realized they were now outnumbered. Yelling at his remaining companion to follow him, he hightailed it down the street.

The third hunter wasn't ready to call off the fight until both of the women launched themselves at him, driving him to the ground. He looked up at Derek, seeking help he quickly realized wouldn't be forthcoming.

Derek let his eyes go red. "What are you doing here?" he growled.

"What the hell do you think?"

"Who are you after?"

"Any vampire I can find!" He struggled against the two holding him down, swore when he realized that they were a lot stronger than they looked.

"What's your name?"

"Go to hell, bloodsucker!"

"After you."

Fear shadowed the hunter's eyes for the first time. "I'll tell you whatever you want to know if you let me go."

A faint scuffle warned Derek that the first hunter had regained consciousness. He turned in time to deflect the knife aimed at his back. The blade scraped along his forearm. It stung like hell. Grabbing the man by his arm, Derek threw him down the street. There was a sickening thud when the hunter skidded, headfirst, into a brick wall. The coppery scent of blood rose in the air.

The red-haired vampire looked up at Derek. "Are you through questioning him?"

Derek stared at the hunter. "Depends on whether he has any answers for me."

The hunter cleared his throat. "What do you want to know?"

"Who are you? Why are you here? Did someone send you?"

"My name's Ashby. I was hunting vampires when I came across these two in the Den." The fact that he found it hard to believe the two old ladies were vampires, or that they had taken him down, was evident in his voice. "I followed them here."

"You weren't after me?"

Ashby shook his head.

"You're lying," Derek said. "Who sent you?"

Ashby shook his head again, harder this time, as if that would convince them he was telling the truth.

Derek glanced at the red-haired vampire, who sank her fangs into the hunter's neck.

The hunter let out a shriek. "McDonald's after Mara!

Word on the street says she's willing to lay down a lot of credits for information regarding Mara's whereabouts."

The redhead reared back. Delicately wiping a bit of blood from the corner of her mouth, she looked at the other woman, then at the hunter. "Lou McDonald?"

The hunter nodded.

The white-haired vampire shook her head. "I would have thought she'd be retired by now."

"Who's McDonald?" Derek asked.

"Only one of the most dangerous slayers in the world."

Derek grunted softly. And then he stared at the two old women, wondering why he hadn't put two and two together sooner. He didn't know the redhead's name, but there was a connection between them that he didn't understand. "Which one are you?" he asked. "Edna or Pearl?"

"We never meant you any harm," the redhead said. "It was purely research."

"Be quiet, dear," the other woman said.

"Hush, Pearl." The redhead smiled at Derek. "I'm Edna. I only drank from you so I could find you again."

"Why would you care where I was or what happened to me?"

"Because of the werewolf gene, of course," she replied, as if he wasn't too bright. "Didn't your mother tell you about it?"

"Yeah, she told me. You're lucky she wants you alive, or you'd be history now."

Edna swallowed hard, thinking that, at the moment, Derek looked even more dangerous than his infamous mother.

"Stay the hell out of my sight," Derek said. "Both of you. And get rid of that body down the street."

Edna nodded, then glanced at the hunter trapped beneath her and Pearl. "What shall we do with this one?"

"Whatever you want," Derek muttered darkly, and left them there, the hunter's cries for help ringing in his ears.

Derek spent the rest of the evening in Sheree's bedroom. Sitting in a chair by the window, he watched her sleep, wondering what the future held for the two of them. Wondering what would happen to him during the next full moon. He wasn't afraid of changing into a wolf. He could do that now. But a werewolf? Would he become one of the monsters so popular in the movies? A slavering, bloodthirsty creature who terrorized the countryside, killing indiscriminately? Would his werewolf form be different from the wolf he could assume at will? When he shape-shifted, he remembered who and what he was. Would that be true in werewolf form? Would he recognize those he knew, or attack them without mercy?

He glanced at Sheree, sleeping peacefully, one hand tucked beneath her chin. What was he doing bringing her into his life? What if he killed her? There was no way he'd ever be able to live with that. Maybe he was worrying needlessly. Maybe, come the full moon, nothing would happen. His father had carried the werewolf gene with no ill effects. Hopefully, his son would also be spared.

He sensed the coming of dawn even before the first faint rays of sunlight lightened the sky. It manifested itself in a sudden prickling in every nerve and cell in his body, a tingling that would become excruciating if he was caught in full sunlight.

He brushed a kiss across Sheree's cheek before he left the house.

Mara was waiting for him on the front porch. "What

NIGHT'S PROMISE   137

happened? There's blood on your shirt and in the air." She took a deep breath. "Did you kill someone?"

"A hunter."

She lifted one brow.

As succinctly as possible, Derek told her of the night's events.

"Lou McDonald? Why would she be hunting me after all this time? I never did anything to her." Mara shook her head. "She helped your father find me when I was pregnant with you. And then Logan and I went to her for help when you were kidnapped."

"Once a hunter, always a hunter."

"Like Edna and Pearl." Mara blew out an exasperated sigh. "If it's the last thing I ever do on this earth, I'm going to get rid of that meddling twosome."

Chapter Twenty-One

Derek had not dreamed since he was thirteen, but tonight his fears about becoming a werewolf followed him to sleep. This, however, was more of a nightmare, and even though he knew he was dreaming, he was helpless to escape. . . .

Unlike shape-shifting, transforming into a werewolf proved to be agonizing as bones, muscle, tissue, and flesh stretched and crackled. He writhed on the ground, howling in pain until it was over. Then, bounding to his feet, he raced through the dream's darkness. Streetlights turned into trees, the pavement into earth. He ran tirelessly until he came to a clear pool. Pausing, he stared at his reflection. When he shape-shifted, the creature he became was a handsome thing, fur thick and black, eyes gray, body perfectly formed. But the creature that stared back at him now was hideous— the snout too long, the ears big and misshapen, the body out of proportion.

He whined low in his throat, then turned away and began to run again, his jaws dripping saliva as he scented prey ahead.

He found her caught in a thicket.

It was Sheree, as he had known it would be.

She screamed when she saw him, struggling with renewed

effort to free herself from the briars that were tangled in her clothing and hair.

Snarling softly, he padded toward her, the scent of her fear magnifying his lust for her life's blood. For flesh . . .

In his sleep, Derek recoiled at the thought of consuming human flesh. But the werewolf in his dream would not be denied its prey.

Sheree screamed again as he sank his teeth into her throat, her hoarse cry of pain and fear mingling with his own.

It was the sound of his own tormented cry, and that of his mother calling his name, that woke him. He stared up at her, his body bathed in sweat, his breath coming in ragged gasps.

"It's all right," Mara said, brushing a lock of damp hair from his brow.

"I had a nightmare."

"You were dreaming?" Such a thing was unheard of.

"Yeah."

"Do you want to talk about it? It might help."

"I was a werewolf."

"Go on."

"Sheree . . ." He took a deep breath. "She was my prey."

"A nightmare, indeed. But it's over now."

Sitting up, his back propped against the headboard, he wiped the sweat from his brow with a corner of the sheet. "I shouldn't be with her. I'm a predator. She'll always be prey."

"I disagree. Your dream was a reflection of your fears. You told me yourself that being with her calms you."

"What if that's no longer true when I'm a werewolf?"

"If you're afraid of what you might do, I can lock you up before the full moon. Then we can see how it affects you. Perhaps nothing will happen."

"And if I turn into a ravening monster?"

"Let's worry about that if and when it happens."

"Tell me about Susie McGee."

Mara sat on the edge of the mattress, ankles crossed. "She was your typical wife and mother until she was bitten by a werewolf. Her husband, Rick, was part of a gang of hunters. Pearl's grandson was also one of them. They didn't hunt just vampires, but any and all supernatural creatures. Edna and Pearl had captured several of them so they could experiment with a serum they had invented. It was intended to make all supernatural creatures revert to human."

Her brow furrowed as she called up the past. "As I recall, it worked on a couple of newly turned vampires, but it had no effect on the shape-shifters. Since they're born that way, they had no true humanity to revert to. Its effect on the were-wolves was mixed. Susie was one of their guinea pigs. She would have died if Rafe hadn't turned her. She never really got the hang of being a werewolf, but being a vampire seemed to suit her. She fell in love with a shape-shifter and they got married."

Leaning forward, his mother kissed him on the forehead. "Get some sleep now."

Slipping under the covers, Derek thought about Susie McGee. First a werewolf, then a vampire, but not both at the same time.

As darkness dragged him back down into oblivion, he thought, given a choice, he'd rather be a vampire.

Chapter Twenty-Two

Sheree glanced out the living room window. The sun was just setting. Derek would be there soon. Peeking out the narrow window beside the front door, she saw Mara sitting on the porch, reading a magazine. The vampire had been there since early morning. Sheree had asked if she wouldn't be more comfortable inside, but Mara insisted she was fine where she was.

It made Sheree feel cherished, knowing that Derek and his mother were both protecting her.

Hurrying into her bedroom, Sheree ran a comb through her hair, brushed her teeth, then changed into the blue skirt and sweater she had bought earlier in the day, with Mara offering advice.

She had just applied fresh lipstick when the doorbell rang. Excitement fluttered in her stomach as she ran down the stairs to open the door.

Derek whistled softly when he saw her. "You look great."

"Thank you."

He crossed the threshold, then drew her into his arms, all his doubts about being with her disintegrating when he kissed her.

"I missed you, too," Sheree said, smiling. "What shall we do tonight?"

"Whatever you want."

"I'm happy to stay home, if you are."

"Fine with me."

In the living room, she sat on the sofa and he settled close beside her, one arm sliding around her shoulders.

"How was your day?" he asked.

"Okay. Your mom and I went shopping and then out to lunch. Well, I had lunch. I asked her to come inside, but she refused. It must make for a long day, just sitting there on the porch."

"It's a warning to any vampire, any hunter, who's thinking about hurting you," Derek explained.

"Still . . ."

"Don't worry about it. Time doesn't pass the same for us as it does for you. Vampires can, I don't know how to explain it, sort of shut down so they don't notice the passage of time."

"Really?"

"Really."

"Can I ask you something?"

"Anything. You don't have to ask my permission."

"When we were shopping today, I couldn't help noticing that your mother's reflection didn't show in the mirror. Until you told me otherwise, I always thought that was a myth."

"I wish it was."

"Does it ever make you feel like you're invisible?"

"Worse. It makes me feel as if I don't exist."

Reaching up, she caressed his cheek. "I'm glad you do."

"I am, too, now."

His words warmed her heart. Cupping his face in her palms, she drew his head down and kissed him, gasped as his arms tightened around her.

"Sorry," he murmured, releasing her. "Sometimes I forget how fragile you are."

"Fragile?"

He chuckled. "Honey, I could break you in two with one hand tied behind my back."

"Well, that's comforting!"

"Guess I shouldn't have said that out loud."

"Don't be silly. I know how strong you are. I've seen you in action, remember?"

"Sheree . . ."

"I'm not afraid of you, Derek."

"You should be!"

"I think we already had this discussion. Stop worrying and kiss me again."

"Don't say I didn't warn you," he muttered, and drew her back into his embrace.

Kissing Derek was like nothing Sheree had ever known. She reveled in the strength of his arms around her, in the masterful way he held her and kissed her, the tenderness in his touch as he caressed her. More than his physical strength, she sensed the preternatural power inherent in his kind. Why hadn't she noticed it before? Was she sensitive to it now because she knew what he was? Or had he been shielding it from her until now? The power danced over her skin, a constant reminder that he wasn't like other men.

She pushed him down on the sofa, then straddled his thighs.

He arched one brow, a faint smile playing over his lips, as she unbuttoned his shirt, then ran her fingertips over his chest and belly.

"Careful now," he warned.

"I'm tired of being careful."

He raised himself up so she could remove his shirt.

"Hey," he said when she tossed it on the floor. "That's Armani."

"I'll buy you another one." Her gaze moved over him in blatant appreciation. His shoulders were broad, his stomach ridged with muscle. She traced his biceps, explored the curly black hair on his chest, ran her fingertips along his waistline.

"You're playing with fire, girl."

"Am I? You don't feel like fire. Are vampires always so cool to the touch?"

He nodded. "We don't need to breathe as often as you do. Our hearts beat more slowly."

Her questing fingers stilled as she waited for him to go on. There was so much about him she didn't know. She glanced at his forearm. A faint red line marred his pale skin.

His gaze followed hers to the faint red line that stood out against his pale skin. "I got that when I was five or six. Fell off my bike and landed on a piece of glass. Any wounds I get now heal almost instantly and leave no scar."

"But you can't be up during the day?"

"I can, for short periods of time, as long as I stay out of the sun's light, but I prefer the night. My mother assures me that, in a year or two, the sun will no longer affect me." He drew in a deep breath, let it out in a soft huff. "I could do it now if I drank from her, but . . ." He shook his head. The thought of drinking from his own mother was abhorrent in ways he didn't care to contemplate. "Any more questions?"

She shivered when he ran his fingertips over her lower lip. Though his touch was cool, heat spread through every nerve and cell in her body.

In a move so quick it was over before she realized it was happening, he rolled over, tucking her body beneath his. She recognized the hunger in his eyes, felt her body's primal instinct to flee from danger.

Derek growled low in his throat, his hunger sparked by

the scent of fear on her skin, the sudden, rapid beating of her heart. Closing his eyes, he took a deep breath.

"I'm not afraid," Sheree said, forcing herself to relax. "And I'm not prey. But if you're thirsty . . ." She turned her head to the side. "Drink, Derek."

He growled again, though it was more of a purr, and then he bent his head to her neck and took what she offered.

Sheree closed her eyes as his fangs brushed her skin. How was it possible that something so unnatural—so revolting— could feel so wonderful? She should push him away, never see him again, but she knew she would not—could not. There was something remarkably intimate about letting him drink from her, about knowing that her blood was nourishing him. A little voice in the back of her head reminded her that she would die if he took too much. But even that didn't seem to matter as pleasure rippled through her.

She felt bereft when he lifted his head. His tongue laved her skin, sealing the wounds, and then, murmuring, "Forgive me," he buried his face in the curve between her neck and shoulder.

"There's nothing to forgive." Sheree sifted his hair through her fingers, then softly whispered, "I love you."

"I . . ." Derek cursed inwardly, afraid to tell her he loved her, afraid to believe she loved him. Those three words had started feuds, brought kings to their knees, changed the fate of nations.

He had no idea what havoc those words might cause in his life.

Or hers.

Dammit, he had to say something.

"It's all right," Sheree said. "I didn't mean to say it out loud, but"—she made a vague gesture with one hand—"I couldn't keep it in any longer."

Sitting up, he raked a hand through his hair, conscious

of her steady gaze. "You remember I told you I'd learned something new about myself?"

"Yes."

"I think I'd better tell you about it before this thing between us goes any farther."

Sheree's heartbeat ratcheted up a notch.

Derek closed his eyes, one hand massaging his brow. How was he supposed to tell her he might turn into a werewolf? She had accepted his being a vampire without much fuss. Time to find out how she felt about werewolves.

"Listen, I don't know how to sugarcoat this, so I'm just gonna say it straight out. My father was a werewolf, but the gene he carried was latent and never manifested. Turns out, I also carry that gene."

"Werewolves are real, too?"

"Yeah."

"Can you be both at the same time?"

"I don't know, but I'll probably find out the next time the moon is full."

She fidgeted a moment; then, murmuring, "Excuse me," she left the room.

He heard the sound of a kitchen cupboard opening, water running, knew she was trying to ease her nervousness. He didn't smell fear on her, which surprised him. But she was ill at ease, confused, unsettled. Well, he could hardly blame her. He felt the same way.

He was debating whether to go to her or just leave when she returned. She hesitated a moment, then perched on the edge of the sofa like a bird poised to take flight at the first sign of danger.

"Do you want me to go?"

"I don't know." She fiddled with the hem of her sweater. "It doesn't change the way I feel about you, but . . . well . . ."

She spread her hands in a helpless gesture. "I don't know what to say."

"It's a lot to take in, I'll grant you that."

"You must be . . . I don't know . . . worried. Upset." Her gaze searched his. "Scared."

He nodded. Scared didn't begin to cover it.

"What do you want to do?" she asked.

"That's up to you."

Sheree bit down on her lower lip, then drew a deep breath. "I think I'm going to go home and visit my parents for a week or two and sort out my feelings."

She was leaving. Hadn't he known that, sooner or later, she would go? And though he knew it was for the best, he was tempted to use his preternatural powers to make her stay because, heaven help him, he was afraid of what he'd do—what he might become—without her.

"Derek?"

"I think that's a good idea." It was, he thought, the biggest lie he'd ever told.

Mara listened quietly as Derek told her about Sheree's decision to go back to Philadelphia. Though he spoke with no inflection, she knew the girl's decision had hurt. Her first instinct was to compel the girl to stay, to love her son the way he deserved. The only thing that stopped her was knowing Derek would hate her for it.

The words *I'm sorry* seemed inadequate, but, in the end, that was all she could think to say.

Later, alone in her bedroom, Mara paced the floor, her heart breaking for her son's pain. For the first time in his life, he had fallen in love. She told herself that Sheree's leaving was probably a good thing, at least for now.

Logan materialized in the room a few minutes later. He

didn't have to ask if there was something wrong. The air was thick with the tension radiating off his wife.

Wordless, he drew her into his arms. "Want to tell me what's wrong?"

"Sheree has decided to go home to her parents and Derek is devastated. I don't know what to do."

"Stay out of it. This is between the two of them."

"My son is hurting, and it's all her fault!"

"Yeah, well, there's nothing you can do about it. He's a big boy now. He doesn't need you to lick his wounds."

She sagged in his arms, her cheek resting on his chest. "I always thought when he grew up I'd stop worrying. He doesn't need this on top of everything else. The full moon will be here before we know it."

He snorted softly. "I'm not looking forward to that, either."

Chapter Twenty-Three

Sheree cried while packing her suitcases, cried when she went to bed that night, sobbed quietly in the taxi on the way to the airport and during the flight to Philadelphia, and sniffled on the taxi ride home.

When her father opened the door, he took one look at her tear-ravaged face and folded her in his arms.

"Whatever it is, ducky, it can't be as bad as all that."

"Oh, Daddy, you have no idea!" And the worst of it was, she couldn't tell him everything.

"It's got to be man trouble," Brian Westerbrooke murmured, draping his arm around her shoulders as he guided her into the living room.

Sheree nodded. "Where's Mother?"

"The hospital was having an auction. Naturally, she's in charge. She took Trudy with her. They should be home in an hour or so."

Trudy Simmons lived in the little cottage behind the house. She had worked for Sheree's parents for as long as Sheree could remember. She was a sort of jill-of-all-trades, taking up whatever slack was left by the maid, the cook, and the gardeners.

"Sit down while I pour you a drink," her father said. "You look like you could use one."

Sheree glanced around the room, trying to imagine Derek in her mother's immaculate parlor, with its pristine white carpets, taupe walls, and Louis XV furniture. There wasn't a spot of dust to be found. Fresh flowers graced the tables. A trio of magazines was set, just so, on the ornate coffee table in front of the high-backed sofa. The drapes were tightly closed against the afternoon sun.

"Here you go, ducky." Handing her a glass of chardonnay, her father joined her on the sofa. "Now, tell me all about it."

Sheree told him what she could, how she had met Derek in a nightclub and quickly fallen in love with him, how he had secrets he couldn't share, and that his life might be in danger.

Brian Westerbrooke listened attentively, nodding now and then.

"I didn't know what else to do," Sheree said, "so I came home."

"Well, that was exactly the right thing to do," Brian said. "We're expected at the Somersets' tonight to celebrate Neil's promotion. I think a party and several glasses of champagne are just what you need to take your mind off your troubles."

Sheree groaned softly as she imagined spending the evening with Neil at the Somersets'. No doubt the Uptons would also be there.

Why had she ever thought coming home would be a good idea?

The Somersets' house was ablaze with lights when Sheree and her parents arrived. Her mother looked elegant in a gown by Dior, her father as handsome as always in

Armani. Sheree had chosen a black, off-the-shoulder frock because the color reminded her of Derek and suited her mood at the same time.

She smiled at Mr. and Mrs. Somerset, tried not to grimace when Neil bowed over her hand and kissed it.

"How lovely you look," he said. "I'm so glad you're home."

Murmuring, "Thank you," she tried to free her hand from his, but he seemed determined to hold it. And then she saw Ralph striding toward them, and she knew why Neil wouldn't let go.

"Sheree!" Ralph gushed. Ignoring Neil, Ralph kissed her on both cheeks. "You look good enough to eat!"

Ralph rescued her hand from Neil's. "The orchestra is tuning up. I believe the first dance should be mine."

"And all the rest are mine," Neil said, smirking.

Resigned, Sheree followed Ralph into the ballroom. Holding her too close, he said, "I knew you'd come back."

"Did you?"

"How could you stay away, babe?" he said with an arrogant smile. "I knew there was something between us when we danced together at Leonardo's wedding."

All too soon, Neil came to claim her. Holding her even closer than her previous partner, he spent the entire time bragging about his promotion, hinting that all he needed was a good woman, like her, to make his life complete.

As soon as the song ended, Ralph claimed her again.

By the end of the evening, Sheree felt like a piece of taffy, having been constantly pulled back and forth.

Glad that the evening at the Somersets' was over, Sheree kicked off her heels, hung up her dress, and fell back on her bed. Her feet were killing her.

Lying there, staring up at the ceiling of her old room, she

fervently wished she had stayed in California. By night's end, she had danced with every eligible man at the party, and foolishly compared them all to Derek, which explained why none of them had appealed to her. None of the men she knew measured up to her vampire. Her vampire, she thought, and wondered if she would ever see him again.

Slamming her fist against the mattress, Sheree chided herself for being such a coward. Vampire or werewolf, what difference did it make? She loved the man inside. And yet . . . how many times had Derek warned her that she would always be prey? Maybe it was time to pay attention. Then again, which would be worse, risking her life to be with the man she loved, or spending the rest of her life without him?

There was really no choice.

Her anger faded as she pictured him in her mind—tall, broad shouldered, as handsome as the devil, as sexy as sin.

Still, she thought, it might be wise to wait until after the full moon before returning to California. And, in the meantime, she could get her parents used to the idea that she intended to marry a California boy.

Assuming he would have her.

Chapter Twenty-Four

"McDonald is here!" Pearl couldn't keep a tremor of fear out of her voice.

"Lou McDonald?" Edna glanced around Drac's Dive. The dance floor was crowded; the bar was packed with couples, and with singles hoping to score. "Where? I don't see her."

"There, at the far end of the bar. The woman in the long black coat."

Edna sent a nonchalant glance over her shoulder. Lou McDonald didn't look very intimidating. She was no more than five feet tall, with light blond hair and skin almost as pale as that of the vampires she hunted. But her eyes, ah, there was death in her cold blue eyes.

"We should leave," Pearl said. "She's not looking this way. If we hurry, we can sneak out before she sees us."

Grabbing Edna's hand, Pearl edged toward the door. She breathed a sigh of relief as she stepped outside, with Edna close on her heels, only to come to an abrupt halt when a woman stepped in front of them. Pearl had never seen her before, but she recognized the stink of a hunter.

Before she could dissolve into mist, the hunter slapped

a handcuff around Pearl's wrist. The silver sizzled against her skin.

Before Edna could react, Lou McDonald had come up behind her with a pair of handcuffs, which she quickly locked in place. With an evil grin, the hunter jabbed Edna in the arm with a needle.

Edna exclaimed, "Oh, shit, we're dead!" as McDonald's accomplice jabbed Pearl's arm.

Feeling suddenly light-headed, Pearl watched Edna collapse on the sidewalk moments before everything went black.

Pearl woke abruptly, instantly aware that thick silver chains bound her to a chair. Wide eyed, she glanced around. A small gray room. No windows. A single door.

There was no sign of Edna.

Lou McDonald stood before her wielding a slender, long-bladed dagger. "I want answers," McDonald said. "And I want them now."

"Where's Edna?"

"I'm asking the questions here. I want to know Mara's whereabouts."

"Mara?"

"Answer me!"

Pearl hissed as the silver blade opened a thin gash in her left arm. Blood flowed in the wake of the blade.

"I can do this all night," McDonald said. "And all day tomorrow."

"You'd torture me while I'm at rest?"

"You bet. Where is she?"

Pearl frowned. "You found us. Why can't you find her?"

"If I could, I would. I think she's using some kind of ancient vamp glamour to shield herself from hunters." The blade scraped down Pearl's right arm. "Now, where is she?"

Fighting the urge to cry out, Pearl sniffed the air. Edna was nearby. Pearl tugged against the chains, but there was no escaping bonds made of silver.

"Just tell me what I want to know and I'll make your death quick and painless. Otherwise . . ." The blade opened another gash in Pearl's left arm. The wounds, which normally would have healed almost instantly, were slow to close. Dark red blood dripped onto the cement floor. The smell of it filled the air.

"I'll tell you," Pearl said, stalling for time, although she couldn't think of anyone who would come to their rescue. "But only if you tell me why you're after her."

"Are you as stupid as you look? Why do you think I want her? She's the most powerful vampire on the planet. I'm a hunter. You do the math."

"She'll eat you for breakfast."

McDonald dismissed the idea with a wave of her hand. "Maybe. But I'm about to retire and . . ."

"And you want to take down the biggest, baddest vampire of them all before you do?"

"That's right. One of us is going down." McDonald tossed the blood-stained dagger from one hand to the other. "Whatever happened to her son? Is he still alive?"

Pearl glanced past McDonald, her eyes widening. "Oh, yes," she said, smiling. "He's very much alive. He—"

"Shit!" McDonald whirled around, the dagger tightly clutched in her fist as she came face-to-face with Mara's son.

"Are you looking for me?" he asked mildly.

"Actually, I'm looking for your mother."

"If you'd found her instead of me, you'd be dead now."

"Where's Edna?" Pearl asked.

Derek's gaze remained on McDonald while he answered the other vampire. "She's feeding."

"My sister!" Lou McDonald's eyes went wide. "Where's Cindy? What have you done to her?"

"I didn't do anything to her. I simply compelled her to free her prisoner."

"Edna." Pearl's brow furrowed thoughtfully. "Of course! She brought you here, didn't she?"

Derek nodded. "I heard her call for help."

"And you came!" Pearl's smile was radiant. "Thank you, dear!"

"Turn Pearl loose," Derek said.

McDonald lifted her chin defiantly. "And if I refuse?"

"You can waste time arguing, or you can let her go. It might not be too late to save your sister. But you're not getting out of this room until Pearl's free. The choice is yours."

McDonald's face went white as a harsh wail reverberated from the adjoining room. Glaring at Derek, she unlocked the chains binding the vampire, then ran out of the room screaming her sister's name.

"Thank you again, dear boy." Pearl's nostrils flared as the scent of freshly spilled blood wafted through the air. "Now, if you'll excuse me . . ."

"Enjoy your meal," he said, smiling, though he thought McDonald's blood would be sour, indeed.

Chapter Twenty-Five

Mara stared at her son in wide-eyed disbelief. "You saved their lives?"

Derek shrugged. "It seemed like the right thing to do."

"I don't understand you. Why would you help those two old bats after what they did to your father? What they did to you?"

"Hey, it's done. Let it go."

"So Lou McDonald and her sister are dead?"

"For all I know, Edna and Pearl could be dead, too. I didn't hang around to find out."

"You would know if Edna had been destroyed."

He shrugged. "Then she's alive. Besides, didn't you say you wanted to keep the two of them around for a while?"

"Yes, I did say that." Mara shook her head. "I can't believe those two meddlesome creatures took out the notorious McDonald sisters."

"They had a little help, Ma," Derek reminded her. "It's me you should be thanking."

"Thank you," she said, her voice sugary sweet.

"That hunter wanted you awfully bad. I overheard her saying she was going to take you out or die trying."

"Well, she should be happy then," Mara said, grinning. "I just hope Edna and Pearl cleaned up the mess."

Derek stalked the dark streets of Hollywood. His hunger, stirred to life by the scent of the hunter's blood, rode him hard. He had no doubt that the two hunters were dead. Their screams had followed him out of the building. He had no sympathy for them. They came looking to destroy his mother and had met their own deaths, instead. Sometimes the good guys won. Sometimes they lost—although in this case, he wasn't sure there were any good guys.

The scent of prey drew him toward an unsavory part of town where he found two drunks fighting over a bottle of rotgut. One of them was bleeding from a shallow cut across his cheek. Closing his eyes, Derek took a deep breath, hands clenching as the smell fueled his hellish thirst.

He could have killed both of the transients in an instant, but he was spoiling for a fight. With a cry, he waded into the battle. As expected, the two men quickly turned on him, their own disagreement forgotten in the face of a new threat.

Restraining his preternatural power, Derek fought both of them, relishing their punishing fists, although the pain was negligible. He didn't try to avoid their blows; instead, he welcomed them. He was a monster. It was what he deserved. Until one of the men pulled a knife from the inside of his boot.

The weapon changed the game. Infused with new courage, the armed man lunged at Derek as the second man flung himself onto Derek's back. Derek hissed when the blade buried itself to the hilt in his chest. It wasn't a fatal strike, but it hurt like hell.

Snarling, Derek jerked the blade from his flesh and drove it into the man's heart. The drunk reeled backward, then spiraled to the ground.

The man clinging to Derek's back slid off and hit the street running.

Grunting with pain, Derek bent over the mortally wounded man.

He had never deliberately baited a human before. Never gone looking for a fight. Or enjoyed killing.

He glanced at the sky, wondering if his hunger and his anger had been sparked by the werewolf sleeping inside him.

Later, after disposing of the body, he wondered what Sheree would think if she could see him now, eyes burning, clothing splashed with blood.

Sheree. His need for her grew stronger with every passing hour.

What was she doing? His jaw clenched as he imagined her with other men—dancing, laughing, letting them steal a kiss or two. Did she ever think of him? Was she planning to come back to California, or had she decided to stay in Philadelphia and marry some puny mortal? He slammed his fist against a nearby wall. Why in hell had he let her go?

He strolled down Hollywood Boulevard, ignoring the come-ons of the streetwalkers, sidestepping a couple who'd had too much to drink.

How had he ever lived without Sheree? She had been away for a week and it seemed like years. He hadn't realized just how empty his existence had been until she was no longer in it.

What would he do if she never came back?

Sheree smiled politely as an elderly man with snow-white hair asked her to dance. She would rather have refused, but since her parents were hosting the party, she was expected to dance with anyone who asked, and pretend she was having a good time.

She had been home for over two weeks, and it seemed like an eternity. Every day had been crammed with activities—an endless round of parties, dinners, charity auctions, and Sunday brunches. Ralph had proposed to her twice, Neil three times. And now her mother had ferreted out a new suitor, James van Horn, who made Ralph and Neil seem vastly appealing by comparison.

Waltzing around the floor with her elderly partner, Sheree decided she'd had enough. Tomorrow, she was booking a flight back to California. She missed her little house. She missed the California sunshine.

She missed Derek.

Relieved when the music ended, Sheree thanked her partner for the dance, and hastened out to the verandah for a few minutes alone.

She had never gotten around to telling her mother she was in love with Derek, but perhaps that was a good thing. Better to make sure he still wanted her before she said anything to her parents. One thing she knew for certain: she wanted him more than ever.

She gazed up at the sky. The moon would be full next week. Was he dreading it? Or anxious to confront his fears once and for all?

Sheree.

She whirled around at the sound of his voice, her heart fluttering with excitement at the thought that maybe he missed her so much, he had come after her.

But there was no one there.

It was late the next night when Sheree arrived at her home in California. She had intended to wait until after the full moon, but after hearing Derek's voice in her mind last night, she couldn't wait any longer. He needed her. She was sure of it.

She knew a moment of trepidation when she unlocked the front door, remembering all too clearly what had happened only a few short weeks ago.

Standing in the entryway, she cocked her head to one side, recalling how Derek had assured her there was no one in the house because it "felt empty." She knew now he had probably used his vampire senses to ascertain there was no one there. A handy talent, no doubt, when people were hunting you. She tried to imagine what it would be like knowing people hated you enough to kill you just because you were different.

Turning on the lights, Sheree moved warily through the house, breathed a sigh of relief when the house was, indeed, empty. After leaving her suitcases in the bedroom, she slipped into her nightgown, then went downstairs to make a cup of tea. She would have to go grocery shopping tomorrow. She had emptied the refrigerator before she left. The cupboards were bare except for the basics.

Sheree carried her tea into the living room, then curled up on the sofa. Back home, she had been certain coming here was the right thing to do, but she was suddenly beset by doubts. Derek was a vampire. He slept during the day. He drank blood to survive. He could read her thoughts. He couldn't give her children. He would never grow any older. His mother was a vampire, the oldest vampire in existence, and he belonged to a family of vampires. . . . What would they think of her? Would they accept her? Would she be safe among them?

Sheree sipped her tea, then put the cup aside. Then there was the whole werewolf thing. What if he turned into a werewolf and couldn't control himself? Would he tear her to shreds?

She had come back determined to convince him they belonged together. But now she wondered if she was wrong. He couldn't change what he was. If she wanted to be with him, she would have to accept his lifestyle, his family, the fact that her life would always be in danger. Most troubling of all was the knowledge that she would grow old and gray and he would be forever young and healthy.

Almost, she could hate him for that.

She was about to go to bed when the doorbell rang.

She froze for an instant; then, feeling like Little Red Riding Hood about to meet the Big Bad Wolf, she opened the door.

"What the hell are you doing here?" Derek asked gruffly.

"I'm glad to see you, too," she retorted, her voice razor sharp.

He glanced up at the sky, his skin prickling. Five nights from now, the moon would be full.

"I know I should have waited," she said, following his gaze, "but I couldn't. You called to me last night, didn't you?"

His gaze softened and the next thing she knew, she was in his arms. "How could I hear you when I was so far away?"

"I've tasted your blood." He pushed a lock of hair behind her ear. "I will always be able to find you, know your thoughts, and let you know mine."

"So, you missed me?"

"You have no idea." He held her close, his forehead pressed to hers. "I shouldn't be here," he rasped. "It's dangerous for you, but I couldn't stay away."

"How did you know I was home?"

His hands moved restlessly up and down her back. "I could feel your nearness calling me."

It was, she thought, romantic and creepy at the same time.

He lifted his head, his gaze searching hers. "You were having second thoughts before I got here."

He had been reading her mind again. How would she ever get used to that? Was she to have no privacy at all?

"I've been going crazy without you," he said quietly.

She looked into his eyes, eyes as gray as winter clouds, and mirrored in their depths she saw her own need, her own loneliness. His fears were there, too. Fear of the unknown. Fear that in a moment of weakness, he might lose control and attack her.

A muscle twitched in his jaw. "You're afraid of me." It wasn't a question, but a statement of fact.

"I'm afraid *for* you," she admitted. "But I'm not afraid *of* you. There's a big difference." Tugging on his hand, she led the way to the sofa and drew him down beside her.

He slipped his arm around her shoulders, and tucked her against his side.

Sheree snuggled against him. Was it possible to be both werewolf and vampire at the same time? What would it mean for the two of them if he changed into a werewolf and stayed that way?

"Is that what you're worried about?" he asked.

"Derek, you've got to stop reading my mind! It isn't fair."

He brushed a kiss across the top of her head. "I'm sorry. I can't help it."

"What frightens you the most?"

"Turning into a beast with no control over my actions."

"That would be frightening, but . . . well, you're a vampire and you don't go around ripping out throats and killing indiscriminately, so . . . maybe there's nothing to worry about."

"I guess it depends on whether or not I remember who I am."

Sheree's eyes widened. "I never thought of that." With no memory of who he was, Derek would truly be a beast. "It's only one night a month, right?"

"So they say." But he could kill a hell of a lot of people in one night. "Sheree . . ." At times like this, he wished she could read his mind.

"What?" She looked up at him, her brow furrowed. And then she knew. "You're worried, wondering if I'll still love you if you become a werewolf. It doesn't matter what you are, Derek. Werewolf or vampire, I'll love you just the same."

"Sheree." Lowering his head, he claimed her lips with his, hoping she knew how much she meant to him, afraid that in spite of her brave words, he would do something to drive her away.

She moaned softly, her body molding to his. Her breasts felt warm and soft against his chest, her lips sweetly yielding. Her warmth, the scent of her desire, stirred his hunger. She let out a little gasp of pained surprise when one of his fangs nicked her tongue. The taste of her blood swamped his senses.

With a growl, he sprang to his feet and turned away from her.

"Derek, I'm okay."

"I'm not." When she started to rise, he barked, "Stay there!" He took several deep breaths, fighting the urge to bury his fangs in her throat. "It's best if I go."

"But . . ."

"There's someone I need to talk to."

"Will I see you tomorrow night?"

"No. Not until after the full moon."

"But I just got here."

"I know, and I'm sorry." Reining in his hunger, he turned to face her. "It's too dangerous, love. I can feel the wolf stirring inside. It isn't safe for you to be near me right now. Or for me to be near you." He raked his fingers through his hair. "Heaven help us both, but I don't think I can face this without knowing you're here."

"You won't have to," she promised, and hoped she wouldn't live to regret it.

Edna looked up from the book she was reading. "Pearl," she whispered hoarsely, "Derek's here!"

Pearl glanced around as though she expected to see him in the room. "What do you think he wants?"

"I have no idea." Edna swallowed hard. "Why don't you answer the door and ask him."

"You answer it!"

Edna laid her book aside and opened the door, just a crack. "What are you doing here?"

"I need your help."

"You . . . need . . . *my* help?"

"That's what I said. Mind if I come in?"

"Could I keep you out?"

"Probably not."

Sighing fatalistically, Edna invited him in. "Please, sit down." She gestured at the sofa, then resumed her seat.

Pearl smiled faintly.

"So, what do you want?"

"Mara says you know more about werewolves than anyone."

"That's true," Edna said, unable to keep the pride out of her voice. "I've been studying them since before you were born."

"Is there a way to tell if I'm going to turn when the moon's full?"

Edna clucked softly. "I'm not sure. I'd need to take your blood. Pearl, get my kit, would you?"

With a nod, Pearl went into the other room. She returned a short time later carrying a large brown case. "Where do you want it, dear?"

"On the table by the window." Edna hurried to the table and lifted the lid on the case.

Derek peered over her shoulder, staring at the contents: a number of test tubes and bottles in various sizes, cotton swabs and cotton balls, rubber tubing, and several other objects he didn't recognize.

Edna withdrew a syringe and a glass vial. "Roll up your sleeve."

He did as she asked, watching curiously as she filled several vials with dark red blood.

With that done, she lifted a microscope from the case, then prepared several slides. After pulling a chair up to the table, she peered into the microscope.

Hands clenched at his sides, Derek paced the floor while Edna studied one slide after another. An hour later, she blew out a sigh.

"Well?" Derek growled.

"It's hard to be a hundred percent certain, but I'd say the werewolf gene is active, at least to some degree."

"If I change, will I remember who I am?"

"That I can't say."

"Will I be able to resist it?"

"No. You'll be compelled to change the first time. You might be able to resist in the future, but that will depend on how strong the trait is, and your ability to fight it. I do know that the pain will be excruciating if you try to resist."

"Mara suggested locking me up."

Edna nodded. "She will need a sturdy cage."

"Isn't there a drug of some kind you can give me to keep it from happening?"

"I'm afraid not." Edna glanced at Pearl. "Years ago we concocted a serum we hoped would cure the werewolves, but it wasn't effective. Some died. Even if it had worked, I'm not sure what its effect would be on you, since you aren't completely vampire or werewolf."

Derek raked a hand through his hair. "Your best guess," he said, thinking of Susie McGee. "If I change into a werewolf, will it be permanent?"

"I'm afraid so."

So, that was it. One way or another, he was destined to spend at least part of his life as a monster.

"It might not be so bad," Pearl said. "After all, werewolves are human most of the time. They can walk in the sun. They can have children, eat mortal food, and lead reasonably normal lives."

"Yeah. Except when the moon is full."

On the way home, Derek stopped at an all-night market and bought a pound of raw hamburger.

He stared at the package a moment, then ripped off the paper and swallowed a handful of bloody meat.

And sighed with pleasure.

Mara smelled the raw meat on Derek's breath the minute he entered the house, but wisely said nothing.

"You've been with the old ladies," Logan remarked.

Derek nodded. "Edna took some of my blood. She says the gene seems to be active."

Mara's pale face grew ashen. "What can we do?"

"There's nothing to do until it happens. No way to predict whether I'll turn into a werewolf and stay that way, although Edna thinks it's likely."

"A werewolf," Mara murmured, her deep green eyes reflecting her horror.

"Is there someplace where you can lock me up?"

Logan and Mara exchanged glances.

"It's the only place that will hold him," Logan said.

"What place?" Derek asked.

"Your mother has an old castle high in the mountains of Transylvania. It's been closed for centuries. The land is overgrown. Like all old castles, it has a dungeon in the basement."

"Take me there."

Mara looked uncertain.

"It's the best place for him," Logan said, "even if we decide not to lock him up. There aren't any people for miles, nothing but forest and wild animals."

"Great," Derek muttered. "I'll fit right in."

"I'll go tomorrow morning and prepare our rooms," Mara decided. "You and Logan follow me as soon as the sun sets tomorrow night."

Derek nodded. What would he be when he saw Sheree again? Vampire or werewolf?

Or both?

Chapter Twenty-Six

Sheree spent a restless night. It took her hours to get to sleep, and when she did, her dreams were filled with frightful images of werewolves and vampires ripping each other to shreds or attacking everything in sight, including her.

The sound of someone knocking on the door woke her just after seven A.M. After slipping into her robe, Sheree hurried downstairs. She wished fleetingly that it was Derek, but, of course, at this time of the morning, it wasn't likely.

Wondering who would come calling at this hour, she unlocked the door but left the security chain in place. "Mara!"

"Have I come too early?"

"Oh, no, not at all," she said, removing the security chain. "Please, come in."

Mara swept into the room like a queen granting favors.

"Is something wrong? Is Derek all right?"

"Everything's fine. I was wondering if you'd like to take a trip with me."

"A trip?" Sheree toyed with the collar of her robe. "Where are you going?"

"Romania."

Just the word conjured images of ancient castles and brooding vampires.

"You'll love it. It's a beautiful place."

"I . . ." Sheree blinked. Romania! "I don't know."

Mara's gaze met hers. "Please say you'll come."

Remembering Derek's warning not to stare into a vampire's eyes, Sheree quickly looked away. "Will Derek be there?"

"Of course. He's the reason we're going. You've nothing to fear," Mara assured her. "I will not let anything happen to you."

"My passport's in Philadelphia."

Mara laughed softly. "You won't need it."

An hour later, Sheree had showered, dressed, and packed a bag. Her wooden stake was at the bottom, under her nightgown.

"Are you ready?" Mara asked, her tone impatient.

Sheree glanced around, making sure everything was closed and locked. "Yes, I guess so."

"Then take my hand and we'll be off."

"Why?" Sheree asked, suddenly reluctant to touch the vampire.

Mara caught Sheree's hand in hers. "Because we're traveling by Air Vampire."

Before Sheree could ask what that meant, she felt herself being lifted from the ground. She closed her eyes as a strange buzzing filled her ears, along with the sense of traveling through space at inhuman speed. Nausea roiled in the pit of her stomach.

Just when she thought she might pass out, the world righted itself. Opening her eyes, she found herself standing in the middle of a large room.

Mara smiled at her. "Welcome to Transylvania. Feel free to look around while I prepare our rooms. Here, let me take your bag. You'll be in the first room on the left at the top of the stairs."

Feeling disoriented and a little dizzy, Sheree handed over her suitcase; then, standing in the middle of the great hall, she did a slow turn. The walls were made of gray stone. The leaded windows, set high, were mere slits. She was surprised to see that it was dark outside and wondered briefly what the time difference was between California and Romania.

A fireplace that would comfortably hold a horse and rider took up most of one wall. The mantel was so high, she couldn't reach it. A number of medieval weapons hung above the fireplace. The furniture, scattered in groups around the room, was made of dark, heavy wood; the chairs and sofas were covered in dark red damask. A suit of armor stood in one corner. Large rugs covered the floor; tapestries hung from the walls.

Several doors led to other rooms. Some were vacant; one was a kitchen outfitted with another large fireplace, probably used for cooking in times past. A high wooden table stood in the middle of the floor. Judging by the stains on it, she guessed it had been used for cutting and chopping rather than dining. A rack near the fireplace held a variety of odd-looking utensils and several large iron pots.

A narrow, winding staircase led to the upper floors.

She was debating whether to go up or not when Mara descended the stairs.

"The beds are made," she said, brushing her hands on her skirt. "Your clothes are in the wardrobe. Are you hungry?"

"Yes, a little."

"There's a village at the foot of the mountain. We can get you something to eat there. Logan will stop for provisions before he leaves home."

"When will Derek get here?"

"It will be a few hours yet," Mara said, reaching for her hand. "Ready?"

The village looked like something out of the distant past. It was quaint and charming, as was the restaurant Mara chose. Sheree ordered ham and eggs; Mara asked for a glass of wine.

"Do they know . . ." Lowering her voice, Sheree glanced around. "Do they know what you are?"

"Their ancestors knew. I have not been here in over a century. If the villagers learn the castle is occupied, they may suspect, but they will do nothing."

Feeling uncomfortable, Sheree ate quickly.

When they returned to the castle, Mara told Sheree she was going out for a while and to make herself at home. And then the vampire vanished from the room.

Sheree stared at the place where Mara had been only moments before. What would it be like to be able to just wave your hand and disappear? To cross hundreds of miles like magic? To live forever? While she pondered that, she felt her eyes widen with the realization that Mara had probably gone hunting.

What kind of prey did she prefer? Human? Or animal?

Did she kill when she fed?

Feeling suddenly sick to her stomach, Sheree made her way cautiously up the narrow stone stairs to her room. Inside, she closed the door, then rested her back against it while she surveyed her surroundings.

The room, large and square, was dominated by a bed with red velvet hangings. A rosewood wardrobe—another antique—stood against one wall. A matching four-drawer chest flanked the bed. Sheree shook her head, thinking the castle held a small fortune in antiques.

After leaving the bedchamber, Sheree explored the rest of

the second floor in hopes of finding a bathroom. She found five other bedrooms and a storage closet, but no lavatory.

When she returned to her own room, she spied a chamber pot under the bed. Had she not seen one in an antique store, she would never have known what it was.

Lack of sleep the night before, combined with Mara's mode of transportation, had left Sheree feeling sleepy and disoriented—rather like a princess who had been taken from her own world and dropped into an unknown realm. Stretching out on the bed, she closed her eyes and hoped her own Prince Charming would arrive soon.

Derek glared at his mother. "Why in the hell did you bring Sheree here?" He had detected her unique scent the minute he set foot in the castle. "You know it's dangerous for her to be near me right now. Putting some distance between us is one of the reasons I agreed to come here in the first place."

"You told me yourself that she calms you, and that a few sips of her blood satisfies your thirst. I'm thinking a bit of her blood the night before the full moon will ease whatever transition takes place."

Derek paced in front of the hearth. Maybe his mother was right. But what if she was wrong?

Logan cleared his throat, then pointed at the ice chests at his feet. "Where do you want this stuff?"

"In the kitchen," Mara said, smiling. "Humans are a lot of trouble, aren't they?"

Logan snorted. "At least she's not pregnant!"

Mara sent him a look that could curdle milk. "Very funny."

"I thought so." Lifting a chest in each hand, he headed for the kitchen.

Frowning, Derek stared after Logan, his mind suddenly filling with images of Sheree holding his child. It was impossible, of course, something he had never contemplated. But for the first time in his existence, he regretted the fact that he would never sire a child.

"Now might be a good time for you to go out and get the lay of the land," Mara suggested. "Mark your territory, so to speak."

Nodding, Derek left the house.

The castle stood atop a mountain above the tree line. Standing in the lee of the building, he swept his gaze over the land below. It took only minutes to locate and identify every living creature within miles: wolves, foxes, wild boar, deer. Farther down the mountain, near the village, he identified sheep, goats, cows, and horses.

Flexing his muscles, he began to run along an old deer trail lined with trees and shrubs. Now and then, he heard a rustle in the underbrush as animals scurried out of his path. And suddenly he was in predator mode, his nostrils sifting through the myriad scents in the night for prey, human or otherwise.

When a wild boar broke from cover, Derek let out a shout and gave chase. Moments later, his thirst satisfied, Derek jogged back up the mountain.

He made it inside just as the sun broke through the clouds.

His last thought before he tumbled into oblivion was that he would see Sheree when he woke.

Sheree woke with a start. Jackknifing into a sitting position, she glanced around the room, momentarily disoriented. Where was she? Grabbing her robe, she hurried toward the door, then blew out a sigh as memory returned. She was in a castle in Transylvania.

Mara's castle.

Sheree moved into the hallway, then paused. The house was deathly quiet, she thought, and grinned. Of course it was. She was the only living creature in the place.

She glanced up and down the narrow corridor. Did the vampires trust her enough to take their rest behind those closed doors? Or were they tucked in their coffins down in the dungeon?

The thought made her laugh. She doubted if she could destroy Mara even if she wanted to.

Belting her robe around her waist, she started down the stairs, wondering if Derek had arrived. And even as the thought crossed her mind, she knew he was there, sleeping in one of the rooms above.

Turning on her heels, she ran up the staircase, some inner GPS guiding her down the hallway to the last room on the left. She paused, one hand on the door. Was it locked? But no, it swung open at her touch and she tiptoed inside.

Heavy draperies shut out the morning light. Derek slept on his back, one arm above his head, the other across his waist. His hair was like a splash of black ink across the white pillowcase. A sheet covered him from the waist down.

He was amazingly gorgeous in repose.

Would he wake if she stretched out beside him? Would he be glad to see her, or angry that she had invaded his privacy while he slept?

"I'll be angry if you go away," he murmured, his voice whiskey smooth.

"Oh! You're awake!"

He held out his hand, gesturing for her to join him. She did so gladly, felt a sense of homecoming as his arm curled around her waist.

"I didn't mean to wake you," she said, resting her head on his shoulder.

"I don't mind." His hand caressed her back, slid around to the curve of her breast. Unable to resist, he kissed her cheek, the smooth skin of her neck. "Sheree . . . ?"

She tilted her head back, offering him access to her throat, closed her eyes when he turned onto his side, aligning his body with hers. She felt the gentle pressure of his fangs, sighed with pleasure as he drank from her.

Caught up in the sheer pleasure of his touch, she let her hands drift restlessly along his back and shoulders, tangle in his hair to hold him close. She pressed against him, hating the clothing between them, wanting to feel his skin against hers.

Like magic, her robe and nightgown vanished.

Derek chuckled when she gasped in surprise. "Be careful what you wish for," he murmured, nuzzling her breast.

He kissed her then, a long searing kiss that left no doubt as to what he wanted. His lips moved over hers, coaxing, demanding, as his hands played over her body, learning every hollow, every curve, until she writhed beneath him, desperate with longing, and yet afraid to surrender to him completely.

Drawing back a little, he gazed into her eyes. "You've never been with a man?"

She shook her head, embarrassed to admit she was still a virgin. She had made out with boyfriends in the past, but something had always kept her from going all the way.

He cursed softly, then buried his face in the warm hollow between her neck and her shoulder.

Sheree went still. "Derek?"

"It's all right, love." Lifting his head, he ran his knuckles across her cheek. "It's probably best that we wait."

"But . . . I don't want to wait."

He lifted one brow. "That's not the message you were sending."

"Just because I'm afraid doesn't mean I don't want you."

"What are you afraid of?"

"Well, I've never done it before and . . . and you're a vampire and I don't know if vampires make love like everyone else . . . and . . ." She looked up at him, her gaze searching his as her arms twined around his neck. "I love you."

"And I love you. Enough to wait until you're ready. And FYI, vampires make love like everybody else. Only better." He laughed softly as her stomach growled. "Maybe we should see about getting you something to eat."

"Thank you for understanding."

"I'm not a horny teenager. I can wait." He ran his tongue along the curve of her throat. "You fed me. It's only fair that I feed you."

Swinging his feet over the edge of the bed, he grabbed his pants.

Feeling suddenly shy, Sheree slipped her nightgown over her head, pulled on her robe, then ran her fingers through her hair.

"You're beautiful, love."

"So are you. Love."

Hand in hand, they made their way down to the kitchen.

Derek gestured at the ice chests. "We stocked them with everything we could think of that wouldn't spoil right away."

"Thank you." Lifting the lid of the first one, she found a quart of milk, butter, cheese, a package of roast beef, mayonnaise, and mustard. The second one held paper plates, bowls, cups, glasses, and utensils, as well as a loaf of bread, a box of cereal, packets of sugar and cream, several candy bars, apples, bananas, oranges, peanut butter, jelly, and a package of blueberry muffins. And, thankfully, toilet paper.

Deciding on a glass of milk and a muffin for breakfast,

she carried them into the great hall and sat on one of the sofas.

"I'll take you out to dinner later," Derek promised, sitting beside her.

"I'd like that. Have you ever been here before?"

He shook his head. "First time. Mara's got places all over the world."

"Really?"

"Most vampires who have a few hundred years under their belt keep multiple lairs. They can't stay in one place too long, you know. People start to wonder why they don't age, why they don't have children or visitors. So they keep several places for when it's time to move on."

"Do you have more than one . . . lair?"

"Not yet. I'm still young. I've got a little place in Sacramento. I thought I'd start looking for another one, assuming I'm still a vampire after the full moon." He stretched his legs out in front of him, then asked casually, "Any place you'd like to live?"

The question, which implied a lasting relationship, filled her with warmth. "A few years ago, my parents took me to Italy on vacation. I've always wanted to go back."

She ate the last of the muffin, drained the glass and set it aside.

When Derek slipped his arm around her shoulders, she snuggled against him. "Do you need to rest?"

"No, I'm good." Which was odd, he mused. He usually wasn't able to be awake this long during the day. Another perk of Sheree's blood, he wondered? Or an unexpected side effect of the werewolf gene? There was no way of knowing. But it didn't matter. He was content to stay where he was, with Sheree beside him.

Of course, he couldn't sit there without touching her,

kissing her. Before long, they were stretched out on the sofa, arms and legs entwined. Slowly at first, he explored her body, as she explored his, each caress longer, bolder, more intimate than the last.

And that was how Mara and Logan found them.

At the sound of amused laughter, Sheree bolted upright, her cheeks flaming with embarrassment.

"Ah, young love," Logan remarked, waggling his eyebrows. "Ain't it grand?"

"I doubt if you can remember what it was like, old man." Derek sat up, his arm wrapping around Sheree in an unmistakably male gesture of protection.

"Old man!" Logan looked at Mara. "Are you going to let your son talk to me like that?"

"Do you remember?" Mara asked with a beguiling smile.

Logan's eyes turned smoky with desire. "Want me to show you?"

"Later." She cuffed him on the arm, then looked at Derek. "How do you feel?"

He shrugged. "Fine."

"No cravings?" Mara glanced at Sheree, her brow furrowed.

"No." Derek rubbed his jaw, his expression thoughtful, and then, he, too, glanced at Sheree.

She fidgeted under their combined scrutiny. "What's wrong?"

"I told you so," Mara said with a smug grin.

Sheree looked at Derek. "Told you what? What's going on?"

Derek gave her shoulder a squeeze. "Nothing to worry about. Mara brought you here because I told her that being with you calms me. . . ." He hesitated before adding, "And because your blood satisfies my hunger like nothing else."

"Why would my blood be different from anyone else's?" Sheree asked anxiously. "Is there something wrong with it?"

"Your blood is fine," Mara assured her. "Some believe that certain bloodlines or types have that effect on certain vampires. It's very rare that the vampire and the mortal find each other."

"And you wanted me here because you think my blood will somehow help Derek during the full moon?"

Mara nodded. "Exactly. Now that we've settled that, I'm hungry. Are you coming, Logan?"

"Of course."

"Excuse me," Sheree said, "but can I ask you something?"

"Only if you think you can handle the answer," Mara replied somewhat acerbically.

"Do you . . . I'm not sure what you call it . . . need blood every day?"

"We call it hunting or feeding," Mara replied. "And no, I don't need to feed every day. But I enjoy the hunt. And to answer your next question, I rarely kill my prey these days."

"The same goes for me," Logan said. "Enjoy yourselves, you two. We'll be gone for quite a while."

Clasping hands, the two vampires vanished from sight.

"I hope I didn't make her angry," Sheree said.

"No. It's natural for you to be curious about us." He caressed her cheek with his knuckles. "Anything else you'd like to know?"

"Do you have to . . . to feed . . . every day?"

"No, but I'm a predator, and like most vampires, I also enjoy the hunt."

Sheree shivered as she imagined him stalking helpless humans, throwing them on the ground, burying his fangs in their throats.

Derek snorted softly. "I use a little more finesse than that, love."

"If people knew how wonderful it felt, you wouldn't have to hunt them down. They'd come to you."

His easy laughter filled the air as he pulled her into a bear hug. "Sheree, my love, how did I ever live without you?"

As promised, Derek took Sheree out to dinner that night. Deciding to try the house specialty, she ordered Csirke-paprikás, a chicken stew flavored with paprika, cumin, and chilis. The waitress suggested Sheree add a side of buttered potatoes, which she did. Sheree hadn't expected Derek to order anything, but he asked for a steak, seared on the out-side, and a bottle of wine.

"It's almost the full moon," he said, noting her curious gaze. "The week before it's full, I crave meat." He took a deep breath. "Raw meat."

"Oh. Well, that's . . . interesting."

"No, it's not."

Reaching across the table, Sheree took his hand in hers. "It'll be all right, you'll see."

"I wish I could be sure."

"What are you really afraid is going to happen?"

His hand tightened on hers. "I'm afraid that I'll become a killing machine with no conscience."

Sheree shook her head. "I don't believe that's possible. You're a good man, Derek. I know it in every fiber of my being. I wouldn't be here with you if you weren't."

When the waitress arrived with their dinner, Sheree tried not to stare at Derek's plate. The steak, barely cooked, swam in a sea of blood-red juice.

"I shouldn't have ordered anything," he said, noting the thinly veiled revulsion in her eyes.

"No. Lots of people like their steak rare. I'm told it tastes better that way."

Derek shook his head as he cut the steak into pieces and took a bite. It was remarkably satisfying.

Later, they strolled through the town. It was like stepping back in time, Sheree thought, walking along the cobblestone streets.

"This is where legend says vampires were born," she mused, thinking about Bram Stoker's *Dracula*, and how strange it was to be walking in Transylvania with a real vampire at her side.

Derek shook his head. "No one really knows where the first one came from, or how we came to be. Some believe that it was a curse set upon a man who lusted after another man's wife. Others believe that we're demon spawn, and that vampires cast no reflection in a mirror because we have no soul. There's a small group that believes we are a separate species, and that we evolved along with mankind."

"I've never heard any of those theories before, but I definitely like the last one best. It's an intriguing idea." She glanced around, admiring the quaint shops, the distant mountains, some capped with snow. "It's a beautiful country."

"So they say. You should ask Mara to take you sightseeing before we leave." He slid a glance in her direction. "You should at least visit Castle Dracula while you're here."

"I'd love to. I read a lot about it online."

He lifted one brow. "Researching the undead?"

"Of course. It was a passion of mine."

"Was?"

She punched him on the arm. "You know what I mean."

"How do I know you're not just using me for research?" he asked, eyes glinting with humor.

She batted her eyelashes at him. "Would you mind if I was?"

"You can research me all you want," he said, laughing. "I admit I did quite a bit of it myself growing up."

"You did? Why? I mean, didn't you already know everything there was to know about vampires?"

"More or less, but being one myself, I was naturally curious about what people thought of us. I read everything I could get my hands on about Romania and vampires and Vlad Dracula. To this day, his people regard him as a hero."

"Some hero! I read that he killed over forty thousand people."

"From what I read, it was more like eighty thousand," Derek said. "And that's not counting the number of villages he burned to the ground."

When they reached a narrow alley between two buildings, Derek pulled her into it, then took her in his arms and kissed her hungrily. "I've been wanting to do that all night," he said, his voice husky. And then he kissed her again.

She would have protested but with his arms wrapped around her and his mouth ravaging hers, it was impossible to think of anything but the desire that flamed between them. He backed her against the wall, his body pressing against hers, letting her feel the growing evidence of his desire.

She moaned softly, her hands delving under his shirt, moving restlessly up and down his back and shoulders. His skin was cool beneath her fingertips, the muscles well-defined.

"Derek . . ." She breathed his name, pouring all her yearning into it.

"I know." He could smell the musk on her skin, hear the uptick in the beat of her heart, the scent of her blood as it flowed hot and sweet beneath her skin.

A rush of desire swamped his senses as his arms tightened around her. With a low growl, he lowered his head to her neck.

"Hey, what's going on here?"

A flash of light penetrated the darkness. Derek wheeled around, his eyes blazing red, his lips pulled back to reveal his fangs.

A cop stared back at him. "What the hell?"

Sheree hollered, "Derek, don't!" as he sprang forward, his hands closing around the police officer's neck. "Derek!"

He froze, his whole being focused on the mortal quivering in his grasp. Every instinct urged him to attack. The man was a threat and needed to be eliminated.

"Derek?"

He stiffened at the gentle touch of her hand on his back. "Get away from me!"

"Derek, you don't want to do this," she said quietly. "He hasn't done anything. Please, turn him loose so we can go home."

He growled again.

"If you hurt him, you know you'll regret it later. This isn't who you are."

He took a deep, shuddering breath, then trapped the officer's gaze with his own. "You will not remember this," he said, his voice low, hypnotic. "You will not remember me."

"I will not remember," the officer said.

After sending the man on his way, Derek wrapped Sheree in his arms and willed the two of them back to the castle.

They materialized in the great hall.

After releasing Sheree, Derek went to stand in front of the hearth, his hands braced on the mantel.

Now that the danger was past, Sheree felt suddenly weak. Trembling as with a chill, she made her way to the sofa. Sitting, she scrubbed her hands up and down her arms.

"I wanted to kill him," Derek said, his voice thick with self-reproach.

"But you didn't."

He turned to look at her. "If you hadn't been there, I would have ripped out his heart and eaten it."

It took every ounce of self-control she possessed to keep her horror at his words from showing in her eyes.

But he knew what she was thinking.

He always knew.

Chapter Twenty-Seven

"Transylvania!" Pearl exclaimed. "As in Romania? Home of vampire hunters and werewolves?"

"For goodness' sake, lower your voice." Edna glanced around the crowded nightclub, nostrils flaring as she searched the room for vampires.

Pearl shook her head. "Why on earth do you want to go haring off to Romania all of a sudden?"

"Because that's where Derek is."

"Why would he be there, dear?"

"I can't read his mind," Edna said. "But the reason is obvious. He's gone to wait for the full moon. So we need to go, too. After all, we can't very well watch him shift from here."

Pearl frowned thoughtfully. It made perfect sense, of course, in a twisted, vampire-obsessed sort of way. "I suppose Mara is with him."

"I should think so. Did you ever write that formula down?"

"No. It's still in my head. Why?"

"An idea about the formula's been percolating in my mind the last few days."

"I don't know why, dear. The stuff didn't work."

"I know, but with a bit of recalculating, and the addition of a few new ingredients, I think it might be effective."

Pearl regarded her friend curiously for a moment, then exclaimed, "You don't think Mara's going to come to us for help, do you?"

"Why not? She's got nowhere else to turn," Edna said confidently. "What do you think the weather is like in Transylvania this time of year?"

"How the heck should I know? I've never been there."

"We really are living dangerously these days, aren't we?"

"Yes, we are, dear." Grinning, Pearl lifted her glass. "And it's about damn time!"

Chapter Twenty-Eight

Sheree was surprised to wake the next evening and find Derek sleeping beside her. After bringing her home the night before, he had left her in the great hall. She had no idea where he had gone, or why, though she suspected he had just needed some time alone.

Mara had come home shortly after Derek left. "What happened?" she asked, her nostrils flaring. "Where's Derek?"

"I don't know." As briefly as possible, Sheree had told his mother what had happened in the alley.

"That man owes you his life," Mara remarked. Her gaze moved swiftly over Sheree. "You're unhurt?"

"Of course."

Mara snorted softly. "Derek loves you. I have no doubt of that. But you should be prepared to protect yourself at all times. He is still a predator, and in his current condition, there's no telling what he might do. I know you brought a wooden stake with you. You should keep it handy."

Now, lying in bed beside Derek, Mara's warning came back to her. And yet, looking at Derek while he slept, she found it hard to imagine that he would ever harm her, or anyone else. In sleep, his face was relaxed, all the worry lines gone.

Did Mara know Derek was in her bed? Silly question. Of course she did. Sheree felt a flush warm her cheeks. It was one thing to share a bed with him in her own house; quite another under his mother's roof.

When had he come to her? And why? Sheree recalled his remark about her nearness soothing him, though she didn't understand how her mere presence could suppress either his hunger or his anxiety.

Sheree turned onto her side, studying him as she had the day before. His breathing was slow and shallow. It was a marvel that such an amazing and complex creature loved her. Almost, she could wish to be a vampire just so she could think herself to another country, or dissolve into sparkling mist, or run faster than the human eye could follow.

"I can arrange it, if you like."

"No, thank you."

He opened his eyes, his expression somber. "I should be thanking you."

"Why?"

"You know why. I would have killed that man if you hadn't been there."

"If I hadn't been there, you wouldn't have been in that alley in the first place, and the man's life would never have been in any danger."

"I'm still in your debt. How can I repay you?"

"A kiss will suffice."

Cupping her face in his hands, he kissed her gently, then said, with a teasing grin, "Are you sure you wouldn't like me to bring you across?"

She swatted him on the arm, then sat up, intrigued and repulsed by the idea at the same time. "Have you ever made another vampire?"

He winked at her. "Not yet."

"Do you know how?"

"In theory."

"Is it done the way they do it in the movies?"

"Pretty much. I'd drain you to the point of death, then give you my blood. When you woke the next night, you'd be one of us."

"Does it hurt?"

"I don't know. No one ever turned me."

"You said you'd have to drain me to the point of death. What if you took too much?"

"You would die. None of us, not even Mara, can raise the dead."

It was a sobering thought and quickly obliterated Sheree's curiosity.

Derek traced her lower lip with his forefinger. "You would make a beautiful vampire."

"What do you mean?"

"All vampires have a sort of glamour that enhances their natural appearance. Haven't you noticed?"

Sheree started to say no, but then she thought about Mara and Logan. There was something indefinable about them, an allure she had been unable to put a name to.

Troubled by his words, she looked at Derek. Had she been drawn to him because of some vampiric magnetism she couldn't resist?

"Perhaps, in the beginning," he admitted with a wry grin. "But the attraction between us is very real. Otherwise your blood wouldn't have such a powerful effect on me."

He tugged her down beside him, his arm slipping around her waist to draw her body closer to his. Sheree snuggled against him, her head pillowed on his shoulder, one hand resting on his chest. Butterflies danced in her stomach at the touch of his lips moving in her hair.

"Sheree, I can't believe you're here. Or that you've accepted all this . . ." He made a broad gesture with his hand meant to encompass the castle and everything in it. "I can't help thinking that you were meant to be mine." He kissed her cheek. "That you will always be mine," he murmured, his voice thick with emotion.

She raised herself on one elbow so she could see his face. "Don't you know I'll be yours for as long as you want me?"

"Then you'll be mine forever."

Sheree smiled. It was a wonderful sentiment, but she doubted he'd feel the same when she was old and gray and he was still young and vibrant.

"I will want you until the day death takes you from me."

"I'd like to believe that," Sheree said. "I really would. But, honestly, Derek, can you really see yourself making love to some wrinkled old woman?"

"No." He caressed her cheek. "But I can see myself taking care of you until you draw your last breath."

It wasn't fair, she thought bitterly. Why did she have to fall in love with a vampire? Maybe he meant what he said, maybe he would still love her when she was in her eighties, if she lived that long. But how would she feel about him? Would she love him until her dying breath? Or hate him because he didn't grow old, because she was going to die while he would go on loving and living without her?

"Damn, girl," Derek muttered. "Talk about looking on the dark side of things!"

"If you'd stay out of my mind, you wouldn't know what I was thinking!"

"You're young, love. You've got lots of time to change your mind before you turn into that wrinkled old crone."

"Oh!" Grabbing her pillow, she hit him over the head with it. His laughter only made her angrier and she hit him again and again, her anger gradually turning to laughter until he rolled her onto her back and rose over her. He wasn't laughing now, and neither was she. His dark gray eyes were smoky with desire as he lowered his head and claimed her lips with his.

Wrapping her arms around his back, she pulled him down until his body covered hers. With a shock, she realized he was naked save for a pair of black briefs that did nothing to disguise his gender or his burgeoning desire.

"Sheree . . ." His eyes flashed red and he groaned, the sound torn from the very depths of his being. "Tell me to stop before it's too late."

"Drink, my love," she urged. "You'll feel better if you do."

He went still, his fingers tangled in her hair. She could feel the struggle within him as he fought to control his hunger and his desire. As much as he needed her blood, as satisfying as it might be, she knew that he regretted the necessity—that he was afraid she would think he saw her only as prey.

He whispered words of love in her ear but they weren't needed. Lost in a blissful haze, she had no thought to deny him, didn't care what he took as long as he didn't leave her. After a moment, she felt the warmth of his tongue against her skin, followed by the touch of his fangs at her throat. She arched against him as pleasure flowed from his bite to the very center of her being.

She clutched his shoulders, heard his voice whisper, "Forgive me," and then all thought was swept away in a tidal wave of such sensual pleasure she thought she might die of it.

Die. . . .

For a terrifying moment, the world went crimson. And then black.

"Sheree! Sheree! Dammit!"

Derek's voice, laced with terror, called her from the abyss. With an effort, she swam back through layers of blackness to find him hovering over her, his brow furrowed, eyes shadowed with worry.

He hissed a sigh of relief when she opened her eyes. "I thought . . ." He pulled her into his embrace, his face buried in her hair.

A moment later, Mara and Logan burst into the room.

"Derek, what have you done?" Mara demanded.

With a low growl, Derek grabbed a blanket and wrapped it around Sheree. "You know damn well what I did." He stroked Sheree's face. She was pale, so pale.

"Yes, I know. A little more and she would be dead now."

Logan grabbed Mara's hand and tugged her toward the door. "Let's go," he said gruffly. "We're not needed here."

Muttering, "She might not be so lucky next time," Mara followed Logan into the hallway and closed the door.

"Why is your mother so upset?" Sheree asked.

Derek smoothed her hair away from her face. She was almost as white as the pillowcase. "I nearly took too much."

Sheree blinked at him. Was that why she felt so light-headed? "I feel so strange, as if I could close my eyes and fly away."

"You need nourishment. Come on." Taking her by the hand, he helped her stand, then swept her into his arms and quickly carried her down the stairs.

In the kitchen, he set her on a chair, then reached into one of the ice chests and withdrew a chilled bottle of orange juice. After filling a glass, he handed it to her. "Drink," he commanded. "All of it."

When she drained it in only a few swallows, he filled it again. And then again.

"No more." Shaking her head, Sheree put the glass on the table.

Derek's gaze moved over her face, noting her color had returned. Another few minutes, he thought bleakly, and he would have killed her.

"I'm fine," she said, seeing the worry in his eyes.

"Are you? I could have drained you dry!"

"I trust you," she murmured, cupping his cheek in her palm.

"I only hope that trust doesn't get you killed."

Derek carried Sheree back to bed, stayed with her until she fell asleep, then went into the living room. Logan was stretched out on one of the sofas, ankles crossed, arms folded behind his head.

Mara paced the floor in front of the fireplace, her quickened steps the first clue that something was bothering her.

"What's going on?" Derek asked, sitting on the other sofa.

"Edna and Pearl," Logan answered.

Derek arched one brow. "What about them?"

"They're here!" Mara said. "Why the devil are they following us?"

Logan snorted. "Why do you think? The full moon is only two nights away. I'm guessing they don't want to miss the show."

Derek glared at his stepfather. "It's not a show, dammit! It's my life, and it's hell not knowing what to expect! Do you have any idea what it's like waiting for whatever the hell is going to happen?" He sprang to his feet, hands clenched at his sides. "I can feel it building inside me, waiting to explode."

"Derek," Logan said, "I didn't mean—"

"What if it turns me into a beast I can't control? Dammit, it's hard enough to control what I am now!"

Mara laid her hand on his arm but he shook it off.

Moving to the fireplace, Derek braced his hands on the mantel, staring down at the ashes in the hearth.

"I'm afraid," he admitted, his voice barely audible. "Afraid of what I might do to her in a moment of weakness." He picked up the fireplace poker, his hands tightening around it until his knuckles were white with the strain. "Afraid I'll lose control."

"Derek, listen to me—"

"No!" He rounded on his mother. "You never should have brought her here!" The poker bent in his hands. "If I hurt her . . ."

"Derek," Mara said quietly, "I think she's the answer. You care for her. You've protected her. . . ."

"Sure, when I'm myself." He shoved the poker into his mother's hands. "I want you to lock me up tomorrow before dark."

"You need to drink from her the night before the full moon."

He wanted to refuse but his mother was right. Sheree's blood satisfied him like nothing else. Perhaps if he drank from her before he turned into a werewolf, her blood would suppress the urge to kill.

Moving to the window, he stared out at the darkness. He breathed in and his nostrils filled with the scent of rain. A storm was coming. In the distance, a deer rested in a thicket, while an owl hunted the night for prey.

Prey. It was all around him. Outside, the deer stirred. Before he realized what he was doing, Derek was at the deer's side, his fangs buried deep in the animal's throat. The blood was thick and rich and hot and he drank it all, drank until he was sated with the taste and the smell.

When sanity returned, he rocked back on his heels, horrified by what he had done. He glanced at the moon, barely visible behind the gathering clouds. But he didn't have to see it to know it was there. He could feel its pull on his preternatural senses, feel it calling to the beast lurking inside him.

If he was capable of this when the moon was not yet full, what would he do when its pull was at its strongest, and he at his most vulnerable?

Would animal blood be enough to satisfy him then?

* * *

Mara stood at the window, scarcely aware of Logan's arm around her waist. She didn't have to see what had happened to know what Derek had done. She had sensed his overpowering need to kill, the deer's panic, her son's remorse. Ever since he was a child, Derek had loved the deer, the squirrels, and the rabbits that roamed the countryside around her home in the Hollywood Hills. He had once nursed a wounded fawn back to life. He had occasionally fed on animals, but never any of the deer.

"He'll be all right," Logan said, his voice pitched above the noise of the sudden downpour and the thunder that accompanied it as the storm broke.

"Do you really believe that?" She leaned against him, grateful for his strength, his unwavering devotion. "Because I don't."

"Maybe it's time to pay a call on those two old broads," he suggested.

He ducked out of the way when she whirled around. But instead of hitting him, playfully or otherwise, as he expected, she threw her arms around him.

"Logan, I could kiss you!" she exclaimed. "Why didn't I think of that?"

Chapter Twenty-Nine

Sheree knew a moment of disappointment when she woke alone in bed the following evening. She had hoped Derek would spend the day at her side; now, she wondered where he was.

There was an odd feeling to the house as she tiptoed down the hall, thinking she might spend some time in Derek's bed, in Derek's arms. There was only one more night until the full moon. She knew he was worried about what he might become, what he might do. Perhaps her presence would offer him some comfort.

But his room was empty.

She paused in front of the bedroom Mara and Logan shared but lacked the nerve to knock on their door.

In the kitchen, she tried to determine what was causing her uneasiness. And then she knew. She was feeling the same tension the vampires in the house were feeling.

Sitting at the table, nibbling on a slice of bread and jelly, she was struck by the realization that she was sharing a house with three vampires. And that no one knew where she was, or who she was with. And that her cell phone was dead, and even if it was working, *she* could be dead before help arrived, should she need it. It was a sobering thought.

Muttering, "Stop it," she poured herself a glass of orange juice. She wasn't afraid of Derek or his family, so why was she entertaining such morbid thoughts? Maybe, deep down, she was more afraid than she wanted to admit. Well, who could blame her? Mara was the oldest vampire on the planet. As Derek had said, none of the rules applied to her, although Sheree had no idea what rules vampires adhered to, if any.

And then there was Derek. As much as she loved him, she couldn't begin to imagine the stress he must be under, or how he would react if he couldn't resist the call of the full moon.

Her nerves grew taut as darkness fell. Where were they?

She whirled around when she realized she was no longer alone. "Derek . . . oh." She glanced from Logan to Mara. "Where is he?"

"He asked us to lock him in the dungeon."

"The dungeon! Why? The moon won't be full until to-morrow night."

Mara didn't answer, just stood there, her expression one of unutterable sorrow.

"He's afraid, isn't he?" Sheree asked. "Afraid he might hurt me."

Logan nodded. "That's part of it."

"Did something happen?"

"He killed a deer last night."

"Oh." It was sad, Sheree thought, but surely it didn't warrant such concern.

"He ripped out its throat and drained it of blood," Logan explained. "He was completely out of control."

Out of control. Sheree could easily imagine the carnage if that had happened in the city, among unsuspecting men and women. "Can I see him?"

"Of course," Mara said.

"Just be careful," Logan added.

* * *

The dungeon was located at the bottom of a long flight of narrow stone steps. There were no electric lights, only a few lanterns that cast flickering shadows on the gray stone walls and floor.

A number of small cells lined both sides of the cavernous room. A larger, square cell stood at the end of the corridor. Barefoot and shirtless, Derek paced the confines of his prison. A long silver chain linked his left ankle to a heavy bolt in the floor.

His head came up, his eyes zeroing in on her as she approached. "Go away," he growled.

"No. I don't want you to be alone. Why are you chained to the floor?"

"The silver grounds me so I can't use my preternatural powers to escape."

"Oh." She filed that bit of knowledge away, wondering if she would ever know all there was to know about vampires and werewolves.

"Sheree, I'm sorry I got you involved in all this."

The droop of his shoulders, the regret in his voice, tugged at her heart. Forcing a smile, she said, "It hasn't been all bad."

"Just most of it," he muttered darkly. "Stay there!" he hissed when she moved closer to the bars.

"I want to help." She closed the remaining distance between them, then thrust her arm between two of the bars. "Take what you need."

He recoiled from her as if she was offering him a cup of hemlock. "I can't, love. Not now."

"Now is when you need it the most."

He couldn't argue with that, but he didn't trust himself to stop after a sip or two.

He was still at war with himself when Logan appeared, carrying one of the easy chairs from the living room.

Logan smiled at Sheree. "You might as well be comfortable if you're going to stay down here," he remarked, positioning the chair close to the cell. "Oh, and Mara sent you this." He pulled a candy bar from his pocket and handed it to Sheree. "It used to be her favorite."

"Thank her for me, please."

"Sure. Can I bring you anything else?"

"Not now, thanks."

Logan's gaze moved over Derek. "You doing all right, son?"

Derek nodded, his jaw clenched.

"Well, holler if you need anything," Logan said, and vanished from their sight.

Sheree sank down in the chair, her fingers tracing the logo on the candy wrapper.

After a moment, Derek sat on the floor, his arms resting on his bent knees. "Talk to me."

"About what?"

"Tell me about you. What kind of a little girl were you? Dirty face and pigtails?"

"That was rarely allowed," Sheree said, pretending to be shocked by the mere idea, and then grinned. "I was an only child and my parents spoiled me shamelessly. I'm afraid I took advantage of them, but they never complained. I had enough dresses and dolls for a dozen girls. And horseback riding lessons and ballet lessons. And my very own TV. Of course, what I really wanted most of all was a little sister, because my best friend had one. Did you ever miss having brothers and sisters?"

"Not really. But after I turned thirteen, I missed having friends. I couldn't play outdoors after that and gradually I stopped hanging out with them because it was too hard to explain why I couldn't go outside, and why I couldn't grab a hamburger on a Saturday afternoon, or spend the day surfing."

"What about girls?"

He snorted softly. He had never had any trouble in that department. "Dating was easier in some ways. There wasn't anything unusual about taking in a late movie or going for a walk along the beach after sunset. Things like that. But I never saw the same girl more than two or three times. It was just too hard to hide what I was, to keep coming up with excuses for why I couldn't take them out for an afternoon at the beach or come over for Sunday dinner, or take in a matinee."

Sheree shifted in the chair, thinking he must have had a lonely childhood. How awful, to have to hide who you were, to always be on your guard.

"It wasn't all bad," Derek remarked. "My family spoiled me, too, in their way. I got to do most of the things boys like to do, like hunting and fishing, only we did our hunting and fishing after dark. Logan taught me to wrestle and play baseball, and he took me rock climbing and hiking. . . ." His voice trailed off as his hands clenched at his sides.

"What is it?" Sheree asked. "What's happening?"

"I can feel the werewolf in me trying to get out."

"That's not supposed to happen until tomorrow night, is it?"

"Who the hell knows?" He raked his fingers through his hair, then stood and began pacing the floor, the thick chain rattling with every step.

Rising, Sheree folded her hands around the bars. "Derek, drink from me. Maybe it will help."

He growled deep in his throat, and then, in a blur of movement, he was standing in front of her, one of her arms clutched in his hand, his head bent over her wrist.

As his fangs pierced her flesh, she gasped, surprised by the pain. It had never hurt before.

A low purr filled the air as he drank.

And drank.

Sheree closed her eyes, and when she opened them again, Mara was at her side.

"Derek," his mother said sharply. "Let her go!"

He looked up, his eyes blood red. And then he snarled at her.

Mara dissolved into mist, then rematerialized inside the cell. Gripping her son's arm, she stared into his eyes. "Let her go. Now."

He obeyed instantly, then backed away from her.

A moment later, Mara was again at Sheree's side. Eyes narrowed, she asked, "Are you all right?"

Sheree nodded, too afraid to answer lest she burst into tears. Once she recovered, she asked, "What's going to happen to him?"

"I wish I knew. I brought you here because I thought your blood would soothe him, as it has in the past, but I was wrong. He's losing control of himself, just as he feared he would. I think it might be better if you come upstairs."

"Let her stay," Derek said, his voice filled with guilt. "I need her."

"Don't be a fool. What do you think would have happened if I hadn't stopped you?"

"Sheree," he whispered. "Please stay."

"I don't advise it," Mara said, "but the choice is yours. If you decide to stay, you have only to call me if you need me."

"Thank you."

With a last warning glance at her son, Mara left the dungeon.

Sheree sat in the chair again, watching as the red slowly faded from Derek's eyes. He sank down on the floor, his back braced against the wall. She bit down on her lower lip, searching for something to say, some words of comfort, but nothing came to mind. She had clung to the hope that the full moon would come and go without incident, but it seemed a foolish hope, given what had just happened.

Sheree kept Derek company until the rising sun coaxed him to sleep. Exhausted, she went upstairs to bed, only to lie there, staring at the ceiling, wondering what the night would bring. It seemed a given that he would shift into a werewolf. She wished she knew more about such creatures, but the only information she had came from horror movies. They were compelled to change when the moon was full. They terrorized humans, often killing them in hideous ways. She had never believed in werewolves the way she believed in vampires. Now, it seemed werewolves were also real. If vampires and werewolves existed, why not all the monsters of myth and legend? Fairies and trolls, giants and elves, zombies and leprechauns and the invisible man!

Derek had said little last night, his thoughts obviously turned inward. She could only imagine what he was thinking, feeling. Being a vampire was bad enough, but at least that was something he knew, something he could control, at least most of the time. She knew what he feared was being out of control, that when he was a werewolf he would be a beast with no conscience, no memory of his humanity. That he would savage anything that crossed his path.

Turning onto her side, she closed her eyes, and prayed that the things Derek feared the most would never come to pass.

One way or another, things would come to a head when the moon rose tonight.

Chapter Thirty

"I win!" Pearl exclaimed, tossing her cards onto the table. "That's three games in a row."

"You always were lucky at cards," Edna remarked. "I think you cheat."

"Well, of course I cheat," Pearl said. "Are you just now realizing that?"

"What? You mean to sit there and admit that all these years you've been cheating me, your best and only friend?"

"It's more fun than losing, dear."

Edna had worked herself up into a fine lather when there was a knock on the door of their hotel room.

Pearl met Edna's wide-eyed gaze. "What is she doing here?" she asked in a barely audible whisper.

"Let me in and I'll tell you."

Gathering her courage, Pearl opened the door. "Mara," she said, "how nice to see you again."

"Spare me your fake hospitality. I need your help."

Pearl glanced at Edna. "You need *our* help?"

"The serum you were working on during the war. Do you have any left?"

"No."

"Can you cook up another batch?"

"Are you thinking of trying it on Derek?" Edna looked at Pearl with an I-told-you-so expression.

"I don't know what else to do. This, this . . . whatever it is, is tearing him up inside. I know I should have come to you sooner." Instead, her pride and distrust had cost them valuable time.

"I have the formula memorized," Pearl said. "Of course, there's no guarantee it will work."

"It killed two of the werewolves when you tried it before," Mara said.

"True, and that's what you want to happen now, isn't it?"

"Only if you're sure it will destroy the werewolf gene without killing my son in the process."

"The results with the vampires was mixed," Edna remarked. "It cured two of them, but had no effect on Rafe. Of course, those vampires were very young, as I recall. Isn't that right, Pearl?"

"Yes, dear. With a few modifications, I think we can adjust the formula so it will kill the werewolf gene without hurting the host."

Mara's eyes narrowed. "What kinds of modifications?"

Pearl tapped her forefinger against her lips. "Well, for starters, I think we need to add a bit of wolf's bane for added killing power, and a few drops of your blood."

"My blood? Why? It's already running in his veins."

"A little fresh vampire blood couldn't hurt."

"Can you have the serum ready in time?"

"Goodness, no," Pearl exclaimed. "We have to collect the ingredients and prepare them properly. That will take several days. And it has to cook for at least forty-eight hours."

"We don't have forty-eight hours!" Mara snapped.

Pearl squared her shoulders. "Then you were right. You should have come to us sooner." She cringed when the ancient vampire's eyes went red. *I'm dead*, she thought, and clapped her hand over her mouth.

Mara glared at her, then nodded. "Just do what you have to do." With a wave of her hand, she was gone.

Pearl collapsed in Edna's arms. "I thought I was a goner for sure," she exclaimed.

"I thought we both were."

"We'd better pray this batch works," Pearl murmured, then grabbed Edna by the hand. "Come on, we need to get to work."

"All right," Edna said, "but I want to be near Derek when the moon rises."

"Edna . . ."

"Don't you 'Edna' me. I want to see him change. It's the reason we came here, after all!"

Chapter Thirty-One

Sheree.

She smiled faintly as the sound of his voice penetrated her dreams.

Sheree. I need you.

She rolled over, still half asleep, expecting to see him sitting beside her, but there was no one there. A glance at the window showed the sun had not yet set. Sighing, she closed her eyes again and snuggled under the blankets.

Sheree! Come to me.

It wasn't a request, but a command, one she could not resist. Rising, she drew on her bathrobe, then made her way to the dungeon.

Derek stood near the cell door, his hands wrapped around the bars, his knuckles white. *Get the keys. They're on a nail on the wall.*

She didn't want to obey but she was powerless to resist. The keys felt like ice in her hand.

Unlock the door, then remove the chain from my ankle.

Her mind screamed for her to refuse, but his will was stronger, his voice irresistible. She jabbed the key in the lock, then stepped into the cell.

"Release me," he said, and she had no choice but to obey.

Kneeling, she unlocked the thick silver cuff that bound him.

"You will stay here," he said. "You will not call my mother or Logan. Do you understand?"

She nodded.

"Good girl." Taking the keys from her hand, he left the cell, locked her inside, then tossed the keys on the chair. "I'm sorry," he murmured, and then he was gone.

Sheree wrapped her hands around the bars. Everything within her screamed for her to call for help, but try as she might, she could not form the words.

Moments later, Mara and Logan materialized in the dungeon. Mara wore a nightgown; a pair of jeans rode low on Logan's hips.

"What happened?" Mara unlocked the door with a wave of her hand.

"I don't know. He made me come down here somehow. I wanted to refuse, but I couldn't."

"Mind control." Mara looked at her husband. "He's stronger than I thought. I'm going after him."

"I want to go, too," Sheree said. "Just let me get dressed."

"No. Logan, stay here with her."

Logan rubbed his jaw. "I think I should go with you. In his condition, it might take two of us to handle him."

"Someone has to stay with Sheree in case he comes back." Mara lightly stroked his arm. "I'll be all right."

"Just be careful. We don't know what he's capable of now," Logan admonished, but the warning fell on empty air. Mara was already gone.

Beckoning for Sheree to follow him, Logan said, "Come on, girl, it's going to be a long night."

* * *

Derek ran through the hills with no destination in mind. His ankle burned where the silver had touched him, but he paid it little heed. All he wanted was to be alone. He felt a small degree of guilt for forcing Sheree to turn him loose, but it had been to keep her safe. Once he realized he could bend her will to his, he knew he had to get out of the castle and put as much distance between the two of them as he could.

He had been running for close to an hour when he caught the scent of a strange vampire. A young male, coming toward him in a hurry, eager for a confrontation. Confident of its outcome.

Slowing, Derek lifted his head, his gaze darting left and right. The vampire appeared as little more than a blur as it raced toward him.

Spoiling for a fight, Derek held his ground, his feet firmly planted as he waited for the vampire's attack.

With a cry, the other vampire launched himself toward Derek, his hands forming into claws as he reached for Derek's throat. But Derek was ready for him. With a hiss of triumph, his own hands locked around the other vampire's neck and he drove him backward, slamming him against the trunk of a tree, his fingers digging deep into the vampire's throat.

Vampires rarely drank from one another, Derek thought as he sank his fangs into the other man's jugular, but this fledgling had a lot to learn.

At the touch of Derek's fangs, the vampire bucked wildly, his hands clawing at Derek's back, shredding skin and tissue, but the pain didn't register. The vampire's blood was thick and rich. Derek drank deeply, absorbing the other vampire's power into himself, drank until there was neither blood nor fight left in his opponent.

He removed the dead vamp's tattered shirt and used it to

wipe his mouth; then with preternatural speed and power, he quickly buried the body.

Clearing his mind of all thought, he ran for miles, effortlessly, but there was no outrunning the werewolf snarling inside him.

The first pain hit him a short time later. It stole the breath from his body and he howled in protest. He had, on occasion, shape-shifted into a wolf, but that was done quickly, painlessly. This was excruciating, and he howled again.

The next jolt sent him to his hands and knees. The wolf was born moments later in a swift, agonizing transformation that shredded his jeans.

The world looked different through the eyes of the werewolf.

Springing to his feet, he shook himself. As a vampire, his senses were keen, but his werewolf senses were sharper still. Stimuli poured in from all sides, even through the pads of his feet. Exultant, he began to run, needing to feel the earth beneath his paws, the sting of the wind in his face.

To hunt.

To rend human flesh and drink blood.

A house materialized out of the darkness and he ran toward it, nostrils flaring. There was prey inside, two adults and three children.

He had almost reached the house when a familiar scent was borne to him on the wind. Mara. But she couldn't stop him. No one could stop him.

When he reached the dwelling, he didn't slow down. The flimsy front door gave way to his weight and he bounded across the threshold, the vampire part of his mind momentarily gloating because his mother could not follow him inside.

The house smelled of cooked food, of floor wax and flowers, of soap and ashes, of human sweat and hard work.

He paused in the living room, then padded down the short hallway to the nursery. The door was open. Inside, a newborn baby slept in a crib painted white.

New life. Fresh, sweet blood. It called to him. The baby for an appetizer, then the little girl and her brother. Then the parents. His mouth watered as he contemplated the feast awaiting him.

He padded toward the crib, his nails clicking on the wooden floor. Rising on his hind legs, he stared down at the infant. She slept on her stomach, a tiny thumb in her mouth.

A low growl rose in the werewolf's throat as it opened its jaws to pick up the sleeping child.

At the sound of heavy footsteps in the hallway, he dropped to the floor, fangs bared. A man stood in the doorway, a rifle in his hands, his eyes wide with fear, his face a pale oval in the darkness.

The man fired the gun when the werewolf lunged at him. The bullet struck the wolf in the shoulder, but it didn't slow him down. After knocking the gun from the man's hands, the werewolf straddled him, his teeth at the man's throat.

Derek! Stop it!

His head snapped up at the sound of Sheree's voice.

Come home, Derek. I'm waiting for you.

The werewolf shook its head, blood and saliva spraying from its mouth.

You don't want to do this. You'll hate yourself if you do. And I'll . . . I'll hate you, too.

He whined low in his throat as the familiar voice whispered through his mind. Sheree. She loved him. And she knew . . . somehow, she knew what he was about to do.

I know you're strong enough to resist this. Please, Derek, if you love me, don't kill anyone. Come home to me.

He stared at the man cowering beneath him. Bright red blood leaked from the bite marks in the man's throat. The scent tantalized the wolf's senses, urging him to kill the man and take the child.

Derek, please come home to me.

He shook his head, the vampire inside him fighting to subdue the werewolf, but to no avail. Grasping the man's shoulder in his jaws, the wolf dragged him, kicking and screaming, into the living room, away from the child.

The farmer's frantic cries roused his wife. She ran into the room, took one look at the wolf, then turned and ran toward the back of the house, sobbing the names of her children.

Mara's scent drew the werewolf's gaze toward the front door. She stood outside watching his every move. There was no condemnation in her eyes. The life of a mortal meant little to her. He could kill the man or not. She was his mother and a vampire. She would understand what drove him.

But Sheree would never forgive him. She knew he was a vampire, but she had never thought of him as a monster. That would surely change if he killed the man and devoured his family.

The wolf stared at his prey again. The man's eyes were filled with terror, the stink of his fear clung to his skin, mingling with the scent of urine. Weak, puny mortal, the werewolf thought derisively. Wetting himself like some frightened child.

Derek, have mercy on the man. Would you deprive his children of their father?

He snarled softly. He had never known his own father, so why should these children have theirs?

Torn, he threw back his head and howled at the uncaring moon.

"Come home with me, Derek." His mother spoke quietly, but he heard her clearly.

Sheree's voice echoed Mara's words. *Derek, come home to me.*

Growling softly, he licked the blood from the man's neck, then loped out of the house.

A moment later, his mother shifted to wolf form. She sniffed the bloody wound in his shoulder, noting that it was already healing.

Side by side, mother and son ran through the darkness.

Mara paused briefly, her gaze sweeping the shadows before coming to rest on Edna and Pearl. Both women bowed their heads, acknowledging her superiority, before Mara raced to catch up with Derek. Together, they continued on to the castle, where Sheree and Logan waited.

Sheree sucked in a deep breath when she saw the wolves. She stared at the larger of the two. No one would mistake this creature for anything but a werewolf. Big and black, it was the most frightening thing she had ever seen. He was taller, more muscular than the other wolf, his features somehow distorted. The fur that covered his right shoulder was matted with dried blood.

It was hard to remember that it was Derek when he started toward her. She told herself that there was nothing to be afraid of, that he wouldn't rip her heart out. But looking at him, she found it hard to believe.

He paused, whining softly when she took an involuntary step backward.

Sheree blinked when the wolf at Derek's side began to shimmer. A moment later, Mara stood there clad in a pair of jeans and a sweater.

Logan glanced from mother to son and back again. "So, what are the damages?"

"Nothing serious. He killed a rogue vampire and would

have killed a farmer and his family if Sheree hadn't stopped him."

Logan glanced at Sheree. "How did you do that?"

"I'm not sure," she replied, staring at the werewolf. "Somehow I knew what he was doing. I saw him in my mind, not clearly, just vague images, but enough to know what was happening." She lifted one shoulder and let it fall. "I begged him not to hurt anyone."

"What about the vampire?" Logan remarked. "Anyone we know?"

Mara shook her head. "It was self-defense, in any case. And if Derek hadn't destroyed him, I would have. He was on my turf."

Logan grunted thoughtfully. Vampires were notoriously territorial. Just because Mara hadn't been to Romania in a hundred years or so didn't mean another vampire could waltz in and claim the land for himself.

Sheree gestured at Derek's shoulder. "Is he all right?"

"The wound has already healed," Mara said.

Whining softly, the werewolf stretched out in front of the fireplace, his head resting on his paws, his gaze fixed on Sheree's face.

He didn't look any less ferocious lying down. Chewing on a corner of her lower lip, trying to tamp down her fear of the beast, Sheree walked slowly toward him.

A low growl that sounded almost like a purr rumbled in his throat as she knelt beside him. Stroking his head with a tentative hand, she whispered, "Thank you for not killing that man and his family."

The werewolf's tail thumped against the floor.

Sheree smiled faintly as she reminded herself it was Derek, but seeing his eyes in the werewolf's face was beyond bizarre.

The werewolf growled when someone knocked at the door.

"What the hell?" Logan exclaimed. "What are *they* doing here?"

"You might as well go and let them in," Mara said with an aggrieved sigh. "They saw the whole thing."

Sheree glanced at the door, wondering who on earth would be coming to call so late at night. Her eyes widened when the two old ladies she had seen in the Den preceded Logan into the room. She noted they were careful to keep a good distance between themselves and the werewolf.

"Pearl, Edna, this is Sheree, a friend of Derek's. Sheree, these are old friends of the family."

Sheree didn't miss the sarcasm in Mara's voice as she introduced the two elderly women.

"So," Mara said, "how's the serum coming along?"

The taller of the two, Pearl, shrugged. "There's really no way to tell."

"After what you saw tonight, do you still think it will work?"

"I am seventy-five percent sure that it will be effective."

"And if it doesn't work, how will it affect my son?"

"I am reasonably certain that it won't do him any harm," Pearl said. "Of course, there's no way to cure him of being a vampire, since he was born that way."

"He was also born a werewolf," Logan remarked.

"True. And that was where we made our mistake before. We were trying to cure the werewolves and the vampires using the same formula. Naturally, it didn't work," Pearl said. "We've learned a few things since then. As I told you before, this new serum should destroy the werewolf gene. . . ."

"Or at least weaken it so that it will no longer have any power over him," Edna interjected. "We're quite certain it will work after what we saw tonight."

"Yes," Pearl said. "Even though he was compelled to shift, he seemed to be in control of the wolf."

"Thanks to Sheree's influence," Mara said.

Pearl and Edna exchanged glances. "What do you mean?"

"Sheree managed to communicate with him. She asked him not to kill the farmer or his family."

The two elderly vampires focused on Sheree, studying her as if she were a bug under a microscope. It was most disconcerting.

"Has he tasted her blood?" Pearl asked.

Mara nodded.

Edna looked at Pearl. "Are you thinking what I'm thinking?"

Pearl nodded. "We need to add her blood to the serum right away. I have a syringe and a vial in my jacket," she said, reaching into her pocket.

Sheree scrambled to her feet and backed away. "No way! I'm not letting you take my blood!"

"If you want to help Derek, then I'm afraid it's necessary, dear," Pearl said.

Sheree glanced at Mara for help that she knew would not be forthcoming. If she refused to willingly let them take her blood, they would just take it by force.

With a sigh of resignation, she rolled up her sleeve and held out her arm. She turned her head, her gaze fixed on the werewolf, while the vampire siphoned her blood.

She fought a hysterical urge to laugh as she wondered if her life could get any more bizarre.

With the coming of dawn, the werewolf retreated. By then, everyone else had gone to bed.

For no apparent reason, transforming from werewolf to vampire was less painful, though it left him aching from head to foot.

Derek washed up in the kitchen sink, then went to his room and pulled on a pair of sweatpants before making his way to Sheree's chamber.

Stepping inside, he closed the door behind him. An indrawn breath told him she was only pretending to be asleep.

"Do you want me to leave?"

Her excitement and trepidation were evident in the sudden quickening of her heart and the faint tinge of fear on her skin.

He was about to leave when she scooted over, drawing back the bed covers in silent invitation.

He hesitated a moment before sliding in beside her, though he was careful not to touch her. Tension stretched between them.

"I want to thank you for what you did," he said quietly. "If it wasn't for you, that man would be dead now, and I . . ."

Her hand, small and warm, found his. "Was it terrible?"

"There aren't words to describe it. I knew what I was doing but I couldn't stop myself. I looked at that tiny infant and all I could think about was ripping it to shreds." He choked back a sob. "If I'd killed that baby . . ." Even when he'd been a new vampire, he had never been out of control, never been tempted to do anything as vile as kill an infant or a child.

"Derek, don't think about it. It's over for now. I just know the old ladies' serum will work and . . ."

"And I'll still be a vampire and you'll still be . . ."

"The woman in love with you."

His anguish was palpable, her need to comfort him overpowering. Whispering his name, she drew him into her embrace, one hand stroking his hair.

His arms went around her. Murmuring her name, he buried his face in her hair. "Hold me."

"I'm here." She could feel him trembling, knew he was appalled by the events of the night.

"Don't let me go."

"I won't. There now, everything is all right. I'm here. I'll always be here."

Slipping a hand behind her head, he drew her closer, his gaze searching hers.

Her name was a groan on his lips as his mouth sought hers in a kiss filled with desire and a desperate need to blot everything from his mind but the woman in his arms.

"Sheree . . ."

"I know," she whispered. "I know." She turned her head to the side, granting him access to her neck.

It wasn't hunger that drove him now, but a deep-seated need to draw her essence into himself, as if he could absorb her goodness along with the sweet taste of her life's blood.

Sheree's hands drifted over his body, arousing his desire and her own as her fingers explored his back, the indentation between his shoulders, the solid column of his neck, the silkiness of his hair.

When he drew back, she cupped his face in her hands and kissed him with all the yearning in her heart. He was a vampire, strong, invincible, and yet he needed her in ways that no other man ever would. He aroused a keen, protective instinct within her that she had never known she possessed. In that moment, she knew she would readily defend his life with her own, if necessary.

"My tigress," he murmured, nipping at her earlobe.

"Reading my thoughts again, are you?" she asked with feigned anger.

A wicked grin was her answer.

Smiling in return, she filled her mind with images of the two of them wrapped in an erotic embrace, then purred, "What am I thinking now?"

"Sheree?" His voice was thick with desire. And doubt.

"Don't you want me?"

"You know I do, but . . ."

"But you're afraid you'll hurt me."

He nodded, his dark eyes haunted.

With a sigh, she kissed his cheek. If he could wait, so could she. She just hoped he wouldn't make her wait too long.

Chapter Thirty-Two

Derek held Sheree in his arms until she fell asleep. Her love continued to astonish him. He wanted nothing more than to possess her fully, to make her his in the most primal way, but he didn't trust himself not to hurt her. She might not be afraid, but he was scared enough for both of them. Except for that one night when he had almost taken too much, a little of her blood satisfied his hunger. Her nearness soothed him. But what if all that changed while they were making love? She was so fragile. He could break her in two without even trying. A few swallows too many and she could die in his arms. Was it just caution that was keeping him from making love to her until he was certain he had his hunger, his desire, and his werewolf under control? Or was something else holding him back? And if so, what the hell was it, except fear of hurting the woman he loved? He shook his head. Damned if he knew.

He thought of the hours he had spent as a werewolf. He had reveled in his strength and power, in the knowledge that he was almost indestructible. Left alone, he would have felt no guilt at all had he killed the farmer and his family. Guilt and remorse were foreign to the werewolf. Only Sheree's voice, declaring that she was waiting for him, that she would hate him if he killed the man, had kept him from tearing the farmer to pieces.

What if that primal urge to rend human flesh overpowered him while they were making love? The werewolf might not feel guilt, but hurting Sheree would destroy the vampire.

He thought of the serum the two old women were concocting and prayed that it would make him wholly mortal, that he would be able to share his entire life with Sheree, give her children. The thought of being susceptible to disease—and death—was far less appealing. He liked the power being a vampire gave him—the physical strength, the invincibility, the preternatural senses that allowed him to see and hear things denied to humans.

Standing under the stars, he gazed out over the valley. If he was totally honest with himself, he didn't want to be human, but it was a sacrifice he was willing to make for the woman he loved. Yet if he could persuade her to accept the Dark Gift, they could have centuries together instead of the few short years allotted to mankind.

For one brief moment, he considered turning her while she slept, then quickly shook the thought away. Becoming a vampire would have to be her choice. All he needed to do was find a way to convince her.

"Just turn her," said a familiar voice from behind him.

"The way you turned Logan?" Derek asked, swinging around to face his mother. "Did he ever hate you for it?"

"If he did, he never said so."

"And if he had?"

Mara made a gesture of dismissal. "Why worry about something that never happened? He loved me before I turned him. He loves me now. Why fret over the past?"

"And what if I turn Sheree and she hates me for it? I'll have ruined her life and my own."

"Your conscience is your one weakness, you know. You

have a sense of right and wrong a priest would be proud of."
Mara smiled wistfully. "As did your father. Come," she said,
linking her arm with his, "I'm hungry and the night is still
young."

Derek felt no need to feed, but, as always, he couldn't
refuse his mother's invitation, or the chance to watch her
hunt. Even after centuries, she found pleasure in finding and
stalking her prey, sometimes with as much cunning and
stealth as a lioness, sometimes striking with the quick pre-
cision of a cobra.

They hunted the dark streets of the city until she found
someone to her liking: a strong young man staggering home
from the local pub.

Derek watched as she worked her vampire magic on him,
slowly seducing him until he would have given her anything
she asked, and then she took what she needed. She fed
quickly, gave him an affectionate pat on the cheek before
wiping her memory from his mind, and sent him happily on
his way, none the wiser.

Derek had to admire her skill.

"Was he not to your liking?" she asked when the man was
out of sight. "If not, I'm sure we can find a pretty young
thing who's more to your taste."

Derek shook his head. Drinking from another woman felt
wrong, like cheating on Sheree.

Mara clucked softly. "A few drops of her blood may satisfy
your craving, but it isn't enough to sustain you indefinitely."

He said nothing, but he knew she was right. Sooner or
later, he needed to feed, and he would have to take more than
Sheree could spare. Much more.

Walking back the way they had come, he mesmerized a
young couple strolling down the street. He drank from them
both before sending them on their way. Their blood was

neither as satisfying nor as sweet as Sheree's, but he felt better immediately.

Like it or not, his mother had been right again.

She laughed softly as they crossed the street. "I'm always right. Haven't you learned that yet?"

When they returned to the castle, Logan was waiting for them. Mara kissed Derek soundly on the cheek; then, with a come-hither smile to her husband, she went upstairs to get ready for bed.

Logan would have followed, but Derek asked him to stay.

"What do you need?" Logan asked, resuming his place on the sofa.

"Did you ever hate my mother for turning you against your will?"

"No. I would have done anything, given up anything I had, to be with her. Why?"

"She thinks I should turn Sheree."

"It's a terrible thing to do to someone," Logan remarked. "You're not only stealing their life, but everything they know, everything they love."

"Then why didn't you hate my mother?"

"I don't know. I guess I should have, but I loved her so damn much, all I wanted was to be with her. Mortal or vampire, I didn't care what I was, as long as we were together."

"But she didn't stay with you."

"No, she didn't. She turned other men after she left me. I don't know how many. She wouldn't tell me, said she didn't remember. It mattered to me once, but as they say, all's well that ends well. It was worth the centuries of misery and loneliness without her to have her with me now."

"And if she said she was leaving?"

"Then I'd let her go. I didn't beg her to stay the first time, and I sure as hell wouldn't do it now." Logan stared into the distance for a moment before saying, "If you bring Sheree across without asking her, there's no telling what her reaction will be. There's a good chance she'll hate you for it, or hate what she's become and destroy herself. Are you prepared to live with the consequences?"

Derek shuddered at the visual Logan's words planted in his mind—an image of Sheree cursing his name as she walked out into the sun's light, screaming in agony as her body burst into flames.

Jaw clenched, he shook his head, hoping to dispel the image, but later that night, it lingered in his mind until the Dark Sleep dragged him down into oblivion.

The next evening, Mara decided it was time to go back home. Though she had fond memories of living in the castle in days gone by, the old place was in serious need of repair and refurbishing, neither of which she was in the mood to tackle just now.

It took only a short time to pack the few things they had brought with them and lock up the place.

Sheree closed her eyes and held her breath as the four of them stood in a tight circle, holding hands.

When she opened her eyes again, they were in the middle of the living room in Mara's house in the Hollywood Hills. "I'll never get used to that," Sheree remarked when the world stopped spinning. "Never."

"Maybe one day you'll be able to do it on your own," Mara said, heading toward the stairs. "Coming, Logan?"

Sheree looked at Derek, one brow raised. "What did she mean by that?"

"Don't listen to her. She's crazy. So, what now? Do you want to stay here, or go to your place?"

"I think I should go home, see if my plants are still alive, and clean out my fridge."

"Whatever you want, love."

When they reached her house, Derek walked Sheree to the door. At her request, he followed her inside to make sure no one was hiding in the closet or under the bed.

"All clear," he said, returning to the living room. "If you need me, just call. On the phone, or in your mind, I'll hear you and I'll come."

"Do you have to go so soon?"

"I guess not."

"Do you mind if I go change? I'll just be a minute."

"Take your time."

Taking her bags, she went up the stairs.

Derek tracked her movements while he made a slow circuit of her living room. He paused in front of a narrow bookshelf. Three shelves were crowded with figurines of vampires, some made out of pewter, others of glass or ceramic. The rest of the bookcase was filled with books and movies about vampires, including several different versions of the movie *Dracula*.

He couldn't help wondering if she still found vampires fascinating.

He turned at the sound of her footsteps, thinking she got prettier every time he saw her. Her cheeks flushed under his admiring gaze.

"It's a little chilly in here," she said, suddenly nervous. "I think I'll light a fire."

"Let me." A wave of his hand, and flames crackled in the hearth.

Sheree stared at him, her eyes wide. "How did you do that?"

"I don't know."

She glared at him. "Don't tell me that's another secret you can't share."

"No," he said, laughing. "I really don't know. I just think it and it happens."

"Can you put it out the same way?"

"Yeah."

"That's . . . amazing, I guess." She curled up in a corner on the sofa. "So," she said, counting on her fingers, "you can dissolve into mist, read minds, start fires with a thought, and vanish in a puff of smoke. What else?"

Sitting beside her, he drew her into his arms. "I can kiss you until you stop thinking."

"Can you?" Sheree gazed up at him, her eyes glowing with affection.

"Shall I prove it?"

"Yes," she murmured, her eyelids fluttering down. "Oh, yes."

His kiss, when it came, was soft, a gentle wooing that warmed her heart and invaded her soul. She clung to him, her hands restlessly moving over his back, tangling in his hair to keep him close. She loved the feel of his body against her own. He was such a strong, masculine man, everything female within her responded to his touch, to his nearness. His hands caressed her and she moaned softly, wishing he would make love to her. She knew that he thought it was dangerous, that he worried about hurting her, but she wasn't afraid.

Frowning, she drew back so she could see his face. "Why is it I'm not afraid of you?"

He lifted one brow. "An odd question at such a time, don't you think?"

"I guess so. I was a little afraid when I first realized you were actually a vampire but I wasn't afraid of *you*, just of what you are. And that didn't last very long. I wasn't afraid when I let you drink from me. Is that normal?"

"I don't think so. What are you getting at?"

"Maybe I'm not normal."

"Maybe you're not."

"I was kidding," she said, suddenly looking worried.

"I know. But your blood, your nearness, soothes me in ways that nothing else does. There's got to be a reason for it, although I can't imagine what it would be." He brushed his knuckles against her cheek. Was it that difference that drew him to her in the first place?

He opened his preternatural senses when he kissed her again, but he detected nothing except warm, willing woman. A woman who wanted him with every fiber of her body, who wished he would forget his fears and make love to her. Was she right? Was he worrying for nothing? As a vampire, he had never been totally out of control the way he had been as a werewolf.

Overcome with gratitude, he drew her back into his arms, hugging her tightly. "I love you, Sheree," he murmured fervently. "I will love you as long as you live."

As long as you live. The words, which should have thrilled her, filled her with a vague sense of sadness. He hadn't said as long as *he* lived, she noted, which could be hundreds of years or more, but as long as *she* lived, a much shorter timeline.

Sheree closed her eyes, refusing to cry. But even as she told herself to be grateful for whatever time Fate allowed her to share with Derek, she heard a quiet voice in the back of her mind.

Derek's voice whispering, *Sheree, my love, only say the word and hundreds of years can be yours, too.*

* * *

"They're gone!" Pearl exclaimed, staring up at the castle. "I can't believe they would go without telling us."

Edna stared at her friend. "Are you serious? I think we're lucky to still be breathing! I don't know about you, but I'll be perfectly happy to get back to Texas and never see Mara or any of her family again!"

But Pearl wasn't listening. "She needs us. *We* have the formula. I've half a mind not to make the damn stuff!"

"Oh, there's a good idea," Edna said, her voice dripping with sarcasm. "Just piss her off some more, why don't you?"

"Let's go pack," Pearl muttered. "There's no point in staying here any longer."

Edna nodded as she grabbed her favorite bright yellow jacket and orange scarf. "I couldn't agree more."

Chapter Thirty-Three

When Sheree woke, it was almost three in the afternoon. Stretching her arms over her head, she wondered if her internal clock would ever get back to rights. Trying to stay up late to be with Derek had been one thing, going to Transylvania quite another. The change in time had really messed her up, until she wasn't sure if she was supposed to sleep when the sun was up or down.

Last night, Derek's words—*Sheree, my love, only say the word and hundreds of years can be yours, too*—had followed her to sleep, and given rise to a nightmare. She had dreamed that Derek had forced her to become a vampire. He had chained her in the castle dungeon, drained her to the point of death, then forced her to drink his blood. Even now, the thought made her gag. How did he stand it? In her nightmare, she had turned into a ravening, red-eyed monster. Out of control, she had attacked everything and everyone—animals, birds, men, women, and children. Even her parents . . .

Shaking the horrific images from her mind, she went into the bathroom to wash her face and brush her teeth.

She wasn't in the mood for breakfast, so she drank a glass of orange juice and washed it down with a cup of coffee.

Needing to be busy, she spent the next three hours cleaning the house from top to bottom. She did two loads of laundry and while waiting for the clothes to dry, she threw everything out of the refrigerator and washed it inside and out.

When that was done, she went upstairs to shower, then changed into a pair of clean jeans and a T-shirt, put on a pair of sneakers, and went for a long walk. She smiled at the people she passed, thinking how good it was to be alive on such a beautiful evening. It would have been perfect, she thought, if only Derek was there beside her.

It was after seven when she returned home. Grabbing her handbag, she drove to the store.

She was trying to decide between chocolate fudge brownie ice cream or mint and chip when she felt a sudden warmth along the side of her neck, as if someone had kissed her.

She smiled with the realization that someone had. Murmuring his name, she glanced over her shoulder to find Derek standing behind her.

"Too bad you don't eat," she said, containing the urge to throw her arms around him. "You could help me decide which kind to buy."

"I'd rather kiss you again."

Tilting her head back, she closed her eyes in silent invitation, sighed when his lips claimed hers.

The sound of someone clearing their throat made Sheree take a step back. Opening her eyes, she saw a middle-aged woman glaring at them over a tub of vanilla ice cream, while the two young girls at her side giggled.

With a shake of her head, the woman pushed her cart past them, muttering, "Get a room, for goodness' sake."

"Good idea." Derek gestured at the contents in Sheree's basket. "Do you really need all that stuff?"

"I'm afraid so."

He fell into step beside her as she made her way to the checkout line, then loaded her groceries into the trunk of her car. He held her door for her before sliding into the passenger seat.

When he was settled, Sheree started the car and drove home, acutely aware of the man sitting beside her. Just looking at him made her smile. His very presence filled her with a sense of warmth and light, which was odd, since vampires were creatures of darkness.

"It must be love," she mused with a glance in his direction.

He looked at her, one brow raised.

"You know very well what I'm talking about, so don't give me that innocent look."

He didn't deny it, only laughed softly. "You've got it backward, love. You're the light to my darkness."

It was, she thought, the nicest compliment she had ever received.

At home, he carried the groceries inside, then stood in the doorway, arms crossed, watching her stow them away.

"Do you ever miss eating?" Sheree asked as she put a loaf of bread in the cupboard.

"Sometimes."

"What do you miss the most?"

"Cheeseburgers. And French fries. And apple pie."

"Some of my favorites, too," Sheree said, smiling. "What happens when you eat?"

"You don't want to know."

"You can eat steak," she mused. "Have you tried eating any other kind of meat?"

"No. Well, just hamburger, but that's really the same thing."

"And the blood?" She put the last of the groceries away. "Isn't it . . . ?"

"Gross? Disgusting? Revolting? No, it isn't."

Turning to face him, she leaned against the counter, her head tilted to the side. "Does it taste the same to you as it does to me when I lick the blood from a cut?"

"Not even close. You know what Dracula said, that the blood is the life? When I drink from someone, I absorb their memories, their thoughts. Their life. As for the taste, it's indescribable. And irresistible."

"I can't even imagine that."

"This is the strangest conversation I've ever had with a woman," Derek remarked.

"Surely some of your other lady friends have been curious."

"I never trusted any of them, few as there have been, to know what I was." Heat flared in the depths of his eyes. "Come here."

"Is that an order?"

"No, love. Merely a request."

Sheree moved readily into his arms, lifted her face for his kiss, sighed when his mouth found hers. It must be love, she mused again. Because everything she learned about him— no matter how bizarre—only made her want him more. Want to help him more.

"Help me? That you have."

"And I don't intend to stop." Pulling his head down, she kissed him, hoping he was reading her mind so he would know how much she loved him, not only because he was as sexy as sin, but because he treated her like an equal. And because he trusted her with the truth.

"With my life," he said, raining feather-light kisses over her cheeks, her brow, the tip of her nose. His hands cupped her hips, drawing her closer, as his tongue slid along the side of her neck. "Let me?"

"Always." Her eyelids fluttered down as his fangs scraped

lightly over her skin. His earlier words whispered through her mind. *When I drink from someone, I absorb their memories, their thoughts. Their life.* It was disconcerting knowing he was privy to her every thought, her every wish, past and present. *Are you reading my mind now? If you are, kiss me.*

She had barely formed the thought when his mouth covered hers, hot and hungry. Sweeping her into his arms, he carried her into the living room. Flames leaped in the hearth. Never taking his lips from hers, he lowered her to the floor, then gathered her into his arms, his back to the fire. His hands played over her body, sending shivers of sensual delight through every nerve and fiber of her being.

At last, she thought. *At last . . .*

When her cell phone rang, she let the call go to voice mail. But then it rang again. Dimly, she realized the ring was her mother's.

After the third call, Derek drew back. "I think you'd better answer that."

Dazed by his kisses, she fumbled inside her pocket for her phone. "Mom?"

"Sheree, it's your dad. He . . ."

"What?" She sat up, the first shivery chill of fear chasing everything else from her mind. "What's wrong?"

"It's his heart. He's in Presbyterian, in ICU."

"I'll be there as soon as I can book a flight."

"No need for that," Derek said after she disconnected the call. "I can have you there in no time at all."

She stared at him a moment, then smiled faintly. "Vampire Airlines?"

"Best in the world. Is there anything you need to take with you?"

"Just my purse and my phone."

Rising, he helped her to her feet. A look extinguished the fire and turned off the lights. "Ready?"

When she nodded, he wrapped her in his arms.

Clutching her handbag to her chest, she closed her eyes.

When she opened them again, they were in the lobby of Presbyterian Hospital.

"You go on up," Derek said, giving her hand a squeeze. "I'll wait for you down here."

"No. Come with me."

He shook his head. "I can't. Too much blood."

"Oh, of course. You won't leave?"

"No. I'll be here."

With a nod, she hurried toward the elevators.

Sheree had always hated hospitals. She didn't like the smell, or the insipid color of the walls, or the ugly floors. But, most of all, she didn't trust doctors.

She found her mother at her father's bedside, his hand clasped in hers. "Mom, what happened?"

Meredith looked up, her eyes red and swollen. "We were at dinner . . . at the Nortons'. . . . He just . . ." She blinked rapidly. ". . . just collapsed."

"What does the doctor say?"

Meredith swallowed hard. "It's not good. He said . . . that I should . . . prepare myself."

Sheree bit down on her lower lip in an effort to keep from crying. Her mother needed her to be strong. She could fall apart later. But looking at her father, at how pale he was, at all the tubes and monitors, it was impossible to hold back her tears.

Nurses came and went. At midnight, Sheree went downstairs on the pretense of getting some coffee.

She found Derek in the lobby, sitting in a chair near the door. He rose as soon as he saw her and she ran into his arms. There was no need to say anything.

"I'm sorry, love," he said, lightly stroking her hair.

She looked up at him through tear-swollen eyes. "Is there anything you can do?"

"Do you want me to make him a vampire?"

"Of course not, but . . . can't you work some kind of vampire voodoo and save him?"

"I don't know." He had heard stories of humans who had been cured of any number of different maladies by an infusion of vampire blood, but he had no idea if such stories were true, or merely wishful thinking.

He looked down into Sheree's eyes. How could he destroy the hope shining there?

"Go get that coffee," he said. "I need to talk to Mara."

Leaving the hospital, he found a quiet place and opened the link between himself and his mother. He had no idea if he could send her his thoughts from such a great distance. If it didn't work, he'd go home and ask her.

What is it, Derek? Where are you?

Philadelphia. Sheree's dad had a heart attack. He's in the hospital. Doesn't look good. Is there anything I can do?

A little of your blood might save him.

So, the stories are true?

Some of them. I don't know if your blood will cure him, but it might strengthen him long enough for the doctors to save him.

Thanks, Ma.

In his mind, he saw her bristle at his use of the word *Ma*, which she thought was demeaning, but which he used with affection.

Let me know what happens. And be careful.

When he returned, Sheree was waiting for him in the lobby, a cup of coffee in each hand. "What did she say?"

"She said giving him a little of my blood might help. It's up to you."

"It's worth a try! Hurry!"

"Wait. You need to get your mother out of the room."

"All right. How long will it take?"

Following her into the elevator, he said, "No more than a few minutes." When they exited the elevator at the intensive care ward, he said, "I'll wait here. When you get her out, I'll go in."

"Okay."

A short time later, Sheree and her mother left the room.

As soon as they were out of sight, he dissolved into mist, then resumed his shape at her father's bedside. Derek forced the man's mouth open, bit into his own wrist, and let a dozen or so drops of his blood drip down the man's throat.

At a sound from the hallway, Derek dissolved into mist once more and left the ICU. In the corridor, the scent of blood and pain and death was overpowering. A thought took him outside, where he took several deep breaths.

Sheree found him there an hour later. The smile on her face said it all. "You did it! The doctor is calling it a miracle." She threw her arms around him, tears of joy trailing down her cheeks. "Thank you!"

Derek held her close. For the first time in his life, he felt truly grateful to be a vampire.

It was after three A.M. when Sheree persuaded her mother to leave the hospital. "You need to get some sleep," she said as they took the elevator to the lobby. "You don't want Dad to see those dark shadows under your eyes."

"We could have lost him," Meredith said, her voice thick.

"You heard the doctor. Dad's going to be fine."

Meredith nodded.

Sheree looked at her mother, a little surprised to realize that her mother's distress had been sincere. Maybe she had been wrong about her parents. Maybe, in their own way, they really did love each other.

"How did you get here so soon?" Meredith pulled a lace hanky from her pocket and dabbed at her eyes.

The question caught Sheree off guard. She couldn't tell her mother the truth, of course. Mind scrambling, Sheree opted for a part of the truth. "I had decided to come home for a visit. A friend of mine has a private plane and offered to save me the price of a ticket. We were on our way to see you when I got your call. Look, there he is now," she said, before her mother could ask any more questions she couldn't answer.

"Thank you for bringing my daughter home," Meredith said after Sheree introduced Derek.

"I was happy to do it, Mrs. Westerbrooke." He gestured at the cab waiting at the curb. "I took the liberty of calling for a taxi."

"That was very thoughtful of you. You'll stay with us, of course," Meredith insisted as Derek opened the car door.

"Thank you, but it isn't necessary." He winked at Sheree as she climbed into the backseat. "I have a place of my own." He was grateful when she didn't argue.

They arrived at the Westerbrooke home a short time later. Sheree's mother bid them good night and immediately retired to her room, leaving Sheree to look after Derek.

"Thank you again," Sheree said. "If it wasn't for you . . ."

He drew her into his embrace as tears of gratitude flooded her eyes. He held her until her tears subsided, then wiped the last of them away with the pads of his thumbs.

"You'd better get some sleep, love. I'll see you tomorrow night."

"Do you really have a place here, in the city?"

"No."

"Then where are you going to spend the day?"

"At Mara's place."

"You heard my mother. You're welcome to stay with us."

"It isn't safe, love. Your mother is here and there are servants in the house. It's best if I leave. Don't worry, I'll see you tomorrow."

"You promise?"

"I'll be here as soon as the sun goes down." Derek shook his head as her thoughts invaded his. Sometimes, as now, being able to read minds was as much a curse as a blessing. "Come on, love, I'll get you tucked in."

"And stay until I fall asleep?"

Nodding, he swept her into his arms and carried her up the long, winding staircase to her room, tucked her into bed after she changed into her nightgown.

"Sweet dreams, darlin'."

"Thank you again," she murmured, and tumbled into sleep's waiting arms.

Derek brushed a lock of hair from her brow, then left the house. He had just enough time to hunt and make it back to California before the sun came up.

Early the next morning, Sheree and her mother were back at the hospital. Sheree was relieved to see that some of the color had returned to her father's cheeks and that he was resting comfortably.

Sitting beside her mother on one of the hospital's hard plastic chairs, Sheree offered a silent prayer of gratitude that she had met Derek. Without him, she was certain her father would have passed away during the night.

For a time, neither of them spoke, both focused on

watching her father's every breath, tracking the lines on the monitors.

After a while, Meredith took a deep breath and turned toward her daughter. "Tell me about the young man who brought you home. Who are his people? Where is he from? What does he do for a living?"

Sheree shifted in her chair as she tried to gather her thoughts. "Derek's from California. His parents have a lovely home in the Hollywood Hills. Old money," she said. Then, hoping to impress her mother, she added, "They also own a castle in Romania."

"Royalty?" Meredith queried, her eyes suddenly alight with interest.

Sheree nodded, remembering that Derek had called his mother the Queen of the Vampires.

"Neil was upset when you left without saying good-bye."

"Oh, Mom, stop matchmaking. I wouldn't marry Neil Somerset for a million dollars in gold. Or Ralph Upton, either. I'm in love with Derek, and nothing you can say is going to change that."

The argument Sheree saw coming died on her mother's lips when Dr. Carlson entered the room. He nodded at Sheree and her mother, then checked his patient's vital signs.

"How is he?" Meredith asked anxiously.

"Much better." He smiled at the two of them. "Someone must have prayed up a miracle."

Sheree grinned inwardly. A miracle, indeed, she mused, and his name was Derek.

Chapter Thirty-Four

During the next two weeks, Sheree's father made a remarkable recovery. She spent her days and early evenings at the hospital, but her nights were spent with Derek. He had never been to Philadelphia, so she took him sight-seeing. Of course, going with a vampire meant they went touring when most of the places were closed. Being whisked into museums when they were no longer open added a bit of excitement to viewing the Rodin and the Woodmere, or touring Independence Hall and the quaint home of Betsy Ross.

Sheree supposed it was inevitable that her mother would continue to delve into Derek's family, since Meredith was enthusiastic about genealogy and had spent considerable time and money tracing the Westerbrooke line.

Derek sidestepped her questions as best he could, claiming, truthfully, that he had no idea who his grandparents were, or where his mother and father had been born.

"Maybe I should just tell her the truth," Derek suggested one night as he and Sheree left the hospital.

"Oh, there's a good idea," Sheree retorted.

"Well, it would certainly keep her busy, trying to trace Mara's ancestry back to the time of the pharaohs."

"Does it ever just boggle your mind that she's so old? I can't even comprehend it."

"She's like a force of nature," Derek said, opening the car door. "You just have to hope you don't get in her way."

Sheree slid into the passenger seat. Sometimes it was hard to imagine that Derek's mother was a vampire. She was easily the most beautiful woman Sheree had ever seen, elegant and graceful. And deadly. For the first time, she wondered how many people Mara had killed. The number was probably in the thousands, considering how old she was.

Derek looked at Sheree, one brow arched in amusement as he started the car. "Thousands?"

She flushed with the realization that he was reading her thoughts, though why it continued to surprise her, she didn't know. "Too many? Not enough?"

"I have no idea, but I'm sure the number is considerable."

"She seems so nice."

"Nice?" Derek laughed as he pulled out of the parking lot. His mother was a lot of things, but he'd never thought of her as nice.

"Well, she's been nice to me."

He couldn't argue with that. Mara had taken a definite liking to Sheree. "So, where do you want to go tonight?"

"I don't know." Home was out of the question. Her mother would be there soon, and she just wasn't up to listening to Meredith quiz Derek about his family. She wasn't in the mood to go to the movies. She wasn't hungry. . . . She slid a glance at Derek. Well, not for food.

His gaze met hers, and the next thing she knew, they were pulling into a motel. She waited in the car while he registered, a million butterflies chasing each other in the pit of her stomach. She knew she was blushing when he got back into the car and drove them to their room.

"You okay with this?" Derek cut the engine, then got out

of the car and opened her door. "It's just a place to talk. I promise not to seduce you," he said solemnly. "Unless you ask me to."

If she hadn't been blushing before, she was now.

Speechless, she followed him inside. It was a lovely room, Sheree noted, but it was Derek who held her attention as he drew the drapes, shutting out the rest of the world.

She stood in the middle of the floor, acutely aware of the double bed behind her. And the tall, dark man standing in front of her.

"We can leave if you want," he said quietly.

She shook her head vigorously, wondering why being alone in a motel room seemed far more dangerous than being alone with Derek in her own home.

"Perhaps because no one knows where you are," he said, obviously reading her thoughts again.

He didn't move toward her, just stood there, watching her.

Predator and prey. The unwanted thought skittered through her mind.

"I think this was a bad idea," he said, moving toward the door. "Come on, I'll take you home."

Her instincts told her to flee while she could. Instead, she grabbed his arm. "I don't want to go home."

"Don't you?"

"I don't know what's wrong with me."

His gaze moved over her, his expression wry. "We've known each other only a short time," he remarked. "In spite of the strong attraction between us, we're still strangers to each other in many ways. Add to that the fact that I'm a vampire, and recently a werewolf, and I'd say you have every right to be uneasy." He trailed his knuckles along her cheek. "I know it upsets you that I can read your mind, but maybe it's a good thing."

"I don't think so."

He shrugged. "I need to know what you're thinking, especially when you don't want to tell me."

Sheree rested her cheek against his chest. How could he be so strong, so invincible, and so vulnerable at the same time? She should be afraid of him, yet all she wanted to do was protect him, comfort him. Love him.

She sighed when his arms slipped around her waist, closed her eyes when his lips brushed the top of her head. Right or wrong, dangerous or not, this was where she wanted to be.

He held her for a long time, then his thumb lifted her chin and he kissed her, slowly, deeply, as if he had all the time in the world.

Which he did, she thought as she kissed him back. She went up on her tiptoes, her arms twining around his neck as she pressed her body closer to his. He might have centuries, but she had only a few years, and she wanted to spend them all in his arms, legally and lawfully.

"Legally?" He whispered the word against her lips.

She drew back so she could see his face. "Will you marry me?"

He stared at her. Once again, she had surprised him.

"Will you?"

It was wrong on so many levels. Foolish to even consider. Dangerous for her in ways she couldn't imagine. And for him, too, because if he hurt her it would destroy him. But how could he refuse when he wanted her, needed her, more than his next breath? "When?"

"Now. Tonight."

He raked a hand through his hair. He had never considered marriage, but one thing he knew, most mortal females wanted a big wedding, a fancy dress, bridesmaids and parties. "Are you sure?"

She nodded, her gaze intent upon his face, her cheeks faintly pink. She looked beautiful and uncertain, and at that moment, he loved her beyond words.

Cupping her face in his hands, he kissed her lightly. "I'd be honored to have you as my wife."

It took only a few minutes of searching on his cell phone to locate a place that performed same-day weddings. The requirements were few: the couple must both be over eighteen and produce a valid photo ID. A marriage license could be obtained on the premises, the wedding performed immediately.

"Are you still sure you want to do this?" Derek asked.

"Yes."

"You won't be sorry later that we didn't get married in a church surrounded by your friends and family?"

"We can always get married with all the hoopla later," Sheree said. "But I want to do this now, before you change your mind."

As promised, there was no waiting. They filled out the license, showed their ID, and five minutes later they were standing in a small chapel decorated in green and white.

The officiator—she didn't know if he was a minister or not—entered the room moments later. He wore a dark suit and a striped tie. And a toupee that was slightly askew and kept slipping sideways until she was sure it was going to land on the floor in front of her. It was all Sheree could do to keep from giggling as she and Derek exchanged vows.

Once outside, the laughter she had been holding back

burst out of her. "Did you see . . . his hair . . . ? It looked like a raccoon perched on top of his head."

"How could I miss it?" Derek's laughter joined with hers. "I just hope the honeymoon lasts longer than the ceremony. And, speaking of honeymoons, where would you like to go?"

Taking a deep, calming breath, she said, "Surprise me."

He thought a moment, then wrapped her in his arms and whisked her to his house in Northern California.

"Where are we?" Sheree asked when the world righted itself again.

"Sacramento. This is my place."

"Oh. I thought you lived with Mara."

"No."

Nodding thoughtfully, she glanced around the living room. It was large, obviously the home of a single man. The walls were white. The seating, centered around a red brick fireplace, was dark leather; the tables were distressed walnut. There were no pictures on the walls, no knickknacks or magazines on the tables. Heavy curtains covered the windows; the floors were wood.

"Want to see the rest?" he asked.

"Of course."

Though it was a large house, there were only four rooms in addition to the front room: two good-sized bedrooms—one furnished, one not—with a full bath between, and a spacious kitchen that had no appliances and had obviously never been used.

"Have you lived here long?" she asked when they were settled on the sofa in front of the hearth.

"I had it built five years ago."

She looked up at him, eyes twinkling. "I'm surprised you included a kitchen."

His gaze caressed her. "Maybe I knew that someday you'd come along and need one."

She smiled as warmth flooded her being.

"I don't know what I'd do without you," he said, his voice so soft she wasn't sure she was meant to hear him.

She turned in his embrace, her lips seeking his as her hands delved under his shirt. He sucked in a breath at her touch, his tongue sliding across the seam of her lips, dipping inside to taste her own. It sparked an immediate response, her whole body throbbing with need, aching for more.

He lifted her onto his lap, his arms cradling her as he kissed her again and again, each one longer, deeper, more intense than the other, until the ache inside her grew almost painful.

In one fluid move, he gained his feet and carried her swiftly into the bedroom, his mouth never leaving hers as a flash of preternatural power removed her clothing and his, leaving her naked in his arms.

A wave of his hand drew back the blankets on the bed. The sheets were cool beneath her heated flesh. It was oddly erotic, his mouth hot as fire, his body cool as it covered hers.

Her hands were restless as they moved over him, exploring the breadth of his shoulders, the width of his biceps, the shallow indentation between his shoulder blades, the coolness of his skin.

He was exploring, too, arousing her with every intimate touch as he learned the contours of her body, the lush valleys, the warm peaks, the hidden places that made her cry out in ecstasy.

Sheree was lost in a world of sensual pleasure such as she had never imagined. She moaned softly, certain she might expire with need, when his body merged with hers. Somehow, she knew what he was thinking, feeling, even as he knew her thoughts and desires. She felt weightless, as if she were floating in air—every touch, every caress, leaving her breathless with the wonder of it, the joy of knowing that he was a part of her now in ways no one else had ever been, or ever would be.

He was hers, body and soul, for as long as she lived.

And in that one timeless moment when their bodies were one, when the rhythm of her heart matched his, she knew a single lifetime in his arms would never be enough.

Sheree gasped as he thrust deep inside her, carrying her beyond ecstasy, her whole being singing, throbbing, to the music of his touch. She clutched his shoulders, sighed as her body spiraled out of control, then sank slowly back to earth.

He shuddered once, then rolled onto his side, carrying her with him, their bodies still entwined.

"Are you all right?" His gaze moved over her, his expression filled with concern. "Did I hurt you?"

"Stop worrying." She smiled up at him, her fingertips stroking his cheeks, the taut muscle along his jaw. "Thank you for making my first time wonderful."

"Believe me, it was my pleasure."

"And mine."

His hands delved into her hair as he rained kisses on her cheeks, her brow, her eyelids. "I love you," he whispered. "You'll never know how much."

"No more than I love you."

"I think I might have gone over the edge if I hadn't had you with me these past few weeks. You don't know . . . I can't explain . . ." He swallowed hard, his arms tightening around her. "If you hadn't stopped me from killing that man and his family . . ." A long, shuddering sigh wracked his body. "I couldn't have lived with the guilt."

Sheree clung to him as images of Derek walking out to greet the dawn flashed across her mind. Horrified by the mere idea, she knew he would have let the sun destroy him if he had killed that baby.

"Don't think about it," she said, running her fingers through his hair.

"I can't help it. I'm afraid of what might happen next time."

"It'll be all right. I'll be with you. And maybe the old ladies' serum will work a miracle."

A miracle, Derek mused. Sheree was the biggest miracle in his life. Would Fate be so kind as to grant him another?

Chapter Thirty-Five

Sheree woke from a wonderful dream, only to discover it hadn't been a dream at all. Derek slept beside her, looking young and vulnerable at rest. Propped on one elbow, she slowly slid the covers down to his waist, letting her eyes drink in the beauty of her new husband.

Husband, she thought. What an amazing word.

If she touched him, would he feel it?

"Depends on where you touch."

She smiled as she placed her hand in the center of his chest, then slid it down, down, beneath the sheet.

He hissed in a breath. "Oh, yeah, I definitely feel that."

She laughed softly, then leaned over to press a kiss to his lips. "I need a hot shower and something to eat."

"They have a word for women like you."

"Really? What is it?"

He cracked one eye open. "Beautiful."

"I love you, too. Go back to sleep."

He caught her hand when she started to rise. "If you need to leave the house, call my mother and have her go with you."

Sheree frowned a moment, then nodded. She doubted anyone knew where they were, but, better safe than sorry.

After slipping out of bed, she went into the bathroom, which was state of the art, from the self-flushing toilet to the self-cleaning bathtub, shower and sink.

She lingered in the shower—which was big enough for two—for a long time, letting the deliciously hot water ease the pleasurable aches and pains in places she'd never had them before.

Mrs. Derek Blackwood. Mrs. Sheree Blackwood.

She couldn't believe she had proposed to him on the spur of the moment and he had accepted without a second thought.

What would her mother think?

Her mother!

Sheree turned off the water, wrapped herself in a towel, and ran into the living room, where she grabbed her cell phone from her handbag and quickly punched in her mother's number. How could she have been so thoughtless as to run off and get married without letting her mother know? Meredith must be frantic.

She answered on the first ring. "Sheree? Thank goodness! Are you all right? I've been calling you all morning."

"I'm sorry, I should have called you last night."

Meredith's sigh of relief was clearly audible. "Where are you?"

"I'm in Sacramento."

"Sacramento? What are you doing there?"

"I came with Derek."

"I see." There was no mistaking the censure in her mother's voice.

"It's not like that," Sheree said, her temper flaring.

"Isn't it?"

"We're not having an affair!" Sheree snapped. "We got married."

Her mother's huff of disapproval came through loud and clear, followed by a loud click as she disconnected the call.

"Well, what did you expect?" Sheree muttered. "Hearts and flowers?" When her stomach growled, she punched in a new number. "Hi, Mara, could you do me a favor?"

Derek's mother materialized in the living room five minutes later. "Is Derek all right?" she asked, glancing around.

"Yes, he's fine. I just, that is, I'm hungry and there's no food in the house."

Mara regarded her through unblinking eyes, nostrils flaring. "Not very hospitable of him to seduce a young woman and not stock the cupboards."

Sheree blushed from head to foot. She had planned to let Derek break the news to his mother, but she couldn't just stand there and let Mara think what she was obviously thinking.

"We got married last night," she said, her cheeks growing even hotter. "We didn't have time to shop."

Mara stared at her in disbelief. "He asked you to marry him?"

"Actually"—Sheree cleared her throat—"I asked him."

"Well, you're certainly not pregnant, so why the rush?"

First her own mother, Sheree thought, blinking back tears. And now Mara. It was just too much.

"I'm sorry," Mara said, "I didn't mean it to sound like that. I'm happy for you both. I just thought that when my son got married, I'd be there, and that Father Lanzoni would perform the ceremony."

"Who's Father Lanzoni?" Sheree sat down, her tears forgotten.

Mara sat beside her, smiling wistfully. "He's an old friend

of ours. He's officiated at all the weddings in our family. He'll be sorry we didn't ask him to officiate at yours."

"Well, Derek and I did talk about having another ceremony in the company of our friends and relatives. The one last night was rather brief, little more than the two of us saying 'I do.'"

"You really are an old-fashioned girl, aren't you?" Mara said, grinning. "Didn't want the honeymoon before the wedding?"

Sheree nodded, her cheeks growing even hotter.

Mara gave her hand a squeeze. "Welcome to the family. Derek is lucky to have you." She laughed softly when Sheree's stomach growled loudly. "Come on, daughter, let's get you something to eat," she said with a wink. "I have a feeling you'll need your strength when the sun sets."

Mara spent the day with Sheree, liking the girl more and more. There was an innocence about her new daughter-in-law that she admired. There was nothing pretentious about her. Honest of heart was the phrase that came to mind. It was a rare attribute among humans and vampires alike.

After taking Sheree to lunch, Mara insisted on taking her shopping at one of the finer clothing stores.

"You want to look your best for Derek, don't you? Every new bride needs a trousseau heavily stocked with sexy nightgowns and pretty underwear."

"I appreciate it, really I do, but"—Sheree gestured at the wealth of clothes scattered in the dressing room—"this is too much. And everything is so expensive."

"Child, I can afford it," Mara replied with a dismissive wave of her hand. "Consider it my wedding gift. And speaking of weddings, I'm going to need a new dress. After all, I'm the groom's mother."

Sheree watched in awe as Mara dismissed the salesclerk with a wave of her hand. She looked at several dozen gowns, rejecting all of them until she found one in emerald green.

She disappeared into a nearby dressing room. Moments later, she stepped out, announcing, "This is the one."

Sheree nodded in agreement. The dress fit Mara as if it had been made for her. The green silk was the exact color of her incredible eyes, and the narrow slit up the side was provocative without being too revealing.

"Now," Mara said, "all we need is to find a dress for you."

"Not today," Sheree said. "I'm exhausted."

Laden with packages, they left the mall a short time later.

"I don't know how to thank you," Sheree said as they climbed into a waiting taxi.

"No thanks are necessary, daughter. Just keep making my son happy."

"I promise I'll do my best."

Derek was reading the newspaper when Sheree and Mara returned. If he was surprised to see his mother, it didn't show, but then, Sheree thought, he had probably sensed that Mara had been there sometime during the day as soon as he woke up.

Laying the paper aside, he raised an inquiring brow when Sheree dumped a pile of bags and boxes on the floor. "Been shopping?" he asked dryly.

"I told your mother we were thinking of having another ceremony, for our families, and . . ."

Rising, he drew Sheree into his arms. "You don't have to say anything else."

"She bought me a trousseau, as well. Just wait until you see all my pretty new nightgowns and sexy undies," Sheree said, waggling her eyebrows. "She took me out to lunch, too. And to the grocery store," she added as the taxi driver carried several plastic bags into the living room.

"This way," Mara said, gesturing for the driver to follow her into the kitchen.

"Good evening, wife," Derek murmured, kissing Sheree's cheek.

She winked at him, wishing they were alone.

"Soon," he promised.

Mara paid the driver and sent him on his way. "Well, I guess I'll be going," she said. "I'm sure you two would like to be alone."

"How very perceptive of you," Derek drawled.

"I shall expect to see the two of you in a few days."

Derek nodded curtly. "We'll be there."

Mara kissed her son's cheek and gave Sheree a hug. "I ordered you a stove and a refrigerator too. They should be here tomorrow afternoon."

"Thanks, Ma."

"You know I hate it when you call me that," she said, but there was no anger in her voice. "Logan sends his love. Call us if you need us."

A wave of her hand, and she was gone in a shower of sparkling green motes.

"So, how was your day, really?" Derek asked.

"Wonderful. Your mother's really fun to be with. And a lot happier about our marriage than my mother."

"Trouble at home?" Sitting on the sofa, he settled her on his lap.

"She's upset that we eloped while my father is in the

hospital, and that I didn't marry the man she picked for me, and . . . Oh, I don't want to talk about her right now."

"We can go back to Philly so you can visit your father if you want."

"Are you sure you wouldn't mind?"

"Of course not. We'll go tomorrow night. I'd take you tonight, but it might be hard to explain how we got from here to there so fast, unless you want to tell your mother you married a vampire."

"That's a secret I think we'd better keep," Sheree said, kissing him on the cheek. "Thank you for being so understanding."

"Now that we've got that settled, maybe you can model some of that new underwear for me."

"Maybe," Sheree said, batting her eyelashes at him. "And maybe you'll model what I bought for *you*!"

Sheree's father was happy to see her. He welcomed Derek to the family, though he expressed his regret at missing the wedding.

"We're going to have another ceremony," Sheree said, squeezing his shoulder. "I'll expect you to be there to walk me down the aisle."

Brian glanced at his wife. "We wouldn't miss it, would we, Meredith?"

"Of course not," her mother replied coolly.

"Dad, when are you going home?" Sheree asked.

"I'm not sure, but it shouldn't be too long now," he replied, beaming. "As soon as the Doc springs me, I'll get my tux pressed and I'll be ready to give the bride away."

Sheree and Derek stayed until visiting hours were over, then walked her mother to her car.

Their good nights were strained at best.

"She'll get over it," Derek remarked, watching Mrs. Westerbrooke drive away.

"You don't know her like I do," Sheree said ruefully. "Come on, let's go home."

"Okay by me," Derek said with a wicked grin. "I can't wait to see more of that new underwear."

Chapter Thirty-Six

The next few days and nights passed without incident. The stove and refrigerator Mara had ordered arrived on schedule. Mara came by to take Sheree shopping again, this time for dishes, silverware, pots and pans, and a toaster. She refused to let Sheree pay for anything, insisting it was a wedding gift.

With Derek's okay, Sheree spent one morning rearranging the furniture in the living room, only to put it all back again the following morning.

Every afternoon, Mara took Sheree to the hospital to see her father so Sheree could spend her nights with Derek. Of course, Sheree had introduced Mara as Derek's sister, since her parents would never believe Mara was his mother, and, at this point, telling them the truth was not an option. Sheree doubted it ever would be.

She had floundered for an answer when her mother had asked how Derek's sister happened to be in Philadelphia, but Mara had stepped in, saying she had been on her way to Boston on vacation when Derek told her he and Sheree were in Philadelphia.

"I couldn't miss a chance to see my brother and his new

wife," she had lied smoothly. "After all, I can go to Boston anytime."

Meredith remained cool toward her daughter, often leaving the room while Sheree visited with her father.

Sheree was hurt at first, but the hurt soon turned to resentment. It was her life; she had a right to marry whomever she wished, and if her mother didn't like it . . . well, that was just too bad.

Sheree didn't mind spending her days with Mara, or even spending time alone, because she knew Derek would be there when night fell. He offered to take her anywhere she wanted to go, but she was content to stay home, as long as he was with her.

They watched TV or played cards or just spent time talking, getting to know each other better. Even though she sometimes felt as if she had known him all her life, she still had a lot to learn. He made love to her every night, sometimes on the floor in front of the hearth, sometimes in bed, once outside on the terrace under the stars.

But time and place didn't matter as long as she was in his arms, as she was now. Though she tried not to think about it, the full moon was only a few nights away. *What if that was all the time they had left?* she thought miserably. What if Pearl's untried serum didn't work? What if, instead of curing him, it . . .

She banished the thought from her mind. It would work. It had to work.

When his arms tightened around her, she knew he'd been reading her thoughts.

"I have to try it," he said quietly. "I can't go on like this."

Night after night, he had listened while she made plans for their upcoming wedding, all the while wondering if it would ever take place.

He hadn't told her how difficult it had been, the last few

nights, to be near her, or how hard it had been not to kill his prey when he hunted, or how he'd been eating raw meat on the sly for the last four nights. His craving for the stuff grew stronger with every passing day.

Knowing how she'd worry, he hadn't been able to bring himself to tell Sheree, but his mother knew. There was no way to hide it from her. Or from Logan.

"Are you all right?" Sheree asked.

"Sure. Why?"

"You seem so far away."

"Sorry." Forcing himself to relax, he nibbled her earlobe, ran his tongue along the side of her neck. "A taste?"

She tilted her head to the side. "You don't have to ask, you know."

He closed his eyes, inhaling the sweet scent of her skin, listening to the excited thrumming of her heart as she anticipated his bite. As always, it amazed him that she was so willing to give him what he needed.

She shivered with anticipation, sighed with pleasure as he drank from her.

It was both heaven and hell, he thought, an addiction for which there was no cure, a hunger like no other.

He sealed the tiny wounds, then kissed his way along the curve of her neck to her cheeks, her lips.

Murmuring his name, she wrapped her arms around him, willing to give him anything he desired. And he desired everything she had—heart and soul, mind and body. There was nothing gentle in his kisses this night. His rough caresses should have frightened her, perhaps, but she reveled in them, and in the certain knowledge that he would never hurt her.

He aroused her again and again, taking her to the point of fulfillment, then backing off, until she writhed wildly beneath him, sobbing for him to take her.

His release came hard upon the heels of her own. It left her feeling totally spent. And totally, forever, his.

After making certain Sheree was sound asleep, Derek dressed and left the room. A thought took him to the house in the Hollywood Hills, where his mother and Logan waited for him, along with Pearl and Edna.

He felt like an animal in an exhibit, the way they all stared at him, as if waiting for him to explode. And that was exactly how he felt, as if he might blow up at any minute and destroy everything and everyone in his path.

"How are you feeling?" Pearl asked.

"Like shit."

"Well, I guess that's to be expected." The elderly vampire's nose wrinkled. "You've been eating meat."

"It's either that or people," he growled.

"You mustn't eat any more," Pearl said. "It only feeds the werewolf and makes it stronger."

Derek dragged his hand across his jaw. "Now you tell me."

"I think she's right," Logan said. "I can smell the werewolf in you. I couldn't last time."

It wasn't surprising, Derek thought. He could feel the beast prowling inside him, eager to be released. It was stronger than before.

Hungrier than before.

"We were discussing how best to handle this before you arrived," Mara said. "We all think it would be wise to go back to Romania and inject you there, inside the dungeon, since we have no idea what your reaction will be."

He nodded, hands tightly clenched at his sides. "What are the odds of my surviving?"

"I'd say very good," Pearl answered. "You're young and

strong, with the best blood of our kind running through your veins. I'd say the worst that can happen is that you turn into a werewolf and remain that way. And once you learn to control the werewolf, as you've learned to control being a vampire"—she shrugged—"your problems should be over."

"Except for the people I kill along the way."

"Yes," Pearl said dryly. "There is that."

"The full moon is on the twenty-fifth," Mara said. "When does the serum need to be administered?"

"With the modifications we've made, I'm thinking it should be taken the night before," Pearl said. "Edna, what do you think?"

"Sounds right to me."

Mara glanced out the window. There were still a few hours until sunrise. "If we leave here by five, we can be there by three P.M. Romanian time." She looked at Edna and Pearl. "You can stay in the servants' quarters in the castle. There are no lights down there, so you should be able to rest comfortably until nightfall."

"What about Sheree?" Derek asked, his voice thick.

"She must go with us, of course."

Derek shook his head. "No!"

"She's all that saved you from killing the last time," Mara reminded him.

"It's too dangerous. No one should go with me except Pearl."

"What?" The old vampire's voice was little more than a squeak.

"Pearl, the serum, and a gun loaded with silver," Derek said. "Let's end this one way or another."

"Pearl is *not* going alone," Edna said, moving to stand beside her friend.

"And I'm certainly not staying here!" Mara exclaimed.

Logan put his arm around his wife's shoulders. "And your mother isn't going without me."

Mara smiled at her husband and then at her son. "We're all for one," she said in a voice that brooked no argument.

"And one for all," Logan added.

"You're all crazy as hell," Derek muttered. But he was damn glad to have his own musketeers at his side.

"You don't have to go with us," Derek said. "I can take you home to Philadelphia. You'll be safer there."

"Are you trying to get rid of me, Derek Blackwood?" Sheree asked, jabbing her finger against his chest. "Because if you are, you can just forget it. I'm your wife now, and my place is with you, wherever that might be."

Touched beyond words, he pressed his forehead to hers, closed his eyes, and breathed in her scent. His life might be a mess, but right now he wouldn't trade the woman in his arms for anything in the world.

"It'll be all right," Sheree murmured. "I know it will."

Lifting his head, he gazed deeply into her eyes. "I love you," he said fervently. "No matter what happens in the next couple of days, remember that."

She nodded, unable to speak past the lump in her throat.

Thirty minutes later, Derek transported the two of them, along with their luggage, to the castle in Transylvania.

Mara was waiting for them in the main room. "Logan is upstairs," she said. "Edna and Pearl are resting."

Derek nodded.

"I'll keep Sheree company while you rest."

"That won't be necessary," Sheree said. "I want to stay with Derek."

"Of course you want to spend as much time together as you can. I'll see you later, then."

"Thanks, Ma."

To his surprise, she gave him a fierce hug before vanishing from their sight.

Upstairs in their room, Derek undressed, then sat on the bed. "You don't have to stay here while I rest."

"I know, but I want to." Standing in front of him, she pulled her sweater over her head and tossed it aside. After stepping out of her sandals and jeans, she pushed him down on the mattress. "I just thought you'd like some company until you fall asleep."

"Is that what you thought?"

"Was I wrong?"

His gaze moved over her hot pink bra and panties. "What do you think?"

Straddling his hips, she leaned forward and licked his chest. "I think you want me."

"I think you're right." Wrapping his arms around her, Derek rolled over, pinning her beneath him, his weight pressing her into the mattress.

She's prey, the werewolf said. *Take her. It will make us stronger.*

Lowering his head, Derek sniffed Sheree's neck, then licked his lips. Young, tender flesh. Warm blood.

"Derek? Derek! You're scaring me."

Hands clenched, he rolled to his feet. "Get out of here."

She didn't argue. And she didn't run. Grabbing her clothes, she backed slowly out of the room and closed the door. Dressing quickly, she went downstairs, where she collapsed on the sofa and let the tears flow. Face buried in her hands, she prayed that the untried serum would work and that this whole nightmare would soon be nothing but a bad memory.

"Sheree, child, what's wrong?"

She looked up at the sound of Mara's voice. "Everything."

"He sent you away."

"It's not just that. It's . . . it's not knowing what's going to happen. What if he stays a werewolf? Will he still be the same Derek he is now? Will he still love me? Will I still love him?" She dashed the tears from her eyes. "What if the serum doesn't work? What if it . . . ?" She couldn't say the words.

Compassion and tenderness didn't come naturally to Mara. She had lived too long, seen too much, killed too many. You couldn't live as long as she had lived and remain sane if you let the feelings of others affect you. She had learned to be strong, to put her needs above those of others. It was the only way to survive.

But she couldn't ignore the pain in Sheree's eyes, or the hurt in her voice. Sitting beside the girl, Mara slipped one arm around her shoulders. "Whatever happens, we are all in this hell together."

Sheree glanced at her surroundings—the high ceilings, the leaded windows, the antique tapestries. "Sometimes it all seems like a dream, especially in this place. I never believed in magic, but I always believed in vampires. At least I thought I did, until I actually met one and he was nothing like I expected."

"What did you expect?"

"I'm not sure. I know now that I was horribly naïve. I thought I could find one and that would be the end of it. But Derek . . . there was something between us from the moment we met. He's so strong. So powerful. And yet he's vulnerable."

She drew in a shuddering breath. "I need him in ways I don't understand. And he needs me."

"Vampires can be complicated creatures. Like humans, we all have our strengths and our weaknesses. Those who are made generally don't change too much. If they were decent people as mortals, they usually retain that decency, at least as much as possible. Those who are wicked tend to become even more wicked. I guess it's inevitable, given all the power that comes with being a vampire."

"But Derek wasn't made."

"No. He carries his father's goodness, and his mother's evil."

Sheree blinked at Mara. "Evil?"

"I've done terrible things in my time." Mara stared into the distance. "I killed people who didn't deserve it and took pleasure in it. I forced the Dark Gift on those who didn't want it and went blissfully on my way. Some, like Logan, survived. Others destroyed themselves."

"You made Logan a vampire?"

Mara nodded. "He should have hated me for it."

"But he doesn't."

"No. But others did. And they're not all dead."

"Did you want to be a vampire?"

"No. I was turned against my will." She slid a glance at Sheree. "I know what you're thinking. If I was turned against my will, why did I do it to others? I have no answer except that I was angry. My sire turned me and abandoned me, and I often did the same. I have no excuse for my callous behavior except that, mortal or vampire, I was selfish and thoughtless."

"Did you turn Pearl and Edna?"

"No. I would have killed them. Back then, they were trying to find a serum to cure the vampires and the were-wolves and the shape-shifters. . . ."

"Shape-shifters?"

"Yes. People who are two-natured—animal and human. Not like werewolves, who are compelled to change. Anyway, Rafe and his wife were caught up in Pearl and Edna's experiments. I was all for killing the old bats, but Rafe was too softhearted. He turned them instead. And now, if Pearl's serum works, I will be forever in her debt. And Edna's, too."

"Who's Rafe? I think Derek mentioned him once."

"I turned Rafe's father, Vince Cordova, on a whim. Such a handsome young man. He married a mortal girl, Cara, and fathered twins, Rane and Rafe. To my knowledge, his twins and Derek are the only vampires ever born to our kind."

"Does Vince hate you?"

"No. We're family now. Rane and Rafe are both married. Rane has a daughter, Abbey. She's in New York, studying to be an actress. Perhaps you'll meet her one day."

Nodding, Sheree squeezed Mara's hand. "Thank you for taking my mind off our troubles for a little while."

"I'm glad I could help. You've been good for Derek. If there's ever anything you want, anything you need, you have only to ask."

"I just want him to be happy."

"No more than I," Mara murmured. "No more than I."

Chapter Thirty-Seven

Derek stood out of sight in the hallway, hands tightly clenched at his sides as he eavesdropped on the conversation between his mother and his wife. He hated being the cause of their concern, but dammit, it wasn't his fault that his mother was a vampire or that she had married a werewolf! He didn't know why the hell he felt guilty, but he did.

Guilty and hungry as hell.

A thought took him outside. The air was cool and crisp, the sky awash with stars. Standing there, he opened his senses, inhaling the fragrance of damp earth and trees. Shoving his hands into his pockets, he strolled around the perimeter of the castle before heading down the mountain.

He hadn't gone far when he sensed other predators nearby. Pausing, he searched the darkness. Three gray wolves stared back at him, their eyes glowing yellow in the moon's light.

Hackles raised, the bigger of the three growled a warning.

Baring his fangs, Derek took a step forward, an answering growl rising in his own throat.

For a moment, he thought they would challenge him and he relished the idea of a fight, hoping it would release some of the tension building in him.

The big male growled again, then, as one, the three wolves turned tail and disappeared into the darkness.

Was it the vampire they feared, he wondered as he continued down the mountainside, or did they sense the werewolf trapped inside, struggling to get out?

He found his prey in a smoke-filled bar on a quiet street. Only the thought of Sheree kept him from tearing into the woman's jugular and draining her dry.

Filled but not satisfied, he sent the woman away and returned home.

The castle was dark. Mara and Logan were in bed, but not asleep.

Edna and Pearl weren't in the castle. Out hunting, perhaps?

Sheree was sleeping, but not in their room.

Frowning, Derek followed her scent up the stairs. He uttered a vile oath when he found her sleeping on a pile of blankets on the floor in one of the unfurnished bedrooms.

He picked her up, blankets and all, and carried her to his bedroom. Still half asleep, she murmured his name as she wrapped her arms around his neck and snuggled against him.

Something melted inside him when she whispered, "Don't go," as he lowered her onto the mattress.

After tucking her under the covers, he tossed the other blankets aside.

"Derek?"

"I'm here."

"Stay with me."

He dragged his hand across his jaw; then, before he could talk himself out of it, he undressed and slid in beside her.

She scooted closer, one arm stretching over his belly, her head resting on his shoulder. She smelled of soap and shampoo. And woman. His woman.

Whispering, "I'm sorry," into the wealth of her hair, he wrapped her in his arms. "Forgive me."

"There's nothing to forgive." She smiled at him in the darkness. "How could I be angry with you for being afraid you'll hurt me?" She stroked his cheek. "Are you all right?"

He nodded. "Why were you sleeping on the floor in the other room?"

"This is where you take your rest. You didn't seem to want to be with me. . . ."

"Sheree, love, I can rest anywhere. And I always want you with me, even when I should know better."

"Are you thirsty?"

"I fed."

"Was it enough?"

He closed his eyes, trying to resist the urge to drink from her. His need made him feel weak, helpless. Hardly the way a man wanted to appear in the eyes of the woman he loved. He was a vampire, top of the food chain, almost indestructible, yet he was humbled by her love for him, and his need for her.

"It wasn't enough, was it? You're still thirsty."

"Are you reading my mind now?" he muttered darkly.

"I don't know, but I can feel your hunger."

With a low groan, he took what she offered. The warmth of her life's blood flowed through him, the sweetness of it soothing the raging beast inside.

Derek woke the next afternoon to find Sheree asleep, pressed close to his side. Frowning, he glanced at the window, surprised to find that he was awake and the sun was shining. He had always been able to be active when the sun was up, if necessary, but he rarely woke before the setting of the sun.

Lightly stroking Sheree's hair, he wondered if it was yet another symptom of the changes taking place inside him.

Sheree stirred, yawned, and then rolled over, her eyes widening in surprise when she saw he was awake. "Is something wrong?"

"Not that I know of."

"But . . ."

"How do you feel about making love in the daytime, wife?"

"I don't know. I've never done it."

He trailed his fingertips down her arm. "Would you like to give it a try?"

"Maybe."

"Maybe?"

"Oh, just kiss me, you idiot!"

Muttering, "Don't ask me twice," he turned onto his side and pulled her body against his.

Before she knew it, her nightgown was on the floor.

"What fast hands you have, Mr. Blackwood."

"The fastest."

Tossing the covers aside, Sheree straddled his hips. She had never seen him fully naked in broad daylight. His skin was cool and smooth beneath her curious fingers, his muscles were well-defined, his chest lightly furred with soft, curly black hair.

He watched her through heavy-lidded eyes, content to let her explore to her heart's content.

He opened his senses and invited her inside, letting her feel what he felt, hear what he was thinking as she aroused him. And then, in the blink of an eye, he turned the tables on her. She welcomed the weight of his body on hers, lifted her hips to receive him, all the while knowing his thoughts, his desires. It was an amazing experience, feeling his passion mingle with her own, the way he held back his own release until, crying his name, she shuddered with pleasure.

He rolled onto his side, his body still a part of hers as her body cooled and their breathing returned to normal.

He whispered that he loved her, and in his mind, she read his regret that the words were inadequate to express how much she meant to him, how desperately he needed her.

"I don't need the words," she murmured, kissing his cheek. "But it's nice to know."

Later, while Derek slept, Sheree bathed and dressed, then went in search of Mara. She found her in the castle's great hall, playing chess with Logan. Since there was no sign of Edna and Pearl, Sheree assumed they were at rest somewhere below.

Mara glanced up when Sheree entered the room. The knowing look in her eyes made Sheree blush clear down to her toes.

"Is it time to go see your father?" Mara asked.

"If you don't mind taking me."

"Of course not." Rising, she pointed a finger at Logan. "Don't be moving any of those pieces while I'm gone."

"Who, me?" He blinked up at her, his expression one of total innocence.

"We won't be long." Leaning down, Mara kissed her husband, then took Sheree's hand. "Ready? Here we go."

When they arrived at the hospital, they found her father dressed and ready to go home.

He smiled warmly when he saw her. "Hey, pumpkin!" he exclaimed, folding her in his arms. "You're just in time to get me out of this place."

"Where's Mother?"

"Oh, she had a meeting with the mayor this morning. I was just about to call her. The doctor decided to let me go home a day early. This way we can surprise her." He nodded at Mara, standing in the doorway. "Miss Blackwood, how nice to see you again."

"Thank you. You're looking much better."

Just then, a nurse bustled into the room pushing a wheelchair. "All set, Mr. Westerbrooke?"

"Yes, indeed, Jeannie." He settled himself in the chair. "Let's go. Grab my suitcase, will you, pumpkin?"

"Sure, Dad."

Sheree and Mara trailed her father and the nurse into the elevator and down to the lobby.

"If you bring your car around to the front of the hospital, we'll meet you there," the nurse said.

Sheree glanced at Mara. They hadn't come by car.

"I'll get it," Mara said. "Just give me a few minutes."

Sheree smiled reassuringly at her father, even as she wondered what car Mara intended to get.

The vampire returned a few minutes later. Keeping her curiosity in check, Sheree followed Mara and her father out of the hospital, felt her eyes widen when Mara opened the passenger door of a late-model sedan.

After settling her father in the front seat and stowing his suitcase in the trunk, Sheree climbed into the backseat.

Mara engaged Brian in small talk on the short ride to the Westerbrooke house.

"I'm not sure I should go in," Sheree said when Mara pulled into the driveway.

"Of course you're coming in," her father said.

"I'm sure Mother doesn't want to see me right now any more than I want to see her."

"Sheree, that's not true!"

"Yes, it is. She's never going to forgive me for marrying Derek."

Brian sighed. "Just give her some time," he urged, getting out of the car.

Sheree joined him on the sidewalk, waited while he got his suitcase out of the trunk. "I'm glad you're feeling better, Dad. I'll call you when I can."

"I love you, pumpkin."

"I love you, too. Take care of yourself."

"You, too."

Blinking back her tears, Sheree slid into the front seat. She waved at her dad as Mara pulled away from the curb.

"I take it your mother's not happy with your choice of a mate," Mara remarked.

"No. She had a husband and a life all picked out for me."

"Well, at least she didn't abandon you in an alley when you were a child."

"Is that what happened to you?"

"It was a long time ago," Mara said. "And yet it still stings."

"I'm sorry," Sheree murmured, though it seemed odd to offer sympathy for something that had happened so long ago. She was curious to know how Mara had survived. Surely someone had adopted her.

"Perhaps I'll tell you the story one of these days."

Sheree nodded, thinking she would love to hear it. But there was something else she was curious about. "Where did you get this car?"

"I . . . uh, borrowed it from a parking lot. And right now, we're going to return it before someone misses it. And then we're going home."

Home, Sheree thought. Nothing had ever sounded so good.

* * *

It was dark when Sheree and Mara returned to the castle. Logan, Derek, Edna, and Pearl were seated in the great hall. Sheree noted they all looked well fed. It was easy to see once you knew what to look for.

Sheree hugged Derek and exchanged greetings with the other three vampires, but her attention was fixed on the large brown case on one of the side tables. She shivered as Edna lifted the lid and rummaged inside. For better or worse, Sheree thought, her future lay inside that ugly brown box.

"So," Pearl said, lifting a small bottle from the case, "tomorrow night we'll administer this and then . . ." She shook the vial, causing the dark red liquid to slosh back and forth.

"And then what?" Sheree asked, her voice sharper than she intended. Her blood was in the mix, after all.

"We'll just have to wait and see," Edna answered.

"Am I supposed to drink it?" Derek asked, eying the bottle's contents.

"Yes, dear. It should be quite tasty, if a little tart."

"The original serum was given by injection," Mara said.

Edna nodded. "But Pearl thinks, in this case, drinking it will be more effective and faster acting."

"What's the gun for?" Sheree asked.

"For you, dear," Pearl said. "It's loaded with silver."

"Why do I need a gun?" Sheree asked, and immediately felt as if she had just asked the stupidest question in the world as all eyes swung in her direction. "Oh."

Derek slipped his arm around her shoulders. "It was my idea. Silver isn't just effective against vampires," he said flatly. "But werewolves, too."

"You don't expect me to shoot you?"

"Damn right! If I come after you, it's the only thing that will stop me."

Logan glanced at Mara. "So, what's the plan? We lock

Derek in the dungeon, slip him the serum, and hope for the best?"

"It doesn't sound like much when you put it that way," Derek said.

"Have you got a better plan?" Mara asked.

"After you lock me up, don't let Sheree out of your sight. I don't want a repeat of what happened last time, if I can help it."

"I want to stay with you," Sheree said.

"No! Not this time. No one knows how this stuff will affect me. I don't want you anywhere near me." He held up one hand, staying the argument he saw coming. "This isn't open for discussion, wife." He placed his hands on her shoulders and gazed into her eyes. "I've put your life in danger too many times already. I won't knowingly do it again."

Pearl cleared her throat. "I think you should feed again tonight," she said, placing the vial back in the case. "Drink as much as you can hold. It will strengthen your resistance. And whatever you do, don't eat any meat."

"All right. Anything else?"

"If Sheree's willing, you should drink from her, as well."

"Of course," Sheree said, "as much as he needs."

"Anything else?" Derek asked gruffly.

"I think that about covers it," Pearl said. "Edna?"

"Nothing comes to mind."

"If we're done here," Derek said, taking Sheree by the hand, "I'm going to go make love to my wife."

Chapter Thirty-Eight

Later that night, Sheree lay curled against Derek's side. He had made love to her with such exquisite tenderness, it had brought tears to her eyes because every kiss, every caress, had felt like good-bye.

He ran his fingertips along her lower lip. "Don't be sad, love."

"Is it possible to be happy and sad at the same time?"

His knuckles slid ever so lightly down her chin to the curve of her throat. "I can't be sad while you're with me." His gaze moved over her face, as if to memorize every line. "However this turns out, always remember I love you."

Sheree blinked back her tears. "Everything will be all right. I have to believe that. You have to believe that. I don't want to go on without you. No matter what happens, we'll face it together."

"All right, wife," he said with a wry smile.

She placed her hand on his chest, her fingers curling in his hair. "Are you tired?"

He snorted softly. "Hardly." His gaze moved to her throat.

"Pearl said you need to feed again."

"Yeah."

"Can I go with you?"

"What?" Sitting up, he raked his fingers through his hair, then swung his legs over the edge of the bed, putting his back toward her. "No way."

"Why not? You watch me eat."

He swung around to face her, eyes blazing. "Dammit, Sheree, it's hardly the same thing!"

"It's not like I don't know what you do."

"Some things are best done in private," he muttered.

"What are you afraid of?"

"What do you think?" His gaze met hers, his eyes dark, haunted.

She read the answer in his eyes before he turned away from her again.

He was afraid, she realized, afraid that she would no longer see him as a man, but as a monster. Even though she knew he was a vampire, even though she had given him her own blood and would gladly do so again, he didn't want her to see him hunt his prey. It was almost as if he was ashamed of what he had to do to survive.

And even as the thought crossed her mind, she knew that was the real answer.

"I'm sorry. I shouldn't have asked such a thoughtless thing." She laid a tentative hand on his back. "Forgive me?"

"There's nothing to forgive."

"You should go."

He nodded once, briefly, grabbed his clothes, and was gone.

"You're an idiot, Sheree Blackwood." With a sigh of exasperation, she pounded her fist on the pillow. "How could you have been so blasted stupid?"

Derek found an upscale nightclub in the nearest city. There had been a time when bars closed, usually around two A.M., but these days, you could always find one that stayed open all night.

He ordered a glass of wine and carried it to a small table in the shadows. There were only a few people in the place at this hour—lonely people who didn't want to go home, or those just getting off work who needed to unwind a little before going to bed. Sad, unhappy people, mostly. One young woman sat alone at the end of the bar. She downed two drinks, one after the other, then sat there, staring at the empty glasses.

Derek sipped his drink, thinking about Sheree's request. Of all the things she could have asked him, that was one thing he had never considered. Growing up, he had watched his mother hunt. At times, she was gentle as she seduced her victims, taking only what she needed, wiping the memory from their minds. But she could be a ruthless predator when the occasion called for it. He had seen her kill on several occasions—quickly, cleanly, with no regrets, no apologies.

Sheree had seen the violence in him, but those occasions had been to protect her life, or his own. She had never seen him hunt his prey; if he had his way, she never would.

When the young woman left the bar, he followed her down the street. Taking care to block his link to Sheree, he called his prey to him and took what he wanted.

It was near dawn when Derek returned to the castle. Sheree was asleep, her cheek pillowed on her hand, her face damp with tears.

"I'm sorry," he whispered.

"So am I."

"I thought you were sleeping."

"I was waiting for you."

"Sheree, I . . ."

"Shh, you don't have to explain. I think I understand."
Sitting up, she brushed her hair behind her ear. "You need to
drink from me."

He shook his head. "No."

"Pearl said . . ."

"I don't give a damn what she said!"

"Please, if it will help, you've got to."

He wanted to lash out, to drive his fist against the wall, to
bewail the fate that had cursed him with the blood of not one
monster, but two. And then, perhaps feeling guilty, that same
fate had sent him an angel to ease his pain.

He groaned low in his throat as he sat on the bed, drew
her into his arms, and took what he so desperately needed.

Derek slept all that day.

Slipping out of bed, Sheree washed up in the basin on the
dresser, thinking how happy she would be to get back home.
She didn't know how people had survived without showers
and hot running water in the old days, but she sorely missed
the wonders of the modern world—especially flush toilets!

After drying off with a fluffy white towel, she pulled on
a pair of jeans and a sweater, then sat on the edge of the bed,
watching him sleep, until Mara insisted she come downstairs
and have something to eat.

"I'm really not hungry," Sheree said, following the vampire
into the kitchen.

"You have to eat," Mara said. "Giving Derek your blood
drains you, whether you think it does or not. You need to
keep your strength up, too."

"Is there anything you don't know?"

Mara smiled faintly. "Derek is my son. Our connection

runs deeper than merely mother and child. Even when we're apart, I know when he's troubled, when he's hurting. Last night, you insisted he needed nourishment. Take your own advice."

Knowing it was useless to argue, Sheree made herself a peanut butter and jelly sandwich and a cup of tea.

Mara sat across the table from her while she ate. "I wish I could tell you not to worry, but we're all afraid. If I lose him . . . I don't think I'd want to go on."

Sheree stared at the other woman, startled by her words. Mara was strong, the oldest, most powerful vampire ever known. It was somehow hard to imagine the world without her in it.

"What kind of talk is that?" Striding into the kitchen, Logan stood beside his wife, glaring down at her. "The two of you are sitting here acting like he's already dead."

"You don't understand," Mara retorted. "You'll never understand!"

"Don't give me that crap. My blood might not run in his veins, but he's my son as much as yours. Now, both of you, stop with all the doom and gloom."

Mara pushed away from the table, then threw herself into Logan's arms.

Cupping her face in his hands, he gazed into her eyes. "I don't ever want to hear you talking like that again, because if you destroy yourself, you'll be destroying me, too, and I'm not ready to go."

Sheree glanced away as they kissed. She couldn't help envying the two of them. They were deeply in love. They would never grow old or sick or helpless. Mara would always be as beautiful and powerful as she was now, Logan as handsome and strong.

As quietly as she could, she left the kitchen and returned to Derek's bedroom. Almost, it would be worth becoming a vampire if it meant spending centuries with him instead of a few short years.

Resuming her place on the foot of the bed, she tried to imagine what it would be like to be forever young and in love.

Sheree was still there when Derek woke that night. Frowning, he sat up, his gaze darting around the room. "What are you sitting here for?"

She shrugged, her gaze sliding away from his.

"Is everything all right?"

"You tell me." The moon would be full tomorrow night. "How are you feeling?"

"Restless." He looked at her throat, then jerked his gaze away. "Hungry."

She turned her head to the side. "Drink, then."

"Not now." Muscles tense, he pulled on a pair of jeans and a T-shirt and stalked out of the room.

Sheree followed a moment later. She found him downstairs, along with Mara, Logan, and Pearl.

The brown case lay open on the table. She tried not to stare at the bottle of red liquid, or the pistol beside it.

Sheree didn't know which unnerved her more, the sight of the vial, or the weapon. The thought of pointing the gun at Derek sent a chill down her spine. The thought of pulling the trigger, even to save her own life, made her sick to her stomach. She would rather die herself than take the life of the man she loved.

"I'm here," Derek said flatly. "Let's get it over with."

"You need to feed before you take the serum," Pearl said. "And with that in mind, we brought you a gift."

Derek's head jerked up, nostrils flaring, when Edna entered the room, pushing a young girl in front of her. The girl's expression was blank; she couldn't have been more than sixteen or seventeen.

"No!" Derek backed away, his expression stricken. "Get her out of here."

"You must feed," Pearl said.

"I've been hunting on my own since I was fourteen," he snarled. "I don't need you to do it for me."

"Derek . . ."

"I said no!" His anger filled the room in a swirl of crackling black sparks. Before anyone could stop him, he shoved the vial into his pants pocket, grabbed the gun and Sheree, and transported the two of them into the hills above the castle.

Setting Sheree on her feet, he shoved the gun into her hand.

"No! I don't want it!"

"You might need it."

She shook her head. "I don't know how to use a gun."

"It's easy. Just point the damn thing and pull the trigger. I'm a big target."

Sheree glared at him, then threw the pistol down the hill. "You can't always have everything your way."

He snorted. "You think I can't find it?"

"I'll just throw it away again."

With a shake of his head, he turned away from her.

Sheree glanced around. There was nothing to be seen for miles but acres of forest. And the moon slowly climbing higher in the sky.

"Derek, what are we doing here?"

"I had to get out of there. All of them watching me, waiting for me to . . . to . . . hell, I don't know what."

She nodded, every instinct she possessed urging her to flee even as the rational part of her mind told her that was the worst thing she could do. He was a predator. She was prey. If she ran, he would give chase.

He paced back and forth, restless as a caged animal. Tension radiated from him like heat from a blast furnace. When he glanced her way, his eyes were tinged with red.

She cringed when he grabbed her hand. "Come on." His voice was rough, like sandpaper dragged over stone.

"Where are we going?"

"You wanted to see me feed, didn't you?"

Before she could reply, they were on a dark street in a city she didn't recognize. Keeping a tight hold on her hand, he tugged her along behind him, lifting his head now and then to sniff the air.

A short time later, he scented his prey. She knew it by the feral gleam in his eyes when they began to follow a middle-aged woman. Sheree wanted to cry out, to warn the woman she was in danger, but found she couldn't.

Helpless, Sheree trailed behind Derek as he followed the woman out of the town square and down a deserted street. When he called to her, she stopped walking.

"You will stay here," he told Sheree.

Nodding, she whispered, "Pease don't kill her."

He didn't answer, only growled softly before going to the woman.

Sheree couldn't be sure, but she thought he spoke to her, and then he folded her into his embrace, his head lowering to her neck, his hair falling forward so Sheree couldn't see what he was doing. But she didn't need to see to know. Almost as if it were happening to her, she knew what Derek was feeling as he drank from the woman. It was more than nourishment, though she had no words to describe it, only a sense of fulfillment, as if she had been empty before.

It was over in minutes. In her mind, she heard him tell the woman to forget what had happened, to go home and rest.

Smiling, the woman went on her way.

Sheree's heart skipped a beat when Derek strode toward her, his eyes dark. His arm slid around her waist, holding her tight as he transported them back to the hills above the castle.

His eyes glittered with a fierce light. "Now you."

She turned her head to the side, heart pounding wildly, hands clenched at her sides.

"Don't be afraid, wife. I won't hurt you."

"I . . . I'm not afraid."

His laughter mocked the fear she couldn't hide. "Aren't you?"

"Just take what you need."

"Ah, Sheree." His laughter stilled as he drew her gently into his embrace and inhaled her scent. "You are all that stands between me and madness." He cupped her face in his hands, lowered his head, and kissed her, a sweetly lingering kiss that chased all the doubts and fears from her mind. Vampire or werewolf, she knew he would never hurt her.

Sheree slid her arms around his neck as he deepened the kiss, sighed as the rest of the world fell away and there was only the two of them, locked in each other's arms at the top of the world. She leaned into him, wanting to be closer, closer, to taste him and touch him, to rake her nails down his back, to mark him as hers.

But there was no time. The moon would be full tomorrow night. He still needed to drink her blood and then the serum.

But he seemed to have forgotten that as he carefully lowered her onto the ground. Aware that this might be their last night together, he made love to her slowly, arousing her again and again, only to pull back, drawing out the pleasure until, at last, he sank into her, his body becoming one with hers, flesh to flesh.

"Heart to heart," she murmured as he moved deep within her.

"And soul to soul." He whispered the words in her ear as, with one last thrust, he carried her to the stars and back.

Much later, when they were dressed again, he pulled the vial from his pocket. Holding it up, he turned it this way and that. It glowed with an eerie luminescence in the moon's light.

"Like the eyes of a monster," he remarked bleakly.

"Like the eyes of the man I love," she corrected, brushing a kiss across his cheek.

His gaze moved to her throat.

"Now?" she asked.

He blew out a breath, then drew her slowly into his arms. As always, only a few sips of her precious blood soothed and satisfied him as nothing else. He sealed the wounds, then, refusing to meet her gaze, he turned his back toward her.

"Derek . . ." She started to touch him, then withdrew her hand. "If things were the other way around and I needed your blood, you'd give it to me, wouldn't you? Without question?"

He nodded curtly.

"How is this any different?"

He pivoted to face her. "It just is, dammit!"

"There's nothing wrong with needing something from the one you love."

He snorted softly.

"What's really bothering you?" She frowned, then snapped her fingers. "It's your stupid masculine pride, isn't it? Needing my blood makes you feel weak." She shook her head. "Why is needing my blood any worse than needing anyone else's to survive?"

"Because I'm not in love with them. When I'm hunting,

they're prey, nothing more. I don't see you that way. And you'd better hope I never do."

"I love you, too." She kissed his cheek, then took the vial from his hand and removed the cap. "What do you think is in here?"

"Wolf's bane. Your blood. Mara's blood. A handful of herbs, a dash of hemlock."

"Hemlock!" Sheree exclaimed. "That's poison, isn't it?"

"Maybe it'll kill the werewolf."

She glowered at him. "And you with it."

"I guess there's only one way to find out."

"Are you sure this is a good idea?" She stared at the vial. In the dark, the contents looked thick and black.

"Have you got a better one?"

She worried her lower lip with her teeth, then shook her head. "No, but I don't trust Edna and Pearl to have your best interests at heart. No one knows what it will do to you." She took his hand in hers. "I'd rather have a husband who was a vampire and a werewolf than no husband at all."

"It's a chance we'll have to take, love. I can feel the moon calling to me. If this shit doesn't work, tomorrow night I'll have to answer."

"I'm scared, Derek. Please don't drink it. I have a bad feeling about this."

He lifted one brow. "Woman's intuition?"

"Maybe. I don't know." She shook her head again. "I just know something's not right."

"I almost killed a man last month," he said quietly. "I don't want to be that out of control ever again."

"I don't know much about vampires, but it seems to me that the more often you drink from me, the stronger our bond becomes. Maybe, between the two of us, we can control your urge to kill."

"And maybe we can't."

"Then let's wait and see what happens. If you can't control it, we can always try the serum next month."

Derek stared at the bottle in her hand. Truth be told, he wasn't crazy about drinking some untested concoction either, but he was desperate enough to try anything that might work. "What if I go on a killing spree tomorrow night? Do you want that on your conscience?"

She squeezed his hand. "You won't be able to kill anyone if we lock you up. This time I'll make sure your mother stays with me so you can't compel me."

"All right, love," he agreed. "We'll try it your way. I just hope to hell we're doing the right thing."

With a sigh of relief, Sheree emptied the bottle's contents onto the ground. Deep inside, she knew it was the right thing to do.

And yet, what if she was wrong?

What if she had talked Derek into something they would both live to regret?

Chapter Thirty-Nine

The morning of the twenty-fifth dawned cold and overcast, with the promise of rain before nightfall. Sheree woke early after a restless night. She'd had nightmares in the past—more so since meeting Derek. But the ones she'd had last night had been horrible in the extreme.

Thankfully, she remembered only bits and pieces, but what she remembered was enough to make her break out in a cold sweat. Derek had turned into the very monster he feared—a soulless beast with no conscience, and no memory of who he had been. He had chased her through an endless forest until, at last, she had found what she thought was a safe hiding place behind a waterfall, only to discover Mara waiting for her, death shining in her cold green eyes.

The worst nightmare had been the last, when Derek—his body twisted into some grotesque creature that was half vampire and half werewolf—tied her to the bed and then invited Mara, Logan, and the two elderly vampires to come in and drink their fill.

Sitting up, bracing her back against the headboard, Sheree wrapped her arms around her waist. What if the serum would have worked? Maybe it would have cured Derek of being both vampire and werewolf, giving them a

chance for a normal life together. Last night, disposing of
the serum had seemed like the right thing to do. Why did it
feel so wrong now, when the serum was gone and it would
take weeks to make a new batch?

Telling herself that she was worrying for nothing, that
everything would be all right, she glanced to her left, where
Derek lay sleeping beside her. Propped on one elbow, she
let her gaze move over him. For a man who was supposed to
be dead and didn't spend hours at the gym, he had a remarkable physique, one she never tired of looking at. Or touching.

He stirred when she slid her fingertips over his chest,
opened one eye when she licked his navel.

"Is there something you want, wife?" he asked.

"Maybe."

"Well, make up your mind," he said, yawning.

"You don't seem very interested," she retorted.

"Don't I?" He gestured at the sheet, tented over his groin.
"Does that look like I'm not interested?"

Flinging the sheet aside, she straddled his hips, then
leaned down to kiss him, her bare breasts grazing his chest.

"Now that's worth staying awake for." He slid his hands
up and down her back. "Oh, yeah," he said, nipping her earlobe. "I could get used to waking up to this."

Sheree smiled and wriggled against him, the movement
eliciting a low groan of pleasure from Derek. But she
couldn't silence the little voice in the back of her mind that
whispered this might be the last morning they ever spent
together.

It was early evening when Sheree tiptoed downstairs.
After taking a few steps, she chided herself for trying to be
quiet in a castle full of vampires. If they were awake, they
could hear every beat of her heart, every breath she took.

For all she knew, they could even hear her when they were at rest.

The place was eerily silent as she made her way into the kitchen and rummaged around for something to eat, only to find that she had no appetite. She couldn't think of anything but Derek. What would happen at moonrise? Had it been a mistake to beg him not to take the serum? What if something terrible happened because she had talked him out of it?

She hadn't known her vampire very long, but she couldn't imagine her life without him.

Too restless to sit still, she wandered around the great hall, studying the tapestries. They were huge, hanging from the ceiling to the floor, some almost as wide as the walls. One depicted a hunting scene, the other a bloody battle. She wondered how old they were, and who had made them, and who, if anyone, had owned the ancient castle before Mara.

Moving to one of the narrow, leaded windows, she stared outside. Raindrops splashed against the window, blurring the view. But it didn't matter. There was little to see but dark clouds and trees swaying in the wind.

Where was Mara? Why did the castle seem more quiet than usual? Had they all gone home and left her behind?

She shook the thought aside. No doubt they were all at rest.

"We need to talk."

Sheree whirled around, startled by the vampire's silent entrance. One look at Mara's face and it was obvious she knew what had happened the night before.

"Why?" Mara asked, her green eyes as cold as glass. "Why would you do such a thing?"

"If you know what I did, then you must know why."

"We're all afraid," Mara said, her expression softening. "Pearl and Edna are in fear for their lives, certain I'll destroy them if the serum doesn't work. Derek is afraid of becoming a true monster, unable to control himself. You're afraid of losing him."

"What are you afraid of?"

The vampire glanced at the fireplace; a moment later, a cheery fire crackled in the hearth. Sheree stared at it curiously. Vampires didn't feel the heat or the cold, so what use did Mara have for a fire?

"I like the sight of the flames," Mara remarked. "As for what I'm afraid of, I'm afraid of losing my son. I'm afraid that the war going on inside him might warp his mind, that he'll become the very thing he's afraid of, and I'll have to destroy him."

"You would do that? Destroy your own son?"

"If it becomes necessary." Mara stared at Sheree, her expression implacable. "If what you've done harms him in any way . . ."

The vampire didn't have to finish the sentence. Sheree heard the threat in Mara's voice. She had no doubt that her own life would be forfeited if anything happened to Derek.

Chilled to the bone and unable to think of a reply, Sheree left the hall. Her legs were shaky as she climbed the stairs to the bedroom she shared with Derek. She had expected to find him asleep, but he was sitting up, his back braced against the rosewood headboard.

"She had no right to threaten you like that," he remarked, holding out his arms.

"It wasn't a threat," Sheree said, hastening into his embrace. "It was a promise." She glanced out the window, wondering what the night would bring.

"Don't worry, love. I won't let her hurt you." His breath brushed her cheek as he folded her into his embrace.

Nodding, she snuggled against him. Derek would protect her against his mother and anyone else, with his life, if necessary. She knew that without a doubt.

But what if he wasn't there?

* * *

"She did what?" Hands spread in a gesture of disbelief, Pearl stared at Mara. "Why would she pour it out? Does she realize how long it will take to make more?"

"It's a matter of trust," Logan said.

"She doesn't trust me?" Pearl sniffed, obviously offended. "I'm only trying to help."

Logan glanced at Mara, surprised by her silence. "We know that," he said. "But Sheree's experience with vampires is limited. I know Mara told her about the two of you, and what went on during the war, when you were trying to cure the supernatural community. All things considered, it's easy to understand why Sheree isn't in any hurry for Derek to become another of your failed experiments."

Pearl threw up her hands in exasperation. "They didn't all fail!"

Logan nodded. Two of their subjects had reverted to being human without any apparent side effects.

"Pearl worked extremely hard on the new serum," Edna said, somewhat indignantly. "We both did. And to see all those hours of work wasted . . ." She shook her head, her eyes flashing red.

"Do you have any more?" Mara asked.

Pearl shook her head. "No. So, what do we do now?"

"Whatever you want," Mara said. "I'll be in touch if we need you again."

"But . . ." Edna looked to Pearl for help.

"Enough!" Mara's voice cracked like a pistol shot. "Be gone, both of you!"

Before Edna could argue, Pearl grabbed her friend by the hand. "Let's go, dear," she said, and whisked her out of the castle.

"I can't help but echo the old broad's words," Logan drawled. "What now?"

"We do as planned. We'll lock Derek in the dungeon and keep Sheree away from him, and hope for . . ." Mara whirled around as Sheree ran into the hall.

Sheree skidded to a halt, one hand pressed to her heart. "He's gone!"

"Gone?" Mara sent an anxious glance at Logan, then looked back at Sheree. "Gone where?"

"I don't know! One minute we were talking and the next I was alone."

Logan glanced at the window. "The moon hasn't even risen yet."

"Where would he go?" Sheree asked, worry for her own safety swallowed up in her concern for Derek.

"I don't know." Mara lifted her head, scenting the air. "He's not in the castle."

"But you can find him, can't you?" Sheree asked anxiously.

Logan looked at his wife askance. "Can you?"

"Of course!" Mara snapped.

"Whoa, girl," he said, his voice harsher than Sheree had ever heard it. "What's going on?"

"Nothing." Mara cocked her head to the side. "He's hunting in town."

Sheree bit down on her lower lip. Why had he gone to town on this, of all nights? It wasn't safe for the people there. It wasn't safe for him.

There had been numerous stories about werewolves circulating through the towns and villages since Derek had attacked the farmer. People from one end of the country to the other were suddenly reporting sightings of werewolves. Curfews had been set. Parents hurried their children inside as soon as the sun went down. Rewards were being offered for the head of the creature. Numerous large dogs and feral wolves had been killed by spooked citizens.

Sheree sank onto the sofa, her worry for her husband increasing with every passing moment. Unable to shake off a growing sense of doom, she rose and began to pace the floor.

"What's wrong?" Mara asked, quickly picking up on Sheree's distress.

"I don't know." Sheree went to the window and stared into the darkness. Where was he? "What if there are other werewolves out there?" Older, stronger? "What if . . . ?"

"There's nothing to worry about," Mara assured her. "Last time I was here, the vampires had chased all the werewolves out of the country."

"What about all the stories of recent sightings?"

"Fear mongering," Mara said, but she sounded less certain than before.

Logan moved up behind his wife and slid his arms around her waist. "Maybe we should go look for him."

Mara leaned against him. "Not yet. For now, we wait."

"If you don't mind," Sheree said. "I think I'll wait in my room."

Mara dismissed her with a wave of her hand.

"Don't leave the castle," Logan warned.

"Don't worry, I won't," Sheree assured him. She ran up the stairs, tears stinging her eyes. Why had Derek left so abruptly? Why hadn't he told her where he was going? Why hadn't he taken her with him?

Frightened for Derek, she paced the floor, then threw herself onto the bed and buried her face in his pillow. His scent filled her nostrils, reminding her of every minute they had spent together—nights filled with passion, the sound of his voice whispering that he loved her, the surprisingly sensual pleasure of his bite, the strength of his arms around her, the sheer wonder of what he was.

Sheree.

She lifted her head at the sound of his voice. "Derek? Derek, are you all right?"

I need you.

Where are you?

Near where we dumped the serum. Come alone. Hurry!

How will I get out of the castle without being seen?

Go down the back stairs at the end of the corridor, turn right, and go out through the kitchen. Hurry, love.

Spurred by the urgency in Derek's voice, Sheree hurried out of her room and down the old stone stairway once used by castle servants.

She paused at the back door. What was she doing, rushing out into the night to meet Derek when the moon was rising?

Sheree? His voice was filled with pain, touched with panic.

How could she refuse when he obviously needed her?

Taking her courage in hand, she stepped outside.

The rain had turned to mist. Thunder rumbled in the distance. Her enemy, the moon, peeked through the lowering clouds.

As fast as she could, she made her way up the side of the mountain. She was panting by the time she reached the top.

Derek was waiting for her. Even in the dark, she could see the shiny wet stain on the front of his shirt.

"You're hurt!"

"Yeah. Dammit!" Grabbing her by the waist, he shoved her to the ground. "They're coming!"

"Who?"

"Hunters! Shit! Stay down!"

Heart pounding, Sheree pressed herself to the ground. She had expected Derek to drop down beside her. She glanced up when she heard him groan, felt her eyes widen as he began to transform in front of her.

Murmuring, "No, oh, no," she watched in horror as he dropped to his hands and knees, his body writhing, stretching as bones popped and ligaments realigned themselves. His clothes shredded, exposing the thick black fur sprouting from his skin.

Throwing back his head, he howled in pain as he fought against the change.

The heart-wrenching howl, the sight of Derek caught between human and werewolf, sent chills racing down Sheree's spine.

"Up there!" A man's shout cut through the night. "I see him!"

No, Sheree thought, her blood turning to ice. Oh, no, please no!

Caught in the throes of the change, the werewolf snarled at the three heavily armed men closing in on him.

In fear for Derek's life, Sheree sprang to her feet. Waving her arms, she ran forward, shouting, "Don't shoot!"

The men hesitated at her unexpected appearance.

"What the hell!" exclaimed one of the hunters.

And then time warped and everything seemed to happen in slow motion.

The werewolf sprang toward the nearest hunter. The man cried out as the werewolf's jaws clamped around his throat. Shaking the man as if he were a rag doll, the wolf hurled him into the shadows.

At the hunter's scream, the other two men opened fire, shooting blindly.

Sheree reeled backward as something slammed into her with the force of a sledge hammer. She stared in horror at the dark stain spreading across her middle. Had she been shot? Why didn't it hurt, she wondered, as, fighting a wave of nausea, she sank to the ground.

Moments later, Logan and Mara appeared.

Mara jerked the weapon from one hunter. Logan disarmed the other. Not wanting to see the fate of the two men, Sheree closed her eyes.

Voices. Low. Worried. Frantic.

The sound of bones popping.

Derek's voice, calling her name.

Why did he sound so far away? Why couldn't she open her eyes?

"Sheree! Sheree! Dammit, Logan, she's dying."

Dying? Was he talking about her?

"Sheree, love, don't leave me!"

It took every ounce of what little strength she had left to open her eyes. Derek was leaning over her, his beautiful dark eyes wet with tears. Mara and Logan stood behind him, faces grave.

"I'm sorry," Derek whispered hoarsely. "I never should have asked you to come out here."

She tried to say that it was all right, that she loved him, but she couldn't form the words. She whimpered, her hands clutching at her stomach as the numbness wore off. Darkness hovered around her, beckoning her, promising peace, an end to pain. Her eyelids fluttered down.

"Sheree! Dammit, don't leave me!"

"She's almost gone." Mara's voice, tinged with regret.

"No!" Derek's tears dripped onto Sheree's cheeks. "No! I won't lose her. I can't."

"Are you sure this is the right thing to do?" Logan asked. "Have you ever discussed it?"

"Would she want this?" Mara asked dubiously.

"I don't know. I don't care!" Choking back a sob, Derek

whispered, "Forgive me, love," and sank his fangs into her throat.

He drank deeply. Torn by guilt, he drank it all—her thoughts, her memories, her hopes and fears. Her love for him.

When she was but a heartbeat away from death, he tore into his own wrist. Pressed the bleeding wound to her mouth. And pleaded with her to drink.

At first, there was no response. And then she swallowed.

Weak with relief, he closed his eyes and prayed.

Prayed that she would find it in her heart to forgive him for stealing her mortality and replacing it with endless night.

Chapter Forty

Darkness surrounded Sheree, deeper and blacker than anything she had ever known. Her body felt light, alien, as if she could, merely by thinking it, float toward the ceiling. Sounds assaulted her ears—familiar sounds, yet magnified until they were almost painful. Her hand moved restlessly over the blanket that covered her; without thinking, she counted each individual stitch while a distant part of her mind wondered how she could do such a thing.

There was someone nearby. His scent was all around her, comforting in a way she couldn't explain.

"Sheree?"

"Derek? Where are you?"

"I'm right here. Open your eyes, love."

She did as he asked, and quickly closed them against the candle's brilliant light. "Hurts."

"You'll get used to it."

"What's wrong with me? Why do I feel so strange?"

"You were badly wounded last night. Do you remember?"

"There were hunters. . . ."

"Yes. What else do you remember?"

"You were shot. You called me to you."

"That's right. I was wounded. Hurting. I . . ." He swore under his breath. "I needed blood. I didn't realize the hunters were so close, or I never would have called you."

"It's all right." She smiled weakly. "I'm fine."

"Open your eyes, love."

Squinting, she glanced around the room. It was the bedroom she shared with Derek, yet it looked different somehow. She saw details she had never noticed before—the hairline crack in the ceiling above the bed, the individual threads in the hangings, each brushstroke in the white-washed walls. Derek stood beside the bed, darkly handsome in a pair of jeans and a black T-shirt.

She sat up, her gaze fixed on Derek's face. Even he looked different. "What's wrong with me? Am I on drugs?"

He laughed softly. "In a way."

Her gaze darted toward the door. "Your mother's coming," she said, and frowned. How did she know that? Mara walked without making a sound.

A moment later, Mara stepped into the room. "How are you feeling, Sheree?"

"I don't know. Something's wrong with me, and Derek won't tell me what it is. Will you?"

Mara glanced at her son.

He shook his head.

"Well, then, I'll leave you to it."

Sheree's eyes widened as Mara left the room. Never before had she been able to see the vampire vanish, but she saw it now. It wasn't that she disappeared; it was merely that she moved too swiftly for human eyes to follow. Human eyes?

Feeling as though something had sucked all the air out of the room, Sheree looked at Derek. "What have you done?"

He clenched his hands. "I couldn't lose you."

"What have you done?" she asked again, her voice rising.

"You took a bullet meant for me. You were dying. I

couldn't let that happen. Hate me if you will. Destroy me if it will make you feel better, but I didn't want to exist in a world without you in it."

"You turned me." It wasn't a question.

He nodded.

"Go away."

"Sheree . . ."

"Get out!" She pounded her fists on the mattress. "Get out, get out, get out!"

Pivoting on his heel, he left the room.

Sheree stared after him. It couldn't be true. She didn't want to be a vampire. No matter how wonderful it might be to wish herself across the country or dissolve into mist or live forever, she didn't want to be one of the undead. She wanted to spend summers at the beach working on her tan, and winters skiing in the mountains. She wanted a family, and . . . oh, Lord, what would her mother and father think? How could she tell them? They would be horrified.

It couldn't be true. She was letting her imagination run away with her. The vampires were playing a cruel trick on her, that's all it was.

Tears of relief rained down her cheeks. Grabbing a corner of the sheet, she wiped her eyes—and stared in horror at the bloody streaks left by her tears.

It was true.

She was a vampire. *Undead. Nosferatu.*

Her wordless cry of denial rang throughout the castle, echoing off the cold gray walls and vaulted ceilings.

Downstairs, Derek buried his face in his hands as Sheree's hoarse cry of pain pierced the very depths of his soul.

* * *

"Pearl, did you feel that?" Edna shook her head as if coming out of a trance.

Pearl looked up from her crossword puzzle. "Feel what, dear?"

"Derek made a new vampire last night. She just took her first breath as a fledgling."

"How do you know?"

"Because Derek's blood runs in my veins. And hers."

"The girl!" Pearl's eyes widened. "He turned the girl? Are you sure?"

"Yes. During the full moon."

"He didn't shift?"

"He did, but Sheree got hurt and he shifted back to human form to save her. Don't you see what that means? He was in control."

"How can you possibly know all that? I mean, I've never known a blood link to be that strong."

Edna shrugged. "I don't know, but it was as if I could see it all happening. It was . . ." She smiled. "Amazing."

"Well, then, I guess Mara won't be needing us for anything else," Pearl remarked. "I'm thinking we should get back to Texas, where we belong, and I'm thinking we should have left yesterday."

"You're probably right. But I'd sure like to stick around and see how Sheree reacts to being a vampire. Just think about it. She was made by Mara's son. That means she has ancient blood running through her veins. She'll be almost as powerful as Derek."

"A force to be reckoned with, to be sure," Pearl agreed. "Now, let's pack."

Sheree felt numb and drained of tears when Mara entered the room. "Hello, daughter."

Daughter. That was funny, Sheree thought bitterly. "I want to go home."

"Then go."

Sheree frowned. Was it as simple as that?

"You're a vampire now. A thought will take you anywhere you wish to be."

Curious to see if that was true, Sheree tossed the covers aside, surprised when they flew across the room and landed in a heap against the wall.

"You also have a vampire's strength," Mara remarked. "I understand your anger, your wish to leave us. No one will stop you. But, like it or not, you are family now. If you need us, you have only to call."

"I won't."

Mara nodded. "Vampires are not only possessive about territory, but about those we love. There is a bond between you and Derek now that can never be broken. It runs deeper than the sharing of blood, deeper even than the wedding vows you exchanged."

"I don't care. He had no right to do what he did without asking me. I can never forgive him for that."

"Never is a long time for vampires. You're a fledgling now. But my blood runs in your veins. You will be stronger than most new vampires, but not invincible. Remember to stay out of the sun." Moving toward the door, she murmured, "Farewell, daughter."

Determined not to shed any more tears, Sheree faced the window. The sky was lowering and gray. Lightning split the heavens. Thunder rumbled in the distance.

Feeling like Dorothy, she closed her eyes, clicked her heels together, and wished for home.

A mighty rushing filled her ears.

When she opened her eyes again, she was standing in her living room in California.

It was seven o'clock in the morning and the sun was up.

Overcome with a sudden lethargy, Sheree dropped to her hands and knees. Grateful that the drapes were closed, she managed to crawl into the hall closet and shut the door.

This is death.

It was her last conscious thought before sinking into an ebony sea of oblivion.

Chapter Forty-One

Sheree woke with the setting of the sun. One minute the world was black, the next, sensory information flooded her mind. She knew where she was and what time it was. She heard an argument coming from the house next door, traffic noise, a faint sound that eluded her at first, and then, with a laugh, she realized it was the sound of a moth fluttering near the ceiling.

But all that faded into insignificance compared to the horrible thirst that plagued her, an all-consuming thirst unlike anything she had ever known.

Because she was a vampire.

Pain knifed through her whole body. She knew instinctively what it meant. She needed to feed. She needed blood. She had watched Derek call his prey to him. Could she do that? Could she summon a stranger to her and drink from him? Just the thought filled her with revulsion, but another part—the ravenous vampire part—demanded to be fed by whatever means necessary.

Where was the best place to find blood?

She knew the answer almost before she asked the question. Hurrying into the bathroom, she came to an abrupt halt when she passed in front of the mirror. She knew a moment of horror with the realization that she cast no reflection. Good thing she didn't need a mirror to apply her lipstick, she thought, and smothered a burst of hysterical laughter as she stepped into the shower. She was amazed at how wonderful it felt. She could feel each drop of water splashing against her skin.

She washed quickly, avoided looking at the mirror as she went into the bedroom and dressed in her favorite Goth gown, boots, and wig.

Moments later, a thought took her to Drac's Dive. It was like being there for the first time. Colors were sharper, brighter, the music was louder, the notes were more distinct, and the smell—people, booze, sweat, fear, desire, lust. And, over all that, the beating of dozens of hearts, the rich, coppery scent of blood.

She stood inside the door, trying to absorb everything at once even as she wondered how to shut out the constant barrage of sounds and smells.

"It takes practice," said a familiar voice. "In time, you'll learn to shut it out."

"Logan! What are you doing here?"

"Derek sent me."

Derek. Something twisted deep inside her at the sound of his name.

"He should be here, not me. He sired you. Teaching you how to adjust to your new lifestyle is his responsibility, but he said you didn't want to see him. Is that right?"

"Yes. I never want to see him again."

"Are you sure?"

"I have no desire to talk about Derek. Just tell me what I need to know."

Taking her by the arm, Logan led her to a booth in the far corner. He gestured for her to sit, then slid in beside her. "I think you already know most of it. All you're lacking is confidence in your abilities. You need to forget all your preconceived notions about drinking blood. Your mind will tell you it's repulsive. Don't listen. Open yourself to your new nature."

"I don't want to be a vampire." She glanced at all the wannabe vampires milling around the club and wondered if they would still wish for someone to bring them across if they knew what it was really like.

"Sheree?"

"I don't want to be a vampire," she said again. And then she smiled. She didn't have to be a vampire. All she had to do was find Pearl and Edna and ask them to whip up a new batch of their serum. It had worked on newly turned vampires in the past. Why not on her?

She groaned as pain knifed through her again.

"Come on," Logan said, "you need blood."

"I don't want to hurt anyone."

"You won't." Taking her by the arm, he led her out of the club and into the shadows at the end of the street. Biting into his wrist, he held it out to her. "Vampires don't usually drink from others of their kind, but tonight we'll make an exception."

Sheree's mouth watered at the sight of the dark red blood slowly oozing from the wound. Shutting her mind to everything else, she grasped his forearm.

"No!"

Startled by Derek's voice, Sheree dropped Logan's arm.

Derek shoved his stepfather away, then stepped between Logan and Sheree. "If you're going to drink vampire blood, Sheree Blackwood, it's going to be mine."

"What are you doing here?"

"I'm looking after my wife."

"Leave me alone. I hate you."

"I don't care. Logan's right. Teaching you how to be a

vampire is my responsibility, and I'm taking over, right now."
Derek glanced at Logan. "You got a problem with that?"

"She's all yours." Shoving his hands into the pockets of
his jeans, Logan strolled back to the club.

"Do you want to feed from me, or learn how to hunt?"
Derek asked.

Sheree started to tell him to go to hell when the pain
doubled her over. She wrapped her arms around her waist,
certain she was dying, and hurting too badly to care.

Stifling a curse, Derek bit into his wrist. "Drink."

She wanted to refuse, but the scent of his blood enflamed
her senses. Grasping his arm in both hands, she lowered
her head and took what she so desperately craved.

Later, she was embarrassed by what she had done.

"No reason to be self-conscious about it," Derek said.
"Come on, I'll take you home."

"I don't need you to take me."

"Don't argue with me, wife," he warned, taking her hand
in his. "I'm bigger. I'm older. I'm stronger."

"You're nothing but a bully!" Eyes flashing defiance, she
tried to wrest her hand from his, but he was right. He was
definitely stronger.

"You must have questions," Derek said. "What do you
want to know?"

"Nothing. I don't intend to be a vampire very long."

"Right. Pearl's formula. The one you wouldn't let me
drink."

"Maybe I should have."

"Well, I've got news for you, sweetheart. I'm not letting
you drink it, either."

"You can't stop me!"

"Can't I?" He jerked her to a stop, then cupped her chin
in his hand, forcing her to look at him.

She had felt touches of his preternatural power before,

but never anything like this. It crashed over her like a wave, stealing the breath from her body, the strength from her limbs.

"I made you," he said. "If I want, I can control your every thought, your every move. Do we understand each other?"

"I hate you."

"So you said. Hate me all you want, love. But you're not taking that formula."

He transported the two of them to her house, stood behind her while she unlocked the door.

She crossed the threshold, then turned, blocking his way. "I rescind your invitation," she said, her voice thick with triumph.

He snorted softly as he stepped across the threshold. After closing the door, he leaned against it. "Lesson number one. I'm your sire. You can't keep me out." Following her into the living room, he said, "Lesson number two. You need to feed every night for the first year or so. I will teach you how it's done."

Sheree flopped onto the sofa, her arms folded across her chest.

"Lesson number three. Holy water and silver will burn you. Fire will destroy you. A stake in the heart will kill you. Lesson number four. Other vampires are your enemy." He dropped into the chair across from the sofa. "We do not share territory willingly. Master vampires, like Mara, will fight to the death to defend what is theirs."

"What about your family?" She didn't want to ask him anything, but she had to know. "They all get along."

Derek stretched his legs out in front of him, elbows resting on the arms of the chair, fingers interlocked. "The Cordova family seems to be the exception to the rule. I think it has to do with the fact that they truly are family."

"Like you and Mara."

He nodded. "Exactly. And you're part of our family, whether you like it or not."

"Am I going to meet them?"

"I think that might be a good idea."

"I still hate you," she said.

"Yeah, I got that."

"Is it okay if I go to my room now, master?"

"It's your house."

She glowered at him, then flounced up the stairs.

"I can live with your hatred, heart of mine," he murmured. "But I can't live without you."

Derek took Sheree hunting at Nosferatu's Den the next night. She had expected to hate it, to be clumsy. Embarrassed. But it came all too easily.

She chose a single man at the bar, one who was attractive and smelled clean. She called to him with her mind and as simple as that, he was hers.

Derek followed the two of them outside, stood behind her as she bent over the man's neck. She hesitated a moment, but the temptation of his blood could not be denied.

"Careful," Derek said. "You don't have to bite hard. Your fangs are razor sharp."

A gentle nip was all it took.

"Not too much," Derek warned. "If you drink your fill, you'll kill him."

She fed from three different men.

"They all taste different," she mused as they left the Den. "Why is that?"

Derek shrugged. "Different blood types, different diets."

"What if they're sick? How will I know?"

"You'd know, but you needn't worry about catching anything. You're immune to human disease."

When they reached her house, she bid him a frosty good night and went to her room. It was like being a prisoner in her own home, she thought irritably, knowing he was downstairs. She was a big, bad vampire now. She didn't need a keeper.

She was trying to read when Derek opened the door and poked his head into the room. "Tomorrow night," he said.

"Tomorrow night, what?"

"I'm taking you to Mara's to meet the rest of the family."

Before she could say yes or no, he dissolved into mist and was gone.

She couldn't help feeling a little nervous at the prospect of meeting Derek's vampire family. What if they didn't like her? What if she didn't like them?

In an effort to put her fears out of her mind, she tried to dissolve into mist. Derek seemed to do it without any effort at all. Why couldn't she? She had tried on several occasions when she was alone in her room, but, try as she might, nothing happened. Had her sire done something to prevent it?

The following evening, Sheree insisted on calling her parents before she did anything else. She was glad when her father answered the phone.

"I was about to send the police looking for you," her father said. "Where have you been?"

"I guess you could say we were on a short honeymoon," she replied.

"I tried calling several times, but wherever you were, there was no service."

"We were in Romania, in the mountains."

"Romania!"

"Derek's mother has a . . . a summer home there. She let us use it for a few days. How are you, Dad?"

"Ready to walk you down the aisle. You know your mom. She says you're not really married until you exchange your vows in a church."

"What? Oh, of course. We haven't decided on a date yet, but I'll let you know as soon as we do. I've got to go now. I'm on my way to meet Derek's extended family."

"You sound a little nervous."

"Well, I guess I am."

"I'm sure they'll love you," Brian said. "I know your mom would love to say hello but she's out."

"That's okay. Tell her hi for me. I love you."

"I love you, too, pumpkin. Good night."

"Are you ready now?" Derek asked.

"I'm hungry."

"You can stall as long as you want, but we're doing this tonight. Everyone is waiting for us."

"Are you always going to be this bossy?"

"Probably. Let's go. Mara hates to be kept waiting."

Mara's house in the Hollywood Hills was lit up like a Christmas tree. Sheree peered out the window as Derek parked the car in the driveway. It looked like every light in the place was on.

Sheree was a bundle of nerves by the time they arrived. She had taken her time choosing her prey, fed as slowly as possible, insisted she needed to feed again.

Derek had indulged her, a knowing gleam in his eye. And now he was opening the front door, escorting her inside. She had no idea what to expect as she stepped into the living room.

All conversation came to a stop, all eyes swung in her direction.

Sheree's gaze swept over them in a glance. All the men were dark haired and handsome, the women lovely.

Mara smiled as she came forward to embrace the two of them. "Derek," she said, "why don't you make the introductions?"

"Sure, Ma. Sheree, this is Roshan DeLongpre and his wife, Brenna. Brenna is the family's only practicing witch."

Brenna was lovely, with waist-length red hair and eyes almost as green as Mara's. A necklace of amber and jet circled her neck.

"This is Vince and Cara, their twin sons, Rafe and Rane, their wives Kathy and Savannah."

Sheree smiled at each one in turn, although she doubted she would be able to tell the twins apart. She noted all the men and women seemed to be in their mid-twenties except for Savannah, who appeared to be in her early forties.

"And this," Derek said, smiling at a lovely young woman with pale blond hair and blue eyes, "is Abbey Marie, Savannah's daughter. She's the only mortal left in the family."

"Pleased to meet you," Sheree said. The girl looked like a younger version of her mother. Was it strange for her to be the only human among so many vampires?

"How are things going in New York, Abs?" Derek asked.

She shrugged. "Not as well as I'd hoped. I think I'm going to give up my aspirations of being an actress."

Rane put his arm around his daughter's shoulders and gave her a squeeze. "Never give up, sweetie."

"Maybe you'd have better luck here in Hollywood," Vince suggested. "I'll bet Logan could put in a good word for you."

"Maybe, but I'd rather make it on my own."

"So," Roshan said, glancing from Sheree to Derek, "I hear there's a wedding in the wind."

Derek nodded. "We decided to have another ceremony so the families could be there."

"Couldn't wait for the honeymoon, eh?" Vince said, giving Derek a nudge.

"The men in our family aren't known for their patience." Rafe slipped his arm around Kathy's waist. "Are they, wife?"

"No." Kathy winked at Sheree. "They're known for other things, though."

Her comment elicited nods from the other women, all except Abbey, who blushed.

"Speaking of sexy men," Cara said, smiling at Abbey, "have you found your Mr. Right yet?"

"No, and I'm not looking."

"She's got plenty of time for all that," her father said.

Abbey rolled her eyes. "Honestly, we have this conversation every time I come to town." She held up her empty wineglass. "I'm going to get a refill."

As Sheree watched Abbey walk away, she couldn't help feeling sorry for the man who would one day court Rane Cordova's daughter. Mortal fathers were protective enough; vampire fathers were sure to be a hundred times worse.

Sheree grew more at ease as the night wore on. Wine and conversation flowed freely. There was an endless supply of chardonnay and humorous stories as the other couples told tales of their courtship. There was no doubt that Roshan and Brenna's was the most fascinating. Roshan had seen a photo of Brenna in a book, fallen in love with her picture, and traveled back in time to rescue her from being burned at the stake.

Sheree could scarcely credit it. Believing in vampires was one thing, but time travel?

"I can see you don't believe me," Roshan said good-naturedly. "Next time we get together, I'll bring that old book with Brenna's picture in it."

Sheree listened with rapt attention as the vampires talked of past wars, of friends and loved ones lost. Pearl's and Edna's names were mentioned several times. And then, out of the blue, Vince said, "I hear there's a hint of werewolf blood in you, Derek."

A muscle flexed in Derek's jaw, and then he nodded. "From my father."

"Is it a problem?" Rane asked.

"No." Derek glanced at Sheree. "I can handle it."

Rafe nodded. "Glad to hear it."

It was near dawn when the party broke up. Two by two, the vampires said their good-byes and departed. Abbey was the last to leave. She hugged Mara and promised to visit again soon, and then, she, too, was gone.

"So," Derek said, "what did you think of them?"

"If I'd met them before you turned me, I never would have known they were vampires. They seem so normal . . . well, except that they're all exceptionally gorgeous."

"So are you."

Ignoring his compliment, she said, "Who's Abbey's father?"

"Nobody knows. Savannah was artificially inseminated."

"Ah. And she remained human until Abbey grew up, didn't she? That's why Savannah looks older than all the others."

Derek nodded. "Are you ready to go?"

"I guess so."

"Let us know when you set the date," Mara said, "and I'll get in touch with Father Lanzoni."

"Let's do it soon and get it over with," Sheree said.

"I take it you're still angry," Mara said dryly.

"You could say that."

"On that happy note, Ma, we'll take our leave."

* * *

"Have you ever met Father Lanzoni?" Sheree asked as Derek navigated the winding road that led to the freeway. "Is he a vampire, too?"

"Yep. He's one of the old ones . He's officiated at the weddings for just about everyone. Is that going to be a problem?"

"No. In spite of my mother's insistence on a church wedding, she's not very religious, and neither is my father."

"Any particular place where you'd like to get married?" he asked.

"No. You?"

"You find a dress. I'll find a place."

"All right."

Derek blew out a sigh of exasperation as Sheree turned her head to stare out the side window.

Like it or not, he was beginning to think she was never going to forgive him.

Chapter Forty-Two

Sheree went shopping for a wedding dress Friday night, grateful that the stores were open late. It was her first time out and about on her own since becoming a vampire and she was excited and scared in equal measure.

She had tried dissolving into mist before leaving the house, again without success. But she forgot all about that when she entered the bridal shop. There were so many dresses to choose from, she didn't know how she would ever decide. It would have been nice to have her best friend along, but Shirley was happily married and living in Delaware. Even if she'd been nearby, Sheree didn't trust herself to be with Shirley, mostly because she was afraid she would be tempted to tell her friend that she was now a vampire. She was dying—a poor choice of words, she thought—to talk to someone about it, someone who wasn't a vampire.

Sheree picked out a half-dozen gowns and took them into the dressing room, thinking she should have let Mara help her pick out a dress that day long ago. At least back then, she would have been able to see how she looked. She loved them all—the knee-length one with the round neck and short puffy sleeves; the floor-length one with a fitted bodice and flared skirt; the ball gown that looked like it belonged to Cinderella; the one with the deep V-neck and gored skirt; the one that looked more like a long white nightgown than a dress.

How was she ever going to make up her mind when she couldn't even see how she looked in any of them! Tears of frustration stung her eyes as she stepped out of the last dress and tossed it aside.

"I like the one with the fitted bodice."

Startled, Sheree whirled around to find Mara standing near the door.

"I thought you could use some help," Mara said.

"Really?" Sheree raised a skeptical brow. "Or did Derek send you to keep an eye on me?"

"That, too. There are still hunters in the area."

Sheree picked up the gown Mara had mentioned. "I like this one, too, but . . . how do you decide what you want when you can't see yourself in it?"

"Well," Mara said with a cocky grin, "if it looks good on the hanger, I just assume it will look fabulous on me." Reaching for the gown, she said, "I'll try it on so you can see what it looks like."

Mara changed out of her jeans and sweater and into the dress in the blink of an eye. "So?"

"It's beautiful. Would you try on the ball gown?"

"Of course." In moments, she twirled around wearing the other dress.

Sheree blew out a sigh. "It's hard to decide. They're both lovely."

"Well, in my opinion, the fitted one suits you best."

"Then I'll take it. Thanks for your help."

"No problem."

"Did someone help you pick out a dress when you got married?"

"Yes, the first time. Cara, Savannah and Kathy went with me. I could see myself in the mirror back then," she said with a wistful smile. "The second time, I don't remember what I wore. All I remember is the look in Logan's eyes." With a shake of her head, she put the past behind her. "Why didn't your mother come with you?"

"I didn't ask her," Sheree replied, pulling on her jeans. "She doesn't approve of my marriage to Derek. I doubt if she'd want to help me pick out a dress. Besides, it would have been hard to explain why I no longer have a reflection."

"True enough," Mara said, laughing. "Anyone you'd like to invite to the wedding?"

"Just Edna and Pearl. And my parents, of course."

"Edna and Pearl?" Mara exclaimed. "Why on earth would you want them there?"

Shrugging, Sheree finished dressing and stepped into her sandals. "I think I hurt their feelings when I dumped their serum. I'd like to make amends." It was only a little lie.

"Well, they wouldn't have been on my guest list, but it's your wedding."

"So, you'll invite them?"

Mara nodded.

"Thank you." Grabbing her handbag and the gown, Sheree left the dressing room.

Mara waited while Sheree paid for the dress, which was carefully zipped into an opaque garment bag.

"So the groom doesn't see it before the wedding," the saleswoman explained with a smile.

Outside, Mara glanced up and down the street, her expression wary.

"Is something wrong?" Sheree asked.

"I got wind of a hunter earlier."

Hunters, Sheree thought bleakly. She hadn't given much thought to the danger they presented to her now that she was a vampire. "How do you know when they're near?"

"You can smell them," Mara replied, a note of disgust in her voice.

"Really? What do they smell like?"

"Death. Come on, I'll see you safely home."

Derek was waiting for Sheree when she arrived. She had invited Mara in, but the vampire had declined, saying Logan was waiting for her. They were going hunting together.

"I see you found a dress," Derek remarked, eying the garment bag.

Sheree nodded.

"We're all set then. I found just the place. It's an old church in Northern California. I think everyone in the family has been married there except for my mother and Logan, who were married at home."

"Did you set a date, too?"

"A week from tomorrow night. Mara cleared it with Father Lanzoni."

Nodding, she placed the garment bag over the back of the sofa. "I'm hungry."

"Come on, I'll take you hunting."

"Your mother said she smelled hunters in town."

"Then we won't hunt in town," he said, taking her hand in his.

Moments later, they were in Texas.

"Texas?" she asked. "Seriously?"

He shrugged. "Why not?"

She shrugged, wondering what the odds were of running into Pearl and Edna.

"Slim and none," he said. "It's a big state, and we won't be here very long."

She nodded agreeably, but, in spite of what Derek had said to the contrary, she was determined to try Pearl's serum. If he read that rebellious thought, he didn't remark on it.

It was still early and the streets of San Antonio were crowded with shoppers and tourists.

"Don't you have to ask the head vampire's permission to be here?" Sheree asked.

"No."

"Why not? Your mother said master vampires are very possessive of their territory."

"Well, that's true enough, but Mara pretty much out-ranks every other vampire on the planet. And as her son . . ." He shrugged. "I guess you could say I have diplomatic immunity."

She grunted softly. "Must be nice."

Sheree had never been to Texas, although she'd once had a friend who was born there. According to Beth Ann, everything in Texas was bigger, better, and less expensive. Sheree didn't know if any of that was true or not, but she was surprised to see men, and even a few women, wearing gun belts in plain sight.

A short time later, they turned onto the River Walk. It was a lovely place, with quiet walkways, tinkling waterfalls, and placid pools. Surprisingly, it was located one block below street level. They strolled past elegant Victorian mansions that were built on what had once been farmland belonging to the Alamo. Walking on, they passed the Pioneer Flour Mill, as well as hotels, restaurants, outdoor patios, and a number of shops.

They eventually ended up at the Alamo. Sheree knew little about the Alamo's history, except for what she had seen in old movies. It was a lovely old place, and the first mission built in the city.

"Too bad it's closed," she remarked. "Maybe we could . . ." She paused, nostrils flaring at an unfamiliar scent carried by a vagrant breeze. "What is that awful smell?"

"Hunters. Three of them."

"How do they know we're here?" She glanced anxiously at the drifting shadows, but saw nothing.

"I don't know, but we're not waiting around to find out." Grabbing her hand, he said, "Come on, we're getting out of here."

Moments later, they were in another part of the city. Derek quickly found a young couple walking down a quiet, tree-lined street. He mesmerized them with a look. "Which one do you want?"

"The man." Sheree fed quickly, carefully. She had never realized how fragile mortals were until she became a vampire.

When she finished, Derek sent the couple on their way.

At home again, he settled into his favorite chair, his legs stretched in front of him, his gaze on his wife. "Are you ever going to forgive me?"

"I don't know." There were aspects of being a vampire that appealed to her—staying forever young, never getting sick, her increased strength. Even the blood part wasn't nearly as bad as she had expected. But there was a whole part of her life that was forever lost to her. She missed her morning coffee. She missed all her favorite foods. She missed jogging in the morning, sunbathing in the backyard, going to lunch at the mall. She could no longer see her reflection in a mirror, or wear her favorite silver jewelry.

But those were superficial things. There would come a time when she would either have to stop visiting her parents or tell them the truth. How else could she explain the fact that her body didn't age? Or why she couldn't give them grandchildren . . . Children, she thought, blinking back tears. She would never have a daughter of her own, never know the joy of holding her child in her arms. . . .

Derek's jaw clenched and she knew he was reading her thoughts again. She let her mind brush his, but it was closed to her. How did he do that?

Uncomfortable with the tension between them, she bid him good night and went to bed.

Derek sat there far into the night, thinking about Sheree. After reading her thoughts earlier, he couldn't blame her for hating him. He had known he would never have children. When he'd turned Sheree, he hadn't thought about what she would be giving up. He had thought only of what he would be losing, had known, in that instant, that he would rather live with her hatred than exist without her. In spite of her anger, he knew that, deep down, she still loved him. He had assumed she would forgive him sooner or later. Sometimes he thought she was softening; at other times he was certain she was going to stay mad for a century or two.

Then again, women were pushovers at weddings. Maybe a repeat of their vows would remind her of how much she had once loved him.

It was a slim hope, at best, he mused, but at the moment, it was the only hope he had.

Chapter Forty-Three

"The wedding's set for a week from tonight," Sheree told her father. "You and Mom will be there, won't you?"

"Of course," Brian Westerbrooke said. "I wouldn't dare miss such a special occasion twice. Just give me the address and the time and we'll be there with bells on."

"Bells optional," Sheree said, smiling, "tux required for walking the bride down the aisle. I don't have the address for the church, so just meet me in front of the Marchand Hotel at eight o'clock Saturday night. Derek and I will pick you up."

"Why all the mystery?" Brian asked.

"There's no mystery. The church is in an out-of-the-way location. It'll be easier for us to take you there. Derek's already made reservations for you at the hotel."

"Very well. I guess a little cloak-and-dagger journey is good now and then." He chuckled softly. "We'll see you Saturday night, pumpkin."

"I love you, Dad."

"Love you, too." He hesitated a moment, then said, "Sheree, I know you're still upset with your mother, but how about doing your old man a favor and letting it go?"

"All right, Dad."

"Great! She's right here, anxious to talk to you."

Sheree ran a hand through her hair as she waited for her mother to come on the line.

"Sheree, how are you?"

"I'm fine, Mom."

"Is there anything you need for your new home?"

"No. I think we have everything we need."

"Well, I'm sure I can come up with something. See you Saturday."

Sheree blew out a sigh as she disconnected the call. Her mother always tried to smooth things over with presents—a beautiful porcelain doll when Meredith missed one of Sheree's ballet recitals, a new bicycle when she missed a mother-daughter tea, a baby blue convertible when her mother missed a high school awards ceremony.

But none of that mattered now. The important thing was to make sure that everything went smoothly on Saturday, and that her parents had no reason to suspect their daughter, her husband, and her new in-laws were all vampires.

Sheree was a bundle of nerves as they drove to the Marchand to pick up her parents.

"Stop worrying," Derek said. "We'll all be on our best behavior, I promise."

"How am I going to explain the fact that nobody eats?"

"You won't have to. The family will fill plates and cast a glamour on your folks that will make them think we're eating."

"You can do that?"

"Easy as dissolving into mist."

"Might be easy for you," she replied sourly. "Ohmygosh!"

"What's wrong?" Derek glanced around, wondering what had put such a stricken expression on her face.

"My father!"

"What about him?"

"He's a camera bug. He's going to want pictures. Tons of pictures."

"What's the problem? I promise to smile."

"But . . . we don't have reflections. Will we show up in the photos?"

Derek laughed softly. "Not to worry, love. Capturing our likeness was a problem in the old days, when film had silver in it, but with digital cameras, it's no longer an issue."

Relieved, Sheree slumped in her seat, only to bolt upright when the motel came into view. "Look! There they are!"

Derek pulled up to the curb and put the car in park.

Smiling, Sheree jumped out of the car and hugged her father and then her mother.

"Good to see you again, sir," Derek said, shaking Mr. Westerbrooke's hand. He complimented her mother on the dress she wore, and they were on their way.

"How far is it to the church?" Meredith asked.

"Not far," Derek replied. "How was your flight?"

"A little bumpy," Brian said. "Gave Mother quite a scare."

"I can't help it," Meredith said, glancing out the window. "You know I don't like to fly. How did you happen to pick this church, Sheree? It seems rather out of the way."

"It's a Cordova/Blackwood family tradition," Sheree said. "They've been marrying here for years."

"I was hoping you'd get married at St. Timothy's, surrounded by our family and friends," Meredith said, a hint of reproach in her voice.

"We can have a reception at home, if you like," Sheree said.

Ever the diplomat, Brian said, "Of course. That's a great idea." He made small talk with Derek during the rest of the drive.

* * *

"Oh, my," Meredith murmured, gazing out at the church and grounds as Derek parked the car. "It is lovely, isn't it?"

Sheree nodded. Located in a secluded glade well off the main highway, surrounded by tall trees and shrubs, the building might have been transplanted from some medieval setting. Moonlight danced across the stained glass windows on either side of the door. The air was filled with the fragrant scent of evergreens; night birds and crickets serenaded them as Derek dropped Sheree and her mother off at a side door so Sheree could change into her wedding gown.

After escorting Sheree's father into the vestibule, Derek walked toward the front of the church. His family was already there, half of them seated on the groom's side, half on the bride's. He frowned when he saw Edna and Pearl sitting in the back row. Damn, those two always meant trouble.

His mother smiled at him from the front row. Clad in a long green gown, she looked as beautiful as always. He paused to give her a hug before joining the priest and Logan, who were waiting for him in front of the altar.

Father Lanzoni was of medium height, with warm hazel eyes and wavy black hair going gray at the temples. He was one of the oldest vampires in existence, but, like the other vampires in the room, he was shielding his true nature from Sheree's parents.

The priest smiled fondly at Derek. "Good evening, my son."

"Father." Derek shook the priest's hand, and then Logan's.

"Thank you for allowing me to officiate at your marriage," the priest said.

"Thank you for coming on such short notice."

"I wouldn't miss it," he said, smiling. "It's always a happy time when I can join two people in love."

Derek looked toward the vestibule as Vince escorted Sheree's mother to her seat.

And then Sheree was there, looking more beautiful than he had ever seen her as she walked down the aisle at her father's side.

Heart pounding with excitement, Sheree glanced quickly at her surroundings. As Mara had promised, it was a beautiful old church. The altar and the pews were carved from oak. Moonlight shone through the stained glass window above the altar. Candlelight filled the chapel with a warm golden glow, lighting the faces of the wooden statues, but it was Derek who drew her gaze and held it. The man had been born to wear a tux. It emphasized his broad shoulders and long legs, complemented the color of his hair and eyes.

Father Lanzoni smiled at Sheree and Derek, then lifted his gaze to their guests. "We are here tonight to celebrate the joining together of these young people. Who gives this woman in marriage?"

"Her mother and I do," Brian said. Squeezing his daughter's hand, he kissed her cheek, then placed her hand in Derek's.

"My children," the priest said, his voice low and yet filled with authority. "You have come here this night to exchange your vows in the presence of this company. The secret of a long and happy marriage rests with the two of you. You have only to remember to put your loved one first and your own desires second. Treat your loved one as you would be treated. Never forget the way you feel this night and I promise that the love and devotion you have for one another will grow stronger with each passing day.

"I will pronounce the words that bind you together legally, but the true joining must take place in your own hearts, your own souls.

"Sheree Westerbrooke, do you take Derek Blackwood, here present, to be your lawfully wedded husband, to love and to cherish, for now and ever more?"

For now and for ever more, not until death do you part. "I do."

"Derek Blackwood, do you take Sheree Westerbrooke, here present, to be your lawfully wedded wife, to love and to cherish, for now and ever more?"

"I do."

"Then, by the power vested in me, I pronounce you, Derek and Sheree, husband and wife, lawfully and legally wed. Derek, you may kiss your bride."

Very carefully, Derek lifted her veil, then drew her into his arms. "I love you, wife," he murmured. "Are you still angry with me?"

"Not as much as I was. Kiss me."

He kissed her gently at first, and then with greater passion, until the guests burst into applause.

Leaning forward, Father Lanzoni whispered, "Save some for later, my son."

"Yes, later," Derek promised, catching his bride's gaze with his own.

Mara had laid out a feast fit for a king. In addition to salmon and lobster and all the trimmings, there was a beautiful cake and a champagne fountain, as well as several bottles of red wine. Sheree couldn't help thinking all that food was a terrible extravagance, since only her parents and Abbey Marie were able to enjoy it.

The lights were low. Soft music played in the background.

Brian Westerbrooke mingled with the other guests, obviously impressed by Mara's home in Northern California and the many expensive paintings and antiques, yet completely at ease with those around him.

Her mother was polite and friendly, if a little standoffish. Sheree wondered if, somehow, her mother sensed that the people she was mingling with weren't people at all.

The Cordova men all toasted the bride and groom.

Edna and Pearl wished them well.

Kathy, Savannah, and Abbey welcomed her into the family.

Sheree spoke to everyone present, biding her time until Derek was deep in conversation with Roshan and Logan before she took Pearl aside.

"What is it, dear?" Pearl asked.

"I don't want to be a vampire," Sheree said, glancing left and right to make sure they were still alone. "Can you make more of your serum for me? Not the one you made for Derek, but the other one. The one you said worked on newly turned vampires."

"Yes, of course, but are you sure that's what you want?"

"I'm sure. Will you make me some?"

"Have you discussed this with Derek?"

"No, and I don't want you to mention it to him or anyone else. Not even Edna."

"I'll have to think it over, dear. Derek . . ."

"He turned me without asking if it was what I wanted," Sheree said. "I don't need his permission to undo it."

"It will take me a week or so," Pearl said. "I'll be in touch. Thank you for inviting us, but I think we'll be going now."

A week or two, Sheree thought. All she had to do now was keep Derek from finding out.

The party lasted until well past midnight. After changing out of her wedding gown, Sheree thanked Mara for everything, and then she and Derek drove her parents back to the

Marchand. Her father had a meeting late the next afternoon and they were flying home in the morning.

"Don't be strangers, you two," her father said, giving her a hug.

"We won't."

Shaking Derek's hand, her father said, "Take good care of my little girl."

"Yes, sir."

Sheree hugged her mother. "If you ever need to come home," Meredith whispered, "don't be too proud to do so."

"Thanks, Mom. I love you, too."

A last hug for her father and Sheree got into the car. She hated to see her parents leave but she was glad the evening was over. She'd been stressed out all night, afraid someone would do or say something that would arouse her parents' suspicion.

"Stop worrying," Derek said as he pulled away from the curb. "They didn't suspect a thing."

"I know, but I was worried when Mom remarked that everyone looked as if they'd stepped out of a fashion magazine. I could see her checking Kathy's skin, looking for signs of a facelift. And I almost slipped up and introduced Vince as Rafe's father instead of his brother. It would have been hard to explain they're father and son, but look the same age."

"All's well that ends well," Derek said, chuckling. "Are you ready to go home?"

"Yours or mine?"

He ran his hand along her thigh. "Mine is closer," he purred, "and we are on our honeymoon."

It was hard to remember she was angry with him when he was so near, when his scent, the mere touch of his hand, stirred her desire. Not willing to let that anger go, she thought about all she had lost when he turned her into a vampire. His being a vampire hadn't been a problem. She had been willing to make adjustments in her own lifestyle to accommodate his. He preferred the night. He drank blood. She could accept those things. But, even though she was perfectly happy to have a husband who was a vampire, that didn't mean she wanted to be one, too.

Jerking his hand from her thigh, he growled, "Would you rather I had let you die?"

"Stop reading my mind! And for your information, I wanted to *find* a vampire. I never wanted to *be* one!"

When he braked for a red light, she jumped out of the car and dashed into the darkness, running away from a decision she hadn't made. Like a petulant child, she blamed Derek for her unhappiness, for turning her without asking her permission. She was being irrational and she knew it; even if he had asked her, she had been incapable of a response. What would her answer have been?

Derek swore a vile oath as Sheree disappeared from sight. He swerved in front of the car beside him, pulled over to the curb, killed the engine, and went after her.

Sheree ran effortlessly, jumping over block walls without even thinking about it. And all the while, in the back of her mind, she heard his voice asking if she would rather be dead.

She vaulted over a parked car. Of course she didn't want to be dead, but she didn't want to be a vampire, either. All she wanted was her old life back, and she would have it in two weeks.

Slowing, she glanced around. She had no idea where she was. Old buildings hemmed her in on both sides. Most had boarded-up windows. Many were spray painted with gang signs and symbols.

She stopped at the sound of voices. Drunken voices. Coming from the building across the street.

With her preternatural vision, she could see three young men crouched in the doorway, passing a bottle back and forth between them.

One of the men looked up, his eyes widening when he saw her.

Muttering, "Oh, crap!" Sheree tried to dissolve into mist, and when that failed, she whirled around and ran back the way she'd come.

And slammed into Derek.

His arms went around her. "Where the hell did you think you were going?"

"Away from you." She glanced over her shoulder.

"Don't worry, they're too drunk to come after you."

"Just take me home."

"Dammit, Sheree, I'm sorry you're so unhappy, but I'm not sorry for what I did."

She stared up at him, mute.

Blowing out a sigh, he transported the two of them back to his car, drove her to his house. And left her there without a word.

Alone in his bed, she cried herself to sleep, wishing she had never left Philadelphia.

Chapter Forty-Four

The next two weeks were the most miserable of Sheree's life. She never saw Derek, though she sometimes sensed his presence. She thought about going to her own house, but something kept her in Sacramento.

She slept through the days, hunted in the evening, and tried not to think about Pearl, afraid that Derek would read her thoughts and try to stop her.

Where was Derek staying? Was he spending his days at Mara's? Would he come back here if she left? She glanced at the gaily wrapped gifts stacked in the corner. They hadn't opened the presents the night of the wedding; at some point, Derek had dropped them off at the house. She had no interest in any of them.

She had no interest in anything except being human again.

She was curled up on the sofa, trying to watch one of the old Iron Man movies, when someone knocked on the door.

When she opened it, a young man dressed all in black stood on the porch.

"Are you Sheree Blackwood?" he asked.

"Yes. Who are you?"

"Here." He thrust an envelope into her hand, and disappeared from sight.

After closing the door, Sheree opened the envelope and removed a sheet of paper. All it said was, "Meet me tomorrow night at Maxie's Dress Shop in the mall on 7th Street. 8 P.M. Tell no one."

After reading the note, she burned it in the fireplace.

Sheree took a cab to the mall, glancing over her shoulder all the way, but there was no sign of Derek. She checked again before entering the mall, then hurried up to the second floor. It took her a moment to find Pearl. Instead of her usual flamboyant attire, the woman was wearing blue jeans, a gray windbreaker, and a blond wig.

Talk about cloak-and-dagger, Sheree thought.

"Here it is." Pearl glanced around, assuring herself they were alone before pressing a small bottle filled with dark red liquid into Sheree's hand. "Drink it before you go to bed tonight. When you wake up tomorrow night, you should be mortal again."

"Should be?"

"There's no guarantee. Edna and I tested it on three newly made vampires. All reverted back to their humanity."

"That's great!"

"So it would seem. But Edna and I turned the three, and our blood isn't as powerful as Derek's. And they hadn't been vampires for more than a few days. And, well, there are lots of variables in something like this. I just want you to be aware of the danger, and of the fact that it might not work."

Sheree nodded. "I understand. What do I owe you for this?"

"Nothing, dear. I just hope it works," Pearl said, and vanished from sight.

Tucking the bottle inside her handbag, Sheree strolled through the mall, her heart pounding with excitement and trepidation. If she had the nerve to take Pearl's formula, she might wake up her old self tomorrow. Did she have the courage?

She paused in front of a candy store and inhaled the myriad scents emanating from inside. It was unfair that she could now detect even the most delectable smells and could no longer enjoy the taste of her favorite chocolates. She could smell fresh popcorn wafting up from the first floor, and pizza, and pretzels.

She felt a sharp pang when she saw a mother and child emerge from one of the shops. She would never have a child of her own. She told herself that lots of women were unable to bear children, that there was always adoption, though she didn't see how that could possibly work, given her circumstances.

Lost in thought, she stood there until a recorded voice announced the mall would be closing in ten minutes.

Sheree was outside, waiting for a cab, when Derek appeared beside her. "Need a ride home?" he asked.

She stared at him, her heart pounding. Did he know what she'd done?

"Of course I know, you little fool." Grasping her forearm, he propelled her down the street to where his car was parked and practically shoved her inside.

His face was a mask of anger when he slid behind the wheel.

"Have you been spying on me?" she asked angrily.

"Damn right!"

Sheree hugged her handbag to her chest. The proverbial shit was about to hit the fan. "So, why did you let me meet with Pearl?"

"I wanted to see how far you would go." He shook his head. "You're willing to risk your life on something that's been tested on three young vampires? I gave you credit for being smarter than that."

"Well, I guess you were wrong."

"I'm beginning to think you need a keeper."

"I'm beginning to think you're a bully."

He pulled up in front of his house, grabbed her by the arm, and transported the two of them inside.

Sheree twisted out of his grasp. Hands fisted on her hips, she glared at him. "It's my life. I'll do what I want."

"No, you won't. I swear, I'll lock you in the dungeon for the rest of your life if I have to, but you're not taking that damn formula."

"How do you know it won't work?"

"I don't, but it's not a risk I'm willing to take."

"Well, I am!"

He took a deep breath in an effort to calm his anger. "Sheree . . ."

"You were willing to take one of Pearl's potions not too long ago," she reminded him.

"And you talked me out of it."

"Nothing you can say will change my mind." Closing her eyes, she tried to dissolve into mist, but nothing happened. "Are you stopping me?" she demanded, her eyes shooting sparks at him.

"No."

"Then why can't I dissolve into mist?"

"I don't know. But it doesn't matter. I'll find you wherever you go." He took a deep breath. "Sheree, please don't do this. I love you. I know that, under all that anger, you love me, too. We can be happy together if you'll let us. Being a vampire isn't so bad. I think you'll find that the good outweighs the bad."

Tears stung her eyes. "I'm not even a good vampire or I'd be able to turn into mist like everybody else."

"Maybe you're trying too hard. Just think about it and it will happen."

"I'm afraid," she admitted, chin lifted defiantly. "I'm afraid I won't be able to get my own form back and I'll be stuck in some nebulous shape forever."

"As far as I know, that's never happened."

Sniffling, she said, "There's a first time for everything."

"So there is. I know you can do it. Try again."

She closed her eyes and pictured herself becoming invisible, and when she opened them again, she was floating above the floor. She couldn't speak, but she could see the room around her. It was like looking through gauze.

She could leave now and he wouldn't be able to see her go. Would he be able to sense her whereabouts in this form?

She willed herself to go higher, and the next thing she knew, she was hovering near the ceiling. There was a cobweb in the corner. For some reason, seeing it made her laugh, which broke her concentration.

With a wordless cry, she plummeted toward the floor.

And landed, with a soft *oomph,* in Derek's arms.

Staring into his eyes, she tried to summon her anger; instead, she remembered all the nights she had spent cradled in his arms, the warmth of his kisses, the sensual pleasure of giving him her blood. Was that pleasure lost to her now that she was a vampire?

"It works both ways, love. Did you find no pleasure in

drinking from me when I made you?" he asked with a knowing grin.

Her gaze slid away from his. "Maybe."

"Maybe?"

She let out a huff of annoyance. Why did she bother lying when he could read her mind? He could read her mind because he was a vampire. She frowned. Well, so was she.

She knew the moment her mind brushed his by the sudden intake of his breath. For a moment, he blocked her, and then, with a sigh of resignation, he let her inside. It wasn't so much his thoughts she read as his feelings—his lonely childhood, his love for his mother, his regret at having never known his father, his respect for Logan. But stronger than all of these was his love—and his need—for her.

It was the reason he had been able to resume his own form when she was dying, even though it should have been impossible for him to banish the werewolf while the moon was full.

It was the reason he had dragged her back from the brink of death.

It was the reason he was here now, even though she had repeatedly claimed she hated him.

How could she not love such a man? "I'm still mad at you."

A faint smile twitched his lips. "I know."

"You can put me down now."

"Maybe I don't want to." His gaze searched hers. "Are you ever going to forgive me?"

She wrapped her arms around his neck. "Persuade me."

A slow smile spread over his face as he carried her swiftly to bed and showed her, with every heated kiss and caress, just how much he loved her.

* * *

Later, while Sheree slept, a satisfied smile on her face, Derek dumped Pearl's serum down the toilet, then tossed the bottle in the trash, thinking how mad his lovely bride would be when she discovered what he'd done.

And how much fun it would be to kiss and make up again in the years to come.

Chapter Forty-Five

Eight months later

Sheree smiled at Derek as he released a young couple from his thrall and sent them on their way. Hard to believe there had been a time when she was upset about being a vampire. Once she accepted it and decided to make the best of it, she wondered why she had made such a fuss in the first place. True, she'd had to give up some of the things she loved, but she'd gained so much more in return.

"Happy, love?" he asked.

"More than happy." Folding her hands over his shoulders, she went up on her tiptoes and kissed him.

His arms slipped around her waist. "So, you've forgiven me for everything?"

"Do you need to ask?"

"Not really," he said, grinning, "but it's nice to hear every now and then."

"Yes, Derek, I forgive you. For everything."

"Good. I forgive you, too."

"Me?" Her brows rushed together in a frown. "What did I do?"

"Nothing, wife." He laughed softly as he caught her hand in his. "I just wanted to see your eyes flash with anger."

She laughed with him. A year ago, she would have sworn she couldn't love him any more than she already did. But since that time, her love for her husband had grown into something beautiful and rare. Having him know what she was thinking, being able to read his thoughts in return, had created a bond between them that grew stronger with each passing day. She was his equal now, no longer in need of his constant protection. Of course, because he was a male vampire, his urge to protect her was instinctive. And kind of sweet.

He had taken her all over the world, showed her wondrous places inaccessible to humans, sights that few knew existed.

Her friendship with Mara had also grown, due in part to their shared love and concern for Derek. He was still compelled to turn into a werewolf when the moon was full, but as long as he drank a little of her blood before the moon rose, he was able to control the urge to kill. A few days before the moon was full, they went to Mara's castle in Romania or to some other uninhabited spot where he could run wild and free. When Derek was certain he could control the werewolf, Sheree often shifted to wolf form and ran with him. It was exhilarating, racing through the night beside him. Mara and Logan occasionally ran with them.

At home, the desire that was never far from the surface sparked to life. Making love to Derek was always an adventure. Tonight was no different. They undressed each other as they made their way into the bedroom, leaving a trail of clothes, like bread crumbs, strewn behind them.

Lying in bed, he kissed her leisurely, starting with her lips and slowly making his way to her toes and back up again.

He whispered love words in her ear as, with hands and teeth and tongue, he aroused her, bringing her to the brink of fulfillment again and again until, with a low growl, she sank her fangs into his throat. He nipped her in return and the resultant sensual pleasure carried them both over the edge.

"I've married a wild woman," he murmured when they lay panting softly in each other's arms.

She raked her nails over his chest. "Do you love me?"

He lifted one brow in wry amusement. "Don't you know?"

"Yes," she said, "but it's nice to hear the words now and then."

He laughed as she repeated the words he had said to her earlier. "I love you, wife. I loved you from our first kiss, and I will love you to our last."

"Love's last kiss." She gazed deep into his eyes, her heart and soul swelling with emotions too deep for words. "May it be a long time coming."

After I finished *Night's Mistress*, I was certain it would be the last book in my Night series. Just proves how wrong you can be. Derek's story just seemed to write itself, always a nice perk for an author. All I had to do was write it as it unfolded. Turns out, it's one of my favorite books. I loved Derek, I loved Sheree, and it was fun to spend more time with Mara and Logan.

I'm hoping Abbey Marie's story is lurking somewhere in the back of my mind. I guess time will tell.

I'd love to hear from you!

Mandy
darkwritr@aol.com
www.amandaashley.net

Thrilling Suspense from
Beverly Barton